I0822666

Rise
of the
Druid Princess

Book One

The Chronicles of the Emerald Isle

Rise of the Druid Princess

Morrighan Llewellyn Lee

Cover Design: Amanda Garis
Editing: Kelly L. Kingston
Interior Design: Morrighan Llewellyn Lee
Map Illustration: Morrighan Llewellyn Lee via Inkarnate

ISBN: 979-8-218-80682-8
Printed in United States of America

Dedicated to all who use fantasy to survive reality.

Content Warning:

Rise of the Druid Princess is a fast-paced fantasy novel inspired by Celtic lore and mythology. Though this work draws inspiration from mythological events, some aspects have been altered or reimagined to better suit the narrative. This book contains explicit language and sexual content.

There are also depictions/mentions of:

- death of a loved one
- genocide
- child abuse
- blood and gore
- sexual assault
- miscarriage

Reader's discretion is advised.

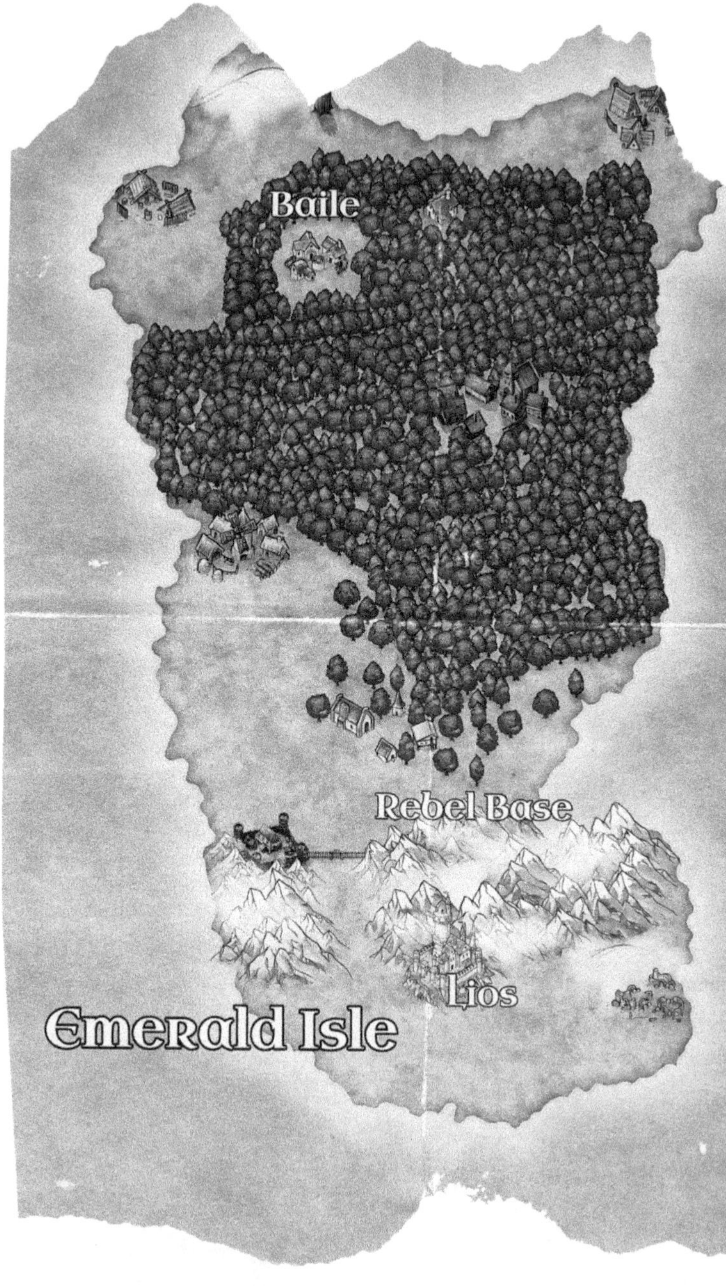

Baile

Rebel Base

Lios

Emerald Isle

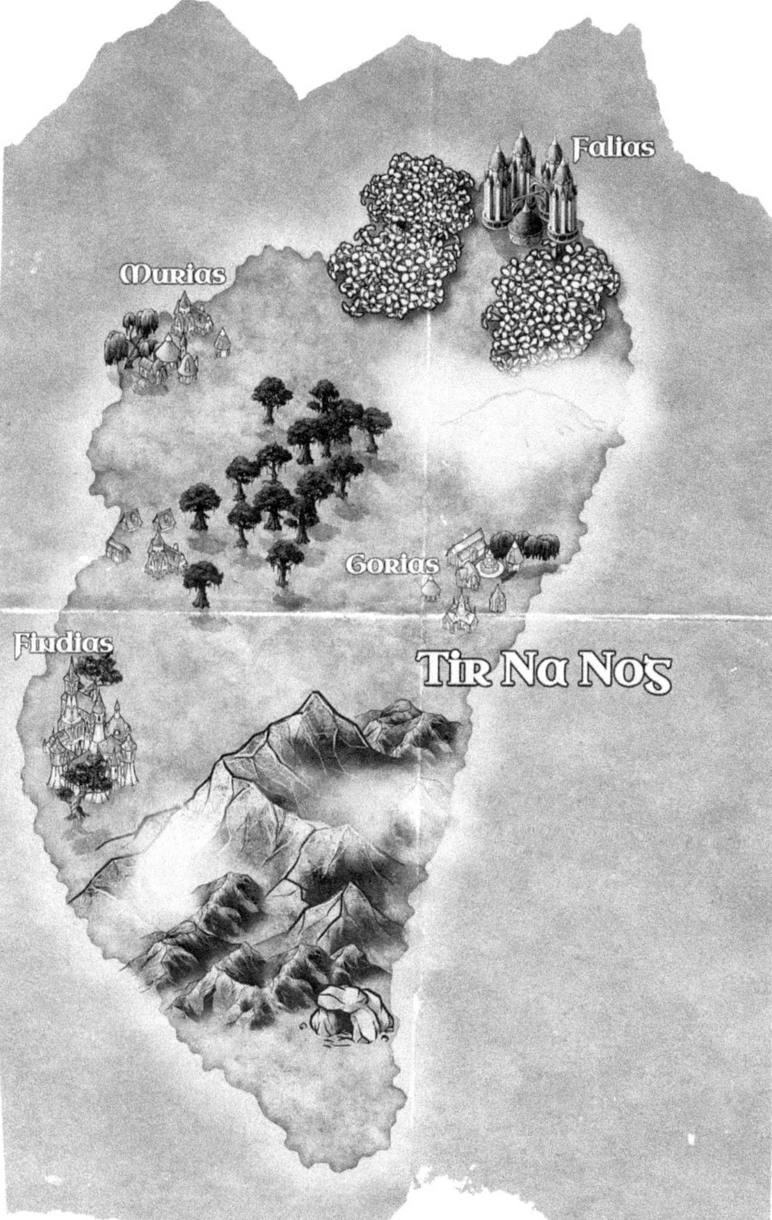
Falias
Murias
Gorias
Findias
Tir Na Nog

Glossary of Magical Beings:

Tuatha Dé Danann:

- o The Dagda – Chief God of the Tuatha Dé Danann
- o Danu – Goddess of the Earth
- o Lugh (the many-skilled one) – God of Light
- o The Morrighan (The Phantom Queen) – Goddess of Battle and Fate
- o Nuada (God of the Silver Hand)
- o Brigid – Goddess of Healing, Smithcraft and Poetry
- o Ogma – God of Knowledge and Wisdom

Aos Si: Fae-like descendants of the Gods. They are eternal beings with accelerated healing. They have heightened strength and speed, as well. They can only be slain by magic or a mortal wound they cannot heal from. They can wield black magic.

The Dullahan: Headless horsemen that are long-dead Druids raised from the dead using black magic. Sunlight is their weakness, for the purity of the light sends them back to the land of the dead.

The Wild Hunt: Warrior wraiths that can be raised from the Land of the Dead. The king/queen of the Druids commands them.

Lesser Fairies: These beings inhabit the Emerald Isle and are not associated with the Aos Si. This includes pukas, mermaid shifters, dragon shifters, leprechauns, and sprites.

Druids: Humans gifted with earth-based magic and elongated lifespan (300-400 years) grant to them by the goddess, Danu. Rightful rulers of the Emerald Isle. They come into their power at 21, when they can begin training to master their gifts. When a Druid comes into their power, the earth quakes in joy. Their magic is drawn directly from the land, and they can manipulate earth and water. They are susceptible to human illnesses.

Seers: Humans gifted with the ability to see the future granted to them by the goddess, the Morrigan. They have an average human lifespan (60-80 years). They are susceptible to human illnesses.

Healers: Humans gifted with the power of healing granted to them by the goddess, Brigid. They have an average human lifespan (60-80 years). They are susceptible to human illnesses.

Scholars: Humans that have the power of knowledge and wisdom granted to them by the god, Ogma. They have an average human lifespan (60-80 years). They are susceptible to human illnesses.

Prologue

"You look beautiful, my Queen," Cara stated, as she finished lacing the back of the queen's gown.

"How many times do I have to tell you? Please call me Deirdre. The formalities are absolutely exhausting, especially in my own home." Deirdre looked at Cara through the mirror. Cara was an older woman in her fifties, a healer from the southern region of the continent. Withered skin with strong lines etched around her mouth and eyes, showing the happiness she had experienced throughout her life. Her hair was the same shade as the storm clouds that constantly loomed over these lands.

Cara was brought to the palace only a year ago when Deirdre became pregnant unexpectedly to aid in the delivery. She stayed to help care for the princess, while Deirdre was away performing her duties as Queen of the Emerald Isle. There was no one she trusted more with the future of the kingdom.

"Nevertheless, you'll be all anyone talks about during the festival,

Deirdre," she coaxed, still fussing with the laces. "All the single nobles will want a chance to dance with such a beautiful thing."

"I am more than a beautiful face for a man to worship," Deirdre shot back, a little too harshly than she had meant to, as Cara winced. Deirdre should have married when she took the throne fifty years ago, but she couldn't relinquish her freedom. Her advisors pressed the issue for many years. She has had many suitors, but none of them would have allowed her to keep her power. They would have expected to run the kingdom in her stead and for her to be the submissive wife.

However, Deirdre had something they did not. Her bloodline was sacred, each child born with greater power than their predecessors. And so, she remained unmarried. She weathered whispers and endured endless pressure from her court, which caused her immense pain for she only wished for her people to love her as they had her father. However, her rule never wavered. She was determined to prove to the court that she was just as capable as any man. Eventually, their doubts quieted, drowned out by her undeniable strength and the prosperity she brought to the kingdom. When she bore a child out of wedlock, the scandal she had expected never came. Instead, the people called it prophecy. The Druids declared the birth a blessing.

Cara meant well, but she did not understand Deirdre's ambition. She offered a quick apology and bowed deeply, murmuring something about tea before hurrying off, leaving Deirdre alone with her reflection. Guilt for how she had spoken to Cara pang through Deidre as she studied the woman who peered back at her in the mirror. Her eyes trailed down the length of her copper hair, which was curled and pinned back from her face—a gold crown was nestled upon her head. She had skin so fair that the splash of freckles across her nose stood out in striking contrast. Her features appeared youthful despite her age. She met the gaze of piercing eyes, the color of jade and lined with kohl, that stared back at her. She held their stare for only a moment before allowing her focus to drift downward to the gold fabric of the dress that clung to every curve. Cara had really outdone herself.

A faint whimper came from the bassinet near the hearth, pulling Deirdre from her thoughts. She leaned over the small bundle, her most prized possession, Aisling, Princess of the Druids. She smiled at her beautiful daughter. Only a few months old, and she already brought life to the once dreary palace.

"Hello, my star. Sleep well?" she whispered, lifting the babe from her bassinet. Deirdre only wished her father could see her. How much she looked like him from her sapphire eyes to her tan skin and dark hair. Deirdre desperately waited for that time to come, though it may never, for it was too dangerous for anyone in the kingdom to ever know who sired the princess.

"Are you ready, my love?" She held her infant daughter close to her breast as she moved to the window across the room. "During Samhain, all the Druids gather here at the palace to celebrate the coming of the new year and to thank the Gods for the year's bountiful harvest. This year has brought many blessings, especially to me."

She beheld the gathering of her people in the fields beyond the walls of Lios, the capital city of the Emerald Isle. The bonfire was already lit, and music could be heard, even from this distance. Her people had much to celebrate to include another year of peace, where all who lived upon the land thrived. Pride bloomed in Deirdre's heart as she watched the celebration unfold.

Cara came back into the room a short time later with a tray containing a steaming tea pot and small cup, setting it on the table in the center of the room. She slowly filled the cup, the smell of clove and chamomile filling the chamber, before turning to the queen, who was still staring out upon her joyous people. "Here, let me take her while you have your tea before we go," she said. Deirdre smiled and pressed a kiss to her daughter's brow before releasing her into Cara's awaiting embrace and taking a seat at the table. Steam floated over the edge of the cup as the queen lifted it to her full lips.

"Thank you, Cara, this is wonderful," hummed Deirdre as she took another. "Are you looking forward to the festivities this evening?"

"Of course!" Cara beamed, her cheeks flushing with excitement. "I have never witnessed such an event."

Deirdre watched her for a moment, amused. "You've lived many years, Cara, yet you still carry the awe of a maiden at her first festival."

"Well," Cara said with a chuckle, "I spent most of those years preoccupied with my patients, not palace galas."

Deirdre leaned back slightly, the cup warming her hands. "You've earned this evening. Let my people spoil you a little."

Cara gave a mock scoff. "Spoil an old woman like me?"

Deirdre tilted her head, a playful glint in her eye. "Old, perhaps. But irreplaceable."

Cara looked down at the baby in her arms, her voice softer. "We do what we can with the time we're given. You both have a bright future ahead."

Deirdre's gaze softened. "I only hope I can give her a world worth growing up in."

"You already have."

Deirdre opened her mouth to reply but was interrupted when the music below came to a screeching halt, replaced by ear shattering screams. The cup Deirdre was holding slipped from her grasp, shattering on the stone floor when she quickly rose and rushed to the window, Cara on her heels. They stared in horror at the scene.

A snake of torches and flashes of dark magic appeared just beyond the celebration. Frantic men, women, and children searched for an escape from the chaos but were unsuccessful in their hunt for safety as they were descended upon by the armed intruders—their lifeless bodies falling to the cool earth. Deirdre leapt into action. Running across the room, she threw open the door, revealing two guards unaware of the event occurring below. "Ready the men," she commanded. "The Aos Si have launched an attack." The two men scurried down the hallway to do as their queen demanded as the door swung shut. Deidre rushed to her wardrobe and withdrew a bundle of black leather.

"The Aos Si? Why would they be attacking us?" Cara asked, awestruck, as she gently laid the baby back in the bassinet.

"Their king is greedy. He has always coveted my lands and the Treasures." Deirdre had an informant on the inside but had not been alerted to a possible invasion. There had been some unrest in Tír na nÓg, but nothing alluding to a threat to the Emerald Isle.

Aisling began to faintly cry, clearly upset by the negative energy permeating the room. Fear for her daughter resonated through her, but she couldn't allow her emotions to get the better of her. Not when she needed a clear head to go into battle. Though her entire body screamed for her to protect the life she brought into this world above all else, she had a duty to her kingdom. "I need you to take Aisling and get as far from here as you can. Head for the temple of Danu, you will be safe there. Go through the mountains, not the pass. They will have posted guards at its entrance to ensure no one escapes. And take my horse. She is the swiftest in the land. None shall outpace her," the queen stated as she began to shed her gown in favor of fighting leathers. Deidre removed another bundle of fabric from the bottom of the wardrobe. She removed the wrappings, revealing the Sword of Light. She strapped it to her hip with practiced hands. Her people didn't stand a chance without the other weapons that had been given to them, but she'd been taken by surprise. She didn't have time to gather the cauldron and spear from where they were hidden, so they would have to do without.

Deirdre turned to Cara, who was franticly packing necessities for the princess, and grabbed her by the shoulders, looking deep into her eyes. "Do not, under any circumstances, come back here until I send for you. One of the Hunt will be sent to collect you when this is settled. She is the Druid heir. They can track royal blood." Deirdre slid a small necklace into Cara's hand—an onyx pendant hung from the chain. "Keep this on her at all times. If anything happens to me, you must protect her with your life. She is important, not just to me, but to the realm."

Cara was at a loss for words. She was a healer, not a warrior, but she was loyal to her queen and loved the young princess like her own. She would do whatever was asked of her without question. Deirdre walked over to the bassinet and swiftly kissed her daughter's forehead. "If I should die, it is up to you to save our people," she whispered to her daughter as a tear trickled down her cheek. "I love you with my entire heart, my star. May we meet again, whether it be in this life or the next."

"I will keep her safe, my queen. You have my word." Deidre turned to Cara, allowing the use of her title to slide, and gave her a slight smile.

"I have appreciated everything you have done for me and will continue to do for my daughter. If I should fall, I need you to make me a promise."

"Anything."

"Do not reveal her identity to anyone, including her. Let her grow up without the burden of destiny unlike I had. I was raised in a palace, not a home. Every choice I made belonged to the crown. I want her to live first, truly live, before duty claims her," the queen sniffled. "Please."

Cara didn't feel it was right to keep such a secret from the young princess, but she could not go against the wishes of her mother. "I promise," she whispered. "When should I tell her?"

Deidre looked upon her sleeping daughter. "Not until the eve of her twenty-first birthday, when she will come into her power. If she grows up waiting for the storm to come, she'll never learn who she is without it. I know what that fear does, Cara. It becomes a shadow that follows you everywhere, every choice you make, every person you love. She deserves more than that. Let her laugh without wondering if it's the last time. Let her fail without thinking the world will burn for it." She swiped her tears away, her voice growing firmer. "If she knows too soon, she'll either try to run from it or chase it. Either path could destroy her before she even understands what she is. However, if she walks into her power as the woman she's chosen to become, she'll be strong enough to carry it."

Cara nodded—her heart filled with sorrow.

"Thank you." Deidre finished the last of her preparations, sealing away the anguish she felt about sending her child away.

Cara gathered the rest of the packs and placed the princess in a sling. The three of them left the room quickly, flanked by the guards who had appeared to have returned only moments before, and rushed down the many flights of stairs to the lower levels of the palace. Soldiers gathered at its entrance, awaiting the command of their queen. Cara watched on with adoration, overcome by fear for the queen she has grown to love.

Deirdre paced in front of the assemblage. "We are under siege by the Aos Si! You have sworn an oath to protect Lios and the people of the Emerald Isle with your life! We will not yield! We will not break! We will see them bleed for having the audacity to attack our great nation!" She unsheathed her sword, pointing it to the sky. "Until the very end!" She roared.

Deirdre spoke a phase in an ancient tongue, long forgotten by most, and summoned the Wild Hunt. A hazy mist rose from the earth, swirling until it solidified into the ghostly silhouettes of men. Their spectral forms joined the ranks, as she led her army out of the palace towards the front gates.

Cara raced to the stables on the other side of the city. She burst through the doors, breathing heavily.

"The Aos Si have invaded. They're attacking the celebration! I need the queen's horse saddled. Now!" She yelled.

The stable boy appeared from one of the stalls, a bridle hanging loosely in his hands. He dropped it at his feet when he saw the look of alarm on Cara's face. He worked quickly, and shortly thereafter, she was upon a horse and headed out of the city via the rear gate. Cara's heart was in her throat, but she was able to expel a shuddered breath when she saw her escape route clear, only a few Lios soldiers standing guard. Before she passed through the gates, she stole a look back down the cobbled street from whence she came. She hesitated for a moment, once again fearing the fate of her beloved queen and the people that lived within the city. She forced herself to turn her attention back to the path ahead and barreled out of the city towards the towering mountains beyond.

Cara paused at the top of the foothills on the other side of the city to watch the events unfold. The screams had faded in the fields below Lios, and the snake of torches now moved towards the front gate. Deirdre and her army awaited the invaders. The Aos Si descended, casting their magic against the gate like a great wall of darkness. Cara sucked in a harsh breath as the gate began to bend to the will of the corrupt magic. The queen responded by sending a magical shield of her own, a shimmering light in stark contrast to the shadows on the opposing side, to reinforce the gate. Cara was filled with what could be false hope. Deirdre was strong and cunning, and she possessed the Sword of Light. She had to survive.

Black smoke encircled the gate, and the shield sputtered and went out. Cara couldn't hear anything from this far away, but she saw when the gates gave way to the army. The Hunt surged forward, their spectral forms moving in a graceful dance with each swing of their blades, as the Aos Si showered arrows of black magic onto the soldiers. Many fell swiftly, their bodies twisting and contorting as the black magic ate away at their skin. The sounds of the battle filtered up towards Cara, the clash of swords and roars of men as they were struck down roiled Cara's gut.

At Deirdre's command, the earth groaned and split open. Massive roots and vines erupting through the cobbled streets, lashing out at the enemy like living whips. Her soldiers rallied their own pure magic following her lead, pushing the Aos Si back towards the ruined gate—their black magic no match for the magic of the Druids.

Deirdre lifted her sword in the air. A beacon of light erupted from its tip, intending to encourage her warriors and instill fear within her enemies. She was prepared to vanquish her adversaries when a perfectly aimed arrow, too fast to be stopped or dodged, caught her in the shoulder. She dropped the sword and clutched her arm with the other. Cara's heart fell. Another arrow pierced Deirdre's thigh. Agony twisted her face as she dropped to one knee.

A young Aos Si male stepped out of the throng towards her, while Deirdre's soldiers were too preoccupied to come to her aid. She attempted to retrieve her sword, but he kicked it out of her reach. Cara watched in horror, her thundering heart now pulsed in her ears, as the last bit of her hope flickered out. Tears streamed down her face. She wanted to look away, but her eyes were trained on the dreadful scene. The warrior circled Deidre with a predatory gaze. Coming up behind her, he brought a blade to her neck. With a flick of his wrist, he slit the queen's throat. Cara gasped for air, watching as Deirdre's lifeless body fell to the ground—her blood staining the cobbled stones of the city street a bright crimson.

The Hunt evaporated in thin air. Tendrils of mist retreated to the earth from which they had risen. Without their queen, they were sent back to the Land of the Dead to await the rise of a new heir that could awaken them once more. The once living vines shriveled and fell limp to the ground. The Aos Si thundered in triumph as the remaining Druid soldiers were finished off, for without the Hunt and their queen, their mere numbers could not stand against the Aos Si army. Their shouts of victory carried across the cool fall breeze, filling Cara's ears with the horrendous sound. Rage boiled the blood flowing through Cara's veins as she watched them celebrate.

Aisling let out a faint cry, drawing Cara back to the task at hand. She gazed upon the squirming heir, who seemed to get heavier with the realization of what was at stake. Clara recalled the promise she made to the queen. Many moons ago, Cara dreamed of having a child of her own. Though it was under the worst of circumstances, this was her chance. "Aine," she whispered as the child drifted off into a peaceful sleep, unaware of the upheaval around her. "That will be your name." With one more look at the city with a heavy heart, its streets now swarming with armed Aos Si soldiers, she sped off into the night.

The temple of Danu would no longer be safe, for that would be the Aos Si next stop in the destruction of the Druidic people. With no destination, Cara pushed the queen's steed deeper into the mountains, the air growing cold and thin—fog clouding her face with every exhale. She nestled the Princess deeper into the sling to keep her delicate face warm against the snow that had begun to dust Clara's cloak and tickle her nose. Cara would keep the Princess safe until she came into her power and could reclaim the kingdom of the Emerald Isle, taking her rightful place upon her mother's throne.

Chapter 1

Twenty Years Later

The birds were chirping loudly in the canopy that morning. The sun's rays shone through the breaks between the branches. My basket was full to the brim with the willow bark needed to make tea for my aging grandmother. Her joints continually ached, and it was the only thing that took the edge off. I spent most of my mornings gathering herbs for her and our patients.

My grandmother was a healer, a human gifted with magic from the Goddess, Bridget. Though magic is a dominant gene passed down from our ancestors, mine never manifested. So, she taught me how to identify herbs and use them for different ailments as a child to make up for the deficit. However, she had recently become too frail to use much of her magic, gather herbs, or spend hours on her feet making tonics for her patients. I took over their care to the best of my ability.

I made my way back home with my harvest. It was a beautiful

day, which was uncommon on the Emerald Isle. Most of the time, thick fog and rain covered much of the island. The beauty of the day was contradictory to the mourning that was occurring across the land. Today was Samhain, the anniversary of the fall of the Druid kingdom and the rise of the cruel Aos Si king, Balor. The Aos Si were ethereal beings descended from the Gods themselves, who took over this land twenty years ago.

Our quaint cottage came into view ahead surrounded by towering oak trees. When my grandmother had gotten too weak five years ago, we settled here in the village of Baile at the northern point of the Emerald Isle. We had spent most of my childhood traveling from village to village, never staying in one place long enough for a house to ever feel like a home. My grandmother always told me, though, that as long as I was by her side, she was home.

I did what I could to make the once-neglected cottage feel how the others had not. I spent an entire summer gathering my grandmother's favorite assortment of flowers to plant on either side of the entrance. I used their petals to make paints of varying colors to add detail to the trim of the door and windows.

I went inside, dropping my basket by the hearth. "Is there anything I can get for you, Mamó?" I asked, leaning over the cot in the corner of the small one-room cottage where my grandmother lay. She had not been doing well for a while now. I do what I can to make her comfortable, for there isn't much I can do to heal the effects of time.

I have been making her tea in hopes of prolonging the inevitable. With no magic of my own, I am left with what I can gather in herbs from the forest surrounding our home. However, every day, she gets weaker. She hasn't been able to stand from her cot for weeks now.

She slowly looked up at me and smiled. "No, my love. I do not believe there is much more you can do for me." The way she said this made me believe that there was nothing else I could do for her in this life, not just in this moment. I gave her a tight smile, drawing a blanket over her.

"I will start your tea," I stated before turning back to my discarded basket. She snored faintly while I prepared her tea.

I stoked the fire within the hearth and filled the cauldron hanging above with the water I had fetched before leaving that morning. I added the willow bark and allowed it to steep, while I watched my grandmother sleep. When my mother died shortly after my birth, she took me in. Our life has not been easy, but she did the best she could, especially with the state of the kingdom. My grandmother had a heart of gold. She was loved by everyone she met and cared for everyone so deeply, never asking for anything in return.

Once the tea was ready, I grabbed a cup from the shelf over the hearth and ladled in a small portion. "Mamó, your tea is ready." She woke with a start, fear appearing on her face. I set the cup on the table and knelt by the cot. I took her hand in mine as I whispered, "It's just me. You're okay." I swept her hair from her face. "I didn't mean to frighten you," I said, as I helped her into a seated position.

"No, my love, you are fine. Just a memory, is all. Tea was the last thing I made for your mother before she was taken from us." I instinctively grasped the heavy onyx pendant that hung about my neck. It was the only thing I owned from my mother My grandmother rarely spoke of her. I knew what she looked like based on my grandmother's description of her features. I also knew she was strong, kind, and always looked out for others. Other than that, I didn't know much about the woman who gave me life. It pained my grandmother deeply to talk about her, so I tried not to push her and only took what she gave me. I sealed the information into a part of my heart I had reserved for the mother I never knew.

I decided to change the subject, not wanting to add to the physical pain that was her current existence. "I overheard some of the Aos Si soldiers in the square the other day say that the king is raising the Human Tax again." When the Aos Si took over this land from the Druids twenty years ago, King Balor's first act was to issue the Human Tax. This stated that any human living on his land must pay fifty percent of their harvest.

This tax has risen several times over the years as more of the Aos Si and fairy folk have migrated from Tír na nÓg during Samhain and Beltane when the veil between the worlds is at its thinnest, which allowed easy passage. The humans were now required to hand over seventy percent of their harvest.

Those who could afford it had smuggled their families across the sea to the mainland in the hulls of fishing ships long ago. Those who couldn't were now forced to work their hands to the bone to barely have enough food to make it through to the next year.

My grandmother scoffed, "If he raises it much more, there will be no humans to sow and harvest his crops nor raise and slaughter his animals. What then?" I handed her the cup of tea, gesturing for her to drink. "Before they arrived, everyone had all they needed. Some were more well-off, but no one ever went hungry or unclothed. Our queen made sure of that. Her people never suffered under her rule."

My grandmother had told me many stories of the great Druid queen who once ruled these lands. She was kind but fierce, protecting her people with everything she had. In another life, my grandmother may have been a scholar, humans charged with the protection of knowledge and the once grand libraries, for she tells the most vivid sagas. It feels as though she was there when these events happened.

"You need to stay away from those soldiers, Aine," my grandmother scolded. "They are dangerous and unpredictable."

"I am careful, Mamó. They will be gone within the week, anyway." During Samhain and Beltane, the fairy mound north of our village was crawling with Aos Si soldiers. Many stopped in our small town for provisions on their way through. The village was on high alert during these times, no one left their houses unless absolutely necessary in fear of what the soldiers might do.

"Do you think that anything will ever change?" I whispered hopelessly. There had been a rebellion five years after the invasion, but it was squashed quickly. No one has ever tried since. Now, the humans are too weak to rise against the king and his armies.

My grandmother handed the empty cup back to me and placed her hand on my cheek, "I believe there is still hope, my love."

"How can you still believe that? After everything you've seen?" I asked. As a healer, she had to nurse many back from near death due to malnourishment while we were traveling. Our village was lucky. We had a small band of young men who hunted and smuggled each family enough meat to supplement the loss from the king's taxes, but many did not have such luxuries. Villages closer to the capital have Aos Si overseers who enforce such laws.

"Because…" my grandmother said before she flew into a coughing fit that racked her entire frail body. I ran to the basin to get a glass of water. Once the coughing subsided, I pressed the glass to her lips and helped her sip.

"You should rest. I have a few patients I need to deliver tonics to this afternoon anyway." I helped her lay back down and covered her with the blanket. "I love you, Mamó. I'll be back later." I kissed her forehead and went to gather my supplies into my basket.

"When you return, there is something I need to talk to you about," she whispered as her eyes fluttered shut. I stood staring at her as she slowly nodded off. As much as I would like to wake her up and demand an explanation as to what the hell she was talking about, she needed her rest, and I had patients expecting me.

I left with my basket a brief time later, racking my brain as I meandered down the forest path to the village. Tall oaks loomed on either side of the dirt trail, casting shadows upon the earth as the midmorning sun shone through their twisted limbs. The air was thick with the scent of wet earth and moss, and somewhere deep in the woods, a woodpecker drilled incessantly at the bark of an unseen tree. Under normal circumstances, I would find peace among the familiar whispers of the forest, but my mind refused to settle. I reached the village and went about my business, all the while still determined to drive myself crazy, fretting about what my grandmother had to tell me.

I came to my first delivery and knocked on the rickety door. The door flung open, and a small girl clamped her arms around my waist. "Good morning, Nora," I laughed. Nora was ten but small for her age.

Her family was heavily affected by the king's taxes. Her father was killed in an accident five years prior, leaving her mother alone with four children under the age of five. Within the first year, Nora's youngest sibling succumbed to malnourishment. Her mother had lost her milk due to stress and overworking her body trying to provide for her family, and she was unable to feed the baby. Milk-bearing animals were not farmed this far north, which left her with no options to supplement.

Last year, her other two children caught a fever, and by that time, my grandmother had declined to the point she couldn't utilize her magic without putting her life at risk. She just didn't have the strength to sustain it anymore. I treated their symptoms with herbs but couldn't cure the illness. They didn't make it through the week. Nora was all her mother had left, and she would do anything to keep her from sharing the same fate as her siblings. I came by twice a week to ensure Nora was healthy.

"My mommy said you were coming today!" Nora exclaimed, taking me by the hand and dragging me through the door.

Her mother was standing in the center of the small cottage, hands on her hips. "I have told you numerous times, Nora, that you mustn't attack Aine when she arrives." Nora's mother gave me an apologetic smile.

"She's fine. I miss her just as much when I am away," I smiled. It was true. I looked forward to my quick visits with Nora. She was always so excited to see me, which was a breath of fresh air compared to everyone else. The rest of the villagers were friendly and appreciated all my grandmother and I had done for them, but Nora was the only one I had truly gotten to know. I have spent so much of my time aiding my grandmother and caring for these people that I didn't have time to make friends.

"I don't have much time today, I'm afraid." A frown appeared on her young face. Her amber eyes stared up at me, pleading. "I'm sorry, little one, but I have ten more people to see before dinner time."

"Okay," she pouted. I made small talk with her and her mother while I checked her over. Nora was in overall good health, but her growth had been stunted due to the lack of nutrients. A few months ago, I talked to one of the hunters who I had tended to when he took a stray arrow from a fellow hunter. They gave the two a little extra each time they returned.

"Well, Nora. All looks good." I gave Nora a tight squeeze. "I have to be on my way, but I will be back." I gave her mother a final goodbye as she pried her daughter off me. Although she was doing well right now, I wasn't sure if her little body would be able to fight off any illnesses. She would most likely not make it to adulthood, and that thought caused my heart to constrict.

She wasn't the only child who faced that fate. Unless something changed, the next generation would be dead before they had even gotten a chance to live. I thought back to my grandmother and the hope she had for the future. I hoped she was right.

A few hours later, I exited the home of my last patient, looking forward to a hot meal and resting my tired limbs. I also desperately wanted to know what it was my grandmother had to talk to me about.

I had made it into the forest when my hands began to tingle. I didn't think much of it until the numbness began to travel up my arms. I halted and dropped my basket at my feet. I clenched my hands into fists in an attempt to return the feeling. My breathing quickly became labored, like a great weight had been placed on my chest. I collapsed to my knees as my head began to pound ferociously. As my heart raced and vision blurred, panic sunk deep into my bones. I tried to push myself off the ground, but in my attempts to stand, I fell forward. Just before my face hit the dirt, I swore the earth rumbled beneath me. Then, everything went dark.

* * *

When I came to, the numbness in my body had subsided along with the pounding in my head. My vision was crystal clear —too clear. The world around me shimmered at the edges, colors were more vivid than they should have been. Something was off. I sat up, rubbing my face, only to feel a strange warmth lingering beneath my skin, pulsing faintly like a second heartbeat. Realizing I had been out for a while, for the sun had already begun to melt below the trees, I quickly rose to my feet. Blood rushed to my head, causing my stomach to churn, almost causing me to tumble back down to the earth. I closed my eyes and took a few steady breaths. Once the wave of nausea subsided and my balance was restored, I grabbed my basket off the ground. I ran towards home as fast as my legs would carry me, the trees flying by in my peripheral vision. My grandmother would be in so much pain from missing her evening tea, not to mention worried sick that I didn't come home.

I burst through the door, breathing hard. The cottage was dark and dead silent. I dropped my things to the floor and rushed to the cot. "Mamo?" I knelt beside her, but she was still. "Mamo? I'm home," I said as tears broke free. "Please answer me." I choked on a sob when my grandmother let out a shallow breath and slowly opened her eyes.

"My love," she said as she tried to raise her hand to my face. I carefully took her hand and guided it the rest of the way. Tears rolled down my cheeks and spilled onto her open palm as I leaned into her cool touch.

"I'm so sorry. I passed out on the way back. I don't know what happened. Oh gods, I'm so sorry. Are you in a lot of pain? I'll get your tea," I rattled as I went to stand.

She gained enough strength to grab my wrist. "It came… early," she breathed as she stared into my eyes with a pained expression. "There is… so much… I needed to tell you. I thought… I still had… time."

"What came early? What are you talking about?" I questioned.

"I am… sorry… my love." She closed her eyes and let out a breath, but she didn't draw another.

I panicked, grabbing her into my arms. "No, no, no. You're okay. Open your eyes. Please, just open your eyes." I pulled her close and rocked us back and forth. "Please, you can't leave me." My sobs shook us as I continued to rock.

I stayed that way for a while, cradling her, wishing for more time. My tears had since dried, and the remnants from the salt left behind created trails down my cheeks. Dawn broke through the window before I finally moved. I set her back down on the cot gently and drew the blanket over her head. I knelt down beside her and prayed to the Gods and Ancestors to help guide her on her journey to the Otherworld.

I stood and made my way to the door in a haze. My mind was racing. I would need to recruit a few from the village to help me construct the funeral pyre and plan a wake to honor her life. Everyone loved my grandmother. She had saved at least one life from each of their families. They owed her everything.

I rubbed my onyx pendant and closed my eyes. I prayed that my mother would give me strength to continue on my own. I gave my grandmother's still form one last look before I opened the door and stepped out into the foggy morning light.

Chapter 2

I spent the day preparing for my grandmother's funeral, notifying the villagers of her passing and enlisting their aid. Nora and her mother came to help prepare my grandmother's body for the funeral. Nora's mother prattled on about a disturbance that shook their cottage the night before. When I collapsed, I thought the quake was a figment of my delirious imagination. I pondered the coincidence while we waited.

We washed my grandmother and dressed her in her finest dress made from linen, the color of the periwinkle wildflowers that were her favorite. I bought the fabric, which was a crisp white before I brought the spool home and dyed it with the petals of the flowers she loved so much. I spent months hand sewing the garment together. It was not perfect, for I was no seamstress, but it was her favorite. My eyes burned with unshed tears as I carefully braided her steel gray hair in a crown about her head. Nora came forward and delicately placed her beloved wildflowers in her hair and a bundle nestled in her still hands. "She beautiful," Nora said as she wrapped her arms around my waist. I nodded and kissed the top of her head, her hair tickling my nose.

I gently took Nora's small hand and led her to the chair in front of the hearth, pulling her into my lap, as her mother excused herself to fetch sprigs of lavender and rosemary, herbs of remembrance, to burn with the pyre. "When I was your age, my grandmother used to tell me this story. I loved it so much, I would make her tell it repeatedly. Would you like to hear it?" I asked Nora as she made herself comfortable.

"Yes, please," she responded. Her enthusiasm brought a small smile to my face.

"Once upon a time," I began softly, "in a land cloaked in mist and magic, there lived a queen with hair the color of autumn fire. Her presence lit up even the darkest halls, and though many feared her power, none could deny her grace."

Nora nestled deeper into my lap, quiet and still.

"She was a protector," I continued, brushing my fingers through the girl's curls, "A warrior queen, beloved by her people, who ruled with both strength and mercy. Her voice stirred courage in men's hearts and soothed frightened children during stormy nights."

"She sounds brave," Nora whispered.

"She was," I agreed. "But even the brave can be broken. You see, the queen bore a daughter. Her only child, born under a Hunter's Moon, when the wolves sang and the stars watched in silence. The girl was her heart, her hope… and her greatest secret."

"Why secret?" Nora asked.

"Because not all who wear crowns live safe lives," I said. "But one day, a shadow fell over their kingdom. Dark forces from another realm sought the child. They feared what she might become—feared that she would grow stronger than even her mother."

I felt my throat tighten, but I went on. "So, she did what few would have the strength to do. She gave the child up. Not to nobles or lords, but to a woman hidden deep in the woods—a wise one, with knowledge of the old ways. Someone the queen trusted with her life, and more importantly, with the life of her daughter."

The fire popped in the hearth, and Nora jumped slightly. I drew her closer.

"She left behind only a kiss, and a promise whispered to the trees: 'I will return for you, when the world is safe again.'"

"Did she?" Nora asked. "Did she come back?"

"No one knows," I said truthfully. "Some say the queen fell in battle. Others say she wanders the hidden paths, still searching for her child. But there are those who believe when the time is right, the daughter will find her way back to who she truly is. That the stars have not forgotten her."

Nora sighed. "I hope she finds her."

"So do I," I murmured, pressing my lips to the crown of her head.

Just before dusk, a few of the local men and their wives arrived at the cottage to build the pyre. They worked in near silence—hands steady as they stacked the wood with care. Each branch was chosen with purpose. Thick enough to bear the weight, and dry enough to catch quickly. A bed of kindling was laid first, then larger logs arranged in a crisscrossed pattern, rising like a sacred altar. As the pyre grew, so did the heaviness in the air, thick with grief and reverence. This was not just firewood. It was a farewell built by hand. Once finished, the men carried my grandmother and place her upon the wooden structure. I followed them out with a torch I lit off the hearth.

They all stood back so I could light the pyre. Nora cried into her mother's arms; the others bowed their heads in respect. "Goodbye, Mamo. May the road rise to meet you. May the wind be at your back. May the sun shine warmth upon your face, and the rains fall soft upon your fields. Until we meet again," I whispered the prayer the Druids once spoke over our dead. I brushed the blazing torch along the bottom of the pyre until it was engulfed in flames and stood back with the villagers.

Everyone began to move inside for the wake, but I stood watching the flames licking the sky. Nora attempted to give me a hug, which was thwarted by her mother. She scooped the child in her arms, hushing her as she carried her to the house. Some of the villagers had brought along aged and beaten instruments. The beautiful notes of a fiddle and the steady beat of a bodhran emanate from the open windows of the cottage. Laugher and singing joined the music, along with the sound of pounding feet against floorboards as those inside danced to the rhythm of the jig. The wake was in full swing as I stood alone in the darkness. I wanted to celebrate the life that was cut short but was overwhelmed by memories that passed through my mind. All the laughs, all the tears, and all the hardships. My grandmother's body might turn to ash, but her soul would continue to live on in my heart.

A sound drew me from the thoughts. It was faint, hardly audible over the music, but coming closer. I realized it was the pounding of horse hooves upon the earthen path that led to the village. Turning my attention to the road, I squinted against the darkness, attempting to make out the newcomers to no avail. The hair on my neck stood on end, creating a strange sense of wrongness that washed over my body.

The riders drew closer as the thundering hooves grew in intensity until they paused just out of the light of the pyre. "Who's there?" I called into the darkness. There was no reply. I heard someone dismount, hitting the ground with a thud. The crunch of soil and rock underfoot told me they moved in my direction. "Can I help you with some…" I broke off when the horseman came into the light, dressed in all black, and no head sat upon his shoulders. The Dullahan, were the personal assassins of the King. I had heard stories of their mercilessness. No one unlucky enough to cross their path made it to see the next sunrise. Fear spread through my body as I stared upon him, rooting my feet in place.

"By order of the King, your soul is ours," an eerie voice slithered through the cool night air, invading my ears. If I hadn't been so frightened, I would have been trying to figure out how a headless wraith could talk at all. I stood in shock for only a moment more before I made a break for the cottage. I had to warn the others.

"The Dullahan! Everyone needs to run!" I yelled as I erupted through the door. Chaos ensued as they all tried to push past me. I was knocked out of the way by panicked bodies as everyone ran down the path to their homes, which was now blocked by three horsemen. The one who had dismounted was astride his horse once again with his brethren.

The villagers came to a halt right in front of the horsemen, huddling together. "Please! We did nothing wrong!" sobbed Nora's mother, Nora hiding in her skirts.

The horsemen brought their steeds slowly closer, drawing their swords. I stared in horror, looking at Nora. Her mother was still shouting her pleas when the first sword struck, and she fell to the ground. Nora screamed, clinging to her mother's broken body.

I rushed into the throng, attempting to retrieve Nora, but the others pushed against me as they tried to run once more. I tried to break through the stampede, but one of the horsemen reached Nora first. The rider dismounted and pulled Nora up with her hair. He examined her as the others continued to pick off the villagers.

Those they didn't run through with their swords perished under the feet of their horses. The patch of earth became soaked with bloody mud, and bodies lay about. I slipped and fell, and by the time I rose to my feet, the horseman had Nora upon his steed, fear written across her innocent face. Her pleading eyes caught mine. There was nothing I could do to help her. I was no warrior. I wanted to scream, to run, to fight, but all I could do was watch.

I was a passenger in my own body, carried by instinct as I turned and ran for the forest—my will to live overpowering my desire to help Nora. These woods were no stranger to me, for I had walked among these trees every morning for years. If I could just get to where the thicket became too dense for their horses to follow, I could lose them. I stole a glance back at the massacre just in time to see the last body crumple into the blood-slick mud, limbs twisted at unnatural angles. Nausea rolled in my stomach at the sight of it all.

The horsemen with Nora turned and went back the way they had come, but the rest turned their steeds and barreled toward me as if they sensed my presence. I ran. Fallen limbs grabbed at the hem of my skirt, as I flew through the forest. The deeper I got, the thicker the trees became. I ran for what felt like hours. My breath labored, and my side screamed for me to stop.

There was no sound of pursuit, just the low hum of crickets and the leaves beneath my feet. I stopped behind a large oak, attempting to catch my breath. I peered out from behind the tree, trying to see through the black for my attackers. My teeth started to chatter. It could have been the fear or the cold that was starting to overcome me. I only wore my thin, homespun dress. Without a cloak, I will never make it through the night. I couldn't stay here, so I kept moving.

The Dullahan are headless wraiths. It is said they were once Druids that the King had slain in battle and resurrected to do his bidding. It is also said that the Dullahan cannot withstand the purity of the sun, for it banishes the beings back to the Land of the Dead. So, they only hunt under the cover of darkness. They track their prey with their dark magic. Once a name is spoken by their master, they don't stop hunting until its owner no longer breaths. There is nowhere one can hide where they won't find you. It was obvious that they were after me, but the why remained to be seen.

I kept my pace through the forest. I was moving in the direction of the village in hopes of finding help. As it grew nearer, the smell of smoke and burning flesh permeated the air. I stopped short at the edge of the woods. Flames engulfed the entire town, and bodies littered the streets.

The guilt clawed at my chest with invisible hands. First Nora, then this. It was all because of me. It threatened to overwhelm me as I looked upon the destruction my existence has caused. Sobs racked my body, and tears burned my eyes as I leaned against a tree clutching my chest. My heart felt primed to explode. I needed to keep moving, but I couldn't stop staring at the slaughter. The heat from the fire brushed my cheeks. The crackling flames tore through each building as they collapsed in on themselves. Wood snapped and groaned as beams collapsed, the air filled with sharp pops and low, tortured creaks. I forced my gaze away from the faces of the fallen, afraid of recognizing someone I couldn't afford to mourn.

The sound of hooves upon the path leading from my cottage sobered me. The three horsemen emerged from the forest. I went to grab my onyx pendant again to give me strength, but it wasn't there. In my urgency to escape, it must have been torn from my neck. I didn't have time to dwell on the agony of the loss. So, I turned and ran once more.

* * *

Hours later, the sun began to rise above the horizon, and the birds came awake in the trees. I was pushing myself to keep moving, but I was exhausted. I could barely lift my foot to take another step when I came upon a hollow at the base of a large willow, surrounded by the most beautiful purple flowers. Their subtle, sweet smell embraced me.

The hollow was just big enough for me to squeeze my small frame into. It would give me cover for the day. I could rest and produce a plan. It didn't take long before my eyes fluttered shut, and I dozed off.

I awoke with a start to the sound of footsteps through the underbrush. I covered my mouth to keep from making any noise that would give away my position. I peeked out of the hollow, hoping to find a deer the source of the rustling leaves. To my surprise, a man walked alertly through the foliage, stopping every few steps to kneel and survey the ground before him. He had midnight black hair pulled back from his face in a tight bun, exposing his rounded human ears. He was wearing tight black leather, which was worn by the human hunters in these parts. A bow was slung over his broad shoulder, and a long sword was strapped to his side. He was tall for a human and strongly built. He was sinfully beautiful.

Though he was human, I didn't trust he wouldn't just hand me over for the right price. I shifted my weight to get a better look, causing loose soil to fall from my hiding place. I winced at the soft sound. When I looked back up, the man was gone. It was possible he had moved along and didn't hear my mishap. Nonetheless, I remained perfectly still, holding my breath and listening intently for movement. Finally, I let myself inhale deeply.

With a thud, the man fell from above and landed on his feet in front of the hollow. He yanked me from the tree and threw me to the forest floor. I hit the dirt hard, nearly knocking the air from my lungs. I quickly rolled from my back and got to my knees, readying to run far from the dangerous man before me.

Stepping back, the stranger nocked an arrow in his bow, pointing it at me. I stilled my movements. A moment of surprise passed across his face before he quickly schooled his features. My eyes met his vibrant green ones, the color of the foliage overhead. I caught a glimpse of an emotion within those earthen wells that I didn't understand, along with a hint of amusement as his lip tipped up into a small grin. His fingers twitched on his bow, causing me to put my hands up in front of me to show that I was unarmed and no threat.

"Wait!" I squeaked, worried that my escape might end up being for nothing.

He dropped the bow and inch. The devilish grin grew ever so slightly. "Why are you hiding, little fox?" he purred. I gaped at him. His voice was deep and lyrical, with a bit of an edge. He brought the bow to his side, replacing the arrow in the quiver strapped to his back. Tilting his head like a predator hunting its prey, he stalked towards me.

I was still kneeling in the dirt before him, as he crouched so we were at eye level. "I asked you a question," he pressed. "Why were you hiding?" I was flustered by his presence. My mouth opened and closed like a fish, trying to form words to explain myself.

"The Dullahan" was all I was able to croak out.

"The Dullahan? And what did you do to draw such attention?" He paused, awaiting my answer.

"They slaughtered my entire village to get to me. Please, I mean you no harm. Let me go," I begged. He examined me. I became acutely aware of my current appearance. My dress was torn and stained with mud and blood. Dirt was crusted under my nails and across my skin, where it was left bare. My dark hair was tangled with forest debris. It painted a hideous picture of the events from the night before.

"What is your name?" He asked.

"Aine," I said, praying to every god that he would let me be on my way.

"I am Rion. I am currently out with a hunting party. We are camped in a hemlock grove not far from here. Come with me."

He turned on his heel as I clambered to my feet. I contemplated turning the other way and running like hell, but I have a feeling he is a good shot with that bow. I wouldn't get far. I followed against my better judgment, having to hasten my steps to keep up with his long strides. Although I didn't trust this man, I was daft to think I would survive another night alone.

We walked in silence for a while until we approached a clearing where four tents were pitched. No one was in the camp from the sounds of it. "How many are with you?" I questioned.

"Me and three others," he answered curtly. He led me to the

tent on the far end. "This is mine. I will fetch some water for you to wash up and see if I can find a clean pair of clothes for you to wear." I stood at the entrance as he disappeared into the forest, bucket in hand. The thought of running resurfaced, but where would I go? I had no one left in this world. This was my only chance to survive, though the likelihood was slim to none. My breath came in shallow pants, and my heart throbbed painfully within my chest, mourning all that I had lost. I took a deep breath to steady myself.

The tent was large, with a bedroll on one side and saddlebags on the other. I hadn't seen any horses coming into the camp, but they must have had them out to graze somewhere nearby. I was still standing in the doorway when he returned with a bucket of water, which he placed at my feet. He rummaged through his bag until he procured a white linen shirt and trousers. "They will be big, but they are clean. I will prepare you something to eat while you wash." He gestured inside the tent and turned towards the dwindling fire at the center of the camp. Appreciation pounded in my heart.

"Thank you," I spat out quickly. "I know this is a huge risk." He turned back to me with a nod, then continued to the fire.

I stepped inside the tent and closed the flap. I choked on my emotions. The guilt was back in full force and threatened to overwhelm me once more and the false sense of safety that I felt at that moment. I damned these men to death the moment Rion had stumbled upon me.

I reflected on all the decisions I made last night. I considered the ways that I could have stopped it all. If I had handed myself over, would the Dullahan have left the villagers alive? Would they have left Nora? My life was not worth theirs.

I pictured Nora's terrified face, covered in her mother's blood.

I beat myself down until I was nothing more than a shell. That empty space that I once inhabited slowly filled with hot rage. I will carry this weight with me for the rest of my life.

I took my time removing the soiled gown and shift, the brisk air brushing over my breasts, causing me to shiver. I leaned over the bucket. I didn't recognize the woman looking back at me. I was born with sun-kissed skin, but it had turned sallow. My cheekbones were all sharp angles, and my cobalt eyes were lined with red from fatigue.

I began to pull the leaves and other rubbish from my hair and used my fingers to comb out most of the tangles. I tore off a piece of my ruined dress to use as a rag to wash the dirt from my face and body. The water was freezing, but it felt good to remove the constant reminder of my failures. I unearthed bruises and scratches, as I removed the grim from where limbs had assaulted me.

Once I had determined I was as clean as I was going to get without hot water and soap, I quickly redressed into the clean clothes. I used a thin strip of my dress to tie the trousers to keep them from falling off. The shirt hung well past my knees, so I tucked it into my waistband. I plaited my hair and fastened it with another strip of my dress.

I grabbed my ruined clothing and the bucket and left the tent. I dumped the black water behind the shelter and walked towards the fire where Rion was stirring a pot. I tossed my dress into the fire and watched it burn, along with everything I ever had or loved in this world. Tears rose in my eyes, but I blinked them away.

I sat on one of the stumps surrounding the fire. Rion ladled what looked like some sort of stew into a wooden bowl and handed it to me. We sat in silence while I ate my fill. "My men will be back soon," he said, looking to the sky where the sun had begun to set. "You will be safe here. You can rest, and we will figure out the rest tomorrow. You may use my tent." He took the bowl from me and stood.

"But where will you sleep?" I asked hesitantly. I was already asking too much from this stranger. I couldn't take his bed, too.

"I will be fine," was all he stated while he walked towards the edge of the grove. Rion wasn't much for words, it seemed. I rose from my stump and moved towards the tent when whispering voices arose in the direction Rion had disappeared. The rest of the hunting party must have returned. I hurried inside, having had enough of strangers for one day.

I sat on the bedroll, allowing the events of the previous evening to seep in. I will give myself one minute. One minute to feel the pain. One minute to feel sorry for myself. My grandmother always said my mother was strong, so I would be the same. I pulled back the fur blanket, not bothering to remove my shoes should I have to run again. I tossed and turned for what felt like hours, not able to get comfortable. Every time I closed my eyes, the horrors of the previous night played behind my lids. At last, exhaustion claimed me, pulling me into its cold, unforgiving embrace.

Chapter 3

A soft shuffling stirred me from my sleep in the hours of the early morning. It was still dark, at least from what I could tell from within the tent, but the forest was starting to wake around me with the sweet first notes of birds and rustling of leaves. I lay still, listening for any sound that signaled trouble. I sat up slowly, scanning the tent, but I couldn't see more than a few inches in front of me.

I stood and went to walk towards the front of the tent when I stumbled over a solid hump on the ground and fell flat on top of it. The object made a faint groan, and I realized my error quickly when hands caught my waist. My breath hitched in my throat. "Damn it, woman. Where do you think you are going?" Rion's gruff, sleep-filled voice rose within the tent. Though I couldn't see him, I knew we were face to face by the feel of his breath on my cheek. He smelled of smoke and something I couldn't place.

A flower, maybe, that brought back a memory that was just out of reach.

"I am so sorry. I heard something and was frightened. Now I realize it must have been you. I didn't expect you to be here. I mean, it's your tent, and you have every right. I'm sorry," my anxious rambling and profuse apologies continued as I attempted to scurry off him. He gripped my waist, not allowing me to move.

"You are safe, little fox. I will not allow harm to befall you." Without another word, he released me. I shot up and rushed back to the safety of the warm furs spread out upon the bedroll, hiding my burning face beneath its soft veil. He sounded confident in his ability to protect me, despite the risks involved. However, being in my presence was a death sentence that shouldn't be so easily ignored.

It was quiet for a while, but I didn't think Rion had fallen back to sleep. "Why?" I asked quietly.

"Why what?" he yawned.

"Why would you jeopardize your life and the lives of your men?" I twisted my body in his direction though I couldn't see him.

"You seem worth saving. Now rest. We must pack up camp and get moving by first light, which will be upon us within the hour," he replied with a huff.

"Where are we going?"

"I know a few individuals who may be able to assist you in your current situation." Getting the impression that he was done talking by his abrasive tone, I rolled over and closed my eyes. I wanted to believe there was a person out there that could help me, but unless Rion had a personal connection to the king and was able to sway his decision for my blood, my life was forfeit. The fear formed a tight fist around my throat that forbade the air from escaping my lungs. All Rion could do was delay the inevitable. I would die, and so would he for obstructing the king's will.

* * *

"Hey. Wake up. It is time to go." Rion shook me awake, standing over me with packs in hand. I rubbed the sleep from my eyes. Mornings always used to bring me immense joy, but today, it felt like another step closer to my impending doom.

I peeled the pelts away from my body and hauled myself to my feet. My back ached, and my neck was stiff from sleeping on the hard ground. I exited the tent into the brisk air. Heavy fog blanketed the forest floor beneath the trees beyond the clearing, creating an eerie atmosphere that heightened my anxiety. The sun was hidden from sight behind the thick clouds above. I noticed that the rest of the tents had already been disassembled, horses stood saddled in their place, as I continued to examine my surroundings.

Rion followed close behind, stating, "I'm going to pack up the rest of the camp, then we'll be off." I nodded, not having the energy to speak.

Three other men stood by the dwindling fire, talking and laughing amongst themselves. They all turned to look at me as I hesitantly walked towards them. "So, this is the woman we are risking our necks for? She doesn't look like much," spat one of the men. Shame barreled through me as my cheeks heated, for he wasn't wrong. There was an otherworldly stillness to him—tall and pale, with snow-white hair that shimmered faintly in the dim light, as if touched by frost. His face seemingly stuck in a perpetual scowl, and his pitch-black eyes held only contempt. He was dangerously handsome, much like Rion.

Another man batted his arm. "Ignore Nolan. He's grouchy in the mornings. I am Flynn, my lady," he gestured to the other man across the fire, "and this is Bellamy. It's an honor to make your acquaintance." I glanced at Bellamy and took a second look. Though Bellamy's hair was longer, he and Flynn were identical, both with sun-warmed skin, auburn hair, and the same open, easy smiles that put others at ease. I stared between them, awestruck. They created a striking contrast to the other man's cool reserve. "You're not crazy, we are twins," Flynn said with a wink as he noticed my bewildered expression. "Twice the fun, if you know what I mean." My eyes widened in shock, and my face only heated more. All four men were absurdly attractive and young, appearing to be in their mid to late twenties.

"I, uh, it's nice to meet you all. I am Aine. I didn't mean to put you in harm's way. I am sorry I have put you all in this situation," I apologized, casting my eyes to the ground. Flynn drew my attention by stepping forward and taking my hand in his.

"You have nothing to be sorry for. It would be a privilege to die for such a beauty," he said, a smirk appearing on his handsome face. I know he intended to make me feel better, but it had the opposite effect as I stared into his dark eyes. Unlike Nolan's that seemed to swallow the light, his held flecks of gold that shimmered like the embers of a dying fire.

"Oh, leave her alone." Bellamy slapped his twin on the back. "He's harmless, I swear. Just a persistent flirt."

Nolan grunted and turned to a white horse. "I'll scout out the road ahead to make sure it is clear." He mounted his steed and trotted out of the grove.

The twins turned to me, an apologetic smile on both of their faces. "He takes some getting used to." I nodded with a small smile. I turned back to the tent Rion was now dissembling.

"Can I help?" I grabbed the bag of stakes lying beside where he was crouched and held it open so he could drop in the ones he had already pulled from the ground. "Nolan is right," I mumbled. "He has every right to be upset. Maybe I should just go. I don't want to cause any dissension among your men, and I certainly don't want to see any more people dead because of me."

Rion fought with a stubborn stake, refusing to be released from the ground. "Nolan is a dick, but he is loyal. He will do as I wish, though he may complain the whole time," he grumbled through his teeth. The stake finally gave way, sending Rion tumbling onto his ass. He huffed out a sigh of frustration before finishing his task.

Nolan rode back into the glen just as Rion strapped the final pack to the rear of his horse.

"All is clear ahead. We better get moving," he called, glaring my way. I glance to the ground, guilty tears pricking my eyes.

Rion led the horse over, stopping in front of me. He put his finger under my chin and raised my gaze to meet his. He searched my eyes for what laid within. A wave of fury overcame his face, and he turned to Nolan. "I will only warn you once. You say one more fucking thing, look at her wrong again, and you will have more than the Dullahan to worry about. Do you understand?" he growled. Nolan didn't speak but nodded reluctantly in agreement. A tight knot lodged in my throat at Rion's overreaction, confusion knitting my brows together. I was but a stranger to him. Why did it matter to him how Nolan treated me? I was about to ask him just that when he turned back towards me, face calm, acting as if nothing had happened at all. "You will ride with me until we can get you a horse."

Until now, I hadn't thought about how I would be traveling with them. I had never ridden on the back of a horse before causing my already heightened nervousness to soar. They had been uncommon in our village, only the wealthy could afford their upkeep. Many used small ponies to aid in farming their lands. We had a horse many years ago when we were traveling to pull our small, covered wagon, but she passed soon after settling in Baile. I looked up at the black and white stallion. It appeared taller than it had just a moment before. "I don't know how to ride," I admitted. "I don't even know how to get on it." My ignorance was met by another scoff by Nolan, to which Rion shot a warning glare.

"Start with putting your foot in the stirrup. Hold onto the edge of the saddle to pull yourself up, then swing your other leg over. I will give you a boost." I did as he instructed. He placed his hands at my waist and hoisted me up on the horse, which remained still while I got situated. Rion mounted behind me and placed an arm around my middle, the other hand held the reins. "I will teach you to manage the reins once you get used to the sensation of riding," he spoke into the top of my head, which rested against his chest. The only sensation I could think about, though, was his hand splaying across my stomach and the rise and fall of his chest at my back. I simply nodded and tried to put space between us, which failed miserably as my ass slid back between his muscular thighs.

He nudged the sides of the horse with his feet, and it moved forward with a jerk. If it weren't for Rion's tight hold, I would have tumbled to the ground with the motion. Bellamy and Flynn mounted their horses with grace, and we followed Nolan into the forest on a small trail out of the grove.

My entire body went rigid as we quickened our pace. The edge of the saddle dug into my hands when my grip tightened, and my thighs were pasted to its sides.

"You need to relax. I will not let you fall," he whispered into my hair. I loosened my muscles one by one against their will. I reclined back against Rion to steady myself. He transferred the reins to one hand and pulled his waterskin from one of the saddle bags, offering it to me. I reluctantly removed my hand from the saddle to retrieve it. I took a long drink, the cool water quenching my thirst, before handing it back.

Nolan rode a few paces ahead of us, and Flynn and Bellamy assumed the rear. The men were on high alert as they scanned the trees for threats hidden within. I followed the path of their eyes and attempted to see through the haze of the fog and dense thicket that could potentially conceal unseen dangers. The hair rose along my arms. "I thought the Dullahan couldn't hunt in the day?" I questioned.

"They cannot, but they are not the only beings that lurk in these forests," Rion answered quietly, keeping his voice just above a whisper. I hadn't even thought about that when I was running for my life through the dense foliage.

"Like what?" The unease of the men elicited the same reaction within my body.

"Leprechauns. Banshees. All the horrors that parents used to scare their children into behaving lurk within the mist of these woods, waiting for some dimwit to wonder into the territory so they can lure them to their death," Flynn answered from behind us. "But don't worry, my lady. Nolan's sour attitude should keep them away."

"Fuck off," Nolan grumbled under his breath halfheartedly.

I felt Rion's chest rumble against my back as he let out a chuckle.

I waited until Nolan was far enough ahead, out of hearing range, before I asked Rion, "Is he always this charming?"

Rion let out a long breath before answering. "Nolan is… complicated. He is fiercely loyal, brutally honest, and protective of those he loves. I would not want anyone else at my back in a fight, but he is also temperamental. Let's just say you never want to be on his bad side."

"Seems to me I have already made it there without even trying," I stated.

"He does not know you, nor trust you."

"And you do?"

"No," Rion answered swiftly. "I do not know you, not fully. However, I am a little more trusting of others than Nolan. I am not so quick to judge that which I do not understand." The honestly within his words was surprising, but it felt as though he was keeping something from me. I said nothing for a moment. The woods passed around us in a blur of gray and green, the steady rhythm of the horse beneath us, and that of the others, the only sound between our breaths. I could feel Rion behind me—calm, solid. It unsettled me how natural that felt.

"You don't even know me," I said quietly. "So why help me?" There was a pause, but this time it wasn't Rion who answered.

"That's not really how this works," Flynn said from behind. His voice was soft, free of the usual grin. "You help people when they need it. End of story."

"Especially when they're running from the Dullahan," Bellamy added. "Not exactly something you walk away from untouched." I turned slightly in the saddle, just enough to glance back at them.

"And what if I brought trouble with me?" I asked.

"You did," Nolan said flatly from the front. "But we're already in it. So, it makes little difference."

Flynn gave a low chuckle. """High praise, coming from a man who once glared at a babe suckling on its mother tit."

I ignored Flynn's crass words and looked back toward Rion, who had yet to speak. I could feel his heartbeat where my back pressed against his chest—strong and steady, like he wasn't the least bit uncertain. "It didn't feel like a choice," he said finally, voice barely above a whisper. "Not with you." The others said nothing. The quiet that followed felt thick with meaning, but no one explained it.

We continued for hours, not speaking much besides the occasional small talk. I shifted slightly, trying to relieve the aching in my limbs. My ass had fallen asleep long ago, and my thighs were on fire. I leaned heavily onto Rion, who tightened his arm around me in response.

Chapter 4

It was hard to tell the time without the sun, but it had to be close to early afternoon when my eyes grew heavy with sleep. I fought the urge for a while, the sound of birds chirping above and the breeze ruffling the trees lulled me into a deep sleep.

I awoke suddenly when the horse lurched forward into a sprint. Rion swore under his breath. It has since grown dark, and the sound of pounding hooves filled my ears. "What's going on?" I yelled over the clamor.

"The Dullahan picked up our trail, hold on." The rest of the men were also pushing their horses full speed between the trees, navigating the dark impressively. We came to a clearing, the men quickly dismounting. Rion pressed the reins into my sweat slicked palms, my shaking hands nearly refusing to grasp them. Panic surged as I realized what was happening. "If they make it passed us, run," Rion commanded as the others surrounded his horse, drawing their swords, as they prepared to make a stand. Everyone held their breath as the pounding hooves of our pursuers slowed at the edge of the wood.

"Hand over the girl human, and we'll let you live," said an eerie voice from the black.

"You can fuck right off," Flynn called back.

The Dullahan moved into sight, swords already drawn and black magic rolling out of their free hands. I couldn't let any more people die for me. They surged forward towards my protectors.

"NO!" I screamed, throwing my hands out in front of me, preparing to hand myself over to spare the men before me. A blinding light flooded the clearing, causing me to slam my eyes shut against it.

Silence filled the air. I waited a moment before slowly peeling them open once more. The Dullahan were gone, and the men were staring in my direction. "What was that?" I asked, searching their faces for an answer.

Rion walked slowly to the horse, taking the reins that I had a death grip on. The other men stood planted in the same spot they had been a moment before. None of them seemed overly concerned about what had just occurred. "The light was emanating from your palms," Rion declared as I gaped dumbly at him. "It was magic, little fox. Pure magic." There was no way. The only magic that ran in my bloodline was healing magic, and it did not present in that way. Not to mention that my magic never manifested. Rion inclined his head towards me, drawing my attention away from my thoughts. "There are some things I need to explain to you, in privacy."

"No, you can tell me right now what is going on," I argued.

"Two nights ago, we felt the earth shake beneath our feet. I suspected it was more than a simple earthquake. It felt as though the power held within the land had been awoken once more." He paused briefly before he continued. "It is said that when a Druid gains their power on their twenty-first birthday, the earth trembles in joy."

I let the information sink in for a moment. Rion searched my eyes for a reaction. "When I came across you in the woods, and you spoke of the attack of the Dullahan on your village, I suspected you were that Druid. That is why…"

"No," I interjected. "That's not true. I am human. My grandmother was a human healer, and my mother died in childbirth, who was also, in fact, a human. There must be another explanation."

"There is not. Everyone in the land now knows that a Druid escaped the massacre. The king knows. That is why he has sent the Dullahan after you. They can sense your magic," Rion explained. "That night, magic entered your body. You had to have felt it."

"I felt nothing," I lied. I had passed out that night from over exertion, not because I was some long-lost Druid.

"You are delusional if you cannot see what is going on." His words stung. Rion turned and addressed his men, "We'll camp here tonight."

I went to dismount, determined to make him see that there must be another explanation for what happened, but my foot got caught in the stirrup. Before I hit the ground, strong arms caught me. I looked up into Rion's strong, chiseled face. He looked at me with pity, which made my blood boil.

I pulled myself out of his grasp and tumbled to the ground. Scurrying to my feet, I got in his face. "You don't know what you are talking about. You are what? Twenty-five? Maybe? You wouldn't have been old enough to remember the Druids." Flynn turned, covering a grin.

"I am an educated man," he said simply, insinuating that I was, in fact, uneducated, which made my anger burn hotter. Before I could say what I honestly thought of his behavior, he started unpacking his horse.

The others had already begun doing the same, all trying to ignore the altercation. I let out a huff and stomped to the edge of the clearing. I needed space to work through my emotions. "Don't go far. The Dullahan are gone for now, but they will be back," Rion called after me. I sent a glare over my shoulder.

Flynn clapped Rion on the back and laughed, "Good luck with that one. You're utterly fucked, man." Rion shrugged out of his grasp, mumbling what I could assume was an insult that I could not hear from this distance.

I watched as Rion pitched the tent quickly from my position. The fire was now rolling, and the others were lounging about when I finally decided I had cooled down enough to join them. Nolan was still giving me the cold shoulder but no longer scowling at me, which was progress. Flynn and Bellamy were talking amongst themselves, preparing the evening meal. The aroma of what appeared to be stew bubbling in the small pot made my stomach growl loudly, which caused Flynn to chuckle, "It's almost ready." My face grew hot—not from the warmth of the large fire before me.

"Where is he going?" I asked Flynn who was seated next to me, catching sight of Rion heading back into the forest.

"Checking the perimeter, my lady. He's a big boy. He can take care of himself," he answered. Rion came back into the clearing a while later, wood in hand. He dropped it by the fire and went into his tent. When he didn't emerge, I quickly finished my bowl and got another to take to him.

I bid the rest of the men a good night and retreated to the tent.

I opened the flap to him sitting in the middle of the floor, head in his hand. Hearing my entrance, he looked up at me. I handed him the bowl. He gave me a quick "thank you" as I sat on the bed that he had made up for me.

"I'm sorry for what I said," he said between bites.

"Thank you." I stayed quiet for a bit longer, not wanting to ruin his meal, before I demanded he tell me everything he knows. "There must be another reason. I am human."

He glanced up at me. "To be fair, the Druids were also human."

"That's not what I meant. My grandmother was a healer. If anything, I would have been gifted with her magic, which I was not. You also said that the Druids came into their power at twenty-one, which I won't be for another ten months," I pointed out.

He continued to study me, like I was a puzzle he had yet to figure out. "You must have come into your power early for some reason." He contemplated. "The magic of the land has not had anyone to wield its power for twenty years. Danu must have felt it was your time."

"It just doesn't make any sense. How could I have survived the massacre?"

"Your grandmother, I assume. She was a human healer?" he clarified. I nodded my agreement. "She must have concealed your identity, even from you, to keep you safe. Though I don't know why she never told you the history of the land." I thought about his answer.

"Just before she died, my grandmother said she thought she had more time. That there were things she needed to tell me." It made sense but didn't explain who I was, why I was such a threat that the king felt the need to send his most ruthless mercenaries after me.

Rion swallowed another bite of his supper before speaking. "I believe you are more than just a Druid, Aine." He turned his body fully towards me and I knew what he was about to tell me was more than I was going to be able to take. "Have you ever been told why the Aos Si attacked the Druids?" I shook my head, not trusting myself to speak. I only knew the events of the overthrow of Lios, not what led to it.

"King Balor was married to a human seer in Tír na nÓg. She spoke a prophecy that there would come a day when a Druid princess would be his destruction. To ensure this never happened, he wiped out the entire Druid population, knowing that they all gathered at the palace during their Samhain celebration. However, the Fates cannot be cheated. Though the king tried, they had a different plan." He paused to allow me to ingest the information.

"I believe that your mother was the Druid queen, Deirdre. Who you knew as your grandmother most likely was a healer your mother had employed for your delivery and care." I stared at Rion, absolutely dumbfounded. I couldn't believe what I was hearing.

"What exactly are you telling me?" I already knew the answer but was struggling to comprehend.

Rion breathed deeply before replying, "I believe you are the princess that the prophecy foretold." It couldn't be true. I was nothing. Nobody. My thoughts were swimming, as I stood abruptly and headed for the front of the tent.

"Where are you going?" he asked, following me out into the cool fall air.

"I just need a moment." I said, stumbling behind the tent. Everything I had eaten came up in one big heave. Rion was there in a moment, holding my hair and rubbing my back, murmuring comfort as I attempted to catch my breath.

"If what I believe is true, your name is Aisling, and you are the only one who has the power to liberate us from the king's oppression."

"Please. Just Stop," I begged. I heaved repeatedly, until my stomach lay barren and aching. When I had nothing left to purge, he helped me back into the tent.

I remained quiet until my heart quit racing. "I am just a poor village girl," I said slowly. "I don't know how to fight. I don't even know anything about magic or anything at all for that matter. In the efforts to spare me, my grandmother kept me sheltered with half-truths and lies. The only information I have is what I got from gossip while visiting patients, which wasn't much. How am I supposed to save an entire kingdom from damnation?" Rion sat me back on the bed. A huge weight settled on my shoulders as I tried to digest the gravity of my situation.

"I can teach you to wield a blade and your magic. We have a long journey ahead of us. It will be hard, but I can help you."

I wanted to know exactly where we were going, but another question slipped past my lips, "How can you help me with magic when you have none?"

"My father was a scholar, who moved my family to the mainland after the invasion. I have read many books on Druid magic." He took my hand and knelt before the bed. "But you need to trust me."

Trust was not something I had enough to spare. He would have to earn it. "Why did you come back?" I asked.

"Because these are my people, and I won't leave them to starve and fend for themselves. I was lucky and grew up in luxury. I want my people to feel the same safety," he paused, seeming to contemplate something before he spoke again. "I'm sure you have noticed by now that my men and I are no mere hunting party. I have been traveling through the kingdom recruiting anyone able to rise and fight against the king. Humans are not the only people oppressed by the king's deeds. Many of the Aos Si are angry, as well. They have been gathering in the mountains surrounding the palace, waiting for me to arrive to lead them."

"The last rebellion didn't make it far. What makes you think this one will be any different?" I asked.

"The last rebellion didn't have the rightful Druid heir," he said, like I would make any difference in a war.

"So that is where we are headed then? To the mountains around Lios?" I speculated.

"Yes," confirmed Rion.

I thought back to the attack on the village, Nora's scared face flashed in my mind's eye. "The night the Dullahan destroyed my village, they took a small girl, Nora. I tried to get her out of there, but the horseman had gotten to her first. What do they want with her? Do you think they will kill her?"

"If you showed any sign that you had a connection with her, they may use her to get to you." He watched me intently. Tears welled in my eyes. "She's no good to them dead," he added as if reading the dark turn my thoughts had taken.

"We have to get her out before they decide she isn't worth keeping alive." The tears now spilled down my cheeks. I quickly wiped them away.

"It's not your fault," he attempted to sooth me.

"But it is. All of this is happening because of me. My people were slaughtered because of me. My mother died because of me. My village. Nora. It is all because I exist," I choked.

"No, the blame lies in the king's hands. His hunger for power and greed led to these events. Not you. Together we can make him pay for it all." Rion spoke with such conviction, but I was still unsure.

I started to shiver. I wasn't sure if it was the cold, vomiting, fear or a mixture of all three that caused my teeth to chatter loudly in the quiet tent. Rion gestured for me to get off the bed and pulled back the blankets for me to get in. "Get some sleep. I know you still have a lot of questions, but you need your strength. We can begin training in the morning and produce a plan moving forward." Rion got up swiftly and left the tent.

I pondered all that I had learned. I still had the urge to deny it all. I had woken up this morning thinking I was nothing of value, only to find out I am the redemption of an entire kingdom. The weight of that realization pushed heavy on my shoulders.

Now I understand why Rion was willing to risk everything to ensure my safety. I felt a tinge of disappointment, though I wasn't entirely sure why. I supposed it was due to his dedication to my protection being driven by what he had to gain from me. He cared about the title, the power, the hope that I could bring to his rebellion, not about the actual person behind those things.

Of course I will aid them. I would do anything to see my people freed from the king's hold, to no longer see children die. I didn't have anything else to lose.

Chapter 5

I woke up in a haze. For a moment, I let myself forget all that had happened. I allowed myself to imagine that I was back with my grandmother. A memory of a time when she was healthy, smiling at me over a bowl of morning broth with a side of fresh apples that I had harvested the evening before, bloomed in my mind. A content smile spilled over my face.

The image was instantly shattered when the memory shifted to the night she died. When my life was turned upside down. I let out a sob and opened my eyes. The reality of my situation finally settled like a rock in my stomach. Even the songs of the birds seemed a little less cheerful this morning. I clutched my chest, trying to subdue the intense throbbing pain within. I choked on my cries, attempting to keep them quiet as to not draw any attention to myself. I was still struggling with the revelation that I was the heir to a dead kingdom—that the weight of a kingdom rested upon my shoulders. I gathered all the painful memories and complex emotions and shoved them down within myself to deal with later, for if I was to lead these people, my people, to victory, I couldn't let myself succumb to them.

A quick glance around the tent told me Rion had never come back last night. His blanket was thrown over me instead. I got up and left the tent. Only Rion sat on the ground by the fire, smoke from the dying embers rising into the sky. A flash of a fire-engulfed structure filled my head. I turned away to gather myself, gazing out into the eternal forest that was buzzing with life, refusing to allow my hidden emotions to slip free once more. The trees reached for the cloud-laden sky. Their leaves flipped to reveal the pale green undersides, begging for the rain that left the clouds dark and heavy. The birds sang loudly, swooping between their outstretched branches. The beauty of the forest settled my nervousness, a comfort that I had sought many a time growing up. I took a steady breath and returned my attention to Rion.

"You didn't come back last night," I stated as I dropped to the ground at his side, the damp earth wetting the baggy trousers that still I wore.

"I figured you would want time alone." He picked up a stick and stoked the fire, sparks flying in different directions. I reverted my eyes to the ground, which Rion seemed to notice as he quickly stopped his prodding of the ashes. There was an awkward tension between us. Refusing to make eye contact, I looked around once more.

"Where is everyone else?" The horses were out of sight, but I knew they wouldn't be far off. There wasn't any sign of the other three men.

"Nolan went out to scout. Flynn and Bellamy went to hunt

and gather to replenish our stores. They will not be back for some time." Rion fiddled with the stick he still clutched in his hands. "I know what I told you last night was a lot of process, but we need you if we are going to succeed in this war."

Finally, I met his pleading gaze. The crushing weight of the duty I had to my people pressed my hand. "I will try," I said.

Rion's eye lit up and a small smile appeared on his face. "We also need you strong," he stated as he handed me a small bowled filled with oats topped with chunks of fresh apples. My stomach growled loudly, causing Rion to chuckle—the first sign of amusement that I have seen from him since I emerged from the tent, which lightened the mood a bit. "Once you have finished, we can begin a small bit of training."

It was delicious, the oats were seasoned with some sort of spice giving it a warm, sweet, slightly woody flavor I did not recognize, and the apples were crisp and refreshing. "What is this?" I asked around a mouthful, not really caring about my manners as I did so.

Rion started at me as though I had grown a giant wart on my face that sprouted little gray hairs, like the absurdity of my question was obvious. "It just oats with bits of apple and cinnamon."

"Cinnamon?" I questioned.

"It's a spice that is harvested from the bark of special trees." I had never heard of such a tree, but was so distracted by shoveling another spoonful into my mouth that I didn't feel it was important enough to disrupt my eating. I cleared the bowl, scraping every last morsel from its edges. I was tempted to lick it the rest of the way clean, but I figured there were lines that should never be crossed. Years of starvation and never knowing the feeling of a full stomach my entire life made those boundaries hard to keep.

Rion took the bowl from my hands, setting it on the ground

beside the fire, and pulled a small blade free from the sheath at his side. He handed it off to me. I gripped its hilt hesitantly. "First, you need to be able to protect yourself. We will begin your training by learning how to wield a knife, just until you build some of your strength. Then, we can move on to sword play." He got to his feet, moving to the center of the clearing.

I scrambled to mine and followed his lead. He positioned me across from him, only an arm's length away. I held the knife out in front of me, my hands so sweaty it nearly slipped from my grasp. "Show me a battle stance," he demanded. I looked down at myself and back at him with confusion. "Good Gods, okay," he huffed in frustration. "Start with your legs shoulder width apart." He came to my side and tapped my dominant thigh. "This foot needs to be slightly ahead of the other. This will keep you steady and not easily knocked over. Now square your shoulder towards your attacker."

"I don't have an…" I started before he moved in front of me and smacked my hand. The knife went tumbling to the ground.

"Your grip is weak. It needs to be firm, but keep your wrist a bit loose to allow for smooth movement. Your blade should be an extension of your arm, whether it be a sword or knife."

He picked up the knife and placed it back in my palm, pressing my fingers closed tightly around its hilt like he had instructed. Grabbing my wrist, he pointed the knife at himself. "With a shorter blade, you must be close to your attacker and precise. Do not leave yourself exposed and be quick. Avoid going straight for the chest. If your blade gets lodged in bone, you won't be able to retrieve it." He guided the blade to his side. "Aim for the kidney on an upward angle." He jerked my hand towards himself, demonstrating the amount of force. I pulled back, not wanting to hurt him. He chuckled. The sound was low and resonated deep within his chest.

Though I was supposed to be listening as he prattled on about hesitation and the physics behind force and momentum, all I kept thinking about was how much I wanted to hear that sound again. He noticed my distraction and cleared his throat. "Are you listening?"

"Yes," I answered quickly, too quickly for it to be the truth.

"Mhmm." He gave me an entirely too knowing, lopsided smile before he continued. My ears burned, but I kept my focus on the task at hand from that point on.

We spent the hour working on my form, which was absolutely atrocious according to Rion. Flynn emerged from the trees with a large deer slung over his shoulders, his twin hot on his heels. He flung the carcass into his brother's arms, causing Bellamy to almost lose his balance, when he saw us. "My turn!" Flynn called as he jogged up to us.

"I think not," Rion said with his hands on his hips.

"You think I am going to hurt the princess?" Flynn winked at me. "There are many things I would like to do to her, but harming her is not one of them." Heat flushed my face. I was not used to the crude remarks. I had been around men before, but most of them were married with children. Anyone my age didn't seem to take an interest in me. I would probably be beautiful, if I was more than a bag of bones.

"Oh, fuck off, Flynn," Rion swore. His reaction caught me off guard.

"Maybe you and I can show her how it's done," Flynn remarked with a huge smile. He drew his sword and backed up a few paces. Rion drew his, pure determination written upon his face.

Bellamy laughed from where he started butchering their kill. "You know this never works in your favor," he called. Flynn waved him off and made the first move. Rion blocked his blow with the grace of a soldier. I moved out of their way and came to Bellamy's side.

"They aren't going to actually hurt each other, right?" I asked him, a little worried someone would come back without an appendage by the intensity with which they were fighting.

"No, but Flynn will most definitely get his ass handed to him," he laughed. "Rion is taking it easy, but as soon as he decides the fight is over, he'll end it."

I watched the two with awe. It was like a language that they were both fluent in. The swords sung as they clashed together, the two men their masters. Neither one was breaking a sweat. "Is that all you got?" Flynn goaded. "When I win, I get to teach the princess how to fight. Maybe my lady would rather stay in my tent, ride between my thighs? I'm much better company." With that, rage twisted Rion's face as he kicked out his foot and hit Flynn in the center of his chest. I inhaled sharply as he landed feet away flat on his back, sword flung from his hand. Flynn was gasping on the ground, having had the air knocked from his lungs. Bellamy caught my arm with a blood coated hand to keep me in my place, seeing my intention to rush to Flynn's side.

Rion walked over and stood above him, sword at his throat. "You need to learn to keep your mouth shut. It will be the death of you." Rion sheathed his sword and stormed off.

"You think you'd learn," Bellamy laughed, shaking his head and releasing my arm to continue his work. I was still rooted in place as I watched Rion disappear into the surrounding greenery.

"Someday," Flynn paused to cough, "it will be him looking up at me from the flat of his back." He laid there for a bit before he rolled to his stomach and clambered to his feet.

"Whatever you say brother. Now that you're done poking the bear, come help me with this deer." Flynn hobbled over to his brother to do just that.

"Are you okay?" I asked when I noticed Flynn clutching his side.

"It's nothing that won't heal, princess." He gave me a reassuring smile before he added, "I will be alright."

I excused myself and moved in the direction that Rion had disappeared.

I found him leaning against a tree at the edge of the clearing. Hearing my approach, he looked my way.

I nodded towards Flynn. "What was that really about?" Rion returned to gazing through the trees. I could tell what Flynn said had bothered him.

"He's got a mouth and sometimes he needs to be taught that women are not objects for his entertainment," he said, lips drawing into a tight line.

"He was only teasing. It's definitely not what I am used to, but I can handle it."

"Well, I can't," he growled, turning back to camp.

Nolan rode into the clearing minutes later, relaying that the road was clear. Rion and Nolan packed up camp with my aid, while Flynn and Bellamy finished the deer and packed the meat up to be smoked later this evening. We were back on the road in under an hour. The twins took up the front this time with Nolan, bragging about their hunting success. Rion and I rode at the rear a few paces behind the others. "Will you tell me about the Druids?" I asked, trying to relieve the tension in the air with conversation.

"Well, what have you been taught? No need repeating what you already know." Irritation wafted off him. So much for relieving tension. I knew he wasn't upset with me, but his curt tone hurt. I continued tentatively.

"My grandmother told me many stories about the queen," I paused, realizing for the first time that she was actually telling me of my mother without me even knowing it. I wished to hold my mother's onyx pendant. I wanted to feel its smooth surface under my thumb, to feel close to her. Sadness for its loss renewed as I continued, "She told me that the Druids were gifted earth-based magic from Danu, the Goddess of the Earth. That they could manipulate the earth and water around them. She told me of the events of the invasion, and all that it cost humanity. Other than that, not much else."

"Aye, your mother's death was a great loss. The Druids were a powerful people and had ruled these lands in peace for centuries. They were a force, but the Aos Si had taken them by surprise. They were under prepared for attack, for no one had threatened them before. They had a false sense of security. Over the last twenty years, Balor has strengthened the kingdom's defenses. He knows that at some point, the people of this land will attempt to regain the kingdom. It is why he imposes higher and higher taxes. He is hoping to weaken the population. But it will not protect him from you," he assured.

"If my mother and her army couldn't stop him, what makes you think I can?" I turned my head to peer into his face. The tension from the events that had transpired earlier seemed to fade as his eyes met mine.

"You, little fox, will be more powerful than any before you. The earth's power was split between many at the time. However, you have access to it all." I gaped at him. I was unaware of how the magic of the Druids worked, but the thought that I had access to all the magic of the earth was intimidating. "That is why we need to catch you up to speed. You need to learn how to use your magic with intention. Last night you were in a highly emotional state, and you did it by accident," he explained.

"And how do I do that?"

"You are a conduit of the Earth's power, so we will begin with grounding. It is the act of forming a connection between you and the Earth, allowing you to pull the power into yourself. However, magic comes at a cost. Earth-based magic drains your strength, and if you take in more than you are able, it could kill you." That seemed daunting and terrifying.

"How am I supposed to know how much I can handle?" All the information laid at my feet was starting to feel like a weight tied around my ankles that, if thrown in a deep lake, would drown me.

"We will start small, go slow. You need to be focused and must try to refrain from performing magic while overwhelmed with emotion. That can cause you to take on too much. You also cannot fear it. You are in control, not the other way around. You will eventually build a tolerance to the magic over time, allowing you to eventually control it all."

My attention was drawn to the land around me as I digested his words. The lush underbrush that coated the ground beneath the tall trees, their branches reaching to the sky as if they, too, worshipped the Gods, was a brilliant green. Wildflowers of all colors were scattered about. Their subtle scents sweetened the air around me. It was still a mystery to me how such beauty could thrive beneath the suffocating tangle of branches, proof that even in shadow, beauty could rise. Just as my people will once again.

As I continued my examination, the forest seemed to hum in approval as the soft buzz of the hidden magic stored within prickled my skin. "I can feel it," I murmured, more to myself than the man pressed into my back. Every plant. Every stone. Every precious piece of soil called to me. Though I feared the treacherous road ahead, my body also vibrated with excitement and determination. I spent my whole life feeling powerless to stop the slow decay of the people around me, and now finally, I have a way to help them beyond herbs and tonics.

I couldn't help the smile that overtook my face as I thought of a world where the kingdom thrived once more. Where families had enough food to fill their bellies and happiness to fill their hearts. It no longer felt like an impossible dream, but a tangible reality. "When will we begin?" I asked, turning at my waist so I could see Rion's face.

"Whenever you are ready," he replied. "Tonight, if you wish."

I nodded my agreement enthusiastically, which made Rion's full lips tip up into a grin. I became all too aware that I was staring at his mouth when he cleared his throat. "Uh, yeah. Yeah, that sounds good," I stammered, snapping my gaze forward and pretending the road had become suddenly very interesting. We fell into a terrible awkward silence that had me shifting in the saddle. Rion stiffened behind me, and his hand that was placed on my stomach fell to my thigh.

"I am going to need you to stop that," his voice thick like honey with an underlying pained tone.

"Did I hurt you?" I stopped my movements, becoming concerned that I may have unintentionally caused him pain. He drew in a deep breath, adjusting and tightening his grip on the reins.

"Not hurt, just making it hard to focus is all." My eyes widened as I thought about my position between his thighs.

"Oh" was all I could manage to say past the lump that had formed in my throat. My face was on fire. I tried to move forward in the saddle to create space between us, but the sway of the horse made it nearly impossible, not to mention Rion had moved his hand back to its original placement and held me firm.

We traveled at the back of the group, still submerged in the awkward tension I had created until just before dusk. "We need to set up camp before it gets dark," Rion called ahead to the other men. "We'll head deeper into the wood off the path," he gestured towards the right.

The men veered off the path and we dismounted, leading the horses to a small patch of grass for them to graze. We walked for a bit before stopping at a spot that was mostly clear of roots. "Flynn, go see if you can spot a creek nearby to refill our skins," Rion ordered. Flynn looked like he might argue, but Bellamy shot him a look, and he stomped off.

"I'll get wood," Nolan said, walking off, as well.

I helped Rion unpack the horse and set up our tent. He kept insisting that he didn't need my help, and I was fairly sure I was more of a hindrance anyway, but I refused to sit by and watch. By the time we were done, Bellamy had started a fire with the wood that Nolan had returned with. The smell of the cooking deer made my stomach grumble. Rion strode off into the forest to check the perimeter. "I will come with you," I offered.

"No, you need to eat. It will only take a moment," he assured me before disappearing into the dark among the trees.

I was too hungry to argue, so I returned to the fire, where Bellamy handed me a healthy portion of the fresh meat. The venison melted in my mouth, its gamey taste enveloping my tongue in a warm embrace. I let out a soft hum. I couldn't think of the last time I had enough sustenance to fill my stomach. As long as I can remember, I have gone to sleep hungry.

Rion returned and we all ate in silence. The tension between Flynn and Rion still permeated the air. It created a bubble of anxiety that surrounded the group. No one spoke, afraid that it may burst. Nolan was the first to rise, claiming the first watch. He strode off into the forest beyond. Then, Flynn left for his tent without a word, leaving Rion, Bellamy, and I around the fire.

"You guys need to make up. He's been sulking all day," I said to Rion.

"He will get over it," he grumbled. Man, I thought women were supposed to be the moody ones. "I got to piss," Rion got up quickly and headed into the forest, intentionally avoiding the conversion.

"What is his problem?" I asked Bellamy when he was out of earshot.

"There are things you don't understand, princess," Bellamy shifted uncomfortably.

"Care to explain?" I prompted.

"No, not really. It isn't my place." Bellamy stood quickly when Rion returned, feigning a stretch. "Looks like it's my time to turn in before I take over watch from Nolan. Goodnight, sleep tight, don't let the leprechauns bite," and with that Bellamy disappeared into his tent.

Rion stood warming his hands over the fire. I didn't want to bring up what Bellamy had said. The last thing I wanted was to make him upset with both brothers. He crouched beside me and held out a hand. "Are you ready to begin working with your magic?"

I nodded, though butterflies, or perhaps bees, swarmed in my stomach as I took his hand. He hauled me to my feet in one fluid motion. "Remove your shoes," Rion instructed. "Direct contact with the Earth will help you summon the magic within and form the connection. For the first few tries, I will be your anchor." I removed my shoes like he asked and took his outstretched hands. "If at any time you feel things are moving too fast, find our connection and follow it back." I took a moment to feel his callused hands within mine. I familiarized myself with the connection. I felt something stir deep within me that I could not explain, like a thread tightening around my core and snaking into my heart. Rion drew in a sharp breath. "Good, now close your eyes and breathe with me. In through your nose and out through your mouth. Focus on the feel of your feet on the Earth and keep breathing."

I continued to follow his direction. My heart thundered against my rib cage. I focused on the feel of the moist soil under my bare feet, roots and stone dug sharply into my soles. I felt the ground pulse beneath my feet. My eyes flew back open. "I feel it," I gasp.

"Stay focused." I snapped my eyes back shut. "Now, reach down through the connection and pull the magic into your body. Feel it warm your feet, your legs," Rion guided me, his voice soft as velvet. The heat he described climbed up my legs. "Good, just like that," he whispered his praise, which nearly made me lose all focus. A rush of warmth bloomed in my chest, confusing and fierce. My knees nearly buckled as the magic surged higher, tingling beneath my skin, and mingled with something far more human, a deep desire that I hadn't expected. His voice slid past my defenses like it belonged there. My reaction caught me off guard, raw and intense, and suddenly I wasn't sure if I was standing in a circle of power or falling headfirst into something I couldn't control.

The heat rushed up through my core into my chest, and I let out a gasp. "Too fast, go slow. You're doing great." My focus slipped with his words, the burning sensation from the magic winked out, leaving me feeling hot in a whole other way. My eyes flung open, and he was staring at me.

I caught a glimpse of need in his eyes before he gained control of himself. The fire's light played on his features. His strong jaw, and high cheekbone cast shadows across his face. Short stubble had begun to litter his chin. He was the most beautiful man I had ever had the privilege to lay eyes on.

"That was a really good attempt." He dropped my hands suddenly, shifting uncomfortably. He was being kind because I failed miserably. My limbs felt heavy, but I was nothing if not persistent.

"I want to try again," I stated, offering my hands to him.

"Tomorrow. You need to rest before you can try again." I went to argue, but he held up his hand to stop me. "Please don't. I need you breathing for this all to work." The warmth I had felt from his praise froze within my heart as I was reminded that I am only a tool to him. I needed to get my attraction and emotions under control before they ruined everything.

Chapter 6

The fog was thick as we continued our journey south the next morning. Rion informed me, as I devoured the same oat breakfast as the day before, that we would be stopping at an inn for the night, assuring me that it would be safe. He said we deserved a night where we didn't have to sleep with roots stuck in our backs, but I was not entirely convinced that it was a good decision.

Nestled between Rion's strong thighs felt different after last night. His weight pressed against my back, and his arm weaved around my waist was now more distracting. I silently cursed myself.

Flynn rode up next to us. "We need to come up with a plan before we reach the palace," he said to the group.

"First things first, we need to locate the four magical treasures of the Tuatha Dé Danann. Without them, we don't stand a chance, even with the princess," Rion replied.

The mention of these treasures piqued my interest, taking my mind off the feel of Rion's hands on my treacherous body. I looked between them, confused. "The what?"

Nolan scoffed from the front of the line, "Where on earth were you hiding, under a rock?"

"What did I do for you to hate me so? You don't even know me!" I had had enough of him ignoring my existence, and when he did decide to speak to me, it was an insult. I typically could keep my temper under control, but I needed to understand his position in all of this. He didn't seem like he gave a damn about anything that didn't directly benefit him.

Nolan came to a sudden halt and turned his horse to face Rion and I. "I followed Rion throughout this entire kingdom in search of a way to save us all. When we felt the magic of the land be claimed, I thought we finally had a shot. Then he brought you back. An ignorant little girl, who could very well be our damnation, not salvation," he seethed. "Rion, I know you think she can master all she needs to know by the time we have collected the treasures, but she knows nothing of the world she lives in, the people she came from. We are fucking doomed."

Rion was shaking with rage behind me. "You will watch your fucking tongue, or I will see it freed from your mouth. She has a lot to learn, yes, but she is all we have. The only hope."

Bellamy shifted uncomfortably in his saddle. "I don't believe everything that just spewed from Nolan's wretched mouth, but he did make a good point. We don't have enough time."

"Before you guys continue speaking like I am not here, can one of you explain what exactly these treasures are?" I asked.

Nolan looked about ready to jump from the horse he perched upon and pummel me, his glare burning holes in my skin, as Rion spoke from behind me, "Many centuries ago, the Tuatha Dé Danann were in the midst of a war against the Fomorians, a giant race that used to roam these lands." His voice was tight, as though he spoke through gritted teeth. "At the time, the Emerald Isle was separated by five major clans, four of which had agreed to aid the Gods. Each of the clans was led by one of the Tuatha Dé Danann. The war was won, though the humans had lost many, but their fortitude and loyalty to their Gods did not go unnoticed.

"Each of the clans was blessed with a gift by one of the Gods. Danu blessed her clan with Earth-based magic, as you already know. The Morrighan blessed her tribe with the gift of vision. Both clans were also given a long lifespan. Ogma's clan was gifted with wisdom and knowledge, and Bridget gifted her clan with healing magic. You know them as the Druids, seers, scholars, and healers.

"The Tuatha Dé Danann also brought with them four magical items from their four great cities: Failias, Findias, Goirias, and Murias. The Spear of Lugh was said to be unbeatable in battle. It never missed its mark, ensuring victory for its wielder. The Dagda's Cauldron, which no person came away from unsatisfied. It provided sustenance to all who deserved it. It was also rumored to be able to bring back warriors from the dead. Claíomh Solais, the Sword of Light, was famous for its invincibility and sharpness. It could pierce any armor and, like the spear, never missed its target. The sword was once wielded by the God, Nuada of the Silver Hand.

"Most importantly, Lia Fáil, the Stone of Fal, for when the true heir of the Emerald Isle stood upon the stone, it would roar with joy. When all four are brought together in one place, their wielder becomes blessed with their combined divine power. They could take down an entire army with a single thought." The tension in

Rion's voice lessened, as if he had drifted to some far away place, where he stood watching these events unfold.

"The Gods encouraged the humans to unite under one kingdom, and to determine its ruler, each clan leader stood upon the stone. Whoever the stone chose would also control the four treasures. Everyone took their turn, and the stone chose the Druids. The final gift the Gods gave the Druid leader was the ability to raise and control the Wild Hunt—warrior wraiths that are summoned from the Land of the Dead.

"The first Druid king separated the magical gifts, fearing they were too powerful to keep in a single place. The stone was set into the dais beneath the throne in Lios. The sword remained with the king and the other two were hidden. Should the Druid ever need them to protect the kingdom, they would be retrieved. The location of the treasures was only known by the king, who passed the knowledge to his heir, who passed it on to theirs.

"The kingdom lived in peace under Druid rule for centuries. During this time, the Tuatha Dé Danann disappeared. No one is sure whatever happened to them. Balor took the throne of Tír na nÓg shortly after their disappearance. However, the king grew greedy. He was young at the time and ambitious. Being the ruler of one kingdom did not satisfy his need for power. When his wife – a human seer – told him of his fate, his resolve was set. So, King Balor devised a plan to overthrow the Druids and take the human kingdom for his own. I believe you know the rest of the story."

I took a breath as I consumed the information I had just been presented. "Well, as you said, we need to find the rest of the treasures before he does," I finally said. I wasn't sure of much these days, but I promised Rion I would try. Even though it all felt hopeless at the moment.

Bellamy sighed, "But where do we start? The false king always keeps the sword on him. The stone is literally set in stone, and the other two haven't been seen for centuries."

Nolan finally broke his silence, "We have six weeks until we reach Lios. That's enough time to produce a solid plan, but Rion, you have six weeks to teach the girl to at least use a weapon. She cannot step foot into that palace unless she can protect herself." Six weeks. I had six weeks, and I could barely wield the knife without dropping it. I could feel the panic attack approaching at rapid speed.

"I can get it done," Rion said, still agitated. I didn't know if he was upset with me, Nolan, or the situation in general. "We need to get a move on. We have been stopped long enough, and I want to reach the inn before nightfall."

Rion rode to the front of the group, leading the way. I contemplated everything I had learned. The shoes I had to fill were large, and I didn't know if I would be capable. The weight of responsibility pressed heavy on my chest. If I couldn't figure my shit out, I would cost them everything, including their lives. "I'm sorry I wasn't what you all were expecting," I whispered when we were far enough ahead of the others to not be overheard.

"This plan has been long in the making before we even knew you existed. We would have gone through with it with or without you. However, I do believe that I can teach you enough to keep you alive. Once we have the treasures, we can use their power to regain the land for the last time. Then you will take your rightful place on the throne," Rion encouraged.

"I don't know what it means to rule. What if I can't do it? What if I am nothing like my mother?" Then it dawned on me. "Do you happen to know who my father was?"

"According to the histories, your mother never spoke of who your father was. I am assuming your grandmother did not know?"

"She didn't, at least that is what she had told me. Based on recent events, I don't know how much of her words were true."

"I am sorry. I wish I had the answer for you."

We continued ahead in silence as the sun began to set. The silence was broken when Flynn and Bellamy started discussing the debauchery they had planned for the evening. "I want to wet my lips with the piss they call ale, then find a woman or two to warm my bed for the evening," Flynn exclaimed.

Nolan chimed in, "I don't know how you can think of fucking anything. My ass is surely bruised. I'd never keep pace." Hearing him joke with the twins made me hate him a little less, but just a little.

"I'm just happy to sleep off the ground," Bellamy replied. "I'm tired of waking with a crick in my neck."

"You better get used to it. This will be the only night we can afford the luxury. However, do not let your guard down. We still have about an hour until we reach the village. The sun is already going down, and I do not want to be ambushed while you guys are daydreaming about ale and women," Rion scolded his men.

Bellamy called from behind, "Hey! I am only dreaming of a non-rocky bed." Rion chucked and shook his head.

Though inns were not common anymore, there were a few that got by selling weak brew and hot food to those who could afford it, mostly the Aos Si and hunters. "I am assuming your family did well on the mainland?" I asked Rion. He had decent leathers, horses, and could afford to stay at an inn—his family must have money.

The men continued their discussion of sex and drinking,

while Rion took a minute to reply. "My father became a merchant after we relocated. He did well enough."

"What was it like growing up on the mainland?" I asked, the topic piquing my interest.

He contemplated his answer yet again, before saying, "Things are much different there. They are not ruled by a king or queen, but by a council. It is a conglomeration of Aos Si, lesser fairies, and humans. The land is protected by the God Manannan. He was neutral during the war and decided to create a place that was also neutral. There is a mist surrounding the continent, controlled by the God. You cannot pass through without his permission and that of the council. If you enter without, the mist disorients you. If you emerge, you are on the same side from which you started. If you are allowed entrance, you must relinquish any magic or weapons and take a vow of nonviolence. If at any time you break that vow, it will take your life where you stand." He paused for a moment before he continued, "Anyone can leave at any time, but you will not be allowed passage through the mist again."

I wanted him to tell me about his childhood. Though I was happy to learn about this mysterious land, I wanted to know more about him. "What about you? Were you happy there?"

"I had everything I ever needed." He left it at that. Then, his head flew to the right of the path and halted, throwing up his hand for the others to do the same. I squinted against the night that had descended. I didn't see anything.

"What is it?" I whispered. Rion hushed me harshly. Something was wrong. Then I heard the faint rustling in the bushes. Nolan swore from behind us. I tried to turn to see what was going on, but Rion's large form blocked my view.

"Fuck," he said, quickly dismounting and drawing his sword. I was finally able to see what all the commotion was about. The way we had come was blocked by child sized men, leprechauns. More came out of the forest and cut off the other end of the road. Rion spoke clearly, "We wish no trouble. Please allow us to pass."

One of the leprechauns stepped forward. He must be their leader. "This part of the forest is under our domain, gifted by the king. You are trespassing. We have every right to defend what is ours."

Rion slowly sheathed his sword, raising his hands in front of him to show he meant no harm. "What do you want for safe passage?"

The leprechaun looked Rion up and down, then in my direction, still perched on Rion's horse. He noticed as Rion attempted to block his view. His lips peeled back over his half-rotten teeth into a diabolical smile. "We want her," he demanded, pointing his stubby figure at me.

"No," Rion growled. The leprechaun backed away a step but regained his courage.

"If you won't hand her over, then we want her weight in gold." My jaw dropped, there was no way Rion had that kind of coin, no matter how well off his father was. More leprechauns had now gathered at the edge of the road, completely boxing us in. Though Rion and his men were skilled warriors, from what I have seen, they had the numbers. They couldn't take them all at once.

"That is a steep sum, don't you think?" Rion pressed, giving them a lazy smile. Was he going to charm them to death? "How about this, I will give you two gold coins to add to your horde, and we will be on our way?"

The leprechaun glowered at him and moved forward once again. "You insult us, boy. We will not negotiate. Either give us the girl or the gold."

A look I had never seen crossed Rion's face. "Pity," was all he said before he quickly redrew his sword and lobbed the leprechaun's head from his shoulders. The road descended into chaos, Flynn and Bellamy swiftly dismounted, taking either side of the road and Nolan defended the front from his horse, who took immense pleasure in stomping the small pests.

The leprechauns swarmed Rion, seeing him as the biggest threat. Before they had a chance to gather about the horse as well, I leapt ungracefully down from its back. Grabbing one of the dead leprechaun's swords, which in my hands was the size of a large knife, I ran to Rion's side. I started to indiscriminately stab at the small men.

"Get out of here, you are not ready!" Rion yelled at me.

"There is no way in hell I am leaving you," I called back, chopping and slicing at the leprechauns. They fell quickly under my blade, even though my skill left a lot to be desired.

Rion and I finished off the last on our end and moved to help the others. Flynn and Rion fought back-to-back with deadly precision as I veered toward Bellamy, parrying a leprechaun's strike just in time. Nolan seemed to be doing just fine with the help from his horse's iron hooves that reared and stomped two would-be attackers.

My eyes drifted back to Rion, and in my moment of distraction, one of the leprechaun's blades caught my wrist, splitting the skin deeply. I gasped and dropped my sword to the earth path, falling with a thud. I grabbed the wound, applying pressure to staunch the bleeding. Blood seeped between my fingers, bright and hot, my head swimming at the sight. The sounds of clashing swords were drowned out by the pounding of my heartbeat like war drums in my ears. "Rion!" Bellamy shouted, his voice cutting through the haze. He lunged toward me, shielding my side as two leprechauns pressed forward. His sword flashed as he fought them off, keeping himself between me and the danger.

"I'm fine," I lied, stumbling back, knees weak. I wasn't. The wound burned, and I could feel strength leaking from me with every drop. Bellamy didn't buy my words, his eyes flicked to my wrist, then to my paling face, and he swore under his breath.

I dropped to my knees. As I fell, I grabbed Bellamy's sleeve and pulled him with me. "Rion get the fuck…" he yelled, but his words trailed off. Time seemed to slow as an arrow whizzed past my face. I felt warmth splatter across my face and watched as Bellamy's eyes glazed over before he fell to the forest floor, blood spurting from the gaping wound on the side of his throat. I used my remaining energy to crawl forward, covering Bellamy with my own body. Rion and Flynn came up from behind me, cutting down the remaining of the leprechauns that encroached upon us.

The forest went dead until a cry of agony roared from Flynn. He pushed me off his twin and pulled him into his arms. "Come on, brother. I am nothing without you." Tears rolled down his face as he looked into his brother's eyes. He sobbed, holding his brother to his heart.

Rion knelt by Flynn's side, placing a hand on his shoulder, and recited the ancient prayer of our forefathers, "May the road rise to meet you. May the wind be at your back. May the sun shine warmth upon your face, and the rains fall soft upon your fields. Until we meet again." Nolan finally dismounted and rushed over to his friend. He placed his hand on his other shoulder opposite Rion. I watched as the men grieved their fallen brother. The pain in my heart momentarily overshadowed the throbbing in my wrist.

I attempted to stand, to give them privacy, but my hand came out from under me. I had forgotten my wound and the loss of blood that caused my vision to blur. I hit the ground face first, hard enough to make my teeth clack together. The taste of iron flooded my mouth. Large hands came upon me, flipping me over. "Shit. Shit!" Rion swore, finding the wound quickly and gripping it once more to halt the bleeding. "Nolan, get me the suture kit. Now!" From where I lay, I couldn't see anything, but I heard rushed steps and Nolan's face appeared above me. Flynn came into my view with a chunk of wood, tears still marring his face.

My vision faded in and out. "Am I going to die?" I asked no one in particular, fear overwhelming my senses.

To my surprise, Nolan answered, "Shhh, no." He wiped the tears from my cheek that slipped free. "We must stop the bleeding. Rion, hold her." Rion's strong hand held my wrist out towards Nolan, then he gently laid the rest of his body across mine. His weight was comforting. Nolan nodded towards Flynn.

"Bite this," he said, holding out the piece of wood. I opened my mouth to allow him to slide the wood between my teeth. Without warning, Nolan made his first stitch. I struggled against Rion's hold, letting out a ragged scream.

"Shhh," Rion ran his free hand across my face. I held his stare to give me strength. Nolan continued stitching, and my energy to fight began to wane with each strangled scream and every attempt to wiggle myself free from Rion's grasp. I could barely keep my eyes open. "Stay with me, little fox. I need you to stay awake," Rion whispered into my ear. I couldn't. I was so tired. I closed my eyes one last time and didn't have it in me to open them again.

Chapter 7

I came awake to whispering voices. I cracked my eyes, but the bright candlelight stung, and I snapped them back shut. I knew I was no longer on the forest floor, for rough linen sheets and a stiff blanket covered me. At some point, my clothing had been changed. I recognized the feel of the soft silk shift encasing my body. Heat burned my cheeks at the thought.

Rion's voice caught my attention. "She can't travel like this. It will take a day or so to recover from the blood loss."

"Did you see the wound when we arrived," Nolan spoke quietly, so as not to be overheard. "It was already beginning to heal."

"I saw," Rion answered.

"What does it mean? The Druids were not gifted with accelerated healing."

"Her father must be Aos Si. It would make sense why her

mother kept it secret. Her people would have never accepted their union. It explains a lot, actually." My eyes flew open, and I attempted to rise. I flopped back on the bed, unsuccessful. This caught their attention and Rion shot to my side. "How are you feeling?" He searched my eyes for any sign of pain, as he pushed wisps of my hair out of my face. I felt weak and my head was pounding, but the pain in my wrist was gone.

"I heard what you said," I said, ignoring Rion's concern. "You think I am half Aos Si?" Rion reached for my wrist and turned it for me to look. The wound was only a pink, raised line. I ran my fingers across the new scar. "How long have I been out?"

"Two hours. A wound like that would have taken a human weeks to heal. Even with a healer, it would still take a day to show this much progress." I continued to stare at my wrist. My grandmother once had a patient that cut her hand deeply, while preparing dinner for her family. It did, indeed, take my grandmother hours just to knit the tendons and veins back together.

Yet there was something that just didn't make any sense. "I have had scraps and cuts in the past. They healed at a normal rate. Why would the ability be just now presenting itself?"

Rion cocked his head, contemplating my question. "I am not entirely sure. I wish I had an answer for you."

Nolan dipped his head. "I will leave you to rest." Just before he exited the room, he turned to me and said, "I want to apologize. For the way I treated you. You were extremely brave out there." He left quickly without another word.

Rion sat on the edge of the bed, taking my hand in his. He looked tired and sad. "It was my fault," I choked out. "Bellamy's death was my fault. If I hadn't left my wrist exposed and gotten hurt, he wouldn't have been distracted." I choked. I couldn't contain my emotions for long until my entire body shook with the force of my sobbing.

Rion pulled me to his chest, tangling his hand in my hair. "It was not your fault. If anything, the fault is mine. You were not ready, and it is my responsibility to make sure you are." He pulled back and tilted my chin forcing my eyes to meet his. "We cannot change what happened. We must move on and not make the same mistake again. Once you have recovered, I will train you harder. I will ensure that next time, you are prepared. Okay?"

I nodded—my gaze locked with his. He stared back at me intently before his gaze fell to my lips. I inhaled deeply. His eyes darkened as he leaned forward, placing a gentle kiss against my lips. He pulled back an inch, seemingly surprised by his own actions but also searching for rejection. He traced a line with his thumb down my cheek and across my lips. Rion was gentle, his touch only a whisper.

He leaned his forehead against mine. "I thought I was going to lose you." His voice wavered. For a moment, I allowed myself to believe he cared for me as I had begun to care for him.

I took his mouth again, wanting to feel its softness once more. Rion was holding back, and I had had enough of it. I broke the kiss to rise onto my knees and straddled his lap where he sat at the edge of the bed. My shift gathered at my hips. "You need rest," he murmured.

I swatted at his hands when he tried to lift me from where I was perched. "I need you," I said, my near-death-experience giving me confidence that I didn't feel. I didn't know what I was doing, but I did know that needed him as close as possible.

"Have you ever been touched by a man before?" He inquired. A blush spread across my face. I shook my head, too embarrassed to voice my inexperience. I'm sure he could not say the same. His movements were practiced. The longer I sat straddling him, the more intense my need became.

"Please," I begged. His composure was lost with my words, and he kissed me once more, deeper this time.

Rion hands went to my waist and guided me against him. His hard length pressed into my core, giving away his own desire. I let out a soft moan as the sensation sent me soaring. "Fuck," he groaned at the same time he stood, taking me with him. He laid me out on the bed on my back.

My shift was now pushed up past my hips, leaving my bottom half bare to him. "We have to go slow." He knelt at the side of the bed and pulled me with my thighs closer to him. He lowered his head and slid his tongue along my core. I gasped loudly. He looked up at me, a smirk playing on his lips. Gods, did he look downright sinful kneeling before me.

He continued his ambush, causing me to throw my head back. Another moan, louder this time, emanated from the back of my throat. I had never felt anything so consuming. I rose higher and higher towards the cliff of ecstasy. Just before I was flung over the edge, Rion stopped. "No. Don't stop," I pleaded.

"Little fox, you never have to beg for me to give you pleasure," he said as he slid a finger into my wet heat. He didn't move for a moment, allowing me to get used to the intrusion. "Gods spare me, you're so tight." He kissed my inner thigh and added a second finger. I moaned loudly this time as he began to pump them in and out of me. He lowered his mouth to me once more. It didn't take long before I began to shutter with pleasure. He groaned as I came, "What a good girl."

He slid his fingers out of me and placed kisses as he ascended my body, lifting my shift as he went, until my breasts were bare to him. "You are perfect," he said as he took my nipple into his mouth.

I entangled my fingers in his midnight hair. He switched sides, making sure each one got the attention they deserved. He released me, planting a quick kiss on my lips before he lay beside me. I rolled into him, snuggling against his chest.

I took a moment to catch my breath. I felt amazing, but I wanted to give him the same pleasure. I kissed his neck and snaked my hand down his body. He caught my wrist right before I reached his waistband. I glance up at him. "If you touch me, I will not be able to control myself."

"Maybe I don't want you to control yourself," I replied.

He sighed, "As much as I would love nothing more than to bury myself deep inside you, you really do need to rest." he said, bringing my hand to his mouth and kissing the scar that now sliced across my wrist. "I will not rush you."

"I don't want you to be unsatisfied," I objected.

"Giving you pleasure, gave me pleasure. I am far from unsatisfied." We lay there peacefully for a while before exhaustion began to tug at me again. Rion rose from the bed, pulling me to my feet. He folded down the blankets to allow me to crawl inside, but he didn't follow. He blew out the candle and turned to leave.

"Where are you going?" I asked, sitting up. He came back to the bed and kissed my cheek. "I have first watch tonight, but I will be back. You get some sleep." He turned once more and headed for the door. "Sleep well, little fox." I thought about the event that occurred. Although I have only known him for a few days, I feel as though I've known him my entire life. Like the Fates had woven our lives together from the start. I have spent my life with minimal human connection, and I desperately craved it. Although Rion was probably using me to fulfill a need, I would greedily take all that he offers.

* * *

I woke to the sound of the door creaking open and footsteps trailing across the floor towards the bed. I rolled over, expecting to find that Rion had returned from his turn on watch. It took a moment for my eyes to adjust to the low lighting. I squinted, making out a figure standing by the door. "Rion, what are you doing? Come to bed." The figure moved forward without a word.

The hair rose on the back of my neck. As the figure crept nearer, I realized my costly mistake. The man in front of me was not Rion, for where Rion's sharply defined features should've been, there was nothing. Just empty space above broad shoulders. It was one of the Dullahan.

I scurried towards the other side of the bed, falling to the floor with a heavy thud. I rose quickly to my feet, keeping the bed between us. "You think you can hide from us, princess?" the wraith asked. The last time I had heard them speak, I didn't notice that I wasn't *actually* hearing a voice. He was speaking into my mind—his eerie voice bounced around the recesses of my mind.

I scanned the room, trying to remain calm and think of a solution. It didn't seem that my scream had been heard by any of my companions, so I was on my own. I raised my shaking hands in front of me and focused, trying to sense the magic that had banished them in the forest, but I felt nothing. I gave up quickly as I continued to scan the room.

The horseman blocked my path to the door, but there was

another that led to a balcony. If I could get there, I could jump. I prayed quickly to the Gods, wherever they were, that they would give me strength and that none of his companions lingered below. "I can fucking try," I spat as I rushed towards my escape. He was fast, but I was faster. I flung the doors open and, without stopping to think, jumped.

I hit the ground hard. I rolled and shot to my feet, taking in my surroundings, ignoring the pain that shot up my legs threatening to buckle my knees. I didn't see the other horseman, but they wouldn't be far off. I needed to find Rion. I let the panic seep in for a split second. What if the horseman had gotten to him and the others first? I jogged to the corner of the inn, pressing my back against the wall. I went to peer around to the front of the inn when I was grabbed from behind, a hand covering my mouth.

"Stay quiet." A wave of relief flooded my veins at the sound of Rion's voice. He removed his hand, and I faced him.

"Where were you?" I whispered.

"I went to the stables a few streets down to retrieve my saddle bags. I had just arrived when they came through. Three of them continued down the road, blocking the southern exit to the village. Where is Nolan and Flynn?"

"I don't know. I haven't seen them."

The door to the inn opened suddenly and we fell silent. We both pressed against the wall, becoming one with the shadows, and peered around the corner. The horseman spoke, "I know you are near, princess. I cannot sense your magic, but you couldn't have gone far. You will never escape the king's wrath. We will find you." The horseman mounted his steed, which he had left standing in the road in front of the building.

After he was sure they were gone, Rion muttered, "We have

to find the Nolan and Flynn before he comes back with the others. They will tear this town apart looking for you."

"We can't leave these people to their mercy," I argued.

"There is nothing we can do to stop them." He took my hand and attempted to lead me back inside the inn.

I snatched my hand back, standing my ground. "I can use my magic like the night in the forest. It will give us the time we need to evacuate the city and get out of here."

"No. You got lucky that night. You are also not strong enough to sustain it. You lost a lot of blood last night that your body is still trying to replenish."

"I just jumped from a two-story balcony. I think I am plenty strong enough," I debated.

"I said no," he said through his teeth.

"These people will die!"

Rion grabbed my wrist firmly and pulled me into him, so we were face to face. "I don't give a shit about these people right now. I will not risk you, now come on." He dragged me back inside the inn as I fought against him. All was quiet, completely unaware of the danger that lurked in the shadows.

He hauled my ass up the stairs and into the first room on the left. The men were both asleep, snoring loudly. "Get up." Rion ordered.

Nolan stirred under the covers. "What's going on? We aren't supposed to head out until morning."

"Can you two fucking shut it," Flynn exclaimed. "My head is killing me."

"I can't fucking help that you drowned you sorrows all evening in the bottom of a bottle. We need to go. Now!" Rion shouted.

Nolan noted the urgency and irritation on Rion's face and

rose to his feet. Flynn on the other hand didn't seem like he cared less as he rolled back over, pulling his pillow over his head. Rion lost the remaining control he had over his temper. He yanked the sheet from the bed and Flynn along with it, who went tumbling to the floor. "Get the fuck up, now!" he demanded.

Flynn got to his feet quickly and confronted Rion with an animalist growl, knife in hand. "What the fuck!" he yelled in Rion's face, pressing the blade to the base of his throat.

Rion tried to regain some of his calm. "Look, it is not safe here. The Dullahan just tried to assassinate Aisling while she slept. We must go. I know you are in pain, but…"

"Don't you dare try to pretend like you know any of the pain I feel," interrupted Flynn. Rion flexed his jaw and took a deep breath.

Nolan bustled around the room packing his bags, ignoring the conflict. I, however, held my breath. Rion gave Flynn a look of sympathy. "Flynn, please. We do not have much time before the horseman comes back with reinforcements. We need to go." Flynn glared but followed the command of his leader.

"Meet us downstairs in five minutes." Rion pulled me out of the door once more, and we went across the hall into another room, which I realized was ours. Once the door was shut, he handed me a set of black leathers similar to his and a white blouse that were folded on the end table. "Put these on," Rion said.

I threw my grass-stained shift over my head quickly. I hauled on the fitted leather trousers, which stuck to my sweat-soaked skin. "When did you get these?" I asked as I donned the blouse.

Rion came to my aid when I struggled with the laces and buckles on the breast place. "I sent the maid with coin to purchase them as soon as we got here." He procured a pair of vambraces from the table. "So, we don't have a repeat of last night," he said as he strapped them to my arms. He reached for the final item laid upon the table, a belt holding a sheath and small blade. He buckled it around my hips.

I withdrew the blade to inspect it. It was beautiful in its simplicity. "Pointy end forward," he chuckled, planting a kiss on my lips. The tension had dissipated between us instantly. I still wasn't happy about leaving the village unprotected, but I understood Rion's point of view. All feelings aside, they needed me to win this rebellion. In his eyes, it was worth the loss of a few to save the many. I sheathed my new weapon once more and swiftly plaited my hair back from my face.

I followed Rion out of the room and down the stairs, where Nolan and Flynn were already waiting. They both looked at me with wide eyes. "What?" I looked down at myself, thinking maybe I had forgotten to lace the stays on my trousers.

Nolan let out a cough. "Rion, you seemed to have misplaced the princess and replaced her with a warrior." Flynn remained silent, the tension between him and Rion permeated the air, making the small room feel even smaller. I made my way to the door, pulling Rion with me before he maimed his friend. Nolan and Flynn followed close behind. We snuck through the streets, keeping to the shadows of the alleys between the cottages.

Once we reached the stables, the men quickly saddled their horses. Rion helped me mount before he got up behind me, pulling me tightly against his chest. "We are going to have to ride hard to get ahead of the horseman," he warned, turning to his comrades. "We will have to head back north and circle back around." He kicked the horse's flanks hard, and it lurched forward.

We reached the border before the screaming arose across the

village. The guilt it brought upon me sliced deep. Just one more tragedy caused by my existence.

Chapter 8

We kept our pace for hours. Nobody spoke, like we feared the sound of our voices would draw the enemy upon us. The only sound was the pounding of hooves upon the dirt. The forest around us even seemed to understand the need for quiet, for there wasn't even a breeze rustling the leaves. However, echoes of the desperate screams of the villagers we left behind rang in my head. "We need to go back," I stated, finally breaking the wall of silence. "There may be survivors"

"There will be nothing left but ghosts and ash, princess." It was Nolan who answered me, the sympathy that flowed into his voice was a pleasant surprise. I looked at the others, hoping they would have a different answer. Flynn trailed far behind in no position to argue on my behalf, looking as though he may vomit, barely holding himself upright on his horse, and Rion kept his eyes trained on the road ahead, not even acknowledging that I had spoken at all.

"You don't know that," I whispered, though I knew my hope was misplaced. The night the Dullahan initially came for me, they didn't leave a single soul alive in their search. Nolan's icy eyes met mine. I caught a glimpse of the soft-hearted man hidden behind the harsh exterior he portrayed. I didn't need his pity, nor did I want it.

I huffed and tilted my face skyward. Golden rays peeked through the canopy above, casting shadows upon the ground. I allowed the sun that reached towards me to warm my face. "Perhaps you were right," I spoke after a moment, drawing Nolan's attention once more. Confusion twisted his porcelain features. "Maybe I am this kingdom's damnation, not its salvation." Rion's arm tightened around my waist, the first indication that he was listening to the conversation.

"Enough," he whispered against the shell of my ear. The feel of his breath skating across my skin caused a chill to run down my spine. "Your guilty conscious will be your ruination if you allow it. You need to learn to place blame where it is deserved." A tear slipped free and tumbled down my cheek.

Nolan inched his steed closer and leaned over, tentatively taking my hand in his, casting a glance at Rion as if he needed permission. He turned back to me, his eyes drilling into mine. His pupils pulsed as he said, "I was wrong. You are so much more than I had given you credit for, and I am sorry for that." His apology struck deep. He gave my hand one last squeeze before releasing it.

"Ugh," Flynn groaned, having increased his pace to catch up with us. "We need to stop." He barely got the words passed his lips when he gagged, and vomit spewed down his chest and the side of his horse, who didn't seem all to pleased as he stomped his feet and flicked his mane.

"Gods, Flynn," Nolan averted his eyes, looking nearly as green as Flynn.

"Come on, there is a creek nearby," Rion stated. He led the group a mile down the road before veering off into the ticket and down a sloping hill. The creek came into view, stealing the breath from my lungs with its beauty as the sun caused its surface to sparkle. Fish could be seen swimming wildly just below the surface along the meandering current. The trickling of the water over the shale bottom created a tranquil scene, despite Flynn's continued heaving. Birds swooped down, gathering a healthy meal of those fish with undeniable grace. Purple, pink and white wildflowers grew along the bank and waved in the subtle breeze, as if to welcome us to join their dance.

Rion dismounted, helping me down once his feet hit the ground. Nolan did the same and moved towards Flynn, yanking him down off his horse and dragging him to the water's edge, all the while gagging on the way there. Flynn let out a gurgled laugh, "What? Big bad Nolan afraid of a little vomit?"

"Shut it and strip," Nolan commanded. Flynn did as he was told, fighting with his soiled shirt, which stuck to his skin. Nolan finally took pity on him after letting him struggle for a few minutes and pulled it over his head, pasting mysterious chunks from last night's supper onto the side of Flynn's face and head. I turned my back, not wishing to catch sight of something I did not want to see as he started untying the stays to his britches.

I reached into the creek's cool depths. Closing my eyes, I felt as the water ran through my fingers. The calming effect was surprisingly soothing—it was as if the water knew me, knew my touch, like a memory unlocked after years of being suppressed. "Look," Rion's voice pierced through my bubble to serenity. I hadn't even heard him come up beside me.

I peeled my eyes open against their will and peered at him. He glanced at my hand beneath the water, silently guiding my eyes there. The cool liquid had begun to climb towards the crook of my elbow. "Am I doing that?" As soon as I spoke, the water retreated to its basin.

Rion smiled and nodded. "In a way. The water responded to your touch."

"Responded? You talk as if the water is sentient."

Rion smiled, "Not sentient, no, but aware. Water listens. It remembers. It knows when it's being called."

I focused on the flow of the current—the chill of the water. The hum of the magic stored within prickled my skin. I cupped my hands, allowing the cool water to pool in my palms, and brought it to my parched lips. I drank deep before splashing it across my face. Water dripped from the tip of my nose, as I stared out upon the surface, watching the wildlife that depended on its sustenance and refreshment. On the opposite bank, a doe came from the greenery, dipping its head to get a drink as well. Between her legs, a small fawn, its coat still marked with the white spots of youth, followed its mother's lead. I was saddened by the scene, for it was too late in the year for something so small to survive the winter that would soon be upon us. In the distance, I heard a large splash and Flynn curse as Nolan tossed him into the creek, which startled the deer and her offspring, sending them back from whence they came.

"Fuck!" Flynn shivered, more alert than he had been before, standing in the water that just barely covered his most intimate bits. "It's… so… cold," he stammered.

"Sucks," Nolan chided.

I laughed, though it wasn't entirely funny. I felt for Flynn. He didn't just lose his brother, but his twin. The person that had literally been at his side since birth. He took a long inhale before disappearing below the water's surface. Nolan stood on the bank, arms crossed, to monitor the drunken fool to ensure he did not drown. Flynn resurfaced closer to the bank, causing quite the ruckus as he did so. I kept my eyes fixed on his face, for he was most definitely not hidden within the water any longer. "Holy shit, okay, am I clean enough for you?" He exclaimed.

Nolan examined him closely, a small grin spreading across his face. I was shocked at the sight. I didn't know the man knew how to smile. He pointed at the left side of his face, "I think you missed a spot." Flynn reached up to find nothing but damp, clean skin to Nolan's amusement.

Flynn smacked the water and splashed Nolan, soaking the front of his leathers, before flipping him off with a large smile plastered on his face. But Flynn's laugh died as quickly as it came. He fell to his knees at the water's edge. "I keep turning to say something to him," Flynn mutters, "and there's no one there." My heart broke for him in that moment. "How am I supposed to move on without him here," Flynn's voice wavered. He painted a beautiful, tortured picture of a broken man. Nolan went to his friend, sodden boots be damned, and kneeled in front of him. Gripping the back of his neck, Nolan pulled Flynn to his chest in a firm embrace. They began to shake as Flynn's tormented cries engulfed them. Nolan hushed him, whispering words of encouragement and comfort into his hair. Rion joined them in the water, wrapping his long armed around both men.

I felt as though I was intruding on a private moment as the friends grieved Bellamy's loss, their faces gleaming with fallen tears. My own eyes burned as I looked upon them. Their grief renewed my own, of all that I have lost and all I would stand to lose in the future, because whether I liked it or not, these men were all I had left, aside from Nora, wherever she may be.

I stepped away, allowing the rustling of the leaves to drown out their sorrow, before my tears reached my chin. They deserved this moment, uninterrupted. I followed the curve of the stream until their voices faded. The air was damp. Leaves clung to my boots like they, too, were unwilling to let go. The serenity of the scenery was now tainted by pain and loss—the vibrant colors now muted and sad. I kept the thoughts of my grandmother's passing at bay, but only barely as they attempted to push past the barriers of my mind. I came to a fallen tree, suspended slightly above the ground by its large branches, long forgotten and covered in emerald colored moss. I sat upon its cushioned surface, the gentle texture beneath my fingers grounding me.

I teetered the precipice between the pain of the past and fear of the future. It took all of my strength to suppress my rising emotions, to not allow them to take control. I took a series of breaths, counting to three before releasing each exhale. I could have been sitting there for a minute, an hour, or a day before Rion's voice calling my name drew me out of my haze. "I'm here," I called back.

He sauntered into sight and plopped onto the fallen tree, causing it to bow under his weight. "We should be moving on soon," he said, his voice a bit hoarse and sullen.

"Will he be okay?" I asked, Flynn's pained face coming to the forefront of my mind.

"Grief has a way of sharpening some people," Rion replied, as if he knew from personal experience, "and splintering others. You never know which way it will go until it's too late."

"Who?" Rion turned to me with a puzzled look on his face. "Who was it that you lost?" I clarified.

Rion shifted uncomfortably, taking a large breath before he responded. "I have lost many, little fox. Too many." I wished I could take his pain and bare it so that he did not have to, to steal it away so that he would not have to feel the loss of yet another person he cared for. Before I knew what I was doing, I reached out and caught the single tear that escaped the corner of his eye, wiping away any evidence of its existence. He watched me, his verdant gaze flickering with restrained emotion. Something deep within me pulsed to life, curling and tightening around my heart.

He brought his large hand up to my face, capturing a piece of hair that had worked its way free from my braid in our escape the night before and placed behind my ear. He ran the back of his hand down my cheek. I leaned into his touch, my eyes fluttering shut. "You are the most beautiful women I have ever had the pleasure of laying eyes on," he said.

I couldn't stop the sharp laugh that escaped my lips. "I highly doubt that."

He gripped my chin, forcing my eyes to meet his once more. The seriousness of his face caused me to pause. "You may not see it, but I do. Your strength. Your kindness and compassion for those around you. That's what makes you beautiful, not just to me, but to anyone paying attention." His thumb brushed against my cheek. "So don't laugh it away."

I gave him a small smile. I'd only ever seen weakness when I looked in the mirror—wasted muscle, skin too tight over bone, the ghost of the girl I have never been but longed to be. There was nothing beautiful about sunken cheeks and hollow eyes. But when he looked at me… gods, he looked at me like I mattered. Like I was more than just a means to an end. I hoped with ever ounce of my being that he meant the words he spoke.

After a moment of quiet, Rion got to his feet, pulling me with him. "We better get back to the others." As he led me back to the horses, he didn't drop my hand, instead adjusting his grip so that my fingers nestled between his. The small bit of intimacy caused my heart to pound in my chest, for it was unfamiliar but not unwelcome. When we approached the others, already astride their horses, I attempted to withdraw my hand, only to have Rion's grip tighten. Nolan's eyebrows nearly reached his hairline when he noticed our joined hands.

Rion helped me mount, ignoring his friend's subtle judgement. His hands settled on my waist, lifting me as though I weighed nothing at all. When he swung into the saddle behind me, the space between us vanished. His warm chest pressed into my back, and his strong arm wound about my waist, like a snake constricting its prized catch, providing protection and stability. Rion adjusted the reins in his other hand and clicked his tongue, nudging the horse forward with his legs. The horses climbed the steep incline back to the road beyond, leaving the stream and grief behind. Something within me told me that that would not be the last time we wept for a fallen comrade.

Chapter 9

"We can stop here and rest," Rion stated as the sun light began to fade into hues of pinks and golds. Dusk used to be my favorite time of day. The brilliant colors that painted the skies and the quiet that spread over the land, as its inhabitants settled down for the evening, soothed my soul. Now, it was only a source of anxiety—the peace it once brought long forgotten.

Rion dismounted and led the group deeper into the forest. The snapping of twigs and rustling leaves beneath horse hooves sent small critters scurrying into the underbrush. He quickly found a spot suitable for erecting camp among the trees with little jutting roots and large rocks that would jab us in the backs all night.

My body traveled the entire length of his as he helped me down from the horse, who was stamping his feet, eager to graze on the small amount of grass that covered the forest floor. Rion's strong hands dug into my waist as he set me on my feet. We lingered this way, his eyes darting to my lips. I felt heat begin to pool low in my belly. "Get a room," Flynn hollered, shattering the moment, as he threw his saddle bag at his feet and sent his horse to graze among the trees. The joke fell flat with the underlying tone of irritation coloring his words.

Flynn extracted a bottle from his bag and staggered towards us, offering the foul-smelling ale to Rion and I. Rion eyed him wearily as he declined. "Don't give me that look. Like you haven't borrowed anything without permission," Flynn said with a hiccup, giving him an all-knowing smile. He leaned towards me. "When we were young, he stole an entire case of wine from his father. He caught us of course, but not before we had drunk half the case and were vomiting all over his imported rug."

He laughed, the touching exchange in the creek wiped from his mind by the large amount of alcohol he must have consumed on the road. "Bellamy was so hung over, spending the next day shut in our room with the drapes drawn. Our mother threatened to skin us both if his chores weren't done by the end of the day." Amusement faded from his face for a moment, taking another long draw from the bottle. It returned in a flash as he threw his arm around my shoulders. "My brother and I shared everything." His eyes roamed over my leather clad body. "Even our women."

In the blink of an eye, Flynn was standing beside me, then he wasn't. Rion had him flat on his back, blade drawn at his throat. He was breathing heavily, growling in Flynn's face. "No. Stop," I pleaded to Rion. I grabbed his arm, but he knocked me back onto my ass. Nolan ran from where he was pitching his tent and attempted to haul Rion off him. "Rion, let him go. He's drunk and doesn't know what he is saying. Right, Flynn?"

Flynn stared up in horror at his childhood friend. "I didn't know," he spoke quickly. "I swear. I didn't know."

"She is fucking mine," Rion said through his teeth. He allowed Nolan to finally pull him off, and Flynn clambered to his feet. He rushed over to where he had left his packs, and without another word, set to pitching his tent. Rion knelt on the forest floor, shaking with rage, restrained by Nolan, who sat behind him with his arms strapped around Rion's chest to keep him from rushing after Flynn to finish what he started.

"You need to breathe. He is your friend, and he is harmless. You know how he is. He doesn't mean anything by it," Nolan muttered to his friend. I wanted to go to him, to comfort him, but I was rooted in place by shock. Slowly, Rion stopped fighting against Nolan's hold. Once he felt sure Rion wasn't going to get up and gut Flynn, he released his embrace and stood, retreating to his own half-erected tent.

Rion turned to me, and I could have sworn silver strands threaded through his regretful eyes—a trick of the low light. He crawled towards where I still sat on the ground. He placed a curled finger under my chin and forced my gaze to meet his. "I did not hurt you, did I?" His voice was filled with pain. Guilt was etched in his face.

"No, but you scared the shit out of me."

"I am so sorry." He ran his thumb across my lips. I fought the instinct to shy away from his touch. He may not have meant to hurt me, but the fact that he did, lost in a blind rage, shook me to my core.

"That is twice that he set you off. Do you want to explain why?" I asked wearily.

"The thought of any man touching you besides me makes my blood boil." He sighed, obviously done with the conversation. He stood and made his way back to the horse. I sat where he left me, confusion curling around me like smoke. His words echoed in my mind, their meaning both infuriating and intoxicating. What was I supposed to do with that? With him?

Needing something to occupy my hands—and silence my thoughts—I wandered a little way into the trees and began gathering wood for the fire. I took my time, letting the weight of his voice bleed off into the rhythm of snapping twigs and rustling leaves.

Rion had the tent up by the time I returned and left quickly with the excuse of securing the perimeter. Flynn hadn't emerged from his tent after he haphazardly threw it together, either, leaving Nolan and I alone in the dark.

"Can I?" I asked Nolan, gesturing towards the bed of tinder that lined the pit he had dug. He nodded, handing over the flint and steel and nest of horsehair he had been holding. I quickly had a steady fire going.

"Impressive," Nolan said over my shoulder.

"Not really," I laughed. "I learned early. When my grandmother could no longer firmly grip the flint and steal, lighting the hearth became my job."

Nolan sat beside me on the half-rotten log he had dragged from somewhere in the forest beyond. I took the opportunity to find out more about the man I had begun to care for, since he is not determined to tell me anything. "Rion never mentioned he grew up with Flynn and Bellamy."

"We all did. Our parents were employed by his father."

"And what of his mother? He never talks of her."

Nolan shifted uncomfortably. "That is not my story to tell." He patted my shoulder, seeing my disappointment. "He'll tell you when he is ready. Now that we have a fire, I will prepare something to eat." He motioned towards Flynn's tent. "Maybe getting something other than alcohol into the drunken fool will keep him from making any further poor choices."

Nolan made a quick dinner, giving me a healthy portion before he took Flynn a bowl and retired to his tent. I sat alone by the light of the fire, pushing the pieces of venison and leeks around in my bowl without lifting any to my mouth, for my appetite was nonexistent after the events of the evening. I was happy that Nolan was finally warming up to me, but my thoughts wondered to Rion and his peculiar behavior.

I stared into the fire, the flickering flames dancing like the thoughts in my head. They were chaotic, burning, and impossible to catch. I didn't know Rion. Not really. And yet… I felt tethered to him somehow. It wasn't just the way he looked at me, or how my body reacted to his touch. It was something deeper, older, and something I couldn't put into words no matter how hard I tried. We'd only just met. So, why did it already feel like losing him would break me?

I forced down the stew as my thoughts continued to assault me. After about an hour, with no sign of Rion, I stood, prepared to go off and find him when he appeared from the trees. I let out a sigh of relief. "You should eat," I called to him.

He came to me, lifting me off my feet. Instinctually, I wrapped my legs around his waist. He kissed me deeply, hard and fast like he couldn't get enough. I was swept away by the feeling of his lips on mine, quieting the bombarding thoughts that had consumed my mind. It was entirely different from the night before. When he pulled back, I looked into his hungry eyes. Strands of silver laced through them, unmistakable now, shimmering like molten light. Before I could comment, he took my mouth once again. He carried me towards the tent. I drew back slightly, panting. "You haven't eaten all day. You need something in your system," I repeated, though I didn't wish to stop.

His eyes darkened. "I hunger for something else, princess," he purred. Heat rushed straight to my core with his words. He shifted my weight to one arm braced under my ass to part the flap of the tent. He finally put me down and began to meticulously undo the buckles and laces of my breast plate with experienced hands. I attempted not to dwell on that fact as he threw it to the floor and pulled my blouse over my head in one fluid motion. My nipples peaked against the cool air. He ran his thumb against the sensitive bud, which drew a shallow moan from my lips.

He untied the stays on my trousers slowly. Without removing them completely, he slid his hand until he cupped me in his hand. "You are so wet for me," he whispered. My hips moved on their own accord, sliding my sex against the calloused palm of his hand. He grinned, "What a good girl you are." His words and the erratic movement of my hips threatened to send me over the edge. He slowly slid two fingers inside me, causing a loud gasp to expel through my lips. I sucked in a breath, trying to remain quiet. He curled his fingers against my inner wall. "I want to hear you," he coaxed.

"What of the others?" I panted, worried what the other men in the camp would think of our discretions.

"I want them to hear while I pleasure you. I want them to know who this pussy belongs to," Rion rumbled, his voice husky with need. He thrust his fingers deeper, which caused me to cry out. "That a girl," he praised. His thumb found the bundle of sensitive nerves while he plunged into me. The pleasure was almost too much to bear. My body began to shutter as my climax neared, but just before it did, Rion withdrew. I whimpered at the loss of his hand. He drew his fingers into his mouth. I was alarmed and a bit embarrassed until his eyes fluttered shut, a groan escaping his throat.

I tugged at his leathers, fingers fumbling slightly in my urgency, determined to see what he had hidden beneath them. What he'd kept guarded behind the layers of armor. He didn't stop me. Instead, he reached up and helped, unfastening the buckles and straps with practiced ease.

Each piece gave way slowly, falling between us with a soft thud. The smell of sweat and leather rose as he peeled off the hardened outer shell, revealing the warm skin beneath. I watched, my breath caught in my throat, as the lines of his body emerged. I stepped back when the last piece of armor fell to the floor to inspect the immaculate man that stood before me. I trailed my fingers gingerly up his arms—corded muscles hard under the pads of my fingers. I continued my perusal over his broad chest that was covered in round scars. I traced these as well. "How did you get these?"

"My father was an avid cigar smoker and was not always very happy with the trouble I caused as a child," he replied with a dismissive tone. Anger burned deep within me. I imagined a small, innocent Rion being burned by the person that was supposed to protect him at all costs. I was beginning to understand why he wasn't forthcoming when it came to his family and where he had come from.

I dropped my eyes lower, to his thick length standing tall, a small bead of arousal forming at its tip. I stared entirely too long, which caused a chuckle to reverberate in Rion's chest. I wasn't certain I would ever be able to take all of him within me, if that was his intention. "Do you like what you see?" he asked with a smirk. I blushed, drawing my gaze back to his face.

Rion pulled me against him, his erection pressed into my stomach, as he kissed me fiercely before laying me down upon the furs. He peeled me out of the leather trousers that stuck to my sweat-slicked skin, pushing my thighs apart. It was his turn to admire me bare before him. He slid his hand through my center, his thumb finding that sensitive spot once more. "You are so fucking perfect." I relished his words.

He bowed his head so his mouth could take the place of his hand. His thick tongue slowly teased at my entrance. I cried out once more, louder than before. "You taste so sweet," he paused to say before he consumed me. I screwed my eyes shut and came hard against his mouth, moaning his name. He wrung another out of me before pulling back to watch me come back to myself.

I slowly opened my eyes, taking in the mountain of a man kneeling before me. I slowly rose to my knees, attempting to be seductive in my movements, though I am not confident that I was successful. "My turn," I purred nonetheless, looking up at him through my lashes. Before he could object, I reached between his legs and took him in my hand. Rion was absolutely huge, my fingers barely able to wrap around him fully. His gruff moan filled the tent to my satisfaction. I kept my touch light and ran my thumb over his head, coating it with the moisture gathered there.

He wrapped his hand around mine. "Like this," he breathed. He tightened his grip around mine and stroked my hand down to the base and back up slowly. He removed his hand to allow me to continue on my own. I watched him come undone under my touch. "Fuck, that feels so good," he groaned.

He stood abruptly, grabbing the back of my neck. He rubbed the tip of his erection on my lips. "Open," he demanded. "I want to feel your mouth wrapped around my cock." I did as he asked, parting my lips to allow him to slide in slowly. He shook, trying to keep his composure, and moaned loudly.

I fisted the base of his shaft as he started pumping in and out of my mouth, shallow at first. Rion moved his hand from the back of my neck and entwined his fingers in my hair. He remained slow until he could no longer contain himself. Rion thrusted deep in my throat, gagging me, which was his undoing. My eyes watered, a single tear escaping down my face.

He kept a steady pace during his claiming, keeping his attention fixed on the sight before him, until his movements became sporadic and desperate. He came with a shout, his seed shooting down my throat and spilling out of my mouth. He withdrew and ran his thumb along the corner of my mouth. "You look downright delectable covered in my cum." The indecency of his statement should have sent a wave of discomfort through my being, but it only stood to heighten my arousal.

He grabbed his shirt where it lay on the floor and wiped away the evidence of his climax from my face. He flopped on the bed, pulling me into his embrace. "Was that okay?" I blushed, hoping that he was satisfied.

"You were fantastic, little fox," he answered. "Nothing you do could ever be wrong." Pride filled my chest as I closed my eyes. He twirled my hair around his finger mindlessly. As my consciousness faded, worries of the future consumed me. As a Druid, I had a long life to live. Rion did not, and I may very well be falling for this man. Meaning, there would come a time when he would not be by my side. There was also the fact that Rion has yet to explicitly profess his affections. What if he did not feel the same? What if I was simply a pawn in his game—a warm body to fulfil his male urges? These questions assaulted my mind as I slowly drifted off, clouding the events that had just transpired between us.

Chapter 10

The morning came all too soon. Rion's chest was pressed tightly against my back, and his arm was flung over my body, legs entangled in mine. He was still snoring soundly, the faint rumble vibrating through me. I kept my eyes closed, not allowing the uncertainty from the previous night to ruin the fantasy. I carefully rolled over as to not disturb Rion to gaze upon his sleeping form. I brush his disheveled hair away from his face. He looked peaceful. "You know. It is not polite to stare," he startled me. I had been so enchanted by his otherworldly appearance that I hadn't noticed when his soft snores had ceased. Rion chuckled and drew me closer to him. We were both unclothed, the skin-to-skin contact completely addictive.

"We should probably get up and get dressed," he yawned, nuzzling his nose into my neck. "You need to get something to eat before we begin training this morning. Plus, Nolan is going to be pissed that I did not turn up for my watch last night, though he probably knows why," Rion said with a wink. I blushed as the memories of last night's activities flooded my mind. I was most definitely not quiet, nor was Rion, and I was completely dreading facing Flynn and Nolan's judgement. "You are gorgeous when you blush," he laughed, flicking my nose with the tip of his finger.

Rion kissed my cheek and rose. He dressed quickly, then helped me back into my clothing. When we exited the tent, Nolan was stoking the fire back to life and Flynn was standing by with a stupid grin on his face. "How did you sleep, Rion?" he insinuated.

"Like a baby," Rion replied.

Nolan choked on a laugh. "Someone is in a good mood this morning. Are we going to be able to make it through the day without anyone's life being threatened, now?" My face heated. Oh gods, they heard everything.

Rion responded, "We shall see."

"You're welcome for covering your shift, by the way. Thought it would be a bad idea to, uh, interrupt your sleep," jested Nolan with a smirk. Flynn covered his mouth to suppress a laugh. I was sure I would die right there of embarrassment.

"Okay, okay. That is enough." Rion said with a shake of his head. He turned his attention to me. "First, breakfast. I am absolutely starving. Then, we train."

A brief time later, I found myself standing across from an unarmed Rion, blade drawn. I listened intently as he reiterated the same techniques as our last training session, "Remember your grip. The vambraces will protect your wrists and forearms, but do not let your guard down. Complacency can be just as deadly as any honed blade. Now take up your fighting stance." He gestured towards me with a wave. I shifted my weight, planting my dominant foot ahead of the other firmly to the earth and adjusted my grip on the knife.

"You must always stay focused. Never take your eyes off an opponent," he stressed as he approached me. "Like I said before, with a short blade, you must get close to them to strike. But, in close combat, you run the risk of your attacker getting a hand on you. This prevents you from using your weapon and could allow them the time to use theirs. You must act without hesitation." He held his arm out to me. "Take my wrist."

I shifted my knife to the other hand and did as he asked. "In most wrist grabs, the thumb is the weak link. That is what you are aiming for." He swiftly rotated his wrist towards my thumb and around the back of my hand, breaking my hold easily and pulling his arm back out of reach. "Now you try."

He took my wrist firmly in his hand. I did as he demonstrated and was surprised when it worked. "Good, but make sure you keep your arm back once the hold is broken. They could simply grab you again. Now do it again, it needs to be instinctual."

This time, he grabbed the wrist of the hand with my knife in it, utilizing the pressure points there to release my grip on the weapon. It fell at my feet. "This time, you need to break the hold, and retrieve your weapon," he challenged.

I broke the hold as before, but he grabbed me again before I could move and recover the knife off the ground. "Too slow there, love," he smirked. He yanked me into him. "You are small and lack strength. You need to make up for it with cunning and speed." I gaped at him, for now all I could think about was every point which our bodies touched.

Before I knew what was happening, he swept my feet out from under me, and I landed sprawled on the ground. He was upon me in a heartbeat. My own weapon pressed gently against my throat. Gasping for air, I glared at Rion. He only smiled. "Like I said, focus is key." He retreated, dropping the knife beside me. I scurried to my feet angrily and retrieved my weapon.

"Again," he demanded. We repeated the exercise, Rion grabbing a different wrist at different angles each time. Every time I lost my weapon, I was unable to get it off the ground before he was upon me again.

The last time, I gave up trying to simply bend down and get it. I broke his hold and took a few quick steps back. I dove at the weapon. Once in my grasp, I rolled out of reach and popped to my feet behind him. I kicked the back of his knee, and he dropped to the ground with a thud. I put him in a head lock, angling my blade under his jaw.

I leaned in, breathing heavily, and whispered against the shell of his ear, "Now what?"

"You end it. No hesitation." I released my arm around his neck but kept the blade in place as I sauntered around to face him. His eyes darkened. "Fuck," he exclaimed. "I have never been more attracted to you than this moment." He was also fighting for breath, but for a completely different reason.

"You are completely at my mercy," I cooed.

An emotion I didn't quite understand flooded his features. "Until the end of time," he vowed. I nearly tripped over my own feet at his admission as I backed away, sheathing my knife at my side, and allowed him to rise. He placed a hand on my check. "You did well, little fox. Later, we can work on grounding again. Once you have a decent handle on both, we will combine the lessons, using your magic to complement your combat technique."

"I got lucky. I still have a long way to go before I can hold my own," I pointed out.

"You do," he agreed, placing a hand on my chest, "but, you have the heart of a warrior. You are brave and strong-willed. That is more than most."

"I'm scared," I admitted. "The thought of going into battle is terrifying, especially after the scuffle with the leprechauns. Sparring with you is different. I know you won't hurt me, but how will I react when someone does?"

"Courage does not mean you cannot be scared. It is the act of facing that which frightens you," he assured.

The rest of the day passed in quiet rhythm, the clip of hooves on soft earth and the rustle of wind through the canopy becoming familiar companions. I found myself growing more confident in the saddle; my muscles no longer protested with each movement, and when we finally dismounted, there was no lingering ache.

As the sun set, we made camp once more beneath a ring of ancient oaks. I looked up at the sprawling branches. I thought of all these trees had seen in their lifetime, of what stories they could tell if they would speak. Golden light filtered through their branches in slanted beams, the last warmth of the sun brushing our cheeks before retreating.

Dinner was simple but comforting—dried meat, foraged roots, and a touch of wild mint Nolan had found on the banks of a nearby stream. We sat in a loose circle around the fire, the flickering flames casting shifting shadows across our faces. No one spoke much, but the silence wasn't strained. It was the kind that settles over people who are growing used to each other.

When the last embers of sunlight faded from the treetops, Rion stood and stretched. "I will take first watch," he offered, his voice low and steady. No one argued. One by one, the others slipped into their tents, the day's weariness claiming them without resistance.

I stayed by the fire a while longer, drawn to the quiet companionship. Rion settled on a rock just beyond the glow of the flames, his sword resting across his lap, eyes scanning the darkened woods. The shadows between the trees seemed to pulse with secrets, but here, beside the fire and beneath the stars, I finally felt safe.

Once he was determined that all was well, Rion shifted his attention to me. "Are you ready to resume where we left off the other night?" Rion inquired. My mind went straight to the thought of his hands on my body, the taste of him on my tongue. He smirked like he knew what I was imagining. "Grounding," he clarified.

"Yeah, yes," I spluttered. "Try not to be so distracting this time." However, that seemed to be an impossible task for the man because just his presence flustered me.

I removed my shoes like I had done before. Standing in front of Rion, I took his outstretched hands in my own. I closed my eyes and focused on my connection to the earth, feeling the power that lies just beneath its surface.

The heat spread quickly up my legs and into my belly. It inched its way up my body, until I was smoldering. "Good," Rion purred. "Now, descend slowly into that power." I remained focused. I let the magic consume me. My skin was buzzing with energy, begging to be spent. "Open your eyes."

I did as he requested. I was stunned by what I saw. My body was emitting a low glow, casting shadows over Rion's face. He was smiling from ear to ear. "Now that you are grounded, you can readily use your magic."

"How?" I asked, excited to see what I could do.

"We will start small with using pure magic, like the light you sent to banish the Dullahan." He released my hands and cupped them together. "Start by attempting to make a small ball of light. Will it to be, and it will be."

I focused intently on my hands. Sweat dripped down my face with the exertion. A faint orb grew in my palms, excruciatingly slow, despite the amount of energy I was expelling. Excitement pulsed in my chest. I took my eyes off the sphere of magic for a moment to search Rion's face for approval, and the light sputtered out. The glow receded from my body and back into the earth from which it came.

Disappointment and exhaustion swept through me, causing me to fall to my knees. "I'm sorry. Give me a minute, and we can try again. I can do better."

Rion crouched in front of me. He lifted my chin, forcing me to look up at him. "Okay. First off, that was a major success. You managed to both ground yourself and manipulate your magic with purpose," he declared. "Second, you are spent. With practice, you will grow stronger and be able to maintain more. It will get easier."

I was bolstered by Rion's confidence in me. I gripped his shirt, pulling him into me. He almost fell forward, catching himself by dropping a knee into the dirt with a genuine laugh. It was the most delightful sound I had ever heard. It was the first time I had heard more than a chuckle out of him.

I kissed him passionately. His tongue slipped against my lips, and I opened for him. He swept through my mouth, pulling a moan from deep inside my chest. We were both breathless by the time he pulled away. "As much as I would love nothing more than to take you to bed, I have watch and you need sleep."

I let out a huff of frustration. I was so tightly wound that I didn't know how I would get any sleep without release. I pushed Rion back, until he was seated on the ground, and straddled him. I hesitantly rubbed myself against the growing hardness beneath me.

Rion's hands flew to my hips. I thought he was going to stop my movements, but instead, he guided me firmly along himself. "You will be the death of me," he rumbled.

I leaned forward and trailed my tongue along his neck. "I need you," I rasped in his ear. I gasped as he quickly flipped us over, his weight pressed into me. I shot a look towards the occupied tents just feet from us. The anticipation of being caught only heightened my pleasure as Rion continued to grind his hips.

He stilled and buried his face in my neck, inhaling deeply. "Aisling." I was still getting used to the name, but it was undeniably erotic coming from his lips. "And you called me distracting. All I think about is your wet pussy and how fucking great it would feel to be inside you. It consumes my every thought." His need radiated from him. His hand moved down my body, and he cupped me through my leathers.

I was vibrating with desire. "Please," I begged.

"Like I told you before, you never have to beg for me to give you pleasure." He flipped me once again, so I was on all fours and tugged my trousers down, baring my ass to him. He gave it a firm smack, the sound like a crack of lightning, which made wetness pool between my thighs.

He inserted two fingers, finding the extremely sensitive spot with expertise. I moaned loudly and tightened around him. "That is a good girl," he praised. His thumb found my clit and drew small circles around it. "Come for me." My body reacted to his words quickly, and my climax claimed me. He kept going, pumping in and out of me with precision. I squirmed trying to get away, but he held me in place. The stimulation was almost too much, overwhelming my senses. My second orgasm hit my full force. I cried out, my body shuddering, as he slowed his movements, allowing me to come down from the intense high.

Rion withdrew his fingers and righted my clothing. Then, he pulled me to my feet. "Better?" he asked. I sluggishly noddled. "Good," he grinned. "Now go to bed." I did as he demanded, no longer having any fight left in me. As I made my way past him to the tent, he gave my ass another good smack. I made my way there in a haze, curling deep in the furs spread out upon my bedroll, completely sated. I decided in that moment that I would never be able to get enough of him.

Chapter 11

The days began to blur together in a steady rhythm of travel, campfires, and quiet conversation. Each morning brought a new stretch of winding forest paths or open meadow, and each night we found shelter beneath the trees or beside the trickle of some forgotten stream.

Two weeks passed without incident, the silence between us growing more comfortable with every mile. I had stopped counting the days, but according to Rion, we were no more than four weeks from the mountains.

There was still much yet to prepare before we reached them—physically, mentally, perhaps even emotionally. Though the journey had been calm, a sense of urgency threaded its way through our quiet moments, like a current beneath still water.

Rion was pushing me harder during training, and we have been riding for longer intervals to try to make up for time we lost after the leprechaun attack. After finally finding success with wielding a knife, Rion deemed I was ready to move on to a short sword, which I now carried alongside my knife. I still struggled with leaving my left side exposed, which earned me several stern talks from Rion, but overall, I was improving quickly. On the other hand, mastering my magic was moving much slower than both of us would like. I could ground myself with little effort but was only able to maintain the solid ball of light for only a few minutes before I lost focus.

I have been so drained by the time I have reached my bed that it only takes a few minutes before I am fast asleep. It's also been weeks since Rion has touched me, neither one of us having the energy. However, the rising sexual tension is getting more than anyone can bear.

Rion caught me in the side with the flat of his sword for what felt like the hundredth time. I rubbed the welt starting to form. "Can you fucking stop that?" I growled at him in annoyance.

"I do not know. Can you stop leaving your side exposed?" he shot back.

"I am trying," I argued.

He stepped forward, getting into my face. "Not hard enough! That will get you killed. You are literally leaving an opening for your opponent."

"I can't help that you make it all seem so easy. You were raised with a sword in your hand. I wasn't. Can you just cut me some slack?"

He rubbed his hand over his face, trying to calm himself. "If you would have followed my directives, you would have had this problem solved by now," Rion ranted. I glared at him, sheathing my sword, and stormed off towards the edge of the forest. "Where do you think you are going? We are not done," he called, hot on my heels. I ignored him.

He caught up to me within a few strides. Rion grabbed my arm and spun me to face him. "You need to focus because if you think for a moment, you will survive a battle, you are sorely mistaken."

I struggled against his hold. "Let go of me, now!" I demanded.

He did no such thing, only moved so that his nose was an inch from mine. "Then listen to my instructions. Follow my demonstrations. It's as simple as that."

Before I knew what I was doing, my unobstructed hand came up and slapped him across the face. My palm stung from the blow and a small red mark appeared on his cheek. He breathed heavily through his nose and let go of arm. "You will never talk to me that way again. I am doing my fucking best. Maybe Nolan or Flynn should take over my sword training. They seem to at least see my potential, not just my flaws." I spun back around and continued my trek back to camp. Rion didn't follow this time, still standing in stunned silence in my wake.

I arrived to find Nolan and Flynn had packed up camp already. Horses saddled and ready to go. "Where's Rion?" Nolan inquired.

"Don't know and I don't fucking care," was my reply.

Flynn whistled. "We could hear you guys from here. Trouble in paradise?" I glared at him. He held up his hands in front of him and backed away.

"Can I ride with one of you today? I can't stand the thought of breathing the same air, let alone sharing a horse with him right now." They looked at me like I had just turned into a three headed hydra right before their eyes.

"I don't think that is a good idea," Nolan finally spoke up. I looked at Flynn, hoping his answer would be different.

"No fucking way. I prefer my head attached to my shoulders," he laughed nervously.

"Fine," I grumbled. I walked off to the watering hole we discovered when we got here. It was serene and just deep enough to bathe in. I was too tired last night to do more than wash my face and arms and hoped that its frigid water would cool my temper.

I stripped down quickly and stepped into the water. I waded out slowly so I could acclimate to the temperature as it attempted to steal the breath from my lungs. Though the nights are growing colder with the approach of the impending winter, the days are still warm.

I stopped in the deepest part of the stream that just covered the swell of my breasts and turned my face to the sky, soaking in the sun's rays that weren't blocked by the incessant clouds. Its warmth felt amazing with the contrast of the chilly water.

I took in a large lungful of air and dunked my head under the surface of the water. I stayed under until my lungs screamed to take a breath, enjoying the peace found underneath. Resurfacing with a splash, I wiped the water from my eyes. The snap of a branch on the bank caught my attention. I spun around to find Rion watching me. Anger from our previous encounter scorched my skin once more. "Go. Away," I emphasized each syllable.

He remained planted where he stood. "You cannot go wandering off by yourself. Finish bathing and get out so we can leave."

"No," I spat at him, mostly just to rile him. I didn't intend to spend much more time in the cold water.

"I am not playing," he retorted.

I wasn't sure if I was trembling from the freezing water or from the rage that surged through me. "Good. Neither am I."

He came closer to the bank, the water licking his boots. "You are being stubborn. That water is too cold. You are going to freeze."

"Like you fucking care. You used me for what you needed, and now you are treating me like shit. I am a tool to you, nothing more." I knew the words that escaped my lips weren't true, though he had still yet to admit his feelings for me, but I wanted to hurt him like he had me. "If we accomplish our plans, I will be your queen. Maybe you should start acting like it."

That was the final straw. Rion charged into the water after me. I backed deeper into the water, putting as much space between us as I could, but he was faster. "Is that really what you think, *your majesty*?" he mocked. He continued to descend upon me. "We are not going to get anywhere if you do not get out of the gods damn stream."

He finally reached me and hauled me over his shoulder. I kicked my feet and pounded my fist against his back as he walked us back out of the water. He put me down on the bank and pointed at my clothes. "Now get dressed." I had half a mind to jump back in the water but gave in to the cold that seeped into my bones. He gave my body a swift glance before turning to allow me to dress in privacy.

He attempted to lead me back with a hand under my arm, but I snatched it back. "Don't touch me," I scolded. When we returned to where we had camped the night before, Nolan and Flynn were nowhere to be seen. "Where are Nolan and Flynn?"

"I sent them ahead. They are going to meet us at a village in two nights," he answered.

"Okay? Why?" Suspicion caused me to finally turn and look him in the eye.

"I have something to show you. Can you just get on the damn

horse?" I wanted to continue to be stubborn but knew that if I refused, he would just through me over the saddle against my will, so I nodded and mounted on my own. He climbed onto the horse behind me and kicked the horse into a steady trot. We set aside our fury, but the tension could be cut with a knife.

I wasn't necessarily angry that he was pushing me harder in training. I understood that we didn't have much more time. However, I was upset with the fact he said I wasn't trying hard enough, because I have been working my ass off to be where they needed me to be, to be who they needed me to be. Something was definitely off this morning. Though he has been tough over the last few weeks, he always praised my progress. For some reason, he was exceptionally irritable.

We trekked through the woods at a meandering pace. Rion didn't seem to be in a hurry to get to where we were going, which he had yet to disclose to me. Actually, he hadn't spoken a word to me since we left. "Are you going to tell me where we are going?" I finally asked.

"You'll see, it isn't far," was the reply I got.

We worked our way through the forest, the sun's rays filtering through the canopy to the forest floor lightened my mood with its beauty. At the end of the path, a small break in the trees appeared. Here, the sun shone at such a bright intensity that it was almost blinding, as the horse stepped from the cover of the trees. I was struck by the beauty of the rolling hills of wildflowers before me. Nestled in a valley between two sloping hills, was a village.

"Where are we?" I gaped.

"This is the village of Moore." He sounded tired and sad.

"It's beautiful." I continued to stare at the sight.

"Aye, it is," he agreed.

I slightly turned in the saddle to peer at his face. His eyes were closed and agony spread across his face, like he couldn't bear to look at the village. "Why are we here?" The suspicion from earlier grew.

"My mother grew up here," he whispered, eyes still shut. I remained still and quiet. Rion had never told me about his mother, and I didn't want to discourage him from doing so. He finally opened his eyes, and they were rimmed with tears. Any anger I still held snuffed out. He looked so broken.

"When she was twenty, my father came to the village to trade and caught her eye. She drew his attention over the weeks he was here, determined to marry him." A tear slid down his cheek. My heart broke into a million tiny pieces as I watched that tear drop from his chin. "Due to the gap in age, her parents did not approve of their union, so they ran off in the dead of night. They conceived me a few weeks later. They were happy for a while, but over time my father grew cruel." I remember the burns on his chest and my temper spiked.

"She and I suffered at his hands for years, and it only got worse after the invasion. I spent years seeking my father's approval, but nothing was ever good enough for him." His voice shook with restrained emotion. "Do you remember the story Flynn told about stealing the wine from my father?" I nodded but remained quiet, completely enthralled in his devastating story. "We were young and stupid. We just wanted to have a little fun, but my father caught us. He sent Flynn and Bellamy home, threatening to fire their parents, then turned to deal with me. My father decided he had had enough of my antics. Though I tried to fight against him, I was no match for his strength.

"He bound my wrists to the arms of a chair, pulled out a

knife, and told me if I wanted to be a thief, I would be punished like a thief. He was inches away from taking my hand when my mother found us. She threw herself at his feet, begging him to spare me. He yanked her up by her hair and screamed in her face, blaming her—for my actions, for my existence, for everything. She offered herself in my place, like she always did when she was aware of his abuse. I had done my best to hide most of it from her, to shield her from the worst of him.

"I struggled against my bounds when my father agreed to her pleas with enthusiasm. She had just healed from the last beating she took for me. He dropped her back to the floor and kicked her. A wicked smile spread across his face when she cried out in pain. He didn't stop until blood leaked from her nose and mouth. I begged for him to stop, to take me, but he ignored my cries. When he finally let up, my mother lay on the floor unresponsive, but breathing." Rion paused, letting out a shuttering breath. Tears flowed freely down both our faces.

"He waited until she regained consciousness, which felt like hours watching her chest rise and fall slowly. He gripped her chin, forcing her to look at him. She struggled against his hold but was too weak to wrench herself free. He kept her gaze as he slid the knife, that had been intended for taking my hand, into her chest, then proceeded to watch the life drain from her eyes. That was the moment I realized what I had to do. I thought about all the people we left behind after the invasion. My mother's family that still lived here, imprisoned by a false king. I was determined never to allow another to live under the control of their oppressor, as I had mine. I bid my time, while I planned my escape from his clutches. I got Flynn and Bellamy on board first then recruited Nolan, and together, we would find a way to free the Emerald

Isle from the Aos Si king. That's why I'm here." Rion focused his attention on the beautiful village below. There was one part of his story I didn't understand.

"What happened to your father?" I whispered.

"He is still alive, and I am still driven to ensure that he will pay for what he has done." He looked at me, locking his pain filled gaze with mine. "Today is the ten-year anniversary of her death and it was all my fault." Now everything became clear. The reason he was so irritable and seemed to be pushing me harder today. He was in pain and taking it out on me. "I am so sorry for the things I said. The way I acted. It's not an excuse, but I needed you to understand," he choked. "Please forgive me."

I patted the hand that was still firmly grasping my middle. "I forgive you." My forgiveness broke something in him, the child deep within that craved it more than anything. "Though, I don't think my forgiveness is what you need. You need to forgive yourself. You were young. It is your father who is to blame."

I looked down upon the village, its beauty long gone, now tainted with such misery. I wish I could take Rion's pain and bear it as my own. He needed us to succeed, not just to free our people, but to absolve him from his guilt. He needed to see that evil didn't always win, and I was bound and determined to give that to him.

Chapter 12

We left the village and tormented memories behind us, entering the forest once more. How such a beautiful place could cause so much pain was beyond me. I didn't know what to say as we rode, so I chose not to say anything at all, instead providing Rion with quiet solidarity. I was so honored and grateful that Rion had finally shown me a part of himself that wasn't superficial.

My heart throbbed as I recounted the story of his mother's death at the hands of his father. He could have taken an entirely different path in his life because of the trauma. He could have allowed it to poison his soul, becoming just like his father. He could have allowed it to consume him, until he was nothing but a broken man. However, his resiliency allowed him to take his pain and drove him to help others who are facing the same fate. I admired his compassion and strength.

Rion picked a spot beneath the sweeping branches of a willow to camp for the evening. As he began to unpack the saddlebags, withdrawing the tent from one of the saddle bags, I stopped him with a steady hand. “Let’s not set it up tonight,” I proposed. “It might be nice to fall asleep to the trees above us instead of canvas.”

Rion gave me a sadden smile. “If you wish.”

I gathered bits of dry tinder scattered across the moss-covered ground, while Rion searched for larger pieces of firewood. Once I had enough, I crouched by the fire pit and carefully built a small mound of kindling at its center. Beside me, I wove a loose nest from strands of hair cut from Rion’s horse’s mane, setting it gently on the ground. Holding the curved steel across my knuckles, I struck the flint against it in quick succession, sending sparks flying toward the nest. I was careful not to graze my fingers as the sparks caught—thin smoke curling upward from the singed hair. Dropping the flint and steel, I snatched up the smoldering bundle and blew into it, steady and sure, until it blossomed into flame. I set it into the tinder and fed the fire slowly, adding larger sticks one by one until the flames leapt and danced in a steady, rolling blaze.

Rion had been off scrounging up a vibrant platter of berries and nuts, along with the dried venison in our packs, that would make a hearty evening meal. We ate our fill, the sweet berries and robust flavor of the venison satiating my hunger, as we talked of small things to keep our minds off of Rion’s traumatic confession.

“You still want to work on magic tonight?” I asked wearily once our plates were clear. I wasn’t sure what he would be up for, especially with how our morning training session had gone.

“Of course,” he replied. “Are you okay to do so?”

I was tired but figured I could probably manage. “Yeah, I’m fine.” I guess ‘fine’ wasn’t really the right word, but we couldn’t afford to lose even one training session at this point.

Luckily, I didn't have to remove my shoes or use an anchor to ground myself anymore. I could feel the connection to the earth all the time, whether I was directly touching it or not. I pulled the magic into my body swiftly. It flooded my system with heat. It was a comforting sort of warmth that I had grown accustomed to, and yearn for, like a hug. I created a ball of light about the size of an apple. The creation of the sphere wasn't the issue but how long I was able to sustain it before it flickered out.

I immediately felt tiredness in my limbs as the magic stole my strength, but I fought against it. Every session, I only focused on the sphere itself, hoping that it would grow under my scrutinizing gaze. I chose to use a different approach this time. I closed my eyes for a moment, thinking of Rion and my people, of the lives that depended upon my success. They needed me, so I could not fail. I opened my eyes once more.

The light grew more intense, the sphere nearly doubling in size. I kept replaying the memories of starving children and their parents too weak to provide for them. I reflected on the tragic story of Rion's mother's death. I remembered all those who have died because I was born. My rage fed the magic.

The breeze began to howl around us. Rion stepped forward. "You are going to have to reign it in. You must remain in control," he coaxed. I heard his voice, but my fury burned hot, and it was endless. The wind picked up, the trees bending under its weight until they creaked in protest. The fire wavered rapidly and winked out, my magic the only thing lighting the forest around us.

"You are going to burn out, please stop," Rion pleaded as he inched closer against the air current. I heard him this time. The pain in his voice. The pain I put there by pushing myself too far. I let go of the anger immediately. The wind ceased and we were plunged into darkness.

I felt Rion's arms quickly wrap around my waist as my legs gave way as soon as the magic returned to the soil. My body was completely spent. He lowered us smoothly to the ground. "That was incredible," pride replaced the pain. I lived for his praise. "You've been struggling for weeks. What changed?"

"Everything," I sluggishly responded. "I thought of all the injustices committed. All the lives that have been stolen. All of the spirits who have been broken. And how their salvation rests upon my shoulders."

He nuzzled his nose into my neck. "I want you to know how very proud I am of you. I know I have not said it lately, but you are truly going above and beyond what I had expected. I guess that is the reason I have been so tough on you, because I do see the potential you hold. You were incorrect in your assumption." His lips replaced his nose with a gentle kiss. "You have never been just a tool."

I placed my hand on his cheek and brought his face up to mine. "I am sorry for everything I said. I didn't mean it." Though I couldn't see his reaction, I felt a sigh of relief brush my face.

"I needed to hear it. I was so stuck in my own head that I did not think about how I was treating those around me. Those I care about. I was so angry with you, but once I thought about your words, I realized my error." He leaned into my hand and kissed my palm. I was struck by yet another confession, that he cared for me.

I contemplated the events of the day, and all that led to that point. "I think we need to work on getting to know each other more." I placed my hand over his heart. It was pounding rapidly beneath my touch. "I want to know the man that lies beneath the rough exterior. You showed a bit of him today, but I know there is more. I want to know the man that has begun to capture my heart." It was the first time I had spoken my feelings for him aloud. A part of me worried he'd reject them, but he placed the sincerest kiss against my lips.

"I am yours, little fox. I have always been yours." I reveled in his words. I know I had only known this man for a short time, and maybe it was my naivety or want for human connection, but I never wanted to leave his side. It felt as though he was the other half of my soul, an instinctual bond that could never be broken.

Rion gathered me in his arms and carried me to the bedroll he had placed below the willow's protective branches, for I was still too weak to stand. He laid me on the furs and claimed the spot at my back, curling his body around mine. He drew circles along my arms and hummed in contentment. I felt at peace wrapped in his arms. As long as he stood by my side, I could do anything. I didn't let the worries of time or lack thereof seep in to decimate this moment. My eyes fluttered shut.

I awoke on my back with Rion's head rested on my chest. The rumble of his snores resonated through my body. His inky hair had become unbound at some point during sleep, and it lay across his face, obscuring it from view. I brushed it back behind his ear. Rion's eyes fluttered behind his lids, and he let out a groan. "We should probably get a move on if we are going to meet the boys before dark," I smiled.

He coiled his arms around me tightly. "Five more minutes," he moaned.

I chuckled at the childlike whine that escaped his lips when I weaseled myself out of his grasp and stood, stretching. He flopped over and threw the covers over his head. "Oh, come on," I said as I pulled at the furs, but he was much stronger than me.

He pulled back and I fell flat on his chest, his arms pinning me to him. "Now what, little fox?" he drawled. The smile that took over his face was brilliant. I kissed him fiercely. The look of amusement faded from his face and was replaced with lust.

I smiled innocently at him. "We have to go."

"You cannot just tease me like that and not do anything about it," he grumbled.

"I don't know what you are talking about. Now let's go." He let his arms fall to the bed beside him with a dramatic sigh, and I rose to my feet again.

"Well, now you are really going to have to give me a minute." The confusion must have shown on my face because he whipped back the furs to make his point. The evidence of his arousal stood proud within its leather prison.

"Oops," I smirked and walked away to prepare the horse for travel.

"That's not nice!" He called from behind me. I just laughed and continued on my way.

After Rion dealt with his little problem, we quickly packed up camp and were on the road once more. We skipped morning training, for I was still not fully recovered from last night and he didn't want to push me.

"When we reunite with Flynn and Nolan, we need to discuss the next steps after reaching the mountains. We have four weeks to have a concrete plan for finding the missing treasures and how to infiltrate the palace to retrieve the sword and the stone," announced Rion a little way down the road.

"Why don't we just kill the king? He doesn't have an heir to take over. It would take days of fighting amongst themselves to determine who would lead them. Problem solved," I inquired.

Rion shifted uncomfortably behind me. "Because he will become a martyr to the people that agree with his decisions, who wish to see the human race suffer. He commands an army of over ten thousand men. The small group of rebels I have collected will not be enough to defeat them." He wasn't wrong. "We need all four treasures before we lay siege to the palace. Without them, we will have no chance. We need to also determine how you can raise the Wild Hunt. Their numbers will be needed, as well, for this to work." I soaked in the information, trying to see a clear plan of attack.

Rion continued, "I might be able to get my hands on a few guards to interrogate to see if the king has any leads on where the spear and cauldron might be hidden. Then we need to figure out how to get in and out of the palace with the other treasures unnoticed."

I thought about how we could slip into the palace without raising any alarms. "I could probably get in unnoticed, if I was alone," I thought aloud.

"Absolutely fucking not," Rion shut me down quickly.

"Think about it. They employ human maids, right? I could disguise myself and would be able to freely walk about the palace. A hulking man draws attention where a non-threatening girl does not." It was genius, and it could work. I just need to know the exact location of the Stone and Sword.

"I am not letting you walk into that place without protection."

"But I wouldn't be unprotected. I can wield a sword, and I will be even more practiced by then. I also have my magic," I argued.

"And the Dullahan?" he questioned. "They would sense your presence before you even reached the gate."

"Well, their internal trackers seem to be a bit off, because they have only shown up twice since we met." Rion didn't seem to have a response to that. I could feel his glare on the back of my head, so I patted his hand trying to appease him.

"We do this together or not at all. I would sooner steal you away to the mainland and leave the Emerald Isle to burn before I would let you enter that palace alone. The responsibility is not just yours," he growled.

I decided to drop the conversation for now. "We can discuss particulars with the others later. We'll find a way." Rion's mood improved quickly after the termination of our discussion.

"After all this is said and done, if we survive, what will become of us?" I asked. If he didn't want to talk about the upcoming war, fine, but perhaps he would speak about the future and the little time we had been given.

"I am not sure I understanding what you are asking." Perplexity was evident in his words.

I don't know if it was my naivety or my hopelessly romantic heart that caused me to ask the next question that slipped past my lips. "Will we marry?"

Rion coughed, completely blindsided by my question. "Well, if that is what you want."

"What do you want?" I countered, determined to make him talk about the emotions he had trapped within his hard head. I shifted in the saddle so I could peer at his face.

"I want you…forever." I looked in his eyes and only saw the truth of his words. My heart swelled with an emotion I was not fully prepared to name. I could very well spend the rest of my life, or rather the rest of his, in his embrace, for as long as he would have me. A part of me feared that, in time, he would grow tired of me, but for now, I could lose myself in the fleeting moments and the fire of our intimacy.

We met Flynn and Nolan on the edge of a large village as the sun slipped over the horizon. Before we arrived, the two men had scouted out a tavern with a couple vacancies. I was a little weary after our last stay, but Rion assured me he wouldn't allow anything to happen again.

The smell of stale ale and piss stoved its way up my nostrils when we walked through the front door, the heavy oak wood slamming behind us. The tavern was packed at this time of day, its inhabitants returning from a variety of labor-intensive work were equally as foul as the air that permeated the establishment. We claimed a table in the corner of the large dining room. Rion gestured to the barmaid, who gathered four glasses, filling them with ale, before sauntering up to our table. She passed out the sour smelling beverages. Rion asked politely for four meals, whatever was hot. She nodded and scurried off, disappearing through a set of double doors behind the bar.

As I peered around the room, I noticed that the population of the tavern was mostly men, besides the barmaid and a slew of scarcely dressed women that milled about entertaining the patrons. "What kind of place do you guys have us staying in," I blushed in Flynn and Nolan's directions.

"Flynn picked it," Nolan explained, pointing to the man on his left, who's eyes were roaming over the half-naked women.

Flynn had a stupidest grin on his face when one of the women asked if there was anything they could do for him. "Hell yeah, there is something you can do for me." She straddled his lap and kissed him passionately. My blush deepened. I wanted to fall beneath the table and shield my eyes like a child scared of monster in the dark. The barmaid returned, two more rounds of drinks balanced on a wooden tray, to let us know our dinner would be ready soon. I surely hoped so, because I couldn't sit here much longer, watching Flynn get his rocks off.

Rion threw his hand over my shoulder, already a few pints of ale in. I had been nursing mine, choking down the warm, disgusting liquid.

He brought his mouth close to my ear, his breath causing shivers to cast across my body, despite the rank smell of alcohol. "Does it make you uncomfortable?" he whispered. His unoccupied hand startled me when it found my thigh.

The girl ground herself against Flynn, which caused him to groan deep in his throat. Rion moved his hand closer to my center. "Or does it turn you on to watch?" My face heated even more, worried that someone might spy his hand under the table. I looked around anxiously.

"Stop, someone could see," I whispered back to him.

He sucked my earlobe into his mouth. I took in a sharp breath to try to stop the moan forming in my throat. "Maybe I want them to watch." Rion's hand slipped home. Flynn was too preoccupied by the girl that was shoving her tongue down his throat to notice much of anything, but Nolan's watchful gaze caught my attention. He also had had much to drink. He gave me a knowing smile, leaning back in his seat and crossing his arms over his chest.

Rion's thumb drew small circles over me as heat flooded between my thighs. The pleasure was only amplified by Nolan watching, which intrigued me. Rion followed my line of sight. He chuckles, "Maybe you do too." He continued, adding pressure. I tried to control my breathing as my climax grew closer. I couldn't believe I was allowing this to happen, but it felt so good I couldn't stop it. I didn't want to stop it.

Rion stopped just before I came. He drained his mug and stood, hauling me to my feet. "Have the barmaid send our food up to our room, and make sure you guys get some rest. Early morning," he called over his shoulder as he led me to the stairs. All he got was a grunt of agreement from Flynn and a wave from Nolan.

As soon as the door was shut to our room, Rion picked me

up and brought his lips to mine. I wrapped my legs around his hips and arms around his neck, our kisses feverish. He pressed my back into the door and ground against me, his erection pressing into my core. "If we did not leave that room, I would have taken you on the table for all to see." I gasped at the explicit words. "I would have shown them all that you are mine," he snarled.

He thrusted me hard into the door with a thud. "I'm ready," I panted. He wanted to go slow, but I needed him inside me more than I needed to breathe.

He paused his movements. "Are you sure?" I nodded frantically at him. "Little fox, I need you to say yes."

"Yes," I breathed.

His lips found mine once more. The passion within this man would bring any woman to their knees before him. He walked us over to the bed in the center of the room. He dropped me to my feet beside it and started to peel my clothes off. Once my chest was bare, he palmed my breast that fit perfectly within his hand. "Gods, it's like you were made for me."

He quickly pushed my trousers down my thighs and helped me step out of them. Rion remained kneeling and looked up at me. Running his hands up the back of my thighs, chills followed his touch. I trembled as he looked up at me. Anticipation built low in my belly, while I watched him trail kisses from my stomach to the crop of hair that grew below. "I need you undressed, now," I demanded.

He bowed his head, "As you command, my queen." Before long, he was standing naked before me. I walked around him, trailing my fingers across his stomach. I pressed my chest into his back as my hand descended to his arousal. I gripped him firmly in my hand like he had shown me and pumped him once. He let out an animalist groan, so I did it again. He stilled my hand with his and turned to face me.

My heart pounded in my chest as his eyes darkened. He pushed me gently towards the bed, until the backs of my knees hit the edge, forcing me to sit. I kept my eyes locked on him. I knew he was holding himself back, that he didn't want to rush this.

Stooping so we were eye level, he ran the back of his hand along the inside of my thigh. I opened them wider to give him better access. I leaned forward and claimed his lips once more, bucking my hips to encourage him to touch me. And when he finally did, my moan filled the room.

His unhurried fingers teased me. Fire rushed through me when he finally drove them inside me. I released his lips and flung my head back, my back arching in response to his intrusion. He kissed my throat that was exposed to him as he curled his fingers, finding the hidden spot within that made me squirm. The wet sound of his fingers fucking me joined my moans.

"You are so ready for me," he said as he bit the base of my neck. He withdrew, guiding me to lay my back against the bed. I watched him intently as he used my wetness to prepare himself.

Nervousness formed in the pit of my stomach while I watched him stroke himself. I was still unsure if I would be able to take all of his length. He halted. "Are you sure you are ready for this?" He must have seen the apprehension on my face.

"Yes," I breathed.

"If at any time, it's too much and you need me to stop, I will. Okay?" I nodded—his compassion drove my need ever higher. Rion placed his knee on the edge and climbed onto the bed. My legs parted as he laid upon me, forcing his erection to slide against my center. My body was ridged with anxiety and pleasure. "Relax your body. I will go slow." He gripped his length and guided it to my entrance.

He pushed in slowly, a little at a time to allow my body to adjust to his size. A deep groan reverberated through the room. Restraint twisted Rion's face as he tried to contain the desire to thrust deep inside me. The mix of pain and pleasure was almost enough to send me shooting for the stars.

He took his time until he was fully seated within me. "You okay?" he asked. I nodded, too lost in the feeling of him to formulate words. He withdrew an inch. "You are such a good girl," he purred as he pushed back in. "And so fucking tight." The pain subsided quickly with his movements and was replaced by pure ecstasy.

I moved my hips to match his agonizingly slow pace. This motivated him to quicken his pace ever so slightly. "Oh Gods," I shouted. I was at the edge of my climax when his thumb found my clit once more. I tightened around him, my body trembling forcefully. His movements became irregular before he quickly pulled out of me and came on the flat of my stomach with a groan.

Rion flopped on the bed beside me. "That was fucking insane," he drawled. I was happy he had words for it because I did not. He looked over to me with concern. "Are you okay?"

"I just don't know what to say." He propped himself up on an elbow so he could look at my face. I smiled and placed a hand on his. "I want to say it was amazing, but it was so much more. I think," I hesitated.

"You think what?" he prompted.

"I think…I think I love you." I sputtered.

"Little fox, I loved you from the moment I pulled you from that hollow, covered in blood and dirt." He placed his forehead on mine. His forehead was sweaty from exertion, but I did not care. We stayed that way for a while before he rose. He cleaned me up with a rag hung over the edge of a small tub in the corner of the room that I had missed in our hurry to be united. I made a note to take a warm bath before we left in the morning.

Rion crawled back on the bed, pulling me into his embrace. A nagging thought pulled me from the peace I found within his arms. "I am going to live a very long time." Tears welled in my eyes when I looked at his handsome face. "You will not. I don't think I could bear this life without you in it."

"These are worries for another day," he soothed me as he pulled me closer. "Let us just enjoy the time we are given." I wanted to do as he suggested but nausea bloomed in my stomach. Once this is all done, we would only have a few years before he started to age, and I did not. I would have to watch him wither away, and there wasn't a damn thing I could do to stop it.

Chapter 13

I woke up just before dawn to find Rion missing from the bed. I looked about the room and spied a freshly filled tub, steam filling the cool air. Excitement thrummed through me at the thought of submerging myself within its warm embrace.

I shot to my feet, wrapping a sheet around me to ward away the chill that met my bare skin. I tiptoed across the icy floor and dipped my hand in the water to find it the perfect temperature. I wondered how I managed to sleep through its filling. I dropped the sheet and sank into the water. A content sigh passed my lips.

The door opened, giving birth to Rion. I looked over my shoulder to give him a smile. He came up behind me and knelt by the tub, wrapping his arms around me. "How are you feeling this morning, little fox?"

"Absolutely delightful," I replied as I laid my head back against the edge of the tub, closing my eyes. Rion's sudden movement caused my eyes to fly open as he grabbed the bar of soap that was perched on the lip of the tub along with the cloth. "What do you think you are doing?"

"I thought I'd bathe you, unless you don't want me to," he added.

"Bathe me? Like...Like all of me?" I stuttered.

He laughed, "Yes, all of you."

I hesitated for a moment before saying, "Okay." Rion ran the cloth across my shoulders and around to my clavicle. I tipped my head back over the brim of the tub, enjoying the sensation. The soap smelled of lavender and honey and left my skin feeling as soft as a newly born babe in its wake. Rion moved down my arms to my hands. He paid close attention to my nails, ensuring the dirt was removed from underneath. His attention to detail was astonishing. He moved on to my breast, which peaked in response.

His hand skated down the flat of my stomach. "I'm going to need you to stand so I can finish," he coaxed into my ear.

My body grew rigid. "I can do the rest," I insisted.

He huffed out a laugh, "You are being completely ridiculous. Please. Just let me do this for you." I thought for a moment before I relented and stood. Though there was a fire in the hearth, a cold draft rushed over my skin causing goosebumps to form over its surface. Rion continued slowly.

He leaned over the edge of the tub and kissed my hip, then my stomach. He slid the warm soapy cloth between my legs delicately. I never thought bathing could be this much of a turn on until that moment. But this was only a tease, a promise for later, because I knew we didn't have the time for such things.

Rion spun me, placing a kiss on the swell of my ass. My heart nervously pounded in my chest for what would come next. He dunked the cloth back in the tub and applied more soap before finishing his task. He took his time, meticulous in his work.

Rion proceeded to wash my legs clear down to the soles of my feet. By the time he was done, I was shivering against the cold and the ache that had started to form low in my stomach. How I wished we had the time to satisfy that need.

I sat back down in the water, which was starting to cool, and he kissed my temple with a smile etched across his face. "I will fetch your clothing, and here is a towel for when you are ready," he said as he placed the plush fabric on the edge of the tub. He walked from the room stating he would prepare the horses and would meet me downstairs when I was ready.

I thought I'd be embarrassed, maybe I should be, but I had spent so much time caring for myself and others that having someone to care for me felt incredible. It ranked a close second to the feeling of Rion moving inside me. Our connection grows and strengthens with each passing day. Without him I don't think I'd be able to breathe, to live. I needed him more than I knew how to express and that scared the shit out of me.

Growing up, I had never wanted to be the type of woman that needed a man to survive. I had the skills to make it on my own, especially now that I have been trained to defend myself. But I could get used to having another to depend on. It hadn't seemed possible before, but now I didn't have to bear it all alone.

The water had gone cold by the time I rose and got dressed. I gathered the rest of my things into my pack and hustled out of the room. The men waited at the same table we had occupied the night before. I blushed as I remembered the events that had occurred at this very table. The woman straddling Flynn. Rion's hand on my thigh.

Rion caught the look on my face, and to save me from some of the embarrassment, jumped to his feet. "Let us get going, yeah?" Rion took my hand and led me through the nearly empty tavern to the door. The men behind me were silent as they followed, though I thought I heard Flynn snicker. Rion halted right before opening it and turned back to me, "I have a surprise for you." A grin took over his face.

"What is it?" I exclaimed. I normally didn't like surprises, but by the look on his face, I knew I'd probably like this one. He opened the door and gestured for me to go first. The horses were tied to the hitching post off to the right, and at the end of the line, stood a beautiful black and white mare. Her mane and tail were long and flowing. My heart warmed. He had taught me to handle the reins of his horse, which I learned was quite a stubborn beast, but I hadn't gotten the chance to ride on my own.

I walked over to her. She was absolutely stunning. I ran my hand down her soft mane and across the exquisite black leather saddle upon her back. She whinnied loudly in response. "She's for me?" I asked, still struck by her beauty and his gesture.

"We had been talking about getting you your own horse. I also thought it would be best if you were presented to your people upon your own steed. You will appear stronger than if you were to show up on mine. They are expecting a leader. A queen. You need to look like one," he explained as he patted her neck. I was disappointed that I wouldn't be sharing a horse with him anymore but incredibly excited to have my own. "She has a good temperament according to the smithy. She's patient and loyal." I gave her a pat as he spoke. She nuzzled her nose into the crook of my neck, leaving sloppy kisses behind.

"Thank you. So much. This means the world." Happy tears

stung my eyes. This was the best gift, well the only gift I have ever received. I flung my arms around Rion's neck, pulling him into a hug.

Nolan and Flynn were already upon their horses by the time I hauled myself onto mine. I decided her name would be Bryn. She was a few hands taller than Rion's I noticed as I struggled to mount her. He stood by to ensure I didn't fall right back off.

Once I was seated, he turned to his own and mounted. The sensation of the horse's movements without Rion bracing me felt strange and off balance. It took more effort to keep my seat, and my thighs burned from the pressure I had to use to keep myself upright. Rion rode at my side. "You are quiet. Is everything okay?" He asked.

I feared that if I spoke, I'd lose concentration and fall to my death. "Yeah," I croaked. "It's just a lot harder than I thought it would be on my own."

He chuckled, "You will continue to grow your strength. In a few days, your skills in a horsemanship will probably give Flynn a run for his money."

Flynn scoffed behind me, "We will see about that. Wanna race princess?" I frantically shook my head. If we went any faster than our current pace, I would definitely eat dirt. All the men laughed. I let out a small laugh myself, but my balance began to slip, so it came out more as a wheezing gasp.

Rion's hand shot out to steady me. "If you die now, you better take me with you," his voice was low and serious.

"Well, tell them not to make me laugh," I gestured to the morons that were still laughing at my gracelessness.

After a few hours, I was able to acclimate to riding on my own, to my delight. Bryn was a gentle creature. She seemed to be mindful of every dip in the road and every hill we climbed, navigating them without direction so I could focus on staying put. Rion's horse, however, did not like her one bit. At one point, he attempted to take a bite out of her when Rion wasn't looking—the little asshole.

I had noticed that the closer we got to the capital, the thinner the forest got. We started to pass by more civilians, merchants and travelers, who eyed me and the four gargantuan men that rode behind me. Villages also became more prominent. Keeping out of view would get harder as we went.

The men were arguing behind me about the best way to gain information on the two missing treasures. "I say we just torture the first soldier we come across," Nolan suggested.

Though I want to see the king suffer for his crimes, I didn't believe torturing his soldiers was the best way to gain information. "We can't do that, or we will be no better than he is," I argued.

Rion nodded his head, "I agree. His soldiers follow him out of fear. If we are strategic in who we pick, they will sing without much encouragement."

"I might have an idea," we all turned to Flynn as he spoke. Rion shot a look at Nolan that said *this ought to be good.* "After their shifts, some of the palace guards may be found relieving the stress from protecting the asshat they call king at a local tavern. With enough alcohol, anyone would spill their darkest secrets. We find which one they frequent the most and send someone in."

A look of surprise passed over Rion's face. "That is not a half bad idea. However, none of us would be able to do it," Rion gestured between the three men. "We are undeniably warriors. We would look suspicious asking questions about the spear and cauldron and where to find them."

They might, but I wouldn't. "What if I went in?"

Rion's head spun around. "Absolutely not."

"I could disguise myself as a highborn Aos Si noble girl. Hide my ears with my hair. You could even come with me as a bodyguard. It could work," I argued. Rion had shot down my idea to infiltrate the palace in a disguise, but this way I wouldn't be alone. Perhaps he would agree.

"She has a point. No one would question it. And as a woman, she can ask more questions because she won't be seen as a threat," Nolan defended me. "But it can't be you who goes in with her." A silent conversation passed between the two men when Rion went to object. "I will go. I won't let anything happen to her. I swear." Rion was quiet while he contemplated the plan.

I questioned for a moment why Rion couldn't be the one to go with me, but figured it was due to our relationship. Nolan probably felt it could be a liability. Nolan wouldn't let any harm come to me, but he also wouldn't pull me out at the first hint of danger.

"Rion, please. Let me do this. You can't shelter me from all risk, and I can't expect my people to do anything I wouldn't do myself," I spoke softly.

"Spoken like a queen," he replied. He mulled it over for a few more minutes. I held my breath just hoping he would agree. I had something to prove, not just to him, but to my people and myself. I knew I could do this. "Fine, but you do everything Nolan says." Rion relented. He turned to Nolan, voice threateningly low "And if one hair on her head is out of place when you return, I will personally make you suffer."

I rode closer to him. "I will be okay. If for some reason something goes awry, just know that you have trained me well. I am not the defenseless girl you pulled from the hollow of a tree any longer."

"I know that little fox, but I would rather let this entire kingdom fall than risk having you taken from me." I was struck by his sincerity. He would truly let all the kingdom suffer if it meant I did not. He no longer was on this journey to liberate these people from the oppression he once suffered. He was doing it all for me to ensure that I regained all that was stolen from me.

We moved our horses to the side of the path to allow a family to pass by. The pony hauling the wagon they occupied was old and thin. It wouldn't last them another winter. They would have nothing to plow their fields. The children in the back were also quite thin and lacked the enthusiasm that should shine in every child. The parents looked at us with tired eyes. "We can't allow it to continue," I said to Rion after they had passed. Emotion choked me. "I love you, but this is bigger than us and our wants. We cannot allow our feelings get in the way of our mission."

He looked at me, pride gleaming in his tear-lined eyes. "You will be the best queen this land has ever seen. I will follow you, even into death. If anything ever happens to you, I will not be able to continue this life." I knew what he had said was true, for I felt the same. Love bloomed in my chest as I looked upon the man that now held my heart in his hands.

It was immediately overcome with dread for the future once again. A bad feeling lurked in the shadows of my mind that made everything between us feel fragile, like one well-aimed touch would cause it all to shatter. I gave Rion a tight smile, which caused a look of confusion to contort his face. I nudged my horse ahead to avoid admitting my thoughts, while Flynn and Nolan distracted Rion by discussing specifics of the plan we had conceived.

I tried to dispel the feeling, to banish it with the other things

I didn't want to deal with, but it was stubborn. I cast a backwards gaze to Rion, who was deep in conversation with the others. My intuition screamed that there was something I was missing. Questions that had been left unanswered. That this man who was deeply in love with me, and I him, would lead to my destruction.

Chapter 14

I stared across the clearing to Rion the next morning. He had attempted to question my sudden change in demeanor yesterday, but I simply excused it as exhaustion. He didn't seem convinced but let it go. "What are these two doing here?" I questioned, eyeing Flynn and Nolan who stood off to the side.

"You still have some refining to do with your form, but you need to begin learning how to defend against multiple attackers. Hence their presence." Rion paced in front of me. "I will sit out to observe. I will be able to identify where you need to improve easier that way."

Flynn and Nolan approached me, drawing their weapons. I did the same. Right into it, I guess. "You will need to divide your attention between them. You cannot allow either to get behind you or back you into a corner."

The men began to circle me. I tracked their movements. This

would be harder than sparring with Rion. I knew how he fought, where he would strike and how he would block. I waited for one of them to advance, but they stayed out of the reach of my sword. "Come on, princess. Show us what you got," Flynn provoked me.

I advanced a step, striking out with my sword, that he swiftly deflected. He clicked his tongue. Looking over my shoulder to Rion, he exclaimed, "What the hell have you been teaching her." I took advantage of his moment of distraction. I shot out again, but this time, I smacked his wrist with the flat of my sword. He let out a pain filled grunt and dropped his sword.

Before I was able to apprehend Flynn, Nolan stepped in my path with his weapon pointed at my chest. Flynn quickly retrieved his weapon from the grass and stood alongside his partner. "That was good, princess, and would have worked if I was your only opponent."

Nolan and Flynn attacked as one, two warriors who had spent a lifetime guarding each other's flanks. I struggled to divide my attention between the blades. I successfully parried their advance, but just. I took a few quick steps back while I unsheathed my knife which had been strapped to my thigh. They reestablished their line and pushed forward towards me. I remained planted in my fighting stance.

When they attacked again, I was ready. I blocked Flynn on the right with my sword, and Nolan on the left with my knife. While they prepared for another blow, I ducked low, causing the men to collide their blades together. I rolled to Nolan's side, striking my sword into the back of his knees. They buckled and he fell to the ground. Flynn had attempted to follow me but tumbled over Nolan. Rion laughed, "She's making you two look inept."

Nolan and Flynn scrambled off the ground, glaring at me. I

held my weapons out in front of me, "Give up?" I provoked them.

"Fuck no," Nolan growled.

They separated, moving to either side of me. Rion observed quietly from the side lines as Flynn came at me first, our swords colliding with such force that my arm went slightly numb. He continued his attack, pressing me towards Nolan, who was waiting to catch me in his snare.

I ducked beneath Flynn's next blow, moving behind him. His back was still turned when my sword came to rest on his shoulder. Nolan looked stunned, while Rion laughed once again, "Did I not tell you she's fast. Extraordinary fast." Rion had pounded into my head for weeks that I would not be able to overpower my opponents, that I must be faster and use my small stature to my advantage.

I dropped my sword to my side, while I attempted to catch my breath. "How did you do that?" Nolan gaped.

"Do what?" I breathed.

Rion came to my side and put a hand on my lower back. "I noticed it a few days ago, too."

Flynn had turned to face me and looked just as confused as Nolan. "Anyone want to tell me what I did that was so remarkable?" I pressed.

"You moved with speed that shouldn't be possible for the average human, or even a Druid for that matter," Flynn explained.

"Why didn't you say anything the first time you noticed it?" I accused Rion.

"It was subtle. I needed an outside perspective to observe what was actually happening. Hence, why I did not participate in the exercise. I also had to put you in a situation where you would be challenged. Where you would have to draw upon everything to succeed," Rion gave me a wink trying to quell my irritation. "Unfortunately, you can predict my movements, which is why I enlisted Nolan and Flynn's help."

"Okay, but again, that doesn't really explain my speed."

"It's an Aos Si trait. They are born stronger, faster than the average human. I thought maybe your Druid blood had suppressed that of your father's, because you hadn't presented with any of their power, other than enhanced healing. You should have had access to it since childhood." I reflected upon my memories, searching for any sign that I had been stronger or faster than any of the other children, but came up short.

"I have never been sick," I thought aloud. "My grandmother treated many children that had been unable to fight off simple ailments because they were too frail. I was around the sick all the time and never once became ill, unlike my grandmother, who had come down with a cold a time or two."

"The Aos Si are immune to human ailments, but they still need sustenance to maintain their abilities. It's possible your abilities were suppressed due to the lack of a proper diet. I believe that your ability to heal rapidly was affected by this, as well." Rion's words were shocking. It is jarring to grow up thinking you are a mere human, only to find out you are anything but.

"What are their other natural born abilities?" I hadn't given it much thought and wanted to know what to expect.

Nolan spoke before Rion got a chance to say a word, "Can this conversation continue on the road? We don't want to lose too much of the daylight." We all agreed and set to tearing down camp.

A short while later, we were astride our horses once again. "What else will I be able to do?" It was easy to accept this new development with everything else I had learned about myself. I was actually kind of excited to discover of what I was capable.

"The Aos Si have a few natural powers with which they are born. Along with the increased speed and strength, they have the ability to influence minds and ward against other magic," Rion answered.

"Ward?" I had never heard of such a thing.

Rion tilted his head back and forth trying to figure out how to explain in layman's terms. "It's a kind of magical shield, invincible to the eye."

"Wait," I backtracked. "The Aos Si can control minds?"

"Essentially, yes. They can make you see or hear things that aren't there. Influence your emotions. Control your body against your mind's will. They can also read and speak into your mind. That's how the Dullahan can communicate when they have no mouth to speak with. When the king resurrected them, he gave them that ability in order to communicate." I stared in horror at Rion. The thought of anyone inside my head was utterly terrifying.

"Why did the Aos Si start using black magic when they have all of this at their disposal?" It didn't seem like the cost of using black magic was worth the reward.

"Because it has limitations. Mind control doesn't work on other Aos Si, they learn to ward their minds as children to keep each other out. Any strong-willed individual is also hard to control, and wards are only defensive. Black magic has no such limitations. The king was the first to master it and sway others to do the same. His ambitions led him down a path of no return." Rion shifted in his saddle. I couldn't tell if he was uncomfortable in his seat or with the topic of discussion.

"Where did black magic originate in the first place?" I asked.

Rion replied, "It was the magic of the Fomorians. Where it

came from before that is unclear."

I wanted to have hope, but I couldn't see an end where we don't all end up dead. I am but one person with magic. If we manage to recover the treasures, we could have a chance. But it is possible we won't even get that far. Doubt seeped in and poked holes in all our plans. I second guessed my conviction from yesterday. "Maybe you were right. Perhaps we should just leave and evacuate as many as we can to the mainland. Cut our losses." Images of Rion, Nolan and Flynn dead upon a battlefield soaked in blood flashed through my mind.

"No. I wasn't, and you know it."

"People are going to die," I muttered.

"People are already dying, Aisling." The use of my given name spoke to the severity of the situation. "These people wouldn't survive the trip, and there is no way to get them all out before the king realizes what is happening. It would take years that they don't have. By the time we reach Lios, you will be fully trained. You will have everything you need to make sure this succeeds." Rion made eye contact with me. "Don't let a moment of doubt cloud your judgment. I know you enough to know you would never be able to live with yourself if you had the opportunity to change things but chose not to act."

I nodded. I knew he was right. I closed my eyes and took a deep breath, letting my fears be expelled along with the air from my lungs. I opened my eyes once more. I would do what it takes. I would ensure all the sacrifices made to see us succeed are not made in vain.

* * *

Later that night we sat around the fire, bellies full and content in the silence of the night. The only sound heard were the crickets in the thicket. Rion finally rose to his feet, pulling me with him. Without a word, he led me to our tent. We laid on our bed staring at the canvas ceiling awaiting sleep to claim us. "I want to know more about you," I finally said into the dim.

"What do you want to know?" Rion replied.

I wanted to know everything, but I settled with, "What's your favorite color?"

He chuckled beside me, "It used to be the colors of the sunset. Bellamy and I would sit on the roof of my childhood home and watch the sun fall behind the horizon, casting brilliant oranges and pinks across the sky, and pretend we were on a grand adventure somewhere far away."

"Used to be? What is it now?" I questioned as I turned my head to look at him, though I could only make out the outline of his form beside me.

"The color of your eyes." I could hear the smile in his voice. He ran his thumb down my cheek. "A blue so deep I would happily drown within them." It wasn't the answer I had been expecting, but my heart fluttered in response. "What else would you like to know?"

"What's your favorite food?" I was enjoying the triviality of our conversation. It was what a *normal* couple would want to know about each other, even though we were anything but.

"Growing up, my mother used to make these biscuits that were thin and crisp with a golden edge, their scent wrapping around our home like a warm hug. The blend of ginger, cinnamon, and cloves danced on the air. Each bite was a little burst of warmth, the spice just strong enough to sting the tongue before melting into sweetness. She would make them for me whenever my father was away, because he claimed the smell was nauseating, the only time we were truly happy." The bittersweet tone of his voice hurt my heart. I made a note to make them for him when all of this was over.

"Will you tell me more about her? Your mother?"

He sighed. "She was pure and kind. Always seeing the best in people. It was the best, but also the worst part about her. Her compassion for those around her was what ultimately led to her death."

"It wasn't just her compassion for anyone, but for you. She was your mother. It was her duty to protect you at all costs. I appreciate the sacrifice she made, for without it, I may never have met you. You would have still been under the thumb of your father, would never have been free." Emotion on behalf of Rion threatened to choke me.

"You are right," he whispered back.

"Tell me more. What did she look like?" I pressed, hoping he would shut me out once more.

"She was beautiful. Everywhere she went, her smile and grace lit up the room. Her hair was a golden brown, warm and sun-kissed with hints of honey. I have her eyes." I thanked the forgotten Gods for blessing him with this feature, for it was my favorite. "She would have loved you," he finished.

My entire life has changed in a matter of weeks. The girl I thought I was long gone, slowly being replaced by a woman that would lead a kingdom to victory. If Rion hadn't stumbled upon me, I most likely would have died at the hands of the Dullahan, and the kingdom would have lost their only chance at liberation.

I leaned onto him and kissed him deeply. "I wish I had more

to offer you for everything you have done," I muttered.

"You have given me more than you will ever know, little fox," he replied. He placed a ghost of a kiss on my forehead. "I have spent my entire life waiting for you, and I would have continued to wait an eternity if it meant I got to spend a single moment with you."

There were no words that could accurately express what I felt for Rion. He has shown me love that no one ever had, even my grandmother. Of course, she loved me but only out of duty to my mother. She didn't have a choice. Rion did, and he chose me.

"You are everything I never knew I was missing," I said to him. "I only ever lived in the moment. The future wasn't promised, and I didn't want to hope for something I may never have."

We were close enough now that I could see his eyes. The love he felt for me was shown through the hues of green. Together, it felt as though anything was possible. The feeling was intoxicating. We could make the world bow to us, if we so wished.

I once again thought of our future. A tear rolled down my cheek. Rion's face filled with concern, "What's wrong?"

"There will come a time when I am going to have to go on without you, and I don't think I will be able to bear it," I sobbed. "If we survive this, you will grow old, and I will not."

He pulled me into him, hushing me. "I will never leave you."

His promise sent a wave of fury through me. "But you will," I screamed, as I pulled myself from his grasp and stood. I wasn't really upset with him but the circumstances, which were out of my control. The anger and grief choked me.

Rion got to his feet slowly and stood in front of me. "Even if I am not by your side, I will always be with you," he rephrased his statement. He gradually approached me, "I would never leave you willing. I am far too selfish for that." He caught me by the shoulders, mid pace. "These are not worries for today nor for tomorrow. We have many years before such things matter." He drew me into him. His embrace was warm and soothing. "Please come back to bed. I want to show you just how much I love you." I couldn't deny him.

As he made love to me that night, I made a decision. If it came down to it, I would track down the long-lost Gods and throw myself at their feet. I would beg them to bless him as they had blessed my people. For I would not live another moment without him.

Chapter 15

I stumbled through the city. Bodies lay torn apart at my feet. Aos Si and humans alike were screaming in agony around me. The city streets ran red with the blood of the innocent. I stared in horror at the scene before me. I knelt before a young human soldier. He was still alive, but just barely. His abdomen slayed open by sword or magic.

I grabbed his hand in mine as the tears welled in my eyes. His eyes peeled open slowly. He stared into my soul. Pain laced his features as he whispered, "You were… supposed to… save us." His eyes glazed over as he drew his last haggard breath. I sobbed over his corpse as guilt consumed me like the fire that licked the sky. I had done this. Promised these people liberation, only to lead them to their deaths.

I continued to scan the dead and dying that littered the cobbled stone street. I caught sight of a large man lying face down a few yards off, black hair plastered to the blood coating the back of his head. Panic coursed through me as I stumbled to my feet. I ran as fast as I could without tripping over the others around him.

I fell to my knees, hauling his large form over to reveal his face. Pain struck my heart as Rion's lifeless eyes stared up at me, his green irises lacking the spark of life. I couldn't breathe, couldn't think. He was gone. Gone.

I awoke with a start. Sweat coated my skin and my breathing was rapid. My heart felt as though it may burst from my chest. *It was just a dream,* I told myself. I reached my hand over to find empty space beside me. Rion must have gone out on watch while I was sleeping. I knew I wouldn't be able to fall back to sleep without seeing him, ensuring that he still breathed. I pulled on my boots and cloak and emerged from the tent. It was still dark, the sound of nocturnal animals scurrying about just out of sight filled my ears.

The fire dwindled, only a low glow emitted from the hot coals. I gazed around the campsite, looking for any sign of Rion, as my anxiety began to peek when I didn't initially find him. I made my way to the edge of the wood, peering amongst the trees. Off in the distance, I heard a shout. It came from deep in the forest and was faint. I wasn't sure I had heard it at all until it came again, a bit closer this time.

"Aisling!" Rion cried through the trees. I took off in a sprint towards his voice. "Rion!" I yelled, hurtling myself through the thicket. A branch came out and struck me across my face, but I did not falter. Warmth ran down my face as I continued to run. "Aisling!" Rion called again, but to the right this time.

I turned, keeping pace. "I'm coming!" I shouted. I scanned the blackness pressing in on me. I could barely see a few feet in front of me. I slowed my pace when I almost came face to face with a tree. "Rion! Where are you?" I continued to shout, but he'd gone silent.

Panic rose within me as I continued. What if something happened to him? I slowed a bit more, wildly looking around me for any sign that he'd been through here. Then his voice rose in the wild again, but this time, behind me. I turned and bolted again in the new direction.

I slowed, realizing I must have passed him. I searched the trees and ground around me, looking for his form in the dark. I caught a trail, going off to my left where it seemed someone had walked through the brush. I hoped I wasn't following my own trail, but running aimlessly through the forest was not going to help find Rion. "Rion!" I yelled again, but no answer. The birds started to sing in the canopy above as dawn approached. I walked in silence for a long while. Panic was replaced by dread. I should have awoken Nolan and Flynn. The forest was vast. I was never going to find him on my own.

I thought about running back to camp to get them, but realized I wasn't entirely sure which way camp was. I hadn't been keeping track of my turns, and I knew Rion had to be close.

I continued walking as the sun broke the horizon, casting shadows among the trees. Every so often, I paused thinking I saw movement only to be met by one of those shadows. I could now see the path in front of me, and I stopped. This was a game trail. Animal prints scattered the ground, no sign of anything human. I kicked a rock as tears fell down my cheeks. "Rion!" An agonizing scream that pierced the dense forest. I continued to call his name until my voice was hoarse. He made no reply.

I heard a crack of a stick to my right. I paused and whipped my head around. The trees were packed too tightly together this deep in the wood to see through. The forest seemed to still, the birds going silent along with the breeze that rustled the leaves in the canopy. Anxiety washed over me. I reached to my belt, seeking the hilt of my sword. My hand met empty space. I hadn't strapped it on before leaving the tent and hadn't had time to go back for it before I made the mad dash into the forest. I cursed my stupidity as I continued to scan my surroundings.

Another loud crack sounded. I turned and ran back the way I came. The only sound was that of my boots hitting the dirt. I looked behind me to see if I was being followed. *It was only a deer. It was only a deer.* I chanted in my head.

I turned back to face the direction I was moving when a large, black animal emerged from the forest. I stopped short. Not just any animal, a horse. It was beautiful. The black stallion stood taller than that of the Dullahan's steeds. His mane was long and flowing, hair covering his hooves from view.

His eyes glowed golden in the morning light, like the dying embers of a fire. I reached out my hand and slowly approached. "Hey, boy," I cooed. "How did you get clear out here?"

Just before I touched his snout, an eerie voice reverberated through the air, "I really don't like to be petted." I stood in shock, pulling my hand back to my side as if the majestic beast had bitten me. The horse tilted its head ever so slightly at my confusion, the humanlike intelligence in its glowing eyes unnerved me.

"Did you just talk?" I breathed, absolutely stunned.

"What a magnificent creature you are," the horse purred. My mouth hung open and eyes wide. I was speechless. "The mighty Druid heir. In my forest. What are the odds?" He approached, circling me. I spun with him to ensure I didn't allow him to get behind me. "I can smell the magic following through your veins."

I snapped out of my stupor. "What are you? Who are you?" I questioned the mighty beast.

"I go by many names," he said. "Can take many shapes." Fear pricked at the back of my mind. "I felt your power when you entered my domain. I knew I had to meet that girl who would be this land's salvation," he paused, his voice shifting into one I was so familiar with. "Or its damnation."

My head spun as Rion's voice came from the throat of the horse. "You led me out here." It was meant to be a question, but I already knew the answer. I felt so foolish. I had been so shaken by my dream when I heard Rion's cries that I hadn't even paused to grab a weapon. *Stupid*, I silently berated myself.

"I did. I needed to talk with you, away from prying ears." The horse shook as though it had gotten a chill. A puff of black smoke concealed him from sight for a moment. I was horrified as I watched the smoke dissipate, revealing the most beautiful man I had ever seen.

His hair was black like the stallions and golden eyes peered at me through thick lashes. He was clothed in a simple white linen shirt that pulled against the muscle below and tight black trousers. He appeared to be not much older than me, but the power that emitted from him felt old. Very old.

He approached me. I backed away, matching him step for step, until my back hit a tree. He stopped his assent once he stood directly in front of me and leaned in. I tried to avert my eyes, but he grabbed my chin, forcing me to make eye contact. "I need you to listen to me, princess." He growled. "You are destined for greatness, but your future also holds great sorrow." My nightmare flashed before my eyes. Rion's dead eyes. "To win the war ahead will come at a cost. One you may not be so willing to pay."

I swallowed past the lump in my throat. "How do you know this?" my voice quivered as I asked.

"I have seen it." He tilted his head again. The animalistic gesture churned the fear that sat like a rock in my stomach. "You mustn't trust anyone. Not everything is as it appears." He dropped his hand from my face but didn't back up, still breathing the same air that refused to fill my lungs. He stared into my eyes as if he was searching for something deep within me. His golden eyes saddened. "If anyone can bring this land back to what it once was, it's you." He took one step back, then another.

"What if I can't. What happens then?" I don't know why I asked.

He contemplated my question before he responded, "Then all we hold dear will be lost forever. Come, I will lead you back to your camp." We walked quietly through the trees. My head was filled with so many questions, but I couldn't get any of them to pass my lips. I stopped suddenly when I thought about what he had said. My tongue loosened enough to ask, "What did you mean by not trusting anyone? That things aren't what they appear to be?"

He turned to face me once more. "I meant exactly what I said."

"Okay, so how can I trust what you are saying to be true" I asked angrily.

"I have no reason to lie to you, princess. I only wish to see this land returned to its formal glory," he responded.

"And what of the others that I travel with? They want to see the people liberated from their oppressor," the words flew out of my mouth quickly.

"I agree, but there are things they are keeping from you. Things you deserve to know." I was stunned by his response.

"What kind of things?" I slowly asked.

"I think that is something you should ask them." He turned

back to the direction we were moving and continued to walk. I quickly caught up with him, not wanting to be left in the middle of the forest alone.

What could Rion be keeping from me that would be so bad? I trusted him with my life, my heart. There was no way he would keep something important from me. The man paused again. "This is where I leave you. Continue straight, and you'll make it back." The black smoke engulfed him again, and he was back in the form of a stallion. "Take my warning seriously, princess," he said before he trotted off into the thicket.

I stood frozen, listening for the sound of his retreat, but the forest remained unnaturally still. No birdsong. No breeze. Just silence and the pounding of my heart. His words echoed in my mind, looping over themselves: *Things you deserve to know.* I didn't want to believe him. I *couldn't* believe him. But still… the seed had been planted, and it rooted quickly in the cracks of my trust. I rubbed my arms, chilled, despite the warming light filtering through the canopy. Everything felt *off*, like the forest had shifted in some unseen way. I looked down at my hands—trembling—and took a shaky breath. *He's lying. He has to be,* I thought, but doubt lingered, whispering in my ear as I forced my legs to move forward.

I walked on in a haze of emotion. Before long, the birds began to chirp again, and the unnatural stillness ceased. Thundering feet sounded to my right. Fear pitched my heart rate higher, thinking the horse had returned.

I turned just in time to be engulfed in muscled arms, the scent of smoke and flowers washed over me. "Where the fuck have you been," Rion's panic laced his words. I breathed easier knowing he was alright. "I went to wake you, and you were gone." He pulled back and cupped my face. "You scared the shit out of me, little fox." He roved his eyes over my face, landing on my forehead, where his thumb skidded over the gash I had gotten from the tree limb. I had forgotten about it until now when the pain made me suck in a sharp breath.

I raised my hand, realizing the left side of my face was coated in dried blood. Rion tugged at the hem of his shirt, tearing off a piece of the fabric to wipe away the consequences of my actions. The adrenaline that had kept me moving had evaporated, leaving behind sore muscles and exhaustion that seeped into my very bones. "I'm so sorry. I had a nightmare and came to find you and heard you shouting, or what I thought was you, in the woods, and…" I rambled before he cut me off.

"Okay, okay. Just slow down and tell me what happened." I told him about how I heard him shouting my name, and my run through the forest, desperately searching for him. I had gotten turned around, so there was no way of finding my way back in time to retrieve Nolan and Flynn. I recounted the events that transpired between the man, who presented himself as a black stallion with golden eyes, and I. A look of realization flooded his features, but he didn't interrupt me.

I told him everything the man had said. "He said you guys are hiding something from me."

Rion took a deep breath. "It was a puka, little fox."

"A what?" I had never heard of a puka before.

"They are rare. There used to be a lot more before the invasion, but the Aos Si wiped them out. They would lure children from their beds and convince them to get on their backs to go for a ride. They would eventually return them, but they were never the same, too traumatized by the puka. You shouldn't believe a word that came out of his mouth. He was toying with you." I nodded at his reply. I believed Rion, or at least I wanted to. But his explanation felt too smooth, too practiced. My instincts buzzed, low and constant, like a splinter I couldn't reach beneath the skin. I couldn't shake the feeling that there was some truth to the puka's words, that there was something Rion wasn't telling me.

"How long was I gone?" I peered through the breaks between the limbs high above but could not determine the position of the sun to hint at the time. It had only felt like an hour, but by the way Rion had reacted when he finally found me, I figured it must have been much longer than that. It was not like I was keeping time on my trek through the forest.

"I have been looking for you for two hours, little fox. From what you have told me, I must have missed you by just minutes."

He took my hand, and led me in the direction the strange man, the puka, had instructed me to go. "Let us get back. Nolan and Flynn headed out early this morning to go hunting before I realized you were missing. They should be back by now."

Chapter 16

Rion and I arrived back at camp to find Flynn was butchering a boar he and Nolan must have gotten when they went out to hunt this morning. Nolan stood off to the side. His shirt was torn across his chest and covered in blood. I rushed to his side, pulling at his shirt. "Oh gods! Where are you hurt?" I fretted, trying to inspect the wound. It must be deep to cause that much blood loss. He tried to beat my hands away, but I persisted. If he would just let me see it, I could stitch it and gather herbs to prevent infection.

He unraveled my hands from his clothing, holding my arms away from him. "You need to get your hands off me. I'm fine," he reassured. He shot a look at Rion over my shoulder. "The son of a bitch put up a fight. The arrow only brought him down. I had to do the rest by hand. He reared and caught my shirt. The blood is his." I still wasn't convinced he wasn't injured, but I backed down.

I turned to Rion to contest Nolan›s claim of being 'fine,'

but I stilled when I saw the look on his face. He closed in on me with a deadly calm. Nolan swiftly stepped between us. "Stop!" He commanded Rion. Flynn flew to his feet, shoving me behind him. "You need to take a walk," Nolan stated.

Rion's nostrils flared and he let out an animalistic growl from the back of his throat as he fought the urge to throw the two men out of his way to get to me. They stood at an impasse momentarily, before Rion stalked off reluctantly. I was at a loss for words as I watched him disappear behind the trees. I had seen that temper before but never turned on me.

I turned to the other men, searching their faces for answers. Flynn's face was twisted in rage. "We are never going to survive him! He needs to tell her!"

I paused. "Tell me what exactly?"

"Shut the fuck up, Flynn," Nolan retorted.

"No! He's fucking dangerous and distracted, and she deserves to know why!"

Nolan grabbed Flynn by his collar and growled in his face, "You shut your mouth now, or I will shut it for you. Walk. Away."

Flynn clenched his teeth. "He needs to tell her before he kills someone." He pried himself from Nolan's grasp and headed for his tent. "Or her," he mumbled as he disappeared into the tent.

Nolan knelt by the half-butchered boar and began to cut away the rest of the meat. I crouched beside him. "Nolan, what is he keeping from me?" I pleaded. The puka's words resounded in my skull. *Not everything is as it appears.*

"It is not for us to divulge. Contrary to what it seems, we both love him like a brother. He has always been there when we've needed him. I will not betray his loyalty. I am sorry, but there isn't much else I can say. Rion must be the one to tell you." I straightened and stomped off in the direction of Rion, intent on finding out what it was that he was hiding.

I found him with his forehead leaning against a tree, his face contorted by guilt. The clench in his jaw told me he knew I was there. "I am so sorry," he whispered. I walked closer, hesitantly placing my hand on his arm. He shrugged out of my grasp and walked deeper into the forest.

"What is going on with you?" I asked. *Not everything is as it appears.*

"It's nothing. I'm just tired and on edge." He had his back to me as he spoke.

"I think the puka was right. That there is something you are hiding from me," I tried to keep the irritation out of my voice.

He let out a resigned sigh. "You are right." My heart sank. I was already shaking my head in disbelief when he turned to face me. "I need to explain something to you. About the Aos Si." Rion said after a moment.

"And what I want is for you to tell me is what the fuck is going on with you. You can do more history lessons later." I was starting to get really tired of his avoidance.

"Please," was all he said. His voice held a strange tone.

I let out a huff. "Fine, but afterwards you need to answer my question."

"I will. I'll explain everything." He took a deep breath as he paced. "Back when the first of the Aos Si were born, the Gods came together to bestow a blessing onto their children. One they did not seek to inherit through their blood," Rion began slowly. "There were lengthy discussions about what that gift should be. They spoke of many different magical abilities that would enhance the race, but no one could agree. Then, Aengus Og spoke a single word. Love. He told his fellow deities that they should bless their children with love, a love so strong that it could not be denied."

He paused his pacing for a moment to look at me once again. "A love that could draw two people from the ends of the land to one another." My palms began to sweat at what he was implying. "The Gods decided that each of their children would be blessed with a mate, a single person that was their one true love. They sought the Fates to aid them in this blessing, to ensure that their paths were fated to cross. They obliged the Gods, but they insisted that there would be conditions that must be met for the bond to be complete."

I held my hand up for him to stop. "What exactly are you saying? Are you saying there is an Aos Si male out there that I am supposed to love?" He just stared back at me, which pissed me off. "Rion, answer me. Is that why you are on edge? Do you think some male is going to walk up and claim me as his? I love you. I don't care about some stupid bond." I tried to ease his mind. There was no way I would fall for one of them. A weird emotion, almost like hurt, flashed before his eyes. He schooled his features quickly.

"It is not that simple. The mating bond must be accepted by both parties, then it must be completed. Aos Si males become volatile until the bond is complete, to the point they will kill if they feel the bond has been threatened. And if the bond is rejected, it drives the male mad. Most end up taking their own lives," he explained. I approached him slowly.

Was he afraid for his life, or was he really worried I would fall in the arms of another male? "I love you, Rion. I want you. There is no one that can take me from you." He lowered his head, refusing to look at me. "Did you hear me?" I said, as his eyes snapped into mine. Silver threads spun wildly through his irises. I stepped back abruptly. I had thought I had seen it before, but this was more prominent. "Your eyes," I breathed.

"Little fox. I don't think you understand what I am telling you." He breathed hard through his nose. "What you are seeing are the threads of fate. They are the only thing that I have not been able to conceal."

My mind reeled. "What do you mean?" The answer was close. I could hear it whispered in the back of my mind, but I ignored it.

Light began to emanate from his skin. I took another large step backwards. Rion seemed to grow, taking up more space than he had before. His features stayed the same, but not. An otherworldly grace emanated from him. Dark blue swirls and arcane symbols shimmered across his skin, winding up his muscled arms where his sleeves had been rolled to the elbows, vanishing beneath the fabric before reemerging along the strong line of his neck. But what I couldn't take my eyes off of was his ears. The tips, where they had just been rounded, now rose into points. I gasped, backing away more. Rion was Aos Si. "What is this?" my voice came out a croak.

"I knew you wouldn't trust me if you knew what I was, so I glamoured myself." Hot tears rolled down my cheeks. "My abilities are why we've been able to avoid the Dullahan. I have been warding our camp sites." He attempted to step forward towards me, but I threw my hand up to stop him.

"Don't…Don't come any closer," I begged. It felt as though my entire world was crashing down around me.

"Aisling, please. I didn't want to deceive you, but I had no other choice. Because you're mine. My mate. I couldn't let anything happen to you. I would do anything to keep you safe." I felt as though I was going to be sick. I leaned over, placing my hands on my knees. I tried to calm my racing heart. I thought learning about my heritage was bad, but this was so much worse. "You said you loved me, and nothing would take you away from me. I am the same person you fell for."

Red hot anger flooded my system as I looked up into his eyes, those silver threads flared. "No, you are not. The person I fell for wouldn't have lied to me. What about Nolan and Flynn? They know, don't they? Are they Aos Si as well?"

"They are, yes." I seethed. Rushing to him, I went to slap him across the face, but he caught my hand before it met skin.

"You son of a fucking bitch." I rotated my wrist, loosening his grip like he had taught me, and swept his legs out from under him. I swiped his knife from its sheath at his waist as he fell. I quickly straddled his hips with my blade to his throat. I knew he had let me best him, for the muscles that strained against his clothing were evidence of his strength, but I did not care. I leaned into his face and spoke in a low growl, "You will never touch me again. I want nothing to fucking do with you. Once we reach the mountains, I never want to see you again." I wasn't stupid. I knew I still needed him and his magic to safely reach the rebel base where my army was waiting for me.

"Aisling, I still want to see this land free of the false king's rule. I swear. I told you once that not all Aos Si agree with his actions." He drew a sharp breath when I pressed the blade into his flesh to shut him up, blood welled where it broke the skin.

"That may be true, but I will not be sharing my bed or tent with a liar. I sure as hell won't be sharing my heart with one. I rej…"

Before I could finish my sentence, rejecting this bond between us, Rion interrupted me.

"Don't. Please, don't," his plea fell from his lips. "If you reject it now, I will be no use to you." I thought about his request. If rejection of the bond truly causes the male to go insane, he was right. He would be of no use to me. I was done talking. I rose and stomped back to camp prepared to take on the other two.

Nolan was finishing up with the boar. His face fell when he saw the look on mine. He looked around me to where I assumed Rion was following. His eyes went wide when he saw his appearance. I still palmed Rion's knife, which I now pointed in Nolan's direction. "Show me," I demanded.

"Show you what?" He raised his hands in front of him.

"Show me the lies you have all been keeping from me!" I screamed. Flynn emerged from the tent to see what all the commotion was about. The men looked at one another, then to Rion, before they both glowed, growing and changing as Rion had.

Nolan stood, keeping his hands raised in front of me to show me he meant no harm. "There was no other way, Aisling."

"Save it. I don't want to hear your excuses." I turned and threw the knife at Rion's feet, causing him to take a step back. "We need to get moving. The more ground we cover in a day, the faster I can be rid of you all," I said pointedly in Rion's direction.

The hurt that flooded Rion's features made my heart hurt. I scolded myself for caring and made my way to the tent. I decided to grasp onto the anger, because the pain that I would feel was too much to fathom right now. I quickly packed my bag and strapped my sword and knife to my hips.

I exited the tent, plowing by the men who were solemnly dismantling the camp. I strode over to Bryn, who nuzzled into me. She brought be comfort. I got her saddled and mounted. I waited for the men at the edge of the path. They rode up to me, glamoured once more to appear human. Rion's saddened face was now stone. He showed no emotion at all. "Let's go, princess." The way he said it with such distaste stung.

He rode to the lead, and I followed up in the rear. We traveled in dead silence. Not even Flynn and Nolan spoke amongst themselves. The quiet gave me time to think. I was so mad at him, so hurt that he wouldn't trust me with the truth. But wasn't he right? There is no way I would have trusted him in the beginning had I known what he was, and if it weren't for him, I would have been dead weeks ago.

Although anger thrummed through my veins where my blood should be, I was still madly in love with him. I didn't know whether it was the bond between us that was the cause of my strong feelings for him or if it was truly a matter of the heart, but I needed to find out.

*   *   *

Evening came swiftly. Rion led us from the main road once more. The forest was thinner here, so we had to move deeper in than we had too before. There was more traffic on the road today, as well. Farmers passed with wagons filled to the brim with the final crop of the season. I counted the days in my head, realizing that the final Human Tax collection day was tomorrow. They collect the tax three weeks after Lughnassadh, the Autumnal Equinox, and Samhain, leaving them with little to no food for the winter.

The camp was erected quickly. Flynn and Nolan made some excuse about firewood and scurried off into the forest, leaving Rion and I alone to finish untacking the horses. The tension in the air could be cut with a knife. "I know you're angry with me," Rion spoke smoothly, "but you have to understand why I did what

I did."

I inhaled deeply before speaking. "When were you going to tell me?"

Rion peered over the saddle of his horse. "I thought about telling you a million times. I just didn't know how," he answered.

I thought about every moment we shared since meeting, but there was one thing that just didn't make sense. "Was anything you said about your childhood true? The stories of your mother?"

"My mother was human. They are my people. All of it was true." He looked down at his hands and fidgeted with the buckles of his saddle.

"Your father was Aos Si," I concluded. "Did you really grow up on the mainland?"

"No," he mumbled. "I spent my childhood in Tír na nÓg until the invasion. Afterwards, my father brought us here."

"So, it wasn't all true," I huffed, throwing my saddle at my feet. "How did your mother and father truly meet?"

"He was sent as an ambassador for Tír na nÓg to negotiate trade between the two realms. He traveled for a bit before returning home and that's when he met my mother. They ran away together just as I had said. They were in love once." Rion tossed his saddle down and led his horse to graze.

"And what changed?" I asked.

"Black magic," he responded. "He began to dabble in it when they returned to Tír na nÓg. He slowly became more irritable, easily set off by the littlest things. My mother begged him to stop, but he refused. The power was addictive. It wasn't long before his mind and soul were warped by its use." Rion's voice hardened as he continued, "I never knew him as he was before. I never knew the male my mother loved and who loved her. I never knew the male who wanted me."

"And what of your father's mate? You said every Aos Si had one?" I was desperate to unravel the complex puzzle that was Rion.

"He didn't meet her until after he killed my mother. They will be completing their bond next year," anger lined his voice.

My head spun. I had so many questions, but the most important one came out first, "Does he treat her as he did your mother?"

"No. Though the black magic has made him cold and lacking emotion, the bond is stronger. It's instinctual to protect your mate, to make them happy," he explained. "He would give up everything if she asked him to, but she is quite impressed by the power he wields. Her soul is nearly as black as his. They are perfect together," Rion scoffed.

Rion whipped his head around as Nolan and Flynn arrived back with firewood. "Can we finish this later? I know you have a lot of questions. I will answer every single one of them, but I'd rather do it with at least some privacy." I nodded my agreement to his request.

Rion went to raise the wards around the camp, while I helped Nolan and Flynn get a fire going. "I know you are upset with him," Nolan finally broke the silence, "but try to give him a chance."

"How am I ever supposed to trust him, or the two of you ever again?" The betrayal was still a fresh wound, but if I did not take care of it, it would fester.

"Give it time, but I think you will come to understand why he did what he did." Nolan fed the fire a healthy meal of large logs and smaller twigs until it was roaring, sparks and ash floating towards the heavens.

"Have either of you found your mates?" The concept that

there is a single person the Fates choose for each Aos Si is still strange to me. Humans had the free will to choose that person for themselves, to fall in love and get married. I didn't have that option. Though the bond could be rejected, it would be the end of Rion. The air turned sour in my lungs because the world needed more like him.

"Yes," Nolan spoke quietly. "I lost her, before we completed our bond." The sorrow in his eyes broke me.

"How did you survive?" Rion seemed like such a thing was impossible.

"Rion," he stated. I turned my attention back to Flynn, who had been quiet, to allow Nolan to grieve for his lost mate.

"No. Not yet, but it will happen when it's meant to," Flynn replied to my question. Flynn smirked. "I am surprised though."

"Hmmm?" I didn't know what the hell he was talking about.

"Of all the questions, you have yet to ask the most important one," he laughed. Nolan shook his head, the sadness that had taken over his features a moment ago now wiped clean, but he was also fighting back a grin.

I was so confused. "And what is that?"

"You have yet to ask how old we are." I hadn't even thought about their age. I had been so worried about outliving Rion, and now I wouldn't. It felt as though a huge weight lifted off my shoulders at the thought. It was a weight I didn't even realize I had been carrying.

"How old are the three of you?" I finally asked.

"Nolan is the oldest at forty-seven. I'm forty-five, and Rion is forty-one." The look on my face must have been priceless, while I digested the information, because Flynn barked a laugh. Nolan joined him when I was struck dumb by the information, my mouth open and closing like a fish. My mouth was still agape when Rion returned from the forest.

"Why does she look like that?" Rion asked, concerned.

Nolan spoke because Flynn was still howling in laughter, "Flynn just informed her of our ages."

I looked at Rion as relief flooded his face. "You're forty-one?" I still couldn't wrap my mind around it. He looked to be only a few years older than me. If he were human, he would be nearing the end of his life.

"I am no old man, little fox," he said with a grin. Great, they were all making fun of me. I shot him a playful glare. They continued to tease me as they smoked their kill from that morning.

My world had tilted once more, and I was still trying to grasp it all, but my anger slowly dissipated. The last three weeks have made me realize that I truly didn't know a single thing about the world around me. I watched the flames cast shadows across Rion's face. The beautiful male that came into my life and turned it upside down. The male that stole my heart and claimed it as his, but also willingly handed me his. Was it the Fates making choices on my behalf? Perhaps, but I decided I didn't care. They had made a good choice. If it had to be anyone, I was happy it was him.

Chapter 17

Rion closed the flap to the tent. Darkness closed in around us. We sat on the bed roll, leaving a few feet between us. "What do you want to know first?" Rion asked me.

"I want to know everything. You told me how the bond affects the males, but how does it influence my feelings?" I had already decided I didn't really care about the answer, but I still wanted to understand.

Rion stated, "The bond is an instinctual need to protect your mate, please them, but it has nothing to do with feelings. For most mated pairs, that comes later."

I hadn't been expecting that answer. "So, the love we share? It's real?"

He chuckles, "Yes, little fox. Though, I loved you before I even knew who you were." I felt a shift in the shadows beside me as Rion leaned closer. My eyes had begun to adjust to the low light.

Rion was only a breath away from my face. "I would have torn apart the realms looking for you." He didn't touch me, but his gaze left mine and flicked to my lips. Those silver threads danced wildly in his eyes.

"The silver in your eyes? You called them the threads of fate?" The first few times I had seen it, I thought it was a trick of the light, but they had been increasingly clearer since he told me I was his mate.

"Aye, they tend to only appear before completion when the bond is triggered in some way, threatened or during heightened states of emotion," he paused for a moment. "You have them too, but they are subtle. I have only seen them once." I was taken aback by his response.

"When?" I hadn't had access to a mirror in so long, I wouldn't have even known.

"The night we made love for the first time," he purred. The silver flared brighter, as if the memory set them aflame. "They become permanent after the completion of the bond. When we get closer to Lios, you will see it often."

"And how is the bond completed?"

"First step is the acceptance of the bond by both parties. The time between when it is accepted and competed is the hardest for the male, but the females feel it too. I am already on edge, but it will get worse. I won't be able to stand a male even breathing the same air that was meant for your lungs. This morning when you touched Nolan," he growled, "I wanted to murder him, then punish you for laying your hands on another male." His rage-filled face flashed in my mind.

"I'll accept the bond, Rion. I love you. I was angry, still am, but that doesn't change how I feel." Rion sucked in a breath of relief. "How do we complete it? We can do it now." I told him. I didn't want to wait any longer and risk Flynn and Nolan.

"We can't. It must be completed on Beltane and there is a process to it. Before you accept anything, though, you need to know what you are agreeing to." Rion's relief was short-lived. He was giving me the chance to back out once I had all the information, which only made my resolve stronger.

"Okay. How is it done then?" I questioned.

"We consummate our bond at the height of the moon on Beltane. As our bodies become one, our magic and lives merge with each other. Our power becomes one. Our lives become one, and if one of us were to die, so would the other." Rion took a moment to assess my reaction before he continued, "During the completion, we will need to be under guard, because we are vulnerable. If it's broken at any time before the ritual is complete, it could be fatal." That part stunned me for a moment.

"Wait, we have to consummate it in front of other people." My face heated.

"Yes. We would choose our most trusted soldiers. I would feel safer if it was a battalion of no less than ten. You are too important to risk, to me and to the kingdom." Rion finally reached into my lap and took my hand. "You don't have to make a decision tonight. I know it's a lot, but…"

"I'll do it," I interrupted. I never let fear run my life, and I won't be starting now. I placed my hand on his face. "I'll do it." When I looked into his eyes, I felt a strange sensation, like a puzzle piece fitting into place. The smile that took over his face was radiant. He leaned in and kissed me passionately. I didn't want to break the kiss, but I had one more request. "Will you remove the glamour? I want to see you. The real you."

Rion obliged. He glowed once more. The man that sat before me was glorious. As he had been that morning, he looked the same, but more. It was so hard to explain. He was taller. Every edge was fiercer and more defined. He was perfect.

I ran my fingers along the peak at the top of his ear. He groaned low in his throat. I continued my perusal. I ran my hand down his neck, tracing the swirls that were etched into his skin, and across his chest. His muscles felt denser. "Tell me about these?" I said, referring to the tattoos that now marked his skin.

"They are common among the Aos Si. I got them after my coming-of-age ceremony when I was thirty." It wasn't lost on me that thirty was the point at which the Aos Si came into adulthood.

"What do they mean?"

"Nothing, and everything. They are Druidic symbols." My eyes shot to his face. "When I visited the old shaman female that gave them to me, I insisted upon them, not knowing why they called to me. She attempted to talk me out of it, but there was nothing she could say that would sway my decision." He paused, searching my eyes for a hint of what lied within. "I understand now."

My hand continued down his abdomen, but he grabbed my wrist before I made it to his waistband. "Close your eyes." I did as Rion asked. My hand continued to rest in his. "Do you remember when I used to ground you?" I nodded. "I was using our bond. Do you see it?" I went to shake my head, but I saw it then. A faint silver thread in the dark. It seemed to be floating in the empty space.

I opened my eyes, and he was staring back at me. He pulled me into him and laid down on his back. I rest my cheek against his chest. I attempted to move my hand south once more, but he caught my wrist again. "As much as I would love nothing more, we need to rest. You missed your training session this morning and we need to be up early to make up for the lost time." He brushed my hair from my face. "Sleep now. We have all the time in the world."

* * *

We traveled hard for the next two weeks. The days and nights had begun to grow cold with the impending winter. We left the forest behind us a few days ago, leaving us exposed to nature as we traveled through small villages that littered the outskirts of Lios. Nolan believed we made up for our slow start and were only a few days away from the mountains that loomed in the distance. The pass that led to and from Lios appeared as a large crack through the peaks.

Nervousness took hold. I didn't know what I would say to my people. To the people willing to put their lives on the line to save those who couldn't save themselves. I hoped they wouldn't have the same reaction that Nolan had upon our first meeting. Rion had been pushing me hard in training, waking before the sun rose most mornings to ensure I was ready to lead them. Rion said I was ready, but I wasn't convinced. I have had six weeks of training, and I would be up against those who were raised to be warriors from their first breaths. Those who have hundreds of years of training on me.

I was still struggling with my magic. I have been able to harness my pure magic, which I can use to shield myself and others. However, manipulation of nature didn't come as smoothly. I spent hours staring at a tree branch, doing everything in my power to make it bend to my will, to no prevail. I managed to thoroughly soak Rion with a splash of water from a river four days ago when he taunted me but hadn't been able to recreate what I had done in that moment. Rion says it will come in time, but we didn't have much of that left.

We procured lodging in a stable at the heart of a village. Taverns this far south only catered to Aos Si. I tried to convince the men to remove their glamour, but I still wouldn't be permitted because of my rounded ears. "Why are my ears rounded?" I asked after we had settled in for the night. Flynn and Nolan were both taking turns filling the small space with their snores. "I mean, you are half human," I said to Rion, "but your ears are not."

Rion pondered my question as if it had never occurred to him. "I honestly don't know. Can I see?" He shifted so he could see the back of my ear.

"What is it?" I could tell something was off by his grim expression.

"Your scarred here." Rion gently ran his finger along the shell of my ear. "Your ears were surgically altered. Must have been when you were born to conceal the identity of your father."

"What?" I reached for my ear, but I didn't feel anything. "Why didn't they use a glamour to conceal them?"

Rion shook his head. "Your mother wouldn't have been able to perform the magic to do it. This was also irreversible. It fully conceals your heritage with no risk of anyone knowing."

"How is it you knew, then?"

"I didn't. It was a suspicion. It would have been the only reason your mother never disclosed who your father was. If he was human, there would have been no reason," Rion explained. "I didn't really know until we started training. You were stronger, faster than any human should have been, and improving at an exponential rate." Rion opened his arms to me. I curled up in his grasp as we lay in beds made of straw that poked my skin, causing an itch that no amount of scratch could ease. I took a moment to revel in the feeling of him against me. We had been in such close quarters with the other two to even think about doing anything intimate, and I missed the feel of his hands on my bare flesh.

A gentle wind blew against the stable which caused the shutters to rattle. The horses rustled in the hay we'd given them upon our arrival. I soaked in the peace for it won't be long until we wage war. There will be no time to enjoy the little things.

"Have you ever been to war?" I didn't know if Rion was still awake. He'd been quiet for some time.

"Yes," he whispered.

"What was it like?" I wanted to know what to expect when all hell broke loose.

He took a deep breath. "The smell of death rests upon the land before even the first drop of blood is spilt. All seems to stand still for a moment, then you're in the thick of it. It's loud. So loud. Steel against steel, cries of pain, shouts of commands." I could feel his breath falter a bit, like he was reliving his past experiences. "Then the air stills once more, and it's done."

"Was it worth it? What you were fighting for?" I wanted to know more but could tell by the tension that bunched up his muscles that I couldn't pry too much without him shutting me out.

"No," he mumbled. "It was not." Rion pulled me closer. Exhaustion swooped in before I could utter another word, but I swore as my eyes fluttered shut, Rion whispered, "It almost cost me everything."

I woke to whispering voices and birds chirping in the rafters of the stable. "The girl's name is Nora," Nolan's hushed words jolted me upright.

"Did you say Nora?" I breathed. All three men looked my way. Flynn ran his hand down his face. Rion's face was lined with pain. "What's going on? What about Nora?"

Rion walked over to me and knelt beside the pallet of straw. "Nolan went to retrieve some supplies in the market this morning. There is buzz that the Dullahan are holding a human child hostage at an outpost just outside of the pass into Lios. Her name is Nora." The world spun on its side.

"We have to rescue her," I said with conviction.

Flynn cleared his throat. "It's a trap, Aisling. They are attempting to draw you out since they have been unsuccessful at apprehending you."

I flew to my feet. "I don't give a fuck if it's a trap. We are going."

Nolan stepped in front of me as I attempted to make my way to ready Bryn. "We can't risk you."

I shoved him out of my way, sending him flying to the side. He came to a skidded stop, slamming his back into a pillar. His eyes went wide as I stomped to stand in front of him. I bent at the waist and growled in his face, "My life is no more valuable than hers. Pack your shit and let's go." I spun to Rion, who hadn't spoken a word. "You going to try to stop me, too?" I accused.

He threw his hands up in front of him, "Wouldn't dream of it, little fox. As much as that little display of aggression was a major turn on, I don't want it aimed at me." He winked at me and sent a pointed look to Nolan, who had yet to regain his footing. I didn't give a passing thought to the strength it had taken to put the full-grown male on his ass. "However, we need a plan."

We were back on the road within ten minutes. The men discussed the best course of action to infiltrate the outpost without being noticed, while I prayed to every God who would listen that Nora would still be alive when we got there the following evening. My guilt for leaving her renewed. It was my fault that they had her. Only the Gods know what kind of torture they had subjected her to as a means to get to me. I would be damned if I left her to die a second time.

Chapter 18

Rion and I crouched at the edge a cliff overlooking the outpost below. It guarded the pass into Lios looming behind a heavy iron gate. The only way in or out of Lios was through that gate, which required documentation to pass, or over the mountains. The mountain range was left completely unguarded, for most wouldn't brave the treacherous terrain.

Flynn and Nolan went out scouting to determine which wall was least guarded as soon as the sun fell. The walls, made of stone, rose twenty feet in the air and were lined with torches, casting shadows upon the battlements. Soldiers walked along the rampart and strode through the small courtyard.

There was a multistory wooden building at the heart of the fort, which housed the soldiers charged with defending the pass. Rion claimed that only twenty soldiers and their general occupied the fort at one time. The only sign of the Dullahan's presence was two large black stallions tied to a hitching post within.

Our plan was solid, but my hands shook with anxiety. A lot was riding on everything going as planned. Rion tightened the rope he wounded around his wrist, the only sign he was worried as well. We were going to scale the wall to gain silent entry. If an alarm is raised, we wouldn't stand a chance. We'll be outnumbered quickly. We need time to gain access to the inner structure, where Nora was being held.

"Are you ready?" Rion whispered.

I nodded. "You've taught me well."

"I know there is no talking you out of this, but can I make a request?" Rion turned my way, unwinding the rope from his arm. He grasped my chin, forcing me to remove my eyes from the scene below me and focus on him. "It appears only two of them are here with the girl. Once we find her, you two need to run. Use the rope to propel yourself back down the wall. Flynn, Nolan, and I can deal with the wraiths. Hopefully, before the soldiers are made aware of our infiltration. Bring her back here and wait. We will be right behind you."

I wanted to argue, because I wasn't sure if I would be able to leave him behind. I nodded nonetheless, unable to speak past the lump in my throat. Tears stung my eyes. There was so much that could go wrong. I pushed the thought to the back of my mind. I needed to stay focused.

An owl hooted to our left of the path we took to reach our lookout. No, not any owl, but Flynn. Rion nodded once more before he rose. He slung the rope over his shoulder and pulled me to my wobbly feet. He kissed me fiercely. "I love you," he breathed against my lip.

I found my voice then, "and I you." If we were to die tonight,

I need him to hear those words. We walked down the path and met Flynn and Nolan in the middle. "There isn't anyone guarding the southern wall. It's hard to access, so they probably figured it would be a waste of manpower. The wall is crumbling in places. It will be easy to scale," Nolan stated. We descended the mountain on foot, Flynn leading the way, leaving the horses behind.

The gate was built into the eastern wall of the outpost and nearly against the mountain on the west, only leaving about a two-foot tunnel for us to shuffle through to reach our entry point. The ground was littered with fallen stones from the mountain. The wall was smooth, but the side of the mountain was jagged and ripped at our clothing as we squeezed through the tight space.

As I exited the narrow opening, I took a full breath that I had been unable to take within the tunnel. I gaped up at just how high the wall was. I took a deep breath. I could do this. I had to do this. I thought of Nora's sweet face, which gave me the courage I needed, as Flynn and Nolan began their ascent.

The mortar was cracked and missing between the stones, which left behind perfect hand holds. "You go first," Rion commanded. I took another deep breath before placing my shaking fingers in the first of the holds, resting my foot within another lower down the wall. He rested his hand on my shoulder. "I will catch you if you fall." His attempt to calm my nerves was unsuccessful, but I appreciated his effort.

I heaved myself up and started to climb. *Don't look down. Don't look down.* I chanted to myself. I was about halfway by the time Flynn and Nolan disappeared over the edge. They had made it look so easy. My arms trembled with the exertion. Though I was stronger than I had been all those weeks ago, it took tremendous effort to keep myself going.

The stone dug into my fingers. I was a few feet from the top when I placed my foot in a hold and the rock crumbled. I let out a gasp as I tried to seek purchase with my foot. I stole a glance down. My eyes grew wide, and my breathing became rapid, as I zeroed in on the ground below me. "Eyes up, little fox," Rion whispered, but I was frozen.

Fear overtook my body, and tears rolled down my face. I frantically shook my head. I felt my hands begin to sweat, causing them to slip just a bit. "I can't," I sobbed. "I'm going to fall." I heard shuffling from above.

"Look up, Aisling. Look at me." It was Flynn. I shifted my grip slightly and looked up. He was leaning over the edge with his hand reaching out to me. "There you go. Take my hand. I got you." I would have to let go and propel myself upwards to grab his hand. I went to shake my head to indicate I didn't have the strength left. "Don't you dare give up," Flynn hissed. "You can do this."

I took yet another staggering breath to calm my thudding heart and leapt. Flynn's hand closed around my wrist, "See, I told you, you could do it." He pulled me the rest of the way, hauling me into his arms to hoist me through the battlement. We fell upon the stone. Rion appeared quickly beside me.

His rough hands encased my face to ensure I was okay. I was rattled but physically unharmed. Then he looked to Flynn, who still held me against him. I panicked for a moment until he placed a hand on Flynn's face and leaned his forehead against his friend. "Thank you," he breathed.

Flynn sighed with a breath of relief like he too thought his life was forfeit. "You don't have to thank me. Let's just make it out of this alive, please." Rion tied the rope he was carrying to the battlement and threw the other end down the wall, securing our escape route. We rose to our feet and hurried along the wall towards the turret at the corner, bending low to stay out of sight. I still felt like I might vomit after the scare on the wall, but I pushed through it. We didn't have the time to slow down.

When we reached the door of the turret, Rion took the lead and pushed it open slowly. Its hinges, rusty from neglect, protested with a low whine that caused Rion to pause before slowly pushing it the rest of the way. A steep spiral staircase wound down into the dark out of sight. Rion stepped inside on quiet feet. He looked over the rail to ensure it was clear before he singled us to follow.

We took the stairs two at a time, reaching the bottom swiftly. Rion threw his hand up to halt us. There was no door at the ground level, so he peered around the corner. He pulled his head back to relay what he saw. "There aren't any soldiers, and there is a servant entrance into the building. We should be able to use that to move about unnoticed."

We jogged to the door, keeping our eyes peeled for any stray soldiers and our feet quiet. Nolan pulled the second door open. Flynn shut it behind us a bit too hard, sending a faint echo down the abandoned hall. We all froze in our tracks. Minutes dragged by as we waited to be discovered. When no one came to investigate the sound, we all let out the breaths we were holding. "Okay," I panted. "Where do you suppose they are holding Nora?"

"Try the cellars?" Flynn suggested. "They would be located off the kitchens."

"We'll head that direction. We can search rooms as we go," replied Rion. We snuck through the halls, ensuring we didn't even breathe too loudly. Rion continued to lead the way. How he knew where he was going was beyond me.

Every room we came upon was empty. As we approached

the kitchens, we passed a massive dining hall buzzing with voices. Nolan had suggested we executed our rescue during mealtime to limit the number of soldiers wandering the halls.

The smells of roasted meat and vegetables floated through the hall. My stomach growled loudly. The males turned to me with grins plastered on their faces. "Sorry," I mouthed. I shook my head to focus on the task at hand.

Rion peered into the kitchens before entering. We followed close behind. A middle-aged human woman stood in shock in the center of the room looking like she might let out a scream. Rion placed a finger to his lips. "Please. Be quiet," he whispered. "We are looking for a small human girl being held by the Dullahan. Do you know where she is?"

The woman's gaze shot at me. "You can't be here," she said to me. "You need to leave. It's a trap."

I moved towards the woman, taking her hands in mine. "We figured, but this girl means something to me. I can't leave her in their hands."

The woman's eyes glistened with tears. She looked remorseful as she pointed to the door in the corner of the room. "I didn't see them bring her in, but we were told to stay out of the cellars until further notice," she heaved a heavy sob.

I let the woman's hand fall and looked at Rion, who was already moving to the door. Flynn and Nolan filed in behind him. The door didn't make a sound as Rion eased it open. The air was foul as we descended into the dark. There was a single torch lit at the base of the stairs. I listened for any sign of life, but the air was unnaturally still. The musty smell shoved its way up my nostrils as we descended deeper underground.

I could make out casks lining the walls in the pale light of the torch. "Nora," I whispered.

"Shhh," Nolan scolded me from directly in front of me. I snapped my mouth shut so hard I clacked my teeth together. We walked further into the room. I realized it went further back than I had initially thought. Rion grabbed the torch off the wall and continued to slowly move about the room.

He checked behind barrels of what appeared to be alcohol and baskets of raw vegetables. Shadows danced across the walls as Rion moved the torch. Flynn and Nolan followed his lead, and I searched deeper in the room with no luck. The room was empty.

"There's no one down here," Nolan sighed.

It didn't make any sense. "Then why would the woman lead us down…" I didn't even finish my sentence before I realized. "We need to get out of here."

Rion read the warning on my face, eyes going wide. The woman had led us right into the trap. She had tried to warn us, but we didn't listen. She probably had already informed them that we were here. We turned as one to retreat out of the cellar when footfalls sounded on the wooden steps. "Look what I have caught in my web," an eerie voice rang in my head. "You thought you could evade me."

The horsemen paused his descent, and in his hand, he held Nora by her hair to keep her still. Her eye was swollen, nearly shut and she had a large gash cut across her forehead. Her clothing was ripped and soiled. A strip of cloth was wedged in her mouth. "Aine," she mumbled around the gag. "Help me." Tears rolled down her face. Utter shock at her appearance kept me rooted in place.

"I saw the way you threw yourself in harm's way to try to save this creature. I knew she would come in handy one day." The horseman tossed Nora down the rest of the stairs. The sound of her fragile body hitting the floor made my stomach twist, as she cried out in pain. I attempted to rush to her, but black smoke rushed down the stairs, concealing Nora. "I think not, princess. You stay right there."

Rion grabbed my arm and shoved me behind him. Nolan and Flynn flanked him. "You're going to give us the girl, wraith," Rion spat.

"I'm not giving you anything, traitor." The horsemen retorted. "I'll make you a deal, princess. Come with me, and I will let the girl live." I would do it. I would trade my life for hers. Rion knew that and tightened his grip on my arm. The Dullahan resumed descending the stairs.

He pulled Nora to her feet and unsheathed a blade from his thigh, placing it across her throat. Nora stumbled as she attempted to keep pace with him as he began to circle us. We turned with him to ensure he didn't get behind us. "What will it be, princess?" The horseman baited me. He dug the blade deeper, causing Nora to wince in pain. Crimson dripped slowly down her neck, gathering in the hollow of her throat.

I growled and weaseled out of Rion's grasp. I drew my sword, rushing the wraith in my blind rage. Everything happened so fast. There was a flash of dark magic and large form knocking me into a barrel and to the ground. Pain shot through my side where it had collided with the barrel. The horseman still stood where he had been, but Rion was laying prone on the floor. I ran to his side, falling to my knees beside him. "No, no, no…" I said as I rolled him to his back. The chest of his armor and shirt were singed and torn, and the skin below was blistered. Nolan and Flynn were beside us in a moment. Rion howled in pain as they hoisted him to his feet, bracing him between them.

I went to rush the horseman another time, but Flynn yelled, "Aisling, we need to leave! He needs a healer! Now!"

I looked to the horseman, and to Nora. "Please," she whimpered, the gag distorting her words. "Please don't leave me."

"You leave, she dies. Simple as that," the horseman reiterated. I only had one choice.

My boots scuffed against the dirt floor, as I planted my feet and rallied my magic. I would need to banish the Dullahan back to the land of the dead like I had in the forest. He realized what I was doing too late as I shot a solid ball of my magic into his chest.

He exploded into smoke and disappeared. Nora hit the ground hard. I gathered her in my arms in one fluid motion. She let out a ghost of a whimper. "Shhh. I'm going to get you out of here. Let's go." I led the way up the stairs with Nolan and Flynn hauling Rion on my heels.

We backtracked our way back through the fort. We had only been in the cellars for close to ten minutes, so the dining hall still hummed. I just prayed we wouldn't encounter anyone else as we made our escape. We reached the servants' door quickly.

I finally looked down at Nora cradled in my arms. The front of her clothing was stained red. "No." Her eyes stared unseeing back at me. I let out a sputtering sob. The deep slice across her throat still seeped blood.

"Aisling," Nolan placed his free hand on his shoulder. "She's gone. You're going to have to leave her. You won't be able to propel down the wall with her body."

I shook my head. "No, she can't be. We risked everything. She can't be gone."

"Rion is going to die next if we don't get him to a healer,"

Nolan voice hardened. That snapped me out of my stupor. Rion had finally lost consciousness. The blisters were spreading up his neck. Though I didn't want to leave her, I set Nora's still body at my feet with a sob. My trembling hands were stained with her blood. I took one breath before I switched all emotion off, the only thing running through my head was our escape and getting Rion to safety.

I opened the door and allowed Flynn and Nolan to go first as I guarded their backs. We rushed back up the turret and to the battlement where the rope dangled. A bell sounded over the fort. "Intruders! Intruders!" Someone yelled within.

Flynn and Nolan quickly removed their belts, tethering Rion to Nolan's back with the strips of leather. Flynn went down the rope first, and Nolan next. I turned back to the scene before me. Chaos erupted through the courtyard as soldiers searched for our position.

I had risked everything to save the last person who remained from my old life. I thought Aine died the moment I found out who I truly was, but she didn't. She drew her last breath the moment Nora did. I finally turned and propelled myself down the rope as well.

Rion was once again propped between the other two men once I reached the bottom. I couldn't lose him too. We fetched the horse. Nolan rode with Rion slumped in front of him, leading us to the rebel base. I tied the reins of Rion's horse to my saddle, though he protested ever step of the way, and we raced along the base of the mountain until we came to a path that zig zagged up the side of it. "Will he live?" I hadn't had the heart to ask until now. We slowly began the climb upwards.

"He's dying, Aisling. If we can get him to a healer, he might have a chance, but we don't have much time," Nolan answered. "He was struck by a curse meant for you. It's eating away his flesh faster than he can heal." His voice held his contempt.

He blamed me for this, as he should. Silent tears blurred my lashes and trickled down my cheeks. Nora was dead because of me. Rion was dying…because of me. How many more people would have to die because I still lived?

Chapter 19

White canvas tents, pitched on either side of the path, came into view. Snow floated through the air and covered the ground, a scene straight from a children's story book. Men and women sat around a large fire at the center of the camp. Two men rushed to Nolan when they noticed our arrival to help him get Rion off the horse. "He needs to be taken to a healer immediately," he commanded the men. I dismounted and ran after them. My heart pounded in my chest.

"Colleen!" called one of the men when they closed in on one of the tents. A beautiful human woman appeared in the entrance. Golden strands of hair caught the wind drifting across a pale, freckled face that suggested she was in her early thirties.

"Oh gods. Rion?" she said, holding the flap open to allow the men in. She ignored my presence completely. I ground my teeth together. "What happened?" The woman, Colleen was what the man had called her, asked. The men laid him upon a cot at the center of the room. She dropped to her knees at his side, placing her hand on his cheek.

"He was struck by a curse," I growled. "Can you heal him?"

Colleen sent me a glare over her shoulder. "And who are you?"

Anger thrummed deep in my soul. "I am Aisling, daughter of Queen Deirdre, and heir to the Druid throne."

Colleen's eyes went wide. She stood and bowed deeply. "Your highness. Please forgive me. Yes, I can heal him."

"Good." I approached the cot and fell to my knees. I brushed the back of my hand down his cheek. His eyes fluttered behind his lids. My gaze rose to Colleen's. She stepped back suddenly. Hurt shone in her eyes.

"You're his mate," she whispered. She stood rooted in place for a moment more before she again knelt by the cot. She unbuckled the scorched armor and cut Rion from his shirt and ran her hands gently over the blisters that had spread over his entire face and abdomen.

The blisters on his chest had broken open, the skin slowly turning black and peeling away. I know she was just doing her job, but I couldn't contain the growl that forced its way up my throat at the sight of her hands on him. "It might be better if you waited outside," she suggested. "I am going to have to touch him to heal him. I'd rather not lose my hands in the process."

I checked my temper. "I'm fine. Just fix him." The edge of my voice wavered as I looked down upon Rion's face covered in blisters that were starting to swell and ooze. She nodded and got to work. Warm light bled from her hands. Black smoke rose from Rion's wounds.

"I have to remove the remnants of the magic." she explained.

"Then, his body should be able to heal itself.

"Will it scar?" I asked.

"I believe his face will heal well. However, he may carry the marks on his chest forever. Over time they will fade, but never fully." Colleen's voice lacked empathy, which stoked the fire I was struggling to keep under control. I decided to remain silent, while she healed him.

I looked down at my hands that were covered in Nora's dried blood. Bile ran up the back of my throat. Colleen noticed the look and gestured to the corner of the tent. "There's a basin over there you can use to clean up," she said. I simply nodded and walked over to the table holding a copper bowl.

There was a small brush and soap sitting by a pitcher of water. I poured the water in the bowl and proceeded to scrub my skin and nails, until my hands were pink. My emotions attempted to overwhelm me, but I pushed them back down and stored them away to deal with later. I returned to Rion's side. He was my top priority.

Flynn and Nolan had come by to check on the healer's progress. They brought me a new blouse and leathers. "Burn those," I said when I handed Flynn my soiled clothing. They stayed for a while until they were summoned by the generals for an update on Rion's condition.

Nolan offered to stay. "Flynn can go by himself."

"I'm okay. There isn't anything you can do here. Go with him and make sure he makes it there without falling into the arms of a pretty, young woman on the way." My joke fell flat. Nolan bowed, which threw me off guard. "You don't need to do that."

"Yes, I do, your highness." They left without another word.

I continued to sit by Rion's head for what felt like hours.

The birds had awoken and chittered loudly outside the tent. The morning light leaked in through the flap that remained slightly open.

Colleen finally finished removing all the magic from Rion's wounds. The blisters began to heal rapidly and faded before my eyes. "When will he wake?" I finally broke my silence to ask Colleen.

"It won't be long, now." Just as the words exited her mouth Rion stirred, slowly opening his eyes. "Fuck," he groaned. I shifted to look in his eyes, letting out a breath I didn't realize I was holding.

I flung myself on top of him, sobbing, "I thought you were gone."

"It would take so much more than that to take me from you, little fox." Pain laced his words, but when I attempted to pull away, he gripped me around my middle tightly. "I remember getting hit by the horseman's curse, but everything after that is fuzzy. What the hell happened? Where's Nora?"

I sobbed harder. "She didn't… she didn't make it. I banished the Dullahan with my magic, just like I had done before, but he was faster. He slit her throat right before the magic struck him." I shook with the emotion I had bottled up. All the emotion I had kept neatly packed away surged forth like a river breaking its dam.

"Shhhhh," Rion hushed. "I am so sorry."

"No, I'm sorry. All of this is because of me. Nora's death. You getting injured to save me. All of it" Rion slowly sat us up. Pain flickered on his face when I pulled back to look at him. He brushed the tears from my face.

"First of all, Nora's blood is not on your hands. Secondly, I would have gladly died for you, little fox." He placed his forehead against mine. I inhaled deeply. His scent filled my nose, loosening the sorrow that had my heart gripped in its fist. "We will make them pay. I will ensure you will get the vengeance you rightfully deserve."

Colleen cleared her throat behind me. Rion looked over my shoulder, only now realizing she was there. He winced. "Colleen." He bowed his head slightly. "I hope you are well." Tension choked the room. I had the feeling that they were more than just acquaintances, but now was not the time.

"I am, thank you," she retorted. "You can go. Take it easy today. You're weak from the curse. Your highness." She bowed deeply. I got to my feet and helped Rion stand.

We exited the tent into the frigid air. It was so cold at this elevation, and the air was thin. My chest was tight with emotion and the inability to take a full breath. Rion was still only wearing the shirt he was wearing the night before, but he didn't seem to be bothered by the cold. The camp was alive now with people going about their morning routines. Rion led me through the bustling camp towards a large tent at the center of camp. "Is this yours?" I asked when he gestured for me to go inside.

"Nope," he replied. "It's yours." I gaped at the tent that was three times bigger than the others. I ducked inside and was at a loss for words. The floor was wooden planks. A desk was off to the right with ink and parchment. A large copper tub sat on the left. But, what I was most impressed with was the four-poster bed at the center. Silk sheets and soft furs covered the mattress. "I sent word ahead a few weeks ago to make sure they had everything ready for your arrival. It's not much, but it should do."

"Not much?" I chuckled. "This tent is bigger than the cottage I lived in with my grandmother." I lifted the lid on the trunk at the end of the bed to discover it was filled with clothing. "Thank you, Rion."

He wrapped his arms around my waist from behind and nuzzled into my neck. "I need to gather the generals so I can introduce you. Then you'll need to speak to the people. We need to get our plan in motion." I spun in his arms.

"Tomorrow," I said. "You almost died, Rion, and neither of us has truly slept in days. It can wait until tomorrow."

"Okay," he kissed me gently. "Tomorrow." He kissed me again, more passionately this time. He walked me backwards until the back of my knees hit the bed. I fell back upon the mattress.

"What about 'you need rest' don't you understand," I sighed.

He leaned over me, propping one knee on the mattress between my thighs and braced his hands on either side of my face. "I don't think he cares," he gestured to his erection that was nearly bursting from his trousers. "All I want is to feel the heat of you wrapped around my cock. Fuck rest." He shifted onto his elbows and kissed my neck. I pushed the scrap of his shirt off his shoulders and ran my hands down his muscular back.

His mouth found mine, his tongue sliding across my lip. They parted to allow him access. Rion's strong hands roamed my body, which was still contained within my leathers. He cupped me over my trousers which caused my hips to buck into his hand. I shamelessly ground against his tough. "That's a good girl," he purred in my ear.

"Are you sure… you are up for this?" I stuttered. The blisters on his face were nearly gone, but the wounds on his chest were still an angry pink.

"Yes. I am quite sure," he reassured me.

"Okay, then I need you inside me. Now," I panted. He continued to tease me as he watched me squirm beneath him. Gods, he would be my undoing. He finally pulled me back to my feet and helped me remove my vambraces and leather breastplate. My blouse followed quickly after. Rion gently pushed me back down onto the bed.

He palmed my bare chest, running a thumb over the raised peak. I gasped. He lowered his mouth to the bud and gently flicked his tongue over it. I sucked in a breath and threaded my hand through his hair. Rion moved further down my body leaving a trail of kisses in his wake. My heart pounded with anticipation when he placed a kiss just above my waistband.

My toes curled in my boots. I was going to combust if he kept up with his teasing. He knelt at the edge of the bed, removing my boots and trousers quickly. He paused to remove his own before coming to stand in front of me. He gripped my knees and spread my legs open for him. "Look at you. My beautiful queen, who I will serve until my dying breath."

"Rion. If you don't fuck me now, I will kick your ass and do it myself," my voice didn't come out nearly as threatening as I had wanted.

A feral grin took over his face. "As hot as that sounds," he chuckled as he got to his feet. "I don't think I could bear it, knowing that I'm not the one making you scream." He took hold of my hips and sank himself inside me. I cried out in pleasure, closing my eyes tightly. Explosions of stars painted my lids. "Open your eyes," Rion demanded. "I want you to watch what you do to me."

Rion slid his hand between us. He rubbed his thumb in circular motions against my clit. The combined sensations drove me towards climax. My back arched off the bed. I called out his name as my body began to tremble. My entire body felt as though it was floating among the stars. Euphoria clouded my brain.

He slowed his pace as I came down from my high. He captured

my mouth with his. The kiss was slow and enthusiastic. Rion placed a knee on the bed and nudged me, indicating he wanted me to move further up the bed. We moved without breaking the kiss.

He kept his pace slow. "I love you, little fox," he whispered against my lips. He ran his nose along the side of my face.

"I love you, more than I have ever loved another before," I replied. I had come entirely too close to losing him, and the memory brought tears to my eyes. The fear and grief from the events that had transpired last night broke free from its cage once again.

Rion's movement faltered. "Do you want to stop?"

"No. No, I'm… I'm okay," I croaked.

"You're not, and that's okay." Rion withdrew and sat up against the headboard. He pulled me into his lap, tucking me safely in his arms. His chin rested on my head. I cried until I had no more tears to shed, while Rion rocked us. My eyes were puffy and on fire by the time I was finished.

"I'm sorry," my voice came out hoarse.

Rion gripped my chin and forced me to look at him. "Whatever for?"

"I ruined the moment. I just couldn't contain it anymore." I felt like I lived in a constant state of regret. I struggled at that moment to see how all that we had suffered and lost would be worth the outcome.

"You have nothing to be sorry for. If you need to stop, we stop. Okay?" I nodded, though it didn't quell the guilt. He released me. As I laid my head upon Rion's chest, my thoughts shifted to Nora. The way she smiled every time she saw me. The look of panic on her face when the horsemen held that knife to her delicate throat.

"Nora was only ten. She had so much life to live," I sniffled. "She was always so happy, even though life had never been kind to her and her family. She deserved so much better." I made a silent promise to myself that I wouldn't let another I cared for fall victim to the false king's wrath. I would not lose another damn thing, and I was determined to ensure no one else would either. I fell into a deep sleep with vengeance and blood on my tongue.

Chapter 20

The next morning, I stood in front of a large wooden table at the center of the war tent. Rion and I were dressed in our fighting leathers, armed to the teeth. Four middle aged men, the generals of our small rebel force, stood before me. Flynn, Rion, and Nolan stood off to the side.

I was in charge and that made me uncomfortable. I was a decent fighter now, but I didn't have any experience leading an army. Rion gave me a rundown on war strategy as we got ready this morning, how to address the generals, and what our next steps need to be. "Uh, good morning," I started. Flynn snickered which was met by Rion swatting his arm, though he was also fighting a grin.

I shot them both a glare before continuing, "I am Aisling, daughter of Deirdre, heir to the throne of the Emerald Isle. I am here to help take back what is rightfully ours."

"I am Cian. It is an honor to meet you, Your Highness. We were ecstatic when we felt you come into your power. We thought you had died with your mother," a man with graying, cropped hair said with a bow. The others bowed alongside their comrade. "You look like her."

"You knew her?" He had been the first, other than my grandmother, I had met that had known my mother.

He nodded. "Aye, I was in the infantry stationed in the North when the Aos Si invaded. We all were," he gestured to the men around him. "This is William, Riley, and Seamus. When Rion went about gathering people to aid in a rebellion, we were hesitant because of the failed attempt shortly after the invasion, but he was convincing."

"This time will be different, especially because we have Aisling." Rion stepped to my side. "She still has a little way to go until her magic abilities are ready, but she's a fine swordsman. By the time we are ready to stage an attack, she'll be ready for anything Balor throws at her." I appreciated his confidence in me, but I didn't hold that same sentiment.

"We need to begin by tracking down the treasures the Tuatha Dé Danann gave the Druids. The false king has the sword and the stone, but the spear and the cauldron are still missing. We need to get to them before the he does," I explained to the generals. "We have a plan to figure out what the king knows about their locations. Nolan and I will disguise ourselves and go to a local tavern. The hope is that with enough alcohol, we can get an off-duty guard to tell us what we need to know."

"If you are discovered, you will be executed," Cian stated. Rion stiffened. It had taken quite a bit of persuasion to get him to agree to this plan. "Are you sure there isn't another way that doesn't risk your life?"

"I will be fine. I can hold my own, and I won't be alone. This is the best plan that limits bloodshed," I replied.

"They haven't given two shits about spilling our blood. Why should we care about shedding theirs?" spoke one of the generals, William I believe his name was. His features were as harsh as his words. You could tell life had not been kind to this man.

"If we stoop to their level, we are no better than they are," I snapped. "I will have no tolerance for cruelness. We are building a new kingdom and there will be no room for such things."

William bowed his head and softened his tone, "My apologies, Your Highness."

"I need you all to ready your men. Once we have acquired the two missing treasures, we will need to steal back the other two from under the king's nose. Then, we can launch our attack upon Lios." The generals responded with a nod.

They continued to stare at me. I was confused. What were they waiting for? I looked over at Rion, who was still by my side. "You're dismissed," he commanded the men with an ease I wish I had. The men exited the tent without another word.

"Forgive Will," Rion turned to me after a moment. "He's lost much due to the Aos Si. His wife and three children were killed shortly after the invasion. His village rebelled against the Aos Si male who was appointed as their overseer. He had yet to make it back from his post in the North when the king sent the Dullahan to squash the uprising. All four of those men came from the same village. They have suffered greatly."

I looked to the floor, immediately regretting the way I had spoken to him. I squeezed my eyes shut, berating myself for my inability to manage my temper. "You were right though," Rion said. "We need to be better, do better. It is what I believe your mother would have done." I took a breath and reopened my eyes. There was no time for sulking.

I turned in Flynn and Nolan's direction. "What's the plan for scoping out a tavern?"

"Flynn and I are leaving in an hour to travel to Lios. We will return in five days with a location," Nolan answered. "It will take two days to travel there and another two to travel back without using the pass."

"Okay, and what will we be doing while they are gone?" I asked as I turned my attention back to Rion.

He smiled. "We need to start training your mind against others. You're currently an open book. Before I send you into Lios, you need to be able to keep them out of your head or you could risk the mission."

A realization popped into my head. "Have you been reading my mind?"

"It's hard not to when you are literally screaming your thoughts into my head," Rion replied.

"Wait," I scanned the room, looking at Flynn and Nolan. "What about you guys?" Horror ran through me.

Flynn waggled his eyebrows at me, "I, for one, would love to know what goes on in that head of yours, but Rion would have ours if we even tried. So, no. We have not, but not every Aos Si would be so courteous. If they feel your mind unguarded, they will rip it apart looking for your darkest secrets."

Knowing they hadn't been prodding about in my mind put me at ease. "We are going to get the horses ready and be on our way." Nolan bowed deeply. Flynn followed. I didn't think I would ever get used to that. "Your Highness," they spoke in unison.

I turned back to Rion. "Before we begin, I have a question." It had been nagging me since we had spoken with the generals.

He moved forwards and took my hands in his. "And what is that?"

"Do the soldiers here know what you are? What I am?" I feared that their animosity against the Aos Si might be a problem.

"They do. Bringing you back here safely has instilled a small amount of trust in us. They were still weary of our intentions when we left to gather more rebels three months ago. It is the reason we remain glamoured. It puts the humans at ease."

"You had said there are other Aos Si that don't agree with the king's rule. Where are they?" I had only seen humans milling through the camp.

"While you are in Lios with Nolan, you will also need to gather the Aos Si soldiers that have promised their swords to our cause," he explained. "We won't succeed with the handful of retired human soldiers and farmers."

"How many do we have here right now?" I asked. There were about a hundred tents pitched on the side of the mountain, meaning they could only have about two hundred soldiers.

"We currently have one hundred and eighty-four soldiers recruited, plus the four generals. They each command a battalion of forty-six. I have the word of an additional hundred Aos Si warriors, which will be split between Flynn and Nolan to command. You and I will command the army as a whole."

"I have the ability to raise the Wild Hunt from the land of the dead, but we have not talked about how that can be accomplished. We don't stand a chance without them." I stated.

"What I have heard is that the Druids used a phrase to call them forth from the otherworld, but I do not know what that phrase is. Like the locations of the treasures, it was also passed down through generations of heirs. To my knowledge, no one else knew of it." Rion's confidence faltered a bit, but he quickly regained it. "We will figure it out. We have time before it is needed."

The plan was dependent upon whether I could master my magic by the time we went to storm the castle and had the ability to wield the treasures. Without it, we were doomed. "Well, we better get started then."

Rion led us out into the snow that was dancing through the air. I took a moment to appreciate its beauty. I had only seen snow once in my life. When I was ten, my grandmother was summoned to attend a birth at a small farm at the base of these very mountains on the coast. Their oldest daughter was my age, and she taught me to make snowballs. We played for hours while her mother labored, and my grandmother tended to her.

I bent and scooped a pile of snow in my hand and molded it into a perfect sphere. I tossed it in the air and caught it, zeroing in on Rion's back as he continued to walk in front of me. Before I could think better of it, I lobbed the ball right between his shoulder blades. He stopped suddenly and turned slowly to face me. I couldn't keep the mischievous smile off my face after the astonished look on his face.

"I would watch it if I were you, little fox." He bent at his waist to gather his own handful of snow. He let his snowball fly, and it struck me square in the chest. Before I realized what was going on, he rushed me and hauled me over his shoulder.

I pounded my fist on his back, laughing, "Put me down." He did put me down, right into a large snow drift. "Fuck. It's so cold!" I yelled as the snow made its way past the large fur-lined cloak I wore and connected with my skin.

"Don't pick fights you cannot possibly win," he said with a wink. I threw an armful of powdery snow in his direction. It caught the wind and blew right back into my face. Rion laughed hysterically. I loved that sound more than the beauty of the snow. "Come on, let's get to work," he chuckled as he helped me from the drift.

He led me back to my tent. A small wood stove was lit, heating the interior to a comfortable temperature. The heat was pleasant on my chilled extremities, as I removed my cloak. "So," I started, my teeth chattering a bit due to the cold, "Where do we start?"

You need to learn to build a wall around your mind. Rion's voice purred through my mind.

I stared at him. "How did you do that?"

Rion grinned. *It's easier between mates but harder to block out. If you can shield me out of your mind, you can shield it against anyone.*

I remembered the night he had me feel for the bond, the thread that led between our souls. I closed my eyes, feeling for that connection. I caught hold of it with my mind and sent my thoughts along its length. *Like this?* I asked down the bond between us.

Perfect. His voice reverberated through every corner of my mind. *In order to infiltrate another's mind, you need to project yours towards theirs.*

I kept my eyes closed, so I could focus. I followed the bond until a wall of gold appeared before me. There were engravings all over the wall. I ran my hand along the carvings. *This is my shield.* Rion's voice sounded closer now, like he was standing beside me.

What are these? I inquired about the carvings.

Wards. I figured out how to use them to allow those I trust in without taking down my shield, Rion explained. The strange markings were in a language I didn't understand.

Will you teach me how to ward? I wanted to learn everything I possibly could.

At some point, I would love to. However, there are more pressing matters. You need to build your own shield and harness your Druid magic first.

I pulled back from his gleaming wall and retreated into my own mind. I imagined a golden wall, like the one I'd seen in Rion's mind, rising before me. Nothing happened. I tried again, but instead of a wall of glimmering gold, I pictured thick vines covered in thorns growing and entwining together. They sprouted from the floor of my mind's eye, twisting and turning until a wall of thorns remained. Surprisingly, it took little thought to keep the wall standing firm. Purple flowers grew among the vines. I couldn't identify the foliage, but I knew their fragrance, subtle and sweet. It was entwined within Rion's scent. I recognized it when I fell upon Rion sleeping on the floor of the tent the first day we met.

I finally opened my eyes. "What are they?" I could tell Rion knew what I was speaking of.

"It's fox glove, a deadly plant rarely found in this land. Fields of it grow in Tír na nÓg, though." He seemed to be as confused as I was.

"It's in your scent. I smelled it before I met you too, but I don't know when. It also grew around the hollow you plucked me out of when you came across me in the woods." I tried to pull on any memory that contained the purple flowers but came up empty handed.

"When I was a child, I used to play in the fox glove fields," he recalled.

"I thought you just said the flowers were deadly?"

"They are, to humans, but the Aos Si primarily use from them is for wine, intensifying the effects of the alcohol. It can also be brewed into a tea, leading to the best high of your life," he was talking from experience. "I spent much of my childhood in those fields to hide from my father with Nolan, Flynn and Bellamy," he explained. "The humans believed that fairies lived near the plants. Other's claim the fairies gifted it to the foxes to wear upon their paws to quiet their steps, allowing them to silently approach their pray."

The irony wasn't lost on me. They had been his protection, now they are mine. "Does it work? My shield of… flowers," I giggled.

"Yes. I can no longer read your thoughts, though I can still feel the link between us. We should be able to bypass our shields to communicate through the bond." Rion walked forward. "I do have to say I am impressed." His arms wrapped around my waist. "You figured that out rather quickly. It seems the Aos Si magic comes to you more naturally than that of your Druid ancestors. It was the same way in training when you were utilizing your speed and strength unknowingly."

I pressed my cheek against his chest. I jerked when I felt pride that wasn't my own flood through my body. It came from the bond. It was strange but not unwanted.

A scream rose from beyond the tent. Rion and I looked at one another and rushed into the frigid air. It stole the air from my lungs as we ran towards the cries. A group of people gathered around Colleen's tent. Wails of agony tore from inside. Rion pushed his way through the growing crowd. I stayed close to his heels.

We burst into the tent. In the bed where Rion had just laid the day before, lay a young man. There was blood everywhere and his face twisted in pain. Two other soldiers knelt to one side of the bed while Colleen knelt on the other. Colleen's eyes roamed over

Rion, before returning to her patient. Rion was oblivious, but I saw it for what it was. Longing. I stamped down the possessiveness as Rion demanded, "What the hell happened?"

"We went down to the lake on the other side of the ridge to gather water, like we do every morning," one of the men spoke. "The water was exceptionally cold, so we bet Brian five gold pieces to get in the water." The man on the cot, Brian, let out another painful cry. "He was only in for a moment before he was dragged beneath the surface. We managed to fight off the creature and get him to shore, but not before he was injured."

"Did you see what pulled him under?" Rion's voice was stern but kind, as he questioned the young soldier.

The man nodded his head. "It was a mermaid, sir."

Chapter 21

I thought mermaids were a myth?" I asked Rion as we headed back to our tent. My grandmother had once told me bedtime stories of the ancient shifters that lived in the depths of the sea in their magnificent sunken cities. They were able to live on land as well, shedding their tails in favor of feet.

"Not a myth, but extremely rare. They are not normally aggressive, though. I am going to take a trip down to the lake and see for myself." As soon as we entered the tent, Rion strapped an extra sword to his back and knife to his thigh before he donned his cloak.

"I'm coming with you," I stated as I threw my own cloak over my shoulders. No way in hell I was going to allow him to go alone.

"Fine, but you stay behind me at all times. Got it?" I rolled my eyes at his demand but reluctantly agreed.

We took a path south of the camp that led over the ridge and down the other side. The lake came into view shortly. Its sapphire waters sparkled from the few rays of sun that managed to peak out from behind the clouds. It was hard to imagine that the still waters contained the creature that had caused Brian's injuries.

I was still so enthralled by its beauty that I didn't notice Rion slowed his approach as we reached the edge of the water. Rion let out a grunt when I collided with his back. "Sorry," I mumbled. He gave me a look over his shoulder that caused me to snap my mouth shut.

Rion knelt by the shore, where blood stained the rocks. This must have been where Brian's comrades had pulled him from the water. I squinted at the water, attempting to see what lay beneath when something caught my eye. "What is that?" I asked, pointing to the glimmering object.

Before Rion could reply, a voice danced across the water's surface, "He said one day someone would come to collect the treasure he bestowed upon us." I searched for the origin of the voice, when a woman appeared a few yards from the shore. She smiled warmly at me but shot Rion a glare as he withdrew his sword.

She swam closer, her bronze hair floated in the water behind her. Her emerald tail swished, propelling her forward. I was utterly speechless. She was the most striking creature I had ever seen. "Aisling, daughter of Deirdre, rightful heir to the Emerald Isle, have you come to collect our treasure?"

"How do you know who I am?" I asked as I stepped closer to the mermaid before me, completely forgetting my promise to Rion.

"We heard your name whispered upon the breeze. We knew you would come." She held her hand out to me. I noticed that her skin was iridescent, like the mother of pearl that coated the inside of an oyster's shell. I was inches away from grabbing it when Rion pushed me behind him and pointed his blade towards the mermaid.

"What was placed in your charge?" he demanded.

"You are no Druid and have no claim to what we have been charged with protecting," she hissed in his direction.

I shot Rion a glare but stayed put. I peered around his hulking form to ask, "Tell me, what is it you have that you believe I have come to collect?"

"You must come with me, and I will show you, princess." She once again reached her hand out to me.

Rion turned to me. "There is no way I am letting you go with her. You know that right? She's luring you."

"Rion, I think she has one of the treasures. I saw something in the water right before she appeared." The mermaid waited patiently watching our debate. "I will be fine." I patted the hilt of my sword at my side. "Brian was taken by surprise. I won't be," I assured him. I could see the internal war he waged within himself before he moved off to the side. I reached out to the mermaid and took her cool, wet hand.

"If any harm comes to her," he growled. "I will fucking slaughter you."

"I promise, Your Highness, she will be returned safely to you." I didn't have a chance to question the title she used for Rion before I was pulled beneath the lake's icy surface.

We moved swiftly through the frigid water. My cloak pulled harshly against my throat as we descended into the deep. I unhooked the clasped to prevent it from hanging me.

Before I knew it, my feet landed on the floor of the lake. I had closed my eyes when my face hit the water. I opened them once more. The mermaid was only inches from my face. Bubbles rose from her mouth as she smiled at me and gestured to the golden object that sat before my feet, half buried in the clay that formed the bottom.

My lungs were on fire, desperate for air. I hadn't gotten a full breath before she hauled me down with her. Panic set in quickly. I reached out for the golden object, trying to pry it from its clay prison, but it wouldn't budge.

Spots formed in my vision. I wasn't going to be able to stay under the water much longer before drowning. The mermaid sensed my discomfort and attempted to pull me away, back to the surface. I refused. I didn't want to leave it behind, and I wasn't sure if I would be allowed a second attempt to retrieve it. I had a feeling this was some sort of test to see if I was worthy of the object they protected.

I fought against the innate need to draw a breath and kept pulling. The edges of my vision started to grow darker. *Move!* I screamed at it in my mind.

Little fox! What's going on? Get out of there! Rion yelled back into my head. The object moved slightly in my grasp. I ignored Rion's pleads. I almost had it when my grip slipped causing me to stumble back. I broke. I slammed my eyes shut and let out a gargled, frustrated scream. I threw my hands out in front of me, using everything I had to make the water bend to my will.

I expected the water to rush into my mouth and fill my lungs, but I realized slowly that I could breathe. I thought for a moment that I had blacked out and Rion had dove in to save me. However, when I opened my eyes, a dome of water surrounded me. The golden object sat at the center. I could see clearly that it was a cauldron that was buried in the earth. Excitement rose up inside me. The mermaid looked on beyond the dome. She, too, seemed excited as she swam around erratically.

I fell to my knees and dug out the remaining mud from around the cauldron. It was smaller than I had envisioned, about the size of a helmet. I pulled it to my chest and allowed the water to slowly fill up the pocket of air I had formed. Before it reached my chin, I drew in a large breath.

The mermaid swam back to my side and gripped my arm. The surface grew closer as she pulled me back up to dry land. A ray of sun guiding us back. My face hit cool air as I emerged from the water. Rion was by my side in an instant hauling me back to shore.

He ran his hands over every inch of my body searching for injuries. His hands stilled when he saw what I had cradled in my arms. "The cauldron," he breathed. I could feel the magic radiating off the object I held. It caused the air to buzz around us.

"The first king gave us the cauldron to protect until the crown needed it once more," the mermaid spoke from the shallows. "I am sorry about your men. We were unaware of who they answered to. The false king has slaughtered many of our people," remorse coated her words.

Rion and I looked at the beautiful being before us. She reached her hand out to me once more. Rion stiffened but didn't interfere when I extended my own to her. "All we ask, Your Highness, is that you allow us to remain in these lands, like your forefathers and mother before you."

"You have my promise," I spoke with authority, "that you will be given the same rights and privileges that I wish to restore to my people." She bowed her head gracefully and disappeared once more within the depths of the lake.

I started to shiver against the cold that had settled deep in my bones. Rion unhooked his cloak and placed it on my shoulders. "What happened down there? I heard you scream through the bond," he asked as he did the clasp.

I told him all that had happened in the short amount of time I was underwater. Pride shone in his eyes and flooded our bond. "You did it," he smiled.

"Who would have thought all I needed was a little… encouragement," I put it lightly.

He helped me to my feet, shaking his head. "You scared the shit out of me, little fox. Another few minutes and I would have dived in after you." Another shiver racked my body, and my breath bloomed out in front of me.

"Let's get you back and warmed up, then we can figure out what to do with this," he gestured to the cauldron he had taken from my frozen grasp.

We began our journey back to the camp. "Can the Aos Si die of hyperthermia?" I asked as my teeth chattered. I was pretty sure I was going to do just that. Sharp pains shot up my legs and into my ass with every step, and my nose felt as though it may fall right off.

"No," Rion chuckled, "But it still does not feel great."

I was so stiff by the time we got back to our tent. I mustered enough energy to remove my weapons and peel the soaking clothing away from my skin, while Rion fetched buckets of warm water to fill the tub. I wrapped myself in the furs from the bed until the tub was brimming with steaming water.

"Where the hell did you get this?" I hissed as the hot water hit my chilled skin as I stepped in. Pins and needles shot up my legs. It took all of my remaining strength not to jump back out of the water.

"There is a hot spring in a cave just off the path," Rion replied.

"Well, why didn't we just go there? Why haul buckets?" Seemed like a major waste of time to me.

"It is where everyone else bathes, little fox," he knelt behind the tub and kissed my neck, causing my head to fall back into his chest. "I do not think I could remain in control if another man saw you naked."

"Oh," was all I said. He ran his hands up my arms that rested on the edge of the tub. When he reached my shoulders, he massaged the tensed muscles. His thumb moved in circles at the base of my neck, releasing the tension there. A moan leapt from my lips.

He continued to massage every knot from my shoulders and upper back. I was finally warm by the time he was done. Rion stood and procured a bar of soap. "While you finish your bath, I am going to gather the generals and make them aware of recent events." The cauldron lay forgotten on the bed. The magic emanating from it left a constant ringing in my ears.

"How do we even use it?" I asked before he stepped back out into the snow.

"Honestly, I don't know," Rion answered.

I sank deeper into the tub until the water lapped over my chin. "Great, another thing we have to figure out," I mumbled. Rion left with a chuckle not seemingly bothered by the uselessness of the hunk of metal that I had risked my life to retrieve.

At some point, I had fallen asleep wrapped in the warmth of the water, which had now cooled. I looked around to see Rion had not yet returned. I quickly washed and got dressed in a sheer shift from the trunk at the end of the bed. I was impressed to find it was a perfect fit, like it had been made for me.

I was in the middle of figuring out how to empty the tub when Rion finally returned. He stomped the snow off his boots and brushed it from his cloak. "It's really coming down out there," he stated as he removed the cloak and hung it over the desk chair. He stopped in his tracks when he saw me, bucket in hand, prepared to bail the water. His mouth hung open like a fish out of water.

"What?" I asked. "I was going to empty the tub. I wasn't sure if there was some sort of drain, but figured this would work…" He cut off my rambling.

"Forget the tub." His face was overcome with want and need as his eyes trailed over my body, stopping at where my nipples were peaked against the thin fabric. I dropped the bucket to the ground. I pressed my thighs together to stem the pulsing that erupted from his gaze. "Get on the bed, now," he demanded.

A spark of stubbornness shot through me and a grin formed on my face. "Make me," I taunted. He was on me so fast I didn't have time to prepare.

"Gladly," he growled as he gripped my waist and threw me over his shoulder. The hilt of his sword almost knocked my front teeth out.

He tossed me on the bed before him. Rion was a picture of death, donned in shining black leather and armed to the teeth. He removed his weapons, letting them hit the floor with a thud. Taking his time, he removed his armor and clothing. Anticipation built in my stomach with every roaming glance he sent over my body.

When he finally stood bare before him, he flipped me onto my stomach. Grabbing me by my waist, Rion lifted my ass in the air. I braced my knees on the edge of the bed. *How do you want it?* He purred into my mind. *Hard and fast?* He plunged his fingers deep inside me. I gasped at the pleasant intrusion. *Or painstakingly slow?* He withdrew slowly. I attempted to rock back onto his hand, but his other one kept me in place.

I want to hear what you want, little fox. I want you to tell me in explicit detail how you would like me to fuck you. His voice in my head made my need amplify tenfold.

"I want you to fuck me hard. I want you to make me scream your name, so everyone knows that I am yours and you are mine." I didn't recognize the sultry voice that exited my mouth.

"Fucking, gods," he groaned as he replaced his fingers with his throbbing cock.

He did just as I had asked, pounding deep and hard into me. Neither of us lasted long. His name ripped out of my throat, reverberated through the tent and out into the night. My name followed as Rion found his release.

I was sure that everyone in a one-mile radius heard, but there was only one person that I hoped was listening. That bitch, Colleen. My mind went back to the hurt on her face when she realized I was Rion's mate and how she had looked at him earlier that day. Every bone in my body screamed for blood.

We repositioned ourselves under the furs. Rion fell asleep quickly, his soft snores tickled my face that was resting on his chest. I tried to sleep, but every time I closed my eyes, I saw Colleen in Rion's arms. The fire burned hotter within me.

I finally succumbed to tiredness, fantasizing about the look on Colleen's face when I gouged out her longing eyes and fed them to her.

Chapter 22

I woke up in a terrible mood. I trudged through the snow behind Rion who insisted we trained this morning. At least two feet of snow had been dumped overnight. There was no way I would be able to move properly when it was well over my knees.

I was about to tell him just that when he stopped and turned towards me. "I can feel you drilling holes in the back of my head, and the irritation you are sending down the bond. What exactly is the problem?"

What was my problem? He hadn't done anything wrong. When I had finally found sleep the night before, I awoke every few hours from dreams of blood and vengeance. My petty mind could not and would not let go of the look Colleen had sent Rion, but that wasn't his fault.

"Nothing," I mumbled.

"It's not nothing, but if you don't want to talk about it

that's fine." Rion could be fearsome, but he was also incredibly understanding. I pushed aside my irritation. I knew there would be a time when the dam would break, and when it did, everyone around me would be in danger.

Rion led the way as the path inclined. "Where are we going?" I called ahead.

"You have been successful creating shields with your pure magic, now it's time to see what else you are capable of," he replied over his shoulder. "You need to learn to utilize your earth-based magic while you fight. I figured that it would be best to do so away from where you might accidentally harm someone."

We arrived at a suitable, level area a moment later, surrounded by snow-covered evergreens. Rion took a few minutes to pack down the snow to create a smooth circle before drew his sword and paced before me. I mirrored his actions. I had learned that he would take every opportunity to knock me on my ass when I least expected it.

I was glad I no longer had to consciously tap into my power. It was always flowing under the surface of my skin. Now if I could just learn how to use it defensively.

"Earth-based magic allows you to utilize your surroundings in order to incapacitate your opponents." Rion turned in a circle and pointed with his sword to all that lay before us. "All of this is at your disposal." He made it all sound so simple.

"That's all well and good, but I don't know how. I have only managed to utilize my powers under duress," I pointed out.

Rion faced me once more, a large grin stretched across his face. "What occurred at the lake yesterday got me thinking. When you were submerged in the water, you had an easier time accessing your power. Much like when I had you take your shoes off while learning to ground yourself. You can do that without thinking much about it now and without direct contact with the land. I think we can train your magic in the same way." Excitement radiated off Rion like he had cracked some long-forgotten code.

"So, we should continue with water, since I have had mild success there," I suggested. "But, why are we standing in the middle of the snow when we could have gone back to the lake?"

Rion chuckled. "Because snow is less likely to drown me."

We worked with the snow for three days from morning until night, and I was ecstatic about my progress. I really enjoyed the look on Rion's face when I learned to make snowballs, handsfree, and launch them at his face. He did not share my sentiment, nor did he appreciate the mini avalanche I sent cascading down the mountain and landed on top of him.

As we made our way back into camp that evening, we discussed Flynn and Nolan's return. They should be back by midmorning tomorrow from their reconnaissance mission with the location of a tavern that was frequented by the palace guards. They were also to keep an ear out for any information that may be useful in our endeavor to find the spear and cauldron, though we had already stumbled upon one of the two. Rion hoped that they would discover anything that would prevent me from having to visit Lios.

We approached our tent when a glimpse of golden hair caught my eye. Colleen stood along the path obviously waiting for someone. My blood ran hot in my veins and a growl slipped past my lips. "What does she want," I grumbled. Rion didn't answer as we drew nearer.

She caught sight of us and met us halfway. "We need to talk," she said to Rion.

"The fuck you do," I spat at her. My hand went to the hilt of my knife.

Rion placed a hand on my shoulder and spoke calmly, "Aisling, it's fine. Okay? I'll be right behind you." He gestured to the tent.

I turned my ire onto him and his eyes went wide. "It is not *fine*." I turned to Colleen. "You will stay away from him, or you may find my knife permanently embedded between your ribs," I seethed, but she did not back down.

"I know he is your mate, and I can accept that. However, we have unfinished business. Don't you think I deserve some closure?" she asked. I pulled my knife from its sheath fully prepared to make good on my promise, when Rion grabbed me from behind.

"Stop!" he yelled in my ear. I struggled against his hold. "It's just the bond. You need to stop before you do something you'll regret."

"Oh, trust me. I won't regret it." I stomped on his foot, but he would not release me despite the pain.

"You need to go. Now," he warned Colleen. He picked me up off the ground and carried my struggling form into the tent. When Rion finally let me go, I whirled on him.

"What the fuck was that, Rion!" My voice was unfamiliar, coated in rage.

"You need to calm down and allow me to explain." Rion rubbed his hand down his face. I gestured for him to continue with the knife still palmed in my hand. "Look. The Aos Si sometimes wait centuries for their mates. During that time, they find lovers, even marry. Both parties understand that it's time limited, but they take whatever time the Fates give them. Life is lonely without someone to share it with." He paused. The look on his face told me I was not going to like what was going to come out of his mouth next.

"Colleen and I met ten years ago. My father had thrown me out, and I was traveling through the kingdom with Flynn, Bellamy, and Nolan. We stopped in a small village to gather some supplies, but the villagers had nothing extra to offer. A strange illness had taken hold of the village, and we knew we had to help. I set out to find a healer. The others stayed behind to help aid the ill, for we are immune to human disease as you know." My grip tightened on the hilt of my blade. I didn't want to hear the rest of the story, but I knew I needed to.

I stayed quiet as he continued, "A village over was rumored to have a talented young healer. Colleen immediately agreed to help the sick without a second thought or the risks to herself. We spent weeks together, while she rid the feeble villagers of the disease. She was kind and extremely gifted. We fell for each other quickly." I vibrated with anger. Though I couldn't blame him for relationships that occurred before we met, I couldn't stand the thought of another woman holding his heart or touching his body.

"We were inseparable after that. She was the one to convince me to organize the rebellion a few years ago." Ten years. They had been together for ten fucking years.

"Was she good?" I couldn't help the question that tumbled out of my mouth.

"What" Rion asked seemingly confused.

"In bed? Was she good?" I tried to remain nonchalant, like the answer didn't mean anything to me.

Rion approached me cautiously. "She wasn't you. She wasn't my mate. There is nothing like making love to the very being that was placed on this earth by the Fates specifically for you." He ran his hand gingerly down my cheek, making my eyes flutter shut. My anger melted away ever so slightly.

"There is one more thing I think you should know." My anger returned in full force as I snapped my eyes open.

"What?" I snapped.

"Colleen was with child when I left three months ago." The air felt thinner suddenly, like I couldn't take a full breath. "General Cian told me she miscarried two weeks afterwards. I am assuming that is what she had wished to speak to me about." Rion's face was filled with grief. A sharp pain shot through my chest. To suffer such a loss was a tragedy.

"Oh, Rion. I'm so sorry." For she was not the only one who lost a child. I wrapped my arms around his huge form. My mind cleared rapidly, no longer clouded by possession and rage. `

Rion spoke softly into my hair. "It wasn't meant to be. The Fates had other plans in mind. Anyway, I want you to bear my children. Not her. Some part of me will always love her, but it doesn't even come close to how I feel for you." I didn't have the heart to tell him at that moment that I wasn't entirely sure if I ever wanted to have children, at least not with the kingdom in its current state. However, we had a literal eternity to make such decisions.

"You probably should go speak to her then." I finally relented.

"You promise you'll stay here and not come after her? By the way, I find your possessiveness and aggression extremely attractive," he winked at me.

"Yes. Just go." I pushed him gently away from me with a smile. "But don't be too long. I think it's time I go explore this hot spring everyone keeps talking about." I had discovered through observation that the soldiers tend to bathe after training and before supper. They were all in bed passed out from exhaustion by this time at night.

Rion returned about ten minutes later with a huge red welt on his cheek and a stunned look on his face. "What the hell did you say?" I couldn't help the laugh that bubbled up my throat.

"Well, I had assumed that she understood that when I found my mate, her and I would be over. Seems I assumed wrong." He rubbed the tender spot above his jaw. "She was under the impression that if, and when I found my mate, I would continue my relationship with her as well. We didn't even get a chance to discuss the pregnancy loss."

"So, she hit you?" I was confused as well. I didn't see why any of that would result in physical violence.

"Um, no." I could tell he didn't want to tell me the next part. "She kissed me. And before you get all angry, I immediately pushed her away. Then, I told her she had to leave the camp. That's when she hit me." I was livid that she had the audacity to touch what wasn't hers. However, as much as I hated to admit it, the rebels would need a healer when the fighting began.

"She can't leave until we find another healer, Rion," I stated.

"Well, she'll be no used to use if she's dead. Which is what she'll be if you cannot control the urge to murder her in her sleep," Rion argued.

I knew he was right. I had witness Rion go after his closest friends because of the possessiveness the uncompleted bond caused. Colleen meant nothing to me. This was the first time I had felt its effects, and I didn't know if I could control it. I was going to have to try because we needed her.

Healers had dwindled after the invasion. That was why my grandmother and I traveled from village to village when I was a child. We crossed paths with a few other healers, but they would be long dead by now. The magic gifted to humans had begun to skip generations, sometimes two. It was as if our gifts were fading. However, the reason for the decrease in human magic wasn't entirely unknown.

The king executed any known seers when he took the throne. He had felt the ability was a danger to his reign. A large majority of the scholars had immigrated to the mainland right after the invasion. The Aos Si set fire to all the great libraries because knowledge was power. Any of the scholars that were within refused to leave as the flames engulfed their precious tomes, and they were lost along with them.

Due to the king's taxes, the people required the healers to be able to provide for the Aos Si. So, the healers were the only group of magic-wielding humans that had been allowed to remain. However, the number of children being born and making it to adulthood has been steadily declining in recent years, which results in fewer healers who are experts in their craft. We don't have the time to go on a wild goose chase to find a healer when we have one at our disposal.

I closed the space between us. I placed my hand on the angry welt marring his face. "You need to go back there and tell her not to leave, okay?" Irritation grew within me at the thought of them being alone together after discovering that Colleen believed that Rion would continue their relationship, despite having found his mate. I managed to cram it back down to where it had slithered from.

He placed his hand over mine. Pulling it to his lips, he placed a kiss on my palm. "You are the mate I always hoped I would have, but never thought I deserved. You are the most blessed gift ever bestowed upon me. I would spend all eternity on my knees before you, if that is what you wished of me. I will do everything in my power to be the male you need me to be." I attempted to interject, for he deserved so much more, but Rion silenced me with a kiss. It was slow and sweet.

He pulled away first, leaning his forehead onto mine. The damage done by his father was evident at this moment. He truly couldn't see how much he deserved to feel love and be loved in return. He spent his childhood seeking the approval of a male that never intended to give it. His mother had been his only saving grace, and his father had taken that away, too.

I wrapped my arms around his neck. "Rion, you are everything I didn't know I needed. You have opened my eyes to the world around me and have taught me how to live within it. I would surely be dead, if it weren't for you. Don't for one moment think you don't deserve to have found happiness."

Rion let out a heavy breath. "Do you still want to see the spring?" The question caught me off guard after the emotional moment shared between us. I hoped that he believed the words I had spoken. Rion kept his self-doubt carefully guarded. It was rare when he showed a moment of weakness, but I could tell that moment was over. He had steeled his features, rebuilding the wall that concealed his innermost thoughts and feelings.

"I would love to." I smiled at him. "But after you go to Colleen and beg her to stay. Deal?"

"Deal," he said, placing a soft kiss to my lips. When he returned, he informed me he was able to convince Colleen to stay, but not before warning her that if she valued her life, she would stay about from the both of us.

He made good on his promise, guiding me out of the tent and towards the cave that contained the spring. Torches lined the cavern walls as we descended into the mountain. The air within the cave was much warmer than it had been outside, and the sound of trickling water soon filled my ears. "Wow," I said as the spring appeared before me in all its glory. The damp air condensed along my skin, causing it to become slick with moisture. Steam curled through the cave, laced with the scent of ancient stone, mineral heat, and that sour, volcanic trace of sulfur that clung to the back of one's throat.

Water emerged from a crack in the wall and cascaded down into the pool below, which was crystal clear. The bottom was littered with large boulders that made perfect seating. It was breathtaking. I knelt by the edge and dipped my finger in. It was the perfect temperature. "The pool is fed by two sources," Rion spoke behind me. "Hot water is released from cracks in the bottom of the pool, warmed by volcanic vents deep in the earth, and cold water runs from the waterfall. It creates the optimal environment for bathing, for its not too hot or cold." I found the science behind the hot spring absolutely fascinating.

I heard shuffling behind me. Then, the sound of leather hitting stone echoed through the cavern. I turned to find Rion removing his clothing with a sly grin upon his lips. "Are you going to just gawk or join me?" He didn't have to ask me twice.

I shed the layers of armor and fabric quickly. When I finally sunk my tired body within the warm embrace of the waters, a sense of profound tranquility swept over me, the murmuring falls the only sound. The impending war that preoccupied my mind washed away along with sweat from our rigorous training.

Rion sat at my side with his eyes closed. He too seemed at peace. The stress lines on his forehead, which were always present, receded. His mouth hung slightly agape, and his breathing was even. I admired the beautiful male beside me. He was the epitome of perfection. I would do anything to ensure, once this was over, that we found this kind of serenity for eternity.

Chapter 23

Nolan and Flynn returned when the sun was at its peak, though it couldn't be seen through the thick fog that had rolled in overnight. "We were successful in discovering where the palace guards frequent when off duty, but you are not going to like it," Nolan reported to Rion. We stood in the center of the war tent, staring at a map of Lios that was sprawled across the table before us.

Flynn pointed to a small building furthest from the palace. "The Milkmaid," he finished for Nolan. Rion shifted uncomfortably on the balls of his feet. "The guards are pretty tight lipped. We spent an entire day within its walls, and not a soul spoke of the king or his plans. Though, they were quite preoccupied." Flynn's face was contorted with disgust, while Nolan's features remained neutral. However, the rage in his eyes told a different story.

"Is the tavern unsavory?" I was confused by the wide range of emotions I saw among the men. I raised my glass to sip the wine within.

"Oh, it's no tavern, Your Highness. It's a brothel," Flynn answered. I choked and sputtered the blood red liquid onto the map. Rion stiffened.

"We are not sending her into a brothel. Not going to happen," he said with a shake of his head.

"Well, if you want information, this is where you get it," Flynn stated. "Though, a woman attending such a place for pleasure and not work would draw attention."

"We'll find another way," Rion snapped.

I placed a hand on his arm. The muscles under the linen of his shirt were wound tight. His gaze met mine. "I can do this, Rion. Our plan will need to change to accommodate, but we need this information."

"There is a possibility the king doesn't know a thing. The likelihood that his guards do is even more slim. It is not worth the risk." Rion pulled out of my grasp to pace the room.

"We need that spear, and we don't have any leads as to where it could be. The odds may not be in our favor, but it is the only chance we have. Unless you have another idea, this is what we are doing," I spoke with authority. Though I valued his opinion, I was in charge. This was the first time I pulled rank on Rion. I had unquestionably followed his lead for months now. It was time he did the same.

Rion threw his hands in the air. "Do you know what they do to women, human women may I add, in those brothels?" His voice rose as he descended upon me. "They are essentially slaves, held against their will and forced to service the males of Lios. You will not be going anywhere near that place," Rion growled in my face.

Rage flooded my veins and clouded my mind on behalf of the women Rion spoke of.

"And who are you to tell me what to do?" I spat back. A few months ago, I may have backed down, but not now. I was no longer the frail and meek woman I had been then. If disguising myself as a patron won't work, there is another that would. "Nolan, make sure the horses are ready. We leave for Lios within the hour." I spun and stormed out of the tent before Rion had the chance to speak again. A loud crash came from the war tent that sounded like wood splintering. Rion's voice rose over the clamor as he yelled at his comrades. Before long, I heard the crunch of snow beneath boots close behind me, as I strode through the camp in the direction of the tent.

"Rion, you are not changing my…" I started as I turned to my pursuer. It wasn't Rion that stood in at the center of the path, but Nolan.

"He's right," he murmured, looking at the ground. "Aisling, Your Highness, please reconsider. It is incredibly dangerous. Sleep on it, and if this is still the path you wish to travel, I will be right at your side. I will do whatever is needed to keep you safe, but please think it through, okay?" Nolan's words hit me in the chest with such force that I thought my heart might have quit beating.

I nodded, because I wasn't sure I could speak around the lump in my throat. Without another word, I continued my way to my tent. I agreed to Nolan's plea, but I knew what my decision would be. Not only would I travel to Lios to attempt to discover what the king knew about the missing spear, but I also intended to put an end to the suffering within the brothel. What Rion had to say only steeled my conviction.

* * *

Rion didn't return that night. I lay wide awake, staring at the canvas ceiling above me. I had had enough time to think about the altercation earlier. I was no longer angry with him and understood where he was coming from, for I would have done the same if he were to knowingly throw himself into danger. I had hoped he would return, so we could discuss it further. I couldn't take it anymore and rose from the bed to find Rion. I didn't want to leave without mending the rift between us.

I pulled on my trousers and boots where I had left them lying on the floor earlier and fastened my cloak around my throat. I exited the tent into the brisk, night air. My breath puffed out in front of me as I strolled through the quiet camp. A couple of men sat around a blazing fire, talking in hushed voices. They dipped their chins to acknowledge me as I walked by.

Rion was nowhere to be seen within the camp, so I went to the cave containing the hot spring. My intuition had been correct. Rion sat at the edge of the spring, his trousers pulled up to his knees and his feet soaking in the warm waters. His shoulders slumped, and his head hung forward. The confidence he normally displayed was gone, leaving behind a look of defeat.

"You here to put me in my place again, *Your Highness*." My gut twisted at his words. I removed my cloak and threw it over one of the boulders along the cavern's edge. I kicked off my boots and rolled up my pantlegs, as well, and joined him.

"That was not my intention," I murmured. "However, I am more capable than you give me credit for."

Rion huffed a breath. "My objection had nothing to do with

your competence. I am finding it harder with each passing day to even fathom putting you in harm's way."

I placed a tentative hand on Rion's. "We are about to start a war. It's inevitable. To save these people, we must take the necessary risks to succeed," I reasoned. "Like I said before, I cannot ask of those what I am not willing to do myself."

Rion finally shifted his gaze onto me. The threads of fate swirled in the sea of green that were his irises. "I don't know if I can," he stated. "Every bone in my body is screaming to steal you away from all of this, for your life is worth allowing this kingdom to fall into ruin. My entire world revolves around you. Without you, I am nothing."

"These are your people too, Rion. We can't leave them in the hands of a king that will see them destroyed beyond recognition." I tried to get Rion to see reason, to guide him back to the mission at hand.

"That's the thing, little fox," he whispered, his voice losing all fight. "The only person I care to see make it out of all of this alive is you." I was shocked by his admission.

"And what of Nolan? Flynn? You'd let them die to spare me?" Though I would give my own life to save his, I couldn't stand by and watch an entire kingdom wither and die.

"Aisling, I am not a good person and never claimed to be. I have done things you wouldn't even be able to fathom. This rebellion was my attempt at redemption for all the pain I have caused others, but now I would see it all burn to the fucking ground to spare you," he informed me.

"But what of the pain it would cause me to leave them all behind. Yes, the bond requires you protect me, but didn't you also say it drives one to keep their mate happy?"

"And that is the reason I fight against my instincts. It's the reason I came here instead of to bed, because I couldn't trust myself to make the right choice." Rion's eyes darkened as they drilled into me. I simply stared back into his gaze, not sure what to say.

His eyes flickered back to the pool before him. The silence between us was deafening. "Do you still intend to go to Lios?" he finally asked.

"Yes," I answered in a hushed tone. "I must do something. Nolan still plans to travel with me. You have taught me well, Rion. I am ready to prove myself to my people." Rion only nodded. He removed his feet from the water and stood, looking down at me.

"Fine, but know this. If Nolan allows anything to befall you, he will not live to see another day upon his return." Rion's threat rang through my head long after he exited the cave. The echo of his words created a pit of uncertainty within me. The plan I had begun to form in my mind after leaving the war tent had to work. This was my chance to prove myself to my people and to Rion. To show them all that I could be the ruler they needed.

I left the warmth of the cave and returned to my tent. The bed was empty, still disheveled from where I had been lying. I crawled back into the furs and closed my eyes, willing my mind to go silent. I wished to feel Rion's strong arms wrapped around me as I drifted off the sleep. I hadn't realized how dependent on his comfort I was. His anger at my decision had been palpable in the cave. However, I had something to prove, not only to him, but also to myself.

I fell into a restless sleep, waking every few hours searching for Rion's sleeping form beside me. When the sun finally rose and the birds began to chirp in the evergreens that surrounded the camp, I huffed a long sigh.

I rose from the bed, eyes dry and puffy, and packed a small bag. I had hoped Rion would be waiting to see us off but was disappointed when only one male stood at the mouth of the path that would carry us over the mountains. Nolan had a pack of his own strapped to his back along with his sword and dagger at his hips.

The only way through the mountains was a treacherous journey on foot. I peered back at the camp one last time, hoping to see Rion's face among the people who had started going about their morning chores. Again, I was disappointed. Either he was still angry with me for opposing his demands, or he was avoiding me to keep himself from forcibly making me stay. "We have to get going," Nolan's murmured voice was filled with empathy.

"Okay," I breathed as a single tear fell down my cheek. If I was successful in my mission, he would have to forgive me. I needed to believe that as I followed Nolan.

The further we moved away from the camp, the more I began to second guess my decision. What if Rion was right? When we finally stopped for the evening, I was a bundle of nervous energy. Nolan read me easily enough. "This won't be easy, but I have faith in you." He whispered across the fire that slowly melted a ring in the snow.

"At least one of us does." I sniffled, trying to stem the continuous dripping from my nose from the cold. I tucked myself deeper into my cloak, but it was no use. I lost feeling in my toes a few hours into our journey, as well, and I shook with such a force it loudly clacked my teeth together.

"Come here. You're freezing." I waved him off claiming I would live. "You have done nothing wrong, Aisling. You don't need to punish yourself for doing what you think is right, no matter how anyone reacts to your decisions. You answer to no one but yourself." I was punishing myself, but not for the reasons he thought. When I still refused to move from the rock I was perched upon, he stood and came to my side, pulling me to my feet. He wrapped me in his arms, his cloak with it. I couldn't help the sigh that came forth as Nolan's warmth melted my frozen body.

"Thank you," I murmured through chattering teeth.

We stood that way for a while until the feeling returned to my extremities, though I feared my toes would never be warm again. "Do you think we truly have a chance?" I asked into the warmth of his chest that my cheek was pressed upon. Doubt seeped in through every crack and crevasse of my mind.

"I do," Nolan said simply. "You have proven yourself time and time again. Against all odds you have succeeded."

"There is just so much at stake, Nolan. So much that could go wrong." To my surprise, Nolan placed a single finger under my chin, forcing me to meet his glacial gaze, the cool blue irises piercing my very soul.

"There is much to lose but more to gain. You know better than anyone that these people cannot continue to live this way. To do nothing is signing their death warrant." I knew all he had spoken was true, but it did not change the fact that I would be forced to choose between two evils.

"How do you choose between duty and those you love?" I croaked, because that is exactly the decision I may have to make.

"That is the burden a ruler must carry, and not one that anyone would willingly choose."

"My mother had to make that choice once." I thought of the pain she must have endured as she watched Cara carry me off into the night, never knowing if she would ever see me again. But she had a duty to protect her people, though I am sure she would have rather been the one to ensure my safety.

"Your mother made many sacrifices that night," remorse coated his words, "but those sacrifices were not in vain. Had she not sent you away, you would have perished with the rest of them. She held off the armies so you could escape, for she knew they didn't stand a chance without her and her power."

A whisper echoed deep within my mind—distorted, fragmented, and too faint to understand. I narrowed my eyes. "You speak as if you were there."

Nolan brushed rough fingers over my cheek. "We all were, Aisling." My head spun as I recounted the time I had asked Rion if he had ever fought in a war. He had…the war that slaughtered my people. Nolan saw the conflict that was rising within me, the way my body went ridged. It had never occurred to me that they would have been involved in the invasion. "You need to understand. We didn't have a choice. Rion didn't have a choice. Our fathers were deep in the false king's council."

"There is always a choice," I stated, pulling from Nolan's warmth. The cold wind slammed into me, disorienting me. I dropped to my knees, my breath coming in rapid pants as the realization struck me in the chest like a blade, that these males, who I had blindly followed in the hopes of reclaiming my crown and have come to trust, were a part of the very force to stole everything from me. My home. My mother. My people. My life had become an endless loop of betrayal and broken trust.

Nolan tentatively placed a hand on my shoulder. When I didn't shy away from his touch, he sank to his knees behind me, wrapping his arms fully around me. A scream rebounded off the mountain side. I realized the sound was emanating from me when my throat started to burn with the force.

Nolan said nothing. He just held me, while I let out the pent-up emotions that I had stored away for far too long. I felt the tremble of his hands where they gripped me tightly, how he clung to me as if I was the only thing keeping *him* together. "I am sorry, Aisling," he whispered into my hair after my screaming ceased. "If I could take it back, if I could give my own life to change that night, I would. I know Rion feels the same." I thought of all the time we had spent together the last couple months. Rion's self-hatred and intense guilt wasn't only from the death off his mother, but all he had cost her people. Logically, I knew that if they had refused to participate in the invasion, it wouldn't have mattered. They would have most likely been killed for their disobedience.

A hoarse sob tore from my battered throat. I cried until my eyes were swollen and there were no more tears to be shed. I turned to Nolan, finally meeting his softened features. He wiped the moisture from my face, that had already begun to freeze, solidifying my pain into beautifully tragic crystals of ice. His gentle touch soothed a small portion of my aching heart. "I vow to you, my queen, that I will do everything in my power to ensure all of our wrongs are righted, that all that has been taken from you is restored." Nolan withdrew a small blade from within his cloak. He ran the bald along his palm, blood sweeping from the wound. He squeezed his hand into a fist, the crimson liquid staining the snow as it dripped to the ground. "I swear, on the blood that runs through my veins, that I will fight at your side until my dying breath." I saw it then within his eyes, something I never thought I would from Nolan. Love. Deep and unending.

Before I had a chance to react, he grabbed my hand and drew

the blade across it. He clamped our two wounded hands together. As our blood mixed and mingled, warmth spread up my arm. The burning increased until it struck my heart, nearly stealing my breath away. Then, it rapidly retreated, allowing the cold from the mountain air to seep back in. "What was that?" I breathed.

"A blood oath. I am bound to you, to fulfill my vow." He pushed back his sleeve, unveiling blue markings that now crawled across his skin that pulsed with the magic woven between us. I rolled up my own sleeve, revealing matching swirls and symbols etched into my flesh.

"What if you can't?" I asked as I continued to examine my inked arm.

"If the blood oath is broken, the magic will claim my life in exchange." My eyes shot to his.

"Why? Why would you make such an oath that you may not be able to keep?"

"Because if I should fail, I would rather die than live with that failure, anyway," he stated matter-of-factly. I could feel the magic between us. It wasn't the same as the bond that Rion and I shared, but it was just as powerful, linking our lives together. I looked at the male that had once held such animosity towards me. His faith in me gave me the confidence that I had been lacking. For the first time in weeks, I let myself believe in the possibility of victory and in the strength found not just within myself, but in the bonds forged through trust and shared sacrifice. Tomorrow would bring new challenges, but tonight, I allowed the fragile hope to bloom in my heart.

Chapter 24

Minutes turned into hours, which turned into days of grueling travel through the snowy mountains before we descended the foothills outside the city. My shoulders ached where my pack dug into them, and my thighs burned with every step. Nolan had shed his glamour when the fortified city had come into view, and I wore a simple baby-blue dress that hugged my lean curves, the plunging neckline exposed the swell of my breast and nearly reached my navel, with my cloak pulled snug over my head to conceal my ears.

As we stepped through the main gates of Lios, I observed the city around us. The main roads and alleyways were immaculate. The cobblestones appeared as if they had been polished before our arrival. The buildings that surrounded us on all sides were tall and elegant, built of stone and adorned in gold and silver. There were also smaller wooden structures. Though they were simpler in architecture, they were no less refined.

The people were dressed in ostentatious clothing that emphasized their beauty and flaunted their wealth. The array of colors overloaded my senses, for most of my life I had only had access to linens in shades of brown and white.

I admired purples and pinks of the females' dresses with distaste. The gowns didn't leave a lot to the imagination, with their steep necklines, open backs, and shear skirts. At one point, I would have wished to own such attire. Now, I wanted nothing more than to shed my dress in favor of my fighting leathers. My movements were inhibited by the fabric that gathered at my ankles and restricted access to the long dagger I had strapped to my thigh.

Nolan led us through the throng to a beautiful two-story house with a large sign that read 'The Milkmaid' over the entrance. The sun had begun to set, and males flooded in through the double doors. Nolan led me around the back of the building to the simple door that he and Flynn had scoped out. I checked the handle, finding it was locked. I assumed it was more for keeping people in than keeping them out. I quickly slumped my pack off my shoulders along with my cloak and handed them to Nolan. "I will return in an hour," Nolan exclaimed. "If there is any sign of trouble, you get out of there."

"I'll be alright." I reassured him for the millionth time. Nolan pulled out a set of picks and set to work on the lock on the door. With a subtle click, the door swung open with a creak. I dipped inside, pushing it closed behind me. The air was warm against my chilled face but smelled heavily of sex and sweat, with a hint of incense that attempted to rid the air of the foul odor. I breathed through my mouth as I continued down a long hall.

I came to the end of the hall, looking left and right down the dark intersecting hall that was lined with doors. I turned left, led by intuition. Behind one of the doors came male grunts and shouts of pleasure, mixed with the soft weeping of the woman trapped inside.

I paused by the door drawing a focused breath. I turned the handle slowly to ensure no sound was made. Once it was open wide enough, I peered inside. A woman lay upon the bed. Her lip was busted and fear shone in her eyes as she looked up at the male who towered over her. The makeup she'd been wearing was now smudged across her face.

I gathered my skirts in my hands and palmed my blade. The woman's eyes flickered in my direction as I opened the door a bit more so I could slip in. I shot my finger to my mouth to keep her from alerting the male of my intrusion. She nodded her head slightly. The male none the wiser, too absorbed in his own pleasure to notice the slight dip in her chin.

I snuck up behind him, keeping my footsteps light. By the time he knew what was happening, he was sprawled naked on the floor gasping for breath with my blade at his throat. My knees sat in the pit of his elbows to pin his arms to the floor. The woman scurried off the bed as she covered herself with a sheet. "Go to the back door. Its unlocked." She hesitated for only a moment before she rushed from the room, gathering her clothing from the floor.

I turned my attention back to the male before me. "Make a sound and you die," I growled.

"Wh…what do you want," he stuttered.

I huffed a laugh. "What I want is for your kind to stop thinking humans are here to serve you. That you can use them any way you see fit and suffer no consequences." I pressed the blade into his skin slightly. Blood welled to my delight. I would have to decapitate the male in order to kill him, for no mortal wound would do.

Black magic started to seep from the tips of his finger as he rallied his power. His fear was quickly replaced by anger once he caught sight of my ears. His reeking breath hit me in the face when he leaned into my blade and said, "You don't have the strength to kill me, human. You have no clue of what you have gotten yourself into." I could feel as he reached his mind out to entrap mine. A look of surprise came over his face when he ran into the mental wall.

"I think I know exactly what I have gotten myself into." I shifted so that my weight was above my dagger placed my other hand onto the dull edge of the blade. I leaned into it. The fleshy part of his neck gave way easily, but I had to put in more effort to get the blade to pass through his spine. He struggled for only a moment before his head popped off and rolled to the other side of the room. Blood sprayed into my face and across the floor, but thankfully missed the fabric of my dress. I still had much to do.

I pushed off the man. My stomach rolled as I looked at the blood that covered my hands. I heaved but refused to allow the bile to exit my mouth. I swallowed it back down and went to the water basin that was on a table near the door. I scrubbed the blood from my face and hands quickly, checking the mirror that hung above to ensure I didn't leave behind any evidence of what I had done.

The woman staring back was unrecognizable. Piercing blue eyes and long plaited black hair. My cheek bones were high and sharp, and freckles splattered across a small narrow nose. The last time I had looked into a mirror to admire my reflection was years ago.

I straightened my dress and moved from the room, locking

the door behind me to ensure no one walked in on the mess before I was done. I continued down the hall and checked each room as I passed. They were all empty.

I reached the top of a spiral staircase, voices traveling from below. I descended the stairs which led to a large, crowed room. Aos Si males packed the space, siting on benches or at tables. Human women sat astride their laps and strolled through the room with platters of drinks and food. I stuck to the shadows of the room, trying to gauge my surroundings before I drew attention to myself.

A group of males caught my eye. They wore leathers with the royal crest stitched into the chest plate. My targets. I stepped into the light and walked across the room with a swish of my hips. The males turned in my direction, drawn by my presence. Their eyes traveled down the length of my body with sickening grins plastered on their faces. A shiver tore through my body.

The women among them looked confused, for they didn't recognize me as one of their own. However, they did not correct the males, who had assumed just that. One of the men stood, meeting me halfway to the table. He circled me. "This one's mine, boys," he called to his companions. Disappointment flashed on their faces. I remained quiet, not trusting the vile words that attempted to fly out of my mouth.

I took the man by the hand and guided back to the stairs, leading him to one of the empty rooms on the second floor and shutting the door behind us. The soft click of the latch seemed to echo through the quiet space. The male didn't waste any time, wrapping his arms around me from behind. My skin crawled under his touch. "I have never seen a human as beautiful as you," he whispered in my ear. "You must make your master very happy, for I am sure every male here would pay a pretty penny to be with you." I wanted to vomit as his hands began to roam over my body, leaving no piece of it untouched. I had to play my cards right, if I wanted to discover what the male knew of the king's plan. Then, he would meet the same fate as the other male who thought he could touch what was not freely given.

"Thank you, my lord." I pitched my voice to an octave higher. He placed a kiss on my neck, inhaling my scent deeply. "You are a palace guard?" I asked meekly.

"Mmhmm," he confirmed as he continued his perusal. I was at least grateful he was gentle.

"Do you travel often? I've never been outside of the brothel," I lied. I moved things along as quickly as I dared before he got tired of foreplay and wanted more.

"I have." His answers were short, his mind on only one thing as he began to gather my skirts in his hands. I spun, coming face-to-face with the large male before he reached the dagger I had replaced at my thigh. I gingerly stroked my hand down his face as his grubby hands groped my ass.

"Where are you headed next? Maybe you can come find me once you return and tell me of your adventure." The male sighed as he pressed his body against me. His erection struck my pubic bone. I stifled the urge to push him away from me and run.

"You are a talkative one." He ground against me again. "If you must know, we are headed to the fairy lands to retrieve a weapon for the king," the guard spoke freely, for what was the harm in telling a woman who was forbidden to leave the confines of the brothel.

The spear was in the fairy lands. It's a lead, but not a lot to go on. "What kind of weapon?" I could tell he was getting tired of my questioning. His hands gripped my waist like an iron vise. I knew I would be bruised by morning.

"Why would a whore need to know such things? I am not paying your master for you to speak," he sneered.

"I'm sorry, I was just…" My sentence was interrupted with a close-fisted blow to my face. Pain bloomed across my cheek and into my eye socket. I raised my hand to evaluate the damage. The skin had split over the bone and blood trickled from the wound, dripping from my chin onto my dress.

"Gods, shut the fuck up and strip." I saw red in an instant. I backed up a step, appearing to be following his commands. I kicked out my foot and hit him square in the groin. The male grabbed his crotch and crumbled in on himself with a shout of pain. "You will fucking pay for that whore," he said through gritted teeth.

I ran for the door, but he caught my skirts on the way by causing me to fall hard on my stomach. I gasped for air as I attempted to crawl out of his reach, but he yanked me back. The ripping of fabric filled the room. "Let go of me," I yelled, clawing at the hands that were climbing up my now bare leg. He flipped me to my back and knelt between my legs. Panic rose within me as he grabbed my wrists and held them above my head.

"Stop now!" he demanded, spit spraying my face. I struggled against his hold, but it was no use. He was too strong. I had allowed him too close and now he had full control. I berated myself for the error as I kept trying to free myself. He leaned down, only inches from my face. "I can make this pleasant for you if you promise to behave." Tears pricked my eyes. I was trapped with no way to save myself. My dagger was far out of my reach, and I had no leverage in this position to get him off.

He adjusts his grip, placing both of my wrists into one of his gigantic hands. With his newly freed hand, he started to gather my skirts once more. "Please," I begged. "Please let me go."

"Not going to happen. I will get what I paid for." His hand stumbled upon the bindings of my sheath. "What have we here," he smirked. "The kitten has claws." He withdrew the dagger and examined the sharp blade that glistened in the soft lantern light. "Where did you get such an immaculate weapon. Stole it, I'm sure." A growl emanated from the back of my throat, which only seemed to please him more. In my fury, I leaned up as far as his restraint would allow and spit into his face. All the amusement drained from his face. He took the blade and ran the sharp edge across the bare skin of my exposed thigh. My scream pierced the room. A wicked grin spread across his face as he did it again, a few inches higher. My screams turned into cries for help, which only made him laugh. "Funny thing about places such as this, they don't care what we do as long as you leave the room alive. And even then, there is nothing money can't buy."

After what felt like a thousand lacerations across my thighs, my energy waned. Blood pooled around me, soaking into the back of my dress. Victory shone in the male's eyes as he pushed my skirt to my hips, and I did not put up a fight. He ran the hilt of the knife over the deep wounds he had carved into my skin. Fire surged up my legs everywhere he touched, until he reached the one place I was so desperately trying to protect. I sobbed when he forcefully plunged the hilt deep within me.

Then, a loud bang erupted down the hall as door after door was broken down. The male looked confused when suddenly the door to the room we occupied flung open. The man scrambled away from me, my blade sliding free from my body now held in front of him. Nolan appeared within the door frame flanked by two other Aos Si males. "Aisling!" he screamed as he saw the scene before him. The other males surged forward towards the male cowering in the corner of the room, while he came to my side, carefully gauging the wounds that littered my broken body. He unclasped his cloak and threw it over me. He gathered me off the ground. I whimpered as the movement caused my thighs to rub together. "Shhh. You'll be okay. Everything is okay," he attempted to reassure me as he ran for the door.

Shouts resounded through the brothel, as well as the sound of steel on steel. While I was inside gathering information, Nolan was raising a small force of those who swore their allegiance to the rebellion. My consciousness faded in and out. Nolans concerned face my only view.

He slowed his pace as we reached the gates to not draw any unwanted attention. "Too much ale," Nolan called to the guards with a hint of false amusement in his voice. They laughed, calling back to Nolan that he should keep a tighter leash on his female, but didn't stop us as we strode through, the last of the sunlight fading beyond the horizon. The screech of metal sounded behind us as the gate closed for the night. No one would be allowed in or out until sunrise. My last memory was that of the woman we left behind. "The girls," I managed to croak out.

"They'll get them out," Nolan promised. My eyes fluttered shut, and I was swept away into violent dreams of trauma and horror.

Chapter 25

It was dark by the time we arrived back at the camp. The only faint light was that of the full moon, which was obscured by the dense clouds overhead. My wounds on my thighs had healed into faint, white lines, but the internal scars had only festered on our journey back. We were a day later than we had intended to be, due to the fact we had to wait for my wounds to heal enough for travel. I refused to tell Nolan what had happened inside that room, and he didn't pry, but I was able to relay the information about the location of the spear. "There is a cave on the southern tip of the island guarded by a ruthless dragon shifter," Nolan said. "If it was hidden anywhere, it would be there." Visions of my assault had tormented me so deeply that the mention of a dragon barely stirred me.

"You can't tell Rion," I finally said as we walked through the quiet camp. Nolan's grief-filled face turned to me with a nod. He blamed himself, despite my reassurance that it was not his fault. I knew I would need to tell him eventually, but I valued Nolan's life. The one who violated me was gone, but revenge still needed a face. And for him, Nolan would be close enough.

Nolan bowed as we approached my tent before walking off into the night towards his own. I was utterly exhausted as I threw back the tent flaps, revealing Rion sitting at the desk, composing what looked to be a letter. He looked up at me, and I found a resounding amount of emotion within his eyes. He jumped up from the chair he had occupied and rushed to me, lifting me into his arms. Rion set me down and scoured my body for signs of injury. I plastered a fake smile on my face.

"You're okay." It wasn't a question but a reassuring statement for himself. He inhaled deeply, like he finally was able to breathe fully knowing I had made it back safely. I may be breathing, but I was not okay. "I am so sorry," he apologized as he leaned his forehead on mine.

"It's okay." I understood why he had reacted the way he did. However, his need to protect me, despite the consequences, could cost us the rebellion. "But it cannot happen again. You need to allow me to lead without interference. I appreciate your expertise and experience. I will take your opinion into consideration, but that does not mean I have to take it."

"I understand," he said, softly. "Were you successful?"

Images of the Aos Si propped above me, covered in my blood, flashed in my mind. "We were. The spear is in Tír na nÓg. Nolan believes it is hidden within the Dragon's Den. Nolan was also able to raise a small force to liberate the women of The Milkmaid. The males had a plan of escape and will be joining our forces once they find a safe place to deposit the women." It felt wrong not to divulge the full story, however, Rion was unpredictable. I didn't want him to blame Nolan for a situation I had foolishly gotten myself into.

Rion smiled brightly, which made my withholding of the truth even more painful. "I am so incredibly proud of you," he exclaimed. I gave him a sheepish smile of my own. If he saw through my façade, he didn't mention it.

"We have the next four months to finalize our plan of attack and to ensure the army is ready once we have returned from the island," Rion stated. I gave him a confused look. "We can only travel through the veil when it is its thinnest, which will be during Beltane. And there is the matter of completing our bond." Nerves made my hands sweat.

Rion misread my nerves, stating "We'll see it done, love."

"How are we going to possibly travel to Tír na nÓg, retrieve the spear, and make back before the veil thickens within a day?" It seemed like an impossible task.

"Time moves a bit differently in the fairy lands."

"What do you mean by time moves differently?"

"Two days there tends to be a few hours here. Beltane is celebrated for a week in the fairy lands. It is the time of new beginnings and fertility. Festivals are held across the land with bonfires and the dancing of the May Pole along with other more… exciting festivities," Rion insinuated as he grabbed my ass and kissed my neck. I fought the urge to shy away from his touch, his hands morphing into that of my attackers.

"Oh," was my only reply as his lips traveled across my skin. I forced myself to push the memories aside as his hands slowly explored my body.

I gently pushed him back. "The sun will be up soon, and I

need to bathe. Then, I need to call a meeting with the generals to inform them of what I have discovered." I realized swiftly that I was going to have to tell him what had occurred in Lios sooner rather than later, because I was not going to be able to avoid his touch.

"Would you mind if I joined you?" Rion proposed. I looked at the copper tub in the corner of the tent then scanned his towering form.

"I don't think we will both fight in there together," I said with a forced laugh.

A grin took over his face. "Ye of little faith." He hurried to gather buckets from the spring before I had a chance to reply. Once the tub was full, Rion quickly undressed and stepped into the steaming water. He sat, sloshing water over the sides and gestured for me to join him. His legs were too long, forcing his knees to bend and peak out of the water.

I reluctantly began shedding my clothing. "What is that?" he asked as I removed my blouse, reveling my ink covered arm. He held out his hand, which I took, to examine it more closely.

"Nolan, he made a blood oath to do everything in his power to ensure I gain all that I had lost." I feared for a moment he was angry, but only gratitude painted his face. "He told me that you guys were involved in the invasion." The look of surprise and panic on his face made me quickly state, "I'm not mad. I was at first, but I understand." His anxiety melted away with my affirmation.

His fingers traced the intricate lines of the markings, then over the flat of my stomach. He tugged at my waistband, pushing my pants down my legs. He only got them to my knees until he suddenly stopped, his eyes glued to the other marks I carried. A sharp breath flooded my lungs as his eyes shifted up to mine once more. "And what is this?" Tears welled in my eyes as I looked at my hands, avoiding his. He stood in the tub, water splashed at my feet, as he lifted my chin. I felt his mind brush against my mental wall, asking to be let in. *Show me.* My vines parted like a doorway, allowing him entrance. His body vibrated with red hot rage as he filtered through my memories.

"Don't blame him," I whispered. Rion looked as though he may not heed my pleas, until he seated himself within the tub again, gesturing for me to join him.

I quickly removed my boots, stepping out of my pants, and straddle his lap, laying my head on his chest. Rion brought his arms around me, holding me tightly. "I wish I could bring that prick back to life, for he did not suffer nearly enough for he has done." I felt numb, barely feeling the warm water the surrounded us.

Rion hugged me tighter. *I will never let you out of my sight again. I should have been there.* He spoke into my mind. The intimacy of the action made my heart hammer in my chest. Rion's presence in my mind was comforting.

Why couldn't you go with me?

My father was influential man. I was more likely to be identified than Nolan. I would have exposed the whole operation. Rion stiffened at the mention of his father, like he always did. I wish there was something I could do to soothe the trauma he had sustained at the hands of the man who was supposed to protect him.

I turned my head so I could see his face. "He will pay. I swear to you he will pay for what he did to you and your mother." I grasp hold of the anger—felt it throb within my soul. I let it consume me, for it was better than the pain that threatened to drown me.

His eyes met mine. "I have no doubt." He cupped my face in his hand. "You are beautiful when you promise vengeance, little fox."

The sound of crunching snow erupted outside the tent when Flynn burst inside. His eyes grew wide. "Shit sorry," he exclaimed, turning quickly before he saw something he certainly shouldn't see. "I didn't realize you were back, Your Highness."

Rion covered me with his large hands. "What the fuck do you need?" he growled through his teeth.

"We received word from Lios. Due to an attack on The Milkmaid, the king ordered a search for the males involved with a hefty bounty for their capture. It seems they made it out of the city, but the king posted extra guards at the pass. He also sent a small force to begin canvasing the mountains." Rion jumped from the tub, splashing water all over the floor of the tent.

I clambered out after him and caught the towel he threw in my direction. "We need to move north. Quickly. I hate to give up our vantage point, but if we are discovered now, we won't stand a chance. The men aren't ready to fight," Rion stated before he thought better of the command and turned my way. "I mean, that is what I would suggest, Your Highness."

"I agree, we need to move, now." Flynn left the tent to relay the command. The camp was in chaos when we emerged from the tent. My damp hair froze in the frigid air as we helped dismantle the camp and pack the necessities in wagons that had been stowed at the base of the mountain. We were moving before the sun crested the tallest peak.

Flynn broke off from the group to locate Aos Si allies. "I'll track down the males from Lios, then any others on our way north," he stated before he left.

"We should reach Baile by Beltane, meet us then." Rion held his hand out to his friend, which he took in return. "Be careful."

Rion and I rode at the head of the company, guiding the army along the eastern shoreline to avoid villages and stay hidden. The feel of Bryn beneath me, the roll of my hips as I moved with her stride, anchored me.

The forest came into view by the time evening set it. The journey would be slower now, burdened by the army, most of whom traveled on foot. Rion and I planned the training regimen. Nolan would oversee the soldiers with help from the generals, while Rion continued guiding me in the use of magic.

I found myself at the center of a makeshift war tent later that evening, Rion and Nolan on either side. It was not as grand as the one in the mountains, but it would do. The generals look to me awaiting my orders. "We are going to need to push hard over the next few months, moving quickly in the day. At this pace, we will reach Baile a month before Beltane. Early morning hours every other day will be devoted to training. We travel as far as we can during the day, limiting breaks as much as possible." I feared that the intensity of training and travel would be too much for the frail humans, but we had no other choice. "Once we reach Baile, we will begin preparations to obtain the spear, utilizing the fairy mound a few miles north of the village."

"What of our rations? We were running low before we left," Cian asked.

Rion replied, "We currently have enough to last a week, we will supplement with what can be hunted and gathered along the way."

"An army this large is bound to draw attention. How are we going to avoid being intercepted?" William spoke with disdain. He disagreed with moving the army as a whole and had suggested splitting it into four smaller companies. Rion and I agreed that it would be a poor choice.

Our army was entirely made up of farmers, except for the four generals, Rion, Nolan and I. They had been training, but none of them were naturally gifted in the art of fighting. Without magic of their own and their limited skill, they would never survive if they were attacked. At least together, we had strength in numbers.

"We will continue to move along the coast under the cover of the forest and away from the main roads," I addressed William. "The king still does not know this army exists, and we plan to keep it that way for as long as possible."

William grumbled inaudibly under his breath. I ignored his disrespect, though Rion and Nolan looked like they were about to gut the man. I had had enough. I waved my hand, tired and annoyed. "Your dismissed. Rest and be prepared to move at daybreak."

The generals exited the tent without another word. I huffed a breath of annoyance. Rion glared after the men. "I know I told you to give him a break, but I would like to rescind my request. If he does not find some ounce of respect, I will personally make him crawl before you and beg for your forgiveness."

"I second that," Nolan said through gritted teeth.

"I'm untested. His reaction is totally understandable. It's not the first time someone has found me to be a disappointment," I said pointedly in Nolan's direction. A hint of pink swept across his cheeks.

Nolan reached out to place a hand on my shoulder, keeping one eye on Rion to ensure he didn't lose said hand. "I have never been so happy to be wrong. You have grown into a woman, a warrior, that anyone worth their salt would want to follow. You still have much to learn, but you have proven repeatedly that you have the courage and strength to see this through and come out on the other side victorious." His words pierced my heart.

"Thank you," I replied as I patted his hand. I looked over at Rion, expecting to see rage radiating off him because of the contact, but he couldn't have looked prouder.

Nolan removed his hand and stretched, drawing attention away from the emotional moment. "I better get some rest, as well. I will see you two in the morning." Nolan nearly ran from the tent. Rion let out a laugh.

A smile still lit up his face when he pulled me into his arms. I peered into the endless emerald seas that were his eyes. Nothing but pride and love shone back at me.

Rion led me to the small tent he had erected for us before our meeting with the generals. We laid side-by-side on the bedroll in quiet contentment. I missed the bed we had been forced to leave behind us in the hurry to evacuate the camp. Actually, all my new belongings and luxuries were left behind, minus a few changes of clothing and bars of soap I had shoved into my saddle bags.

Rion's breathing grew deep. Subtle snores escaped his throat. I snuggled close to him and closed my eyes, praying that sleep would soon come for me, as well. There were fleeting moments where I wished I could go back to a time when life was easy. When my days were filled with gathering herbs, caring for my grandmother and patients. When the fate of the entire kingdom didn't lie in my hands.

However, when I looked at Rion, I knew I wouldn't change any of it if I could. He has taught me more about myself, what I am capable of, since we met than I had learned my entire life. The next three months of travel would be strenuous for us all, but with him by my side, I knew we would succeed. Rion was my source of strength. My courage. My home. Without him, I would be nothing but a lost, naive princess without a throne.

Chapter 26

Three months and twenty-three days later, I was standing in what was once the village of Baile. It had now been nearly six months, since I left the village burning to the ground. The charred remains of houses and scorched land, all that was left behind of the once vibrant village. Purple and white speckled flowers grew among the ruins, vines of ivy weaved throughout. I ran my finger along the delicate bell-shaped flower of the foxglove.

Emotion clogged my throat as the long dead guilt wormed its way back in. There was no sign that anyone survived that dreaded night that the Dullahan had come for me. I walked alone down a path I knew like the back of my hand. My surroundings were familiar, yet different. I came to a small clearing. My breath caught as I looked upon the one-room cabin sitting at its center that I had called home for ten years. The building had succumbed to neglect. The roof sagged from rot, shingles missing like broken teeth. The flower beds were overgrown and flooded with weeds. The shutters were half torn from the windows, and vines had begun to climb the moss-covered walls.

My eyes snagged on a large pile of ash on my right. I knelt by the long-burnt pyre. "How things have changed," I murmured. My heart swelled with sorrow. Whether it was to myself or the women who raised me, I did not know. "Why? Why didn't you tell me?" I took a handful of the ash and allowed it to fall from my hand, carried upon the gentle breeze. I wanted to be angry with my grandmother, but another emotion took hold. "I miss you." My words chased the last of the ash that fell from my grasp, slipping through my fingers like sand in an hourglass.

I stood and refrained from going into the tiny cabin. There was nothing here for me anymore but memories of hunger and loss. Any of happy memories left were stored within my heart to be carried with me always.

Instead of returning down the path I had come, I retraced my route of escape from the Dullahan, reliving the night my entire life changed. The forest was alive with the chirping birds and the rustling of small animals in the brush. I watched my footing, branches and roots littered the ground before me, attempting to snag my feet on the way by.

The sheen of metal caught my attention out of the corner of my eye. I knelt and pulled at the silver chain that stuck out from under the dead leaves. I couldn't believe my eyes when I unearthed the large jet-black onyx pendant. I never thought I would ever see the beautiful stone again. The clasp was broken, so I shoved it deep in the pocket of my leather trousers.

"You shouldn't be out here alone." Before I could even recognize the voice, I willed the vines upon the forest floor to tether my intruder to the ground. They wrapped around his legs and ankles tightly. Rion looked pleased with himself when he looked upon his bonds. "That was impressive. No hesitation. Good. Now release them."

A sly smile skated across my face. I circled him just outside his reach. "I don't think I will." My abilities have improved tenfold. The earth completely bent to my will. I tightened the vines ever so slightly. Enough to cause discomfort but not to severely injure. They worked their way up his abdomen, snaring his arms as well. I came up behind him, lips to his ear. "I think I might leave you here. Might do you some good."

I found I enjoyed playing with the prey I caught in my web, especially when it was a six-foot four, raven-haired, Aos Si warrior. While Rion worked on getting me physically ready for the war that was about to ensue, I worked on getting my mind prepared. Emotions like guilt, sorrow, and fear had no place on the battlefield. I sealed those away behind my foxglove wall and replaced them with a slow-boiling rage.

"Now, now, little fox. Is that any way to treat your mate?" Rion let out a gasp as I tightened the vines once more. He struggled for breath. I let him flounder for a moment before I allowed the vines to pool at his feet.

Rion drew a full breath as his eyes darkened. My body responded to the lust within them. I learned quickly while training with him that he also enjoyed being played with. He lounged at me, but I was quicker, sidestepping him. I clicked my tongue at him. "Is that all you have, old man?"

"You better run, little fox, for when I catch you, I am going to fuck you so hard, you won't walk straight for days." I took off at top speed through the trees, Rion hot on my heels. I may be faster, but my moves were predictable.

When I no longer heard his pursuit, I slowed to a steady jog. I kept my ears trained on my surroundings. A branch snapped behind me, causing my head to spin in that direction. I ran smack into a hard chest. Rion's arms pinned mine to my side. Though I could easily get out of his hold, I wanted him to keep his promise.

He backed me into a large oak tree. The bark bit into my back through my thin blouse as he pressed himself into me. "Gods, woman," he breathed into the crook of my neck. He released my arms, which flew around his neck. The ripping of fabric filled the wood as he ripped my trousers from my body. My shirt followed suit, leaving me bare in the forest before him. "You're going to have to stop ripping my clothing," I said breathlessly. "I only have one more set."

He lifted me off my feet. I wrapped my legs around his waist as he braced his hands beneath me to support my weight. He pressed his hard length that was still restrained with his britches against my bare sex. I moaned loudly. "I have to make a trip to a local village for supplies. I'll get you more then." It took many weeks, but I was finally able to keep the traumatic memories at bay and enjoy these moments between us again.

He ground himself against me once more, making all thoughts of ripped clothing filter out of my mind. Rion shifted my weight to one hand and release his cock from its leather prison. He thrusted deep inside me in one stroke. "Fuck," he shouted into the air as a feral moan ripped from my lips.

He did as he promised, savagely pounding into me as my back was rubbed raw from the bark of the tree. The mix of pain and pleasure only heightened the experience, allowing me to reach climax twice before Rion found his. He eased himself out of me and placed me back on my feet. I stood on the tips of my toes and placed a kiss at the corner of his mouth.

I looked down at my naked body and the tattered remains of my clothing. "It's going to be rather strange when I stride back into camp in only my boots." Rion quickly realized his error. Every time my clothing ended up in ribbons, we were within our tent. He stripped off his shirt and handed it over.

He was much larger than I, and his shirt rested more like a dress on my body. The hem ended just below my knees. I gathered what remained of my clothing, and we began to walk back towards Baile. The war encampment was erected among the trees along the village outskirts. "What was it you found back there?" Rion asked as we drew nearer.

I pulled the onyx from my pocket and handed it to him. He turned the stone over in his hand, examining it. "It was my mother's. The only thing I ever had of hers. I lost it when I made my escape from the Dullahan," I explained.

"Hmmm. Interesting." He plopped the stone back into my awaiting hand.

"What's so interesting about a piece of ordinary rock?" I questioned. Though it held sentimental value to me, it was unlikely it meant anything to him.

He cocked his head. "You don't know what that stone does, do you?" I looked at him confused and shook my head. "It is no ordinary stone, little fox. When the Morrigan blessed the humans with the gift of sight, the other Gods felt that the power infringed upon the basic human rights of others. So, they created a gemstone that could blind the seers, keeping those who possessed it hidden from them. It also suppresses a seer's abilities. Knowing the future is sometimes too heavy a weight to bear. Your mother was attempting to shield you from any more prophecies, I suspect."

My mother had continued to protect me, even in death. I thought of all the times I sought the feel of smooth stone beneath my thumb. How it had always given me comfort and a sense of protection.

"I wish I could have had the chance to know her." The pain of her absence threatened to overwhelm me.

Rion placed his arm around my shoulders and gave me a squeeze. "She would be proud of who you have become. Her legacy will live on through you." He placed a gentle kiss on my temple.

The camp was bustling as the men prepared for training. Nolan had been putting them through hard drills, but he believed they would be ready to see combat in just a few weeks. However, we had yet to hear from Flynn. Beltane was only two days away and he had yet to return with the Aos Si. Rion had told me not to worry, but I could tell Flynn's absence was making him anxious.

I had hoped that Flynn would make it back for me and Rion's bonding ceremony tomorrow night. Rion assured me that Nolan would be enough to stand guard while we completed our bond, for I refused to have the entire garrison there to witness our union. I was incredibly nervous, but I trusted Nolan. Aside from Rion, Nolan and Flynn were the only ones that I trusted.

Rion and I oversaw all training maneuvers, since I completed my training. It had given me the opportunity to practice leading an army into battle. We also kept an eye on the Aos Si, flooding the watch tower that guarded the fairy mound, which could be seen from the edge of the forest.

Though I had spent ten years only a few miles from the mound, I had never gotten a glimpse of it. It was a large domed piece of earth covered in vibrant green grass. Heavy fog clouded the top of the hill. We would need to reach the crest to utilize the portal to Tír na nÓg.

Rion didn't seem overly concerned about the fifty extra soldiers that guarded our only passage to the fairy lands. We hope to use the cover of darkness to shield us long enough to reach the top.

The evening came swiftly. Rion kept the camp warded at all times, but he spent the first few hours after the sunset checking the perimeter of the camp. Nolan joined me most nights while Rion was away to keep me company, or perhaps Flynn's absence was starting to eat away at him, as well. "So, I have something I have been meaning to talk to you about," I said around the lip of my wine glass.

"And what is that?" Nolan asked.

"You aren't going to, like, watch? You know? During the ceremony?" This question had been nagging me, since I first found out that the ceremony had to be guarded.

Nolan chuckled. "I will need to remain alert at all times and close to the both of you to keep you both safe." Heat flooded my cheeks. "Once the bond is complete every emotion, every sense will be heightened. Touch, smell, taste. Even your hearing and vision will be sensitive to sight and sound. It is an extremely erotic experience for everyone involved, including the guards." My jaw hit the floor of the tent.

"What the fuck is that supposed to mean?" I was completely awestruck that we were this close, and no one had thought to inform me that Nolan would be affected by the ritual.

Nolan laughed at my reaction, the sound gruff and becoming more familiar with each passing day. "Let's just say, many bonding ceremonies in Tír na nÓg turn into a big fuck fest." I was utterly speechless. "But don't worry, Your Highness. Your mate will not allow anything to occur that you are not comfortable with. Nevertheless, I very much like my cock where it is, and Rion doesn't have a decent track record for sharing." That put my mind at ease, as we finished our wine and stew that he had brought for me.

Rion returned before long. Nolan bid us farewell and strode off into the dark towards his own tent. "So, Nolan had some interesting things to say about the effects that the completion of our bond will have on us… and others." Rion paused mid-step towards our bedroll where I lay. "Care to explain why I had to hear it from him and not you?"

Rion hesitated to devise an explanation. "Well, I have already spoken to Nolan. He will refrain from acting on his impulses. However, there is no saying what either of us will agree to in the moment. I was going to tell you this evening, but it seems he's gotten to it before me."

I could tell he was prepared to call off the ceremony if I wished it, so I hopped to my feet and went to him. "There is nothing that would change my mind about you. Nothing. Whatever happens is meant to be."

The fates had chosen this male for me. They had known he would be what I needed in order to fulfill my destiny. I pushed up onto the tips of my toes and kissed him passionately to show the truth behind my words. "When we are bonded. Our magic becomes one. Does that mean you will get my Druid abilities?" I asked when the kiss had come to an end.

"I don't know. There has never been a bond between an Aos Si and a Druid before. Some Aos Si are stronger in their abilities than others. When pure-blooded Aos Si complete the bond, their magic doubles in strength," Rion replied to my question.

"It would be pretty cool if you did," I chuckled. "I'm sure to Nolan's dismay." He was getting pretty tired of me "practicing" new skills on him. He was not fond of the waterspout I learned to conjure. I had soaked him head to toe in freezing creek water.

Rion shook his head with a laugh. "He's just jealous because he doesn't have cool Druid magic." He placed a quick kiss on the tip of my nose and pulled me to the bed. I pulled my boots off and nestled into the furs. Rion had the unique ability to fall asleep as soon as his head hit the pillow. However, I wasn't sure I was going to be able to sleep. The nerves for tomorrow night and our journey to Tír na nÓg kept my mind alert. There was also a sense of uncertainty. I had a strange feeling that something was going to happen. That we would fail. A nagging feeling kept me awake long into the night. My eyes finally grew heavy, and as I drifted to sleep, an image flashed behind my lids.

It was a similar scene to the dream I had had the night I met the Puka. It wasn't Rion who laid dead at my feet, but a familiar raven-haired woman with unseeing sapphire eyes. My corpse lay not in the streets of Lios but surrounded by what had once been a village now in ruins. Unease chased me into a fitful sleep.

Chapter 27

My stomach was filled with the most obnoxious swarm of butterflies, as I donned the simple silver gown, the only luxury item I had kept from the trunk of clothing from the rebel base in the mountains. It was a single panel of fabric that wrapped around my body and tied at the front. I didn't bother with undergarments, for they would not be needed. I used a small mirror to line my eyes with kohl, stabbing myself multiple times before I was successful. I cursed my shaking inexperienced hands. I finished the ensemble by carefully plaiting my hair into a crown upon my head.

Nolan would be here at any moment to escort me to the spot Rion had chosen deep in the woods and away from prying eyes. I felt on the verge of tears when Nolan finally peeked into the tent. "Wow," he breathed. I gave him a spin, but my stomach wouldn't settle. I stumbled, catching myself on the post holding the tent above our heads.

He moved swiftly to my side. "What's wrong?" I didn't know how to explain to him what I was feeling. I wanted more than anything to complete this bond between Rion and I, but the uncertainty of the future weighed heavy on my shoulders.

Nolan gave me a knowing smile. "Rion is a very lucky male," he said as he wrapped my arm through his bent elbow and patted my hand. "All will go as planned. I will be there to ensure that."

I nodded. "The ceremony isn't the problem. It is everything that could occur after that. If I die, so does he. I am currently the most dangerous person to be bonded to." These thoughts had plagued my dreams the night before and every waking moment since.

"Rion knows exactly what he is doing. Even unbonded, if you were to die, he would follow." Nolan walked us forward and out of the tent. His words put me at ease for the moment.

I looked at the sky and the remarkable sight that I beheld. There wasn't a single cloud to shield my view. No fog hung in the air. The moon sat full and heavy above us, and the stars twinkled and danced. I took a deep breath through my nose. The air around us was laden with the sweet smell of spring blossoms.

Nolan led us along a path through the dense forest. The tree pressed in upon us, blocking out the light of the moon. We came to a small clearing, where the moon reappeared overhead. Rion stood at the center by the light of a small fire. He was dressed in only a flowing pair of black linen trousers. Furs were perfectly placed upon the earth. Nolan stopped a few feet from my mate and bowed deeply. Rion reached his hand out for me to join him. I didn't hesitate to take it. "You look stunning," he whispered at my side. I smiled up at him.

Nolan took a single step forward and got down on one knee, head bent. He removed his dagger from its sheath at his side. "I swear, by blood and steal, to protect you at all cost." He slid the blade along his hand. He clenched his fist, allowing the blood to ooze through his fingers and drip onto the grass at our feet. "To surrender my life to spare yours." He turned his face to ours. Rion placed a hand on his cheek, gesturing for me to do the same. Nolan's cheek was warm under my palm. "To ensure this bond is completed by the light of the Beltane moon." This blood oath was different from the one Nolan and I shared. A single mark was left behind—on the back of Rion's and my hand, and along the side of Nolan's neck. It was in the shape of the crescent moon.

Nolan rose to his feet. Rion pulled him into a hug and kissed his cheek. "I wouldn't want anyone else to share this moment with me." I watched the tender interaction between two friends that had shared a lifetime together before I was even born. Rion released Nolan and turned to me. I struggled not to fidget under his gaze. "Are you ready?"

"Yes," I breathed. He stole my hand and guided me to the furs, where he knelt on both knees. I mirrored the movement. The ebbing silver strands within his eyes were lively in the fire light. They danced in time with the flames. Rion pulled the tie of my robe, allowing the front to fall open. He picked up a small bowl that sat at the edge of the fire containing silver paint. He dipped his fingers in the paint and began to draw spirals along my chest and shoulders.

"The symbols represent the thread of fate that binds us together." He handed the bowl to me, and I replicated the symbols upon his chest. My skin began to buzz with unknown magic that flowed over my body. The sensation was strange but not unpleasant.

Rion took the bowl from my hands.

"Wow," I breathed as the tinkling of my skin intensified. I looked into Rion's eyes. The green had nearly been replaced by silver. He gathered a think piece of twine from the ground beside him and handed it off to Nolan. He took my left hand in his, and Nolan bound them together.

"Repeat after me," Rion instructed. "I promise to love thee wholly and completely without restraint, in sickness and in health, in plenty and in poverty, in life and beyond, where we shall meet, remember, and love again. I shall not seek to change thee in any way. I shall respect thee, thy beliefs, thy people, and thy ways as I respect myself. You are my heart, my shelter, and my strength."

I reiterated the vow word for word. The vibration slowly worked its way down my body, creating a feral need to have Rion's body on mine. Nolan unbound our hands, handed a small box to Rion, and took up his post once more. Rion opened it, revealing a silver ring. The design was beautiful, two hands cupping a crowned heart. "It's a Claddagh. The heart represents love, the crown loyalty, and the hands friendship," Rion explained as he slipped it onto my left right finger, the heart facing inwards. "It was my mother's."

Tears of joy flooded my eyes as I looked at the band. "It's beautiful," I whispered. I shifted my gaze back to him. "I love you." I wished I had something to give him in return.

He cupped my cheek with his hand. "And I you, little fox. You have given so much more than you will ever know." I wasn't sure if I had said the words aloud or spoken them down the bond that was writhing beneath my skin. Rion leaned in and kissed me. I swear sparks flew from where our skin made contact.

He ran his hand from my cheek to my throat, tilting my head for better access. His hand was firm but did not restrict my breathing. A dark part of myself wished he'd tighten grip. A low groan erupted from Rion's throat. His hands flew to my bare waist, picking me up and laid me out upon the furs. Ever touch of his skin on mine, the soft fur against my back, set my body on fire. He lowered his weight upon me. I looked over his shoulder, where Nolan watched our surroundings with an intensity that made me believe that he may have been watching us just a moment before. His presence also heightened my pleasure as Rion's lips roved over my throat and down my chest.

He went painfully slow. A faint glow began to flood the clearing. Wisps of silver came from our bodies and wrapped around us. My heart thundered in my chest as Rion planted a well-placed kiss between my breasts, then he ran his tongue along the curve and back up my throat. I took a staggering breath ready to combust, running my hands along the strong muscles of his back. I whimpered as he pushed off me for a moment to remove his trousers. His cock stood proud in the firelight—the tip wet with the evidence of his desire. I craved him in a way I never thought possible.

The glow of the silver wisps intensified as he found me once more. I wrapped my legs around him as he propped himself on his elbows above me, slowly pressing himself into my entrance. I couldn't contain the scream of pleasure that tore through me. As he began to move, the air around us shifted. Power flowed through my veins. Power that hadn't been there before. Rion's magic merged with my own, creating a shared pool so deep, the bottom was far out of reach. My body pulsed with the new-found power.

As our bodies came together as one, so did our souls. A wave of unity settled deep within my soul, as though it had finally been made whole. I spent my entire life feeling as though something was missing within me. I had always thought it was loneliness, the lack of companionship, but it was him.

Emotions overwhelmed my system. They mixed and mingled with my own. Pride. Love. Joy. An all-consuming and all-encompassing feeling as my heart and soul no longer belonged to myself alone, but also, to the male before me. Sweat beaded at my brow as the bond strengthened, becoming a tangible strand that wrapped around my heart and extended to his.

My senses were overloaded by his touch. The sound of his ragged breaths filled my ears as, he too, succumbed to the effects of the bonding. His strong scent mixed with the sweet smell of spring flowers and sweat consumed me. Release tore through me repeatedly, the comminating effect of our union. However, I never tired.

Rion gave one last thrust and came within me. I stared into his eyes, the threads of fate seemed to settle, but remained stark against the green of his irises. I gradually became aware of my surroundings. I peer once again over Rion's shoulder to where Nolan stood. This time, he was blatantly watching us with lust of his own. Rion followed my gaze to the male. He began to harden again within me. My body reacted in a way I hadn't anticipated, flooding with renewed heat and desire.

I remembered what Nolan had said about the effects that the bonding had upon those present. Rion looked to me then. *Do you want him to join us, little fox?* He purred into my mind. *Do you want the full experience of a bonding ritual?*

My body responded to his words, as I clenched around his length that was still fully seated within me. Before I could think of the consequences, I nodded. A feral grin grew across his face as he gestured Nolan to approach. Rion withdrew and pulled me to my knees once more. Nolan circled us and knelt behind me. One arm wrapped around my body, bracing me against his chest. His other hand encircled my throat. He inhaled deeply. Rion sat back on his heels and watched as Nolan kissed the sensitive spot behind my ear.

Rion got to his feet and grasped the back of my head. He guided my lips to him. They parted to allow him to thrust into my mouth. I moaned against him, which caused his movements to stiffen slightly.

Nolan continued to peruse my body with his free hand that wasn't keeping my head still. It moved down my body, finding the sensitive bundle of nerves. His fingers moved in experienced precision. I soared from the intense pleasure the males wringed from my body. Nolan groaned in my ear, pressing himself into my backside, his arousal evident.

Rion only gave me a moment to draw a breath before he continued to claim my mouth at a feverish pace. I was completely at their mercy. Nolan halted his ministration to untie they stays to his trousers, releasing his erection. Before he touched me again, Rion whispered down the bond. *Does he have your consent?* He withdrew to allow me to answer.

I didn't think twice before murmuring, "Yes." Rion backed up a step to allow me to lean forward. I placed my hands on his thighs. Nolan wedged his knee between mine to spread my legs for him. I was so wet that he found no resistance as he gently inserted himself. His groan filled the clearing.

The lust in Rion's eyes grew as he watched Nolan take me. Nolan's movements were slow and ridged, like he was trying to restrain himself. His fingers found my clit once more and moved in lazy circles. My vision became spotted as the pleasure overtook me, my skin extremely sensitive to touch. My breathing hitched as I was thrown over the precipice.

Rion didn't give me a moment to recover before he filled my mouth once more. Both males moved in tandem as they filled me so entirely. Rion came first, coating my tongue with his release. Nolan withdrew and found his upon my back. Rion dropped to his knees before us, utterly spent. He cupped my cheek in one hand and Nolan's in another. If I hadn't been held up between them, I might have fallen face-first into the grass.

We stayed in our embrace, while we came back to ourselves. I thought once the high of the ritual subsided, I would feel embarrassed or ashamed. I felt neither, only a sense of wholeness that was hard to explain and entirely sated. We didn't speak, barely breathed, for none of us wanted this moment to end. When it did, the reality of the world would sweep in, tainting all it touched.

Rion pulled back and took my hand, placing it on his chest. I was shocked to find his heart beating in sync with mine. "We are one. In every way possible." He smiled at me, then to Nolan who was still pinned to my back. "My brother. Thank you. For everything you have done and will do in the future. I couldn't have been blessed with a better friend." Rion wrapped his arms around the both of us in a tight embrace.

"What happens now?" I asked a bit sheepishly. I didn't know where things lay after all that had occurred between the three of us.

"First, we need to get cleaned up and be off to the fairy mound. We have a few hours before sunrise," Rion answered, which wasn't the answer I was looking for. He seemed to realize that because he added, "We'll figure everything else out later."

Nolan pulled away and straightened his clothing. I turned to him. "I don't know what to say," I admitted. There was a strange feeling I couldn't place.

He placed a kiss on my cheek. "You don't have to say anything. Just take care of him, okay? It's been my job for the last forty years. It's time I passed the torch to someone way more capable than I." Love pierced my chest, but it was not my own. Nolan gathered my clothing from where it was discarded and draped it over my shoulders. Tears glistened in his eyes. "I will leave you now. But please, both of you, come back to me." He rose then and walked back down the hidden path towards the camp.

Rion stood and pulled his trousers back into place as I refastened my gown. He doused the fire before hauling me to my unsteady feet. We walked slowly back to camp, trying to soak up as much of the contentment as we could. When we entered the tent, a bucket of warm water sat at the center, which I assumed Nolan had brought. We washed and dressed quickly. I slid my mother's onyx deep into my pocket as a final touch to my ensemble. Clad in black and armed to the teeth, we set out into the night.

Chapter 28

We approached the fairy mound on silent feet. Guards roamed about the large dark tower that protruded from the ground on the eastern side. A low glow emanated from torches surrounding the ominous structure, and loud voices carried from within as the soldiers enjoyed their own Beltane celebration.

We stuck to the shadows, which were the only thing to shield our approach across the barren land between the forest and the mound. As we grew nearer, the air hummed with the magic from the portal that sat at the crest of the hill, and thick mist hung in the air around us coating our skin with moisture.

The guards spaced evenly along its base were easy to circumnavigate. They were either too drunk or oblivious to our movements within the mist as we slipped between them. The slope was not steep, but my thighs and calves burned, as we ascended in a crouch to stay out of sight. The magic grew more intense the higher we climbed.

The sound of whispering voices reached my ears. Rion threw his hand up over his shoulder to halt my movements. I came up beside him, as we peered at the four soldiers that guarded the shimmering portal within a stone doorway at the center of the mound. It was a beautiful sight to behold. "There is no way to get by them without a fight," Rion whispered. I nodded in agreement and slowly unsheathed my sword to avoid making a sound to alert them of our presence. Rion did the same.

He stood fully and shed his glamour in a flash of light, drawing the attention of the guards. I threw the hood of my cloak over my head to conceal my rounded ears and followed after him. "What do we have here?" one of them asked his companions.

"We don't want any trouble, just passing through to visit family in Tír na nÓg," Rion answered the man as he edged closer.

"Do you have papers?" another questioned. "You must have signed permission from King Balor in order to travel through the portal."

Rion was almost within striking distance as he said, "I think you will find that I don't need papers." He took one more step and swung, catching the guard in the stomach with his sharp blade before he had the chance to draw his own. The man dropped his weapon with an agonizing scream in favor for his innards that spilled from the nasty gash Rion had inflicted. In his panic, the male attempted to shove them back in. It didn't take long before he fell dead at Rion's feet. The three other men were armed in an instant and surrounded us.

I drew upon my magic. The sudden influx of magic flooding my system attempted to steal the breath from my lungs. My control threatened to slip as the ground shook violently as the earth below us cracked open. The guards, along with the body of their dead comrade, fell into the gaping crevice. Their screams were lost as it sealed atop them.

I stood shocked for a moment at what I had done. My magic had felt different—stronger and more volatile, since the completion of the bond. Like it yearned for blood of our enemies. I felt Rion's pride as he tugged my arm urging me to follow him. "That was impressive, but we need to go. Everyone within two miles would have felt that."

We rushed to the portal, but before he could pull me through, Rion paused. "Going through is difficult the first time. You may black out. I vomited the first time I traveled." I took the lead and pulled us through, not worried about his warning, as the shouts of soldiers erupted up the hillside. I felt like I was falling for a moment, then everything went black.

* * *

I awoke in Rion's arms. My eyes fluttered open and were blinded by an intense light. Realizing it was the glaring sun overhead, I attempted to shield my eyes. My head pounded ferociously in time with my heartbeat. "Good morning, sunshine." Rion smiled down at me.

"How long have I been out?" I groaned.

"A lot longer than I would have liked," he replied. "Just over an hour." I looked around and saw that we sat on the slope of a lush green hill. A fairy mound, but not the one we had just been atop. We were positioned below the mist, which allowed a clear view of the world around us. Rion stood and helped me to do the same. I wobbled. My legs threatening to come out from under me. Rion caught me under my arm to prevent me from doing a nosedive.

I took a moment to gain my footing and catch my breath. "Please tell me the next time will not be like that," I coughed.

"No," Rion laughed. "You only have to go through that experience once."

"Thank the fucking gods for that." I took in my surroundings once more. The land was flat and open besides dark green, almost black, trees that grew from the earth in the distance. One could see miles without obstruction. The island was encircled by sparkling blue waters, the smell of the sea carried on the wind, sharp and clean. To the south of the mound jagged, slate gray mountains jutted towards the sky, and to the north was a glorias city of gleaming gold surrounded by rows upon rows of purple flowers. The sun reflected off the city, causing it to appear to produce its own light.

A summer breeze blew over the land, bringing with it the strong scent of foxglove and the sound of waves crashing upon the rocky shores. I closed my eyes allowing it to wash over me. A strong sense of belonging and home rushed through me. "Falias, one of the four great cities of Tír na nÓg. I spent most of my childhood within its walls," Rion muttered. A childhood that haunted his ever step. That drove his need to liberate his mother's people and bring justice to his father.

"We will head towards Gorias." He pointed towards a city that lay between us and the mountains. It was grand, but not as magnificent as Falias. "In order to get to the Dragon's Den on the other side of the mountains and back in time, we will need to borrow a boat. It will be faster to sail along the coast than to attempt the climb over the mountains."

"By borrow, I assume you mean steal." I was wanted, both in the Emerald Isle and here. We couldn't risk being seen, even if news of my survival had yet to reach this realm.

"Aye. If we leave now, we can make it to the city by nightfall." My legs finally felt as though they would support my weight, so I released Rion where I had still clung to him to remain steady. The ache in my head had subsided, though my eyes were still slowly adjusting to the sun. They were not used to its bright rays, for on a clear day back home, there was still a thin layer of clouds hanging in the sky.

Rion led me by the hand down the remaining slope of the hill. Sweat soon coated my skin, which led me to shed my cloak. Even as the sun tracked across the sky and began to dip behind the horizon, the air remained warm. "Is it always this warm here?" I asked Rion.

"It is. The weather is always fair. No snow, occasional rain." A smile was on his lips as he watched me observe Tír na nÓg's beauty. "When all this is done, we will come back so you can get the full experience."

"I would love that," I replied. My mind wandered to what had occurred in the meadow before we left. "What are your thoughts on what happened with Nolan?" I asked Rion, hesitantly. "For months, you couldn't stand any male looking at me the wrong way, but Nolan fucking me was okay? I'm not upset that it had happened, and do not regret it, but I guess I am trying to understand why you allowed it."

"It is a common occurrence for an Aos Si bonding. I knew there would be a possibility, after our bond had been completed, things could escalate. I do have to say, it felt different. I felt no jealousy nor did I feel territorial, only pure love. Knowing that there is another man out there willing to lay his life on the line to protect you gave me a sense of peace. It was also hot as fuck to watch," he added with a wink.

I rolled my eyes. "Is that something you want to continue, is what I am asking?" I clarified.

"Do you love him?" His question didn't feel like a trap, but an honest inquiry of my feelings. I thought about my answer before I replied. After what had happened in Lios, Nolan and I have been growing closer of the last few months of travel.

"I do. It is different from what I feel for you. The love we have is all consuming and innate, but I also cannot deny what I felt last night."

"If it is what you want, I have no problem with it. With the bond now complete, I am no longer threatened by the love of another man." He gripped my hand tightly. "I love you and want you to be happy."

"In any case, it will be time limited. He will eventually find his mate." My words caused a crease to form on Rion's forehead.

"Nolan doesn't have a mate." Sadness and grief wafted off of Rion. It dawned on me that he had told me that once, but it must have slipped through the cracks of my mind.

"What happened?"

"Her name was Aoife. They met when we were children and were inseparable. She was born into a family that was deep in the counsel of the king. She was raised as a warrior and mastered black magic as a child, though the rest of us refused to learn. Nolan tried to convince her that it wasn't worth the price she would have to pay, but she would never listen.

"It is the norm to wait to complete a mating bond until we reach the age of sixteen, if we are lucky enough to meet our mates early. A couple of months shy of their mating ceremony, she was killed when a spell rebounded during training. Nolan attempted to take his own life because the thought of living without her was unbearable. Flynn, Bellamy, and I stayed with him at all times to ensure he never succeeded.

"Losing her changed him. He became cold and irritable. However, since he met you, that harsh exterior has begun to fade. He has started to see the beauty in the world again. Though I would rather have you all to myself, I cannot do that to him. He loves you, maybe more than he ever loved Aoife." Tears brimmed my eyes as Rion told me Nolan's story of love and loss. His selflessness only made me love him more.

We arrived at the outskirts of Gorias as the sun set and allowed the streets to clear before we made our approach. We crept along the shore towards the docks where fishing boats were tethered for the night. Nerves grew in the pit of my stomach, as Rion helped me into one of the bobbing vessels and seated me upon one of the benches that spanned across it.

The scent of salt water filled the air mixed with the unpleasant smell of fish. I had never been on a boat before. I was hoping the contents of my stomach would stay put, as Rion loosened the ropes holding the boat in place and pushed it from the dock with his foot. He sat facing me on the other bench and grabbed the oars from within, positioning them on either side of the boat. He began to row us out to sea before turning us north. The shore disappeared in the night.

I reached over the side and dipped my hand into the dark waters that passed. I got an idea as the water flowed through my fingers. I was careful as I called upon my magic, recalling the destruction it had caused on the mound. The last thing I wanted was to flip the boat, dislodging us into its depth. Gods knew what horrors swam within. I could feel the current of the water moving against the bow of the boat. I changed its direction to flow with us. The boat lurched forward.

Surprise spread over Rion's face when he stilled the oars, and the boat continued on course. I kept a tight rein on my magic so that my control didn't slip. I urged the current to move a bit faster. Rion let out a laugh, "You are an amazing creature, little fox." He leaned forward and planted a kiss on my cheek, which caused me to smile in return.

The salty sea air rushed through my hair. It was freeing in a way I never anticipated such a thing to be. I closed my eyes and pretended I was flying. That I was free from the chains of responsibility for a moment. I opened my eyes once again to face reality.

A strong pungent smell permeated the air. It was overwhelming. I gagged and covered my face with my hand. "Sulfur. When in their dragon forms, shifters produce the gas within special glands. They ignite the gas with a mechanism in their throats, allowing them to breathe fire," Rion explained. "We are getting nearer. Can you move us closer to shore?"

I altered the current beneath the boat. Two glowing orange orbs pierced the black as we pushed forward. "There. Slow the current, and I will row us to shore." I did as he commanded. He took up the oars once more and guided us in. The orbs were in fact two torches. The flames danced in the breeze, illuminating a gaping cave mouth that shot into the side of the slate mountains.

The haul of the boat scrapped against the rocky shore with a growl, the wood creaking under the pressure. Rion jumped into the knee-deep water with a splash. Tugging on the rope that had once tethered it to the dock, he hauled the boat to shore. I took his outreached hand and hopped to the ground alongside him. Gravel crunched beneath my boots as I shifted my weight. The sulfur was even stronger. I refrained from breathing through my nose, electing to breathe through my mouth instead, but it was so heavy I could taste it upon my tongue. "Ready to meet a dragon?" Rion asked.

"As ready as I am ever going to be," I answered nervously. Rion's hand remained in mine as we descended upon the yawning mouth of the cave.

Chapter 29

The air hung thick around us as Rion and I moved deeper into the cavern. Blazing torches lined the walls at even intervals, lighting our way. We had been walking down winding and twisting tunnels for a while now. I had grown accustomed to the smell of sulfur and damp rock as we went. Nausea roiled my stomach for another reason. The fear of the shifter that dwelled within these passages sank deep in my bones like a stone in a raging river. I rubbed my sweat-coated hands down my leather clad thighs, attempting to appease my nerves. The magnitude of what was at stake weighing down on me like the mountain itself.

The only sign of the dragon that was hidden within was heaping piles of gold and silver coins, jewels, and miscellaneous valuable objects. His hoard crowded the tunnels on both sides. "What do you suppose drives their greed?" I whispered to Rion, keeping my eyes trained to the ground to avoid tripping over anything that may be blocking the path.

"It's not greed that fuels their need to acquire wealth. It comes from an instinctual desire to gather and protect things that they consider valuable. It is also ingrained in their nature to protect their domain and guard what is theirs. It is why trespassing in a dragon's hoard is so dangerous. They are unpredictable," Rion kept his voice low as he explained. "Many have tried to enter the Dragon's Den, but none returned nor were heard from again."

I tried to keep the thoughts of doubt that attempted to weasel their way into my mind at bay, but there was a small chance the spear wasn't even here. That we were putting our lives at risk for no reason. I decided to change the subject to get my mind off our potential doom. "If he has the spear and relinquishes it to us, what is the plan then?"

"We need to return to camp and wait for Flynn to return. We cannot make our move until we have more soldiers."

"And what if he doesn't return?" Rion had held out hope, but I wasn't entirely sure that Flynn would ever return.

"He will. I know he will." I gave the back of Rion's head an empathetic look.

"We have to acknowledge that something may have happened to Flynn."

"Just give him more time. He will come. There is no telling where the males from Lios went after the raid on The Milkmaid, or how far they had to go to get the women to safety." Rion's denial was strong, but I dropped it. There was no use arguing any further, but the Emerald Isle was not vast. Flynn should have located them by now.

We were silent as we continued to move throughout the cave system. The tunnels grew narrower the deeper we went, and it became more difficult to avoid knocking over the hoard as we passed. Rion had to turn himself sideways in order to pass through a particularly cramped portion. For the first time, my small stature was beneficial as I easily slipped by. An escape would be nearly impossible if the dragon did not have what we sought and decided to kill us.

The tunnel finally deposited us into a large chamber, seemingly carved by ancient hands, or perhaps the beast itself. At its center, towered the majority of his hoard. Coins of gold, silver, and copper were heaped so high they nearly scraped the ceiling. Gemstones glittered in the light of the torches that surrounded the great room. Rubies, sapphires, and emeralds embedded into golden goblets or encrusted along the bands of crowns.

There were weapons, too. Swords with jeweled hilts, ancient axes etched in long-forgotten symbols of an ancient civilization long dead, and spears blackened by dragon fire. Some still dripped with rust and blood. Broken armor and scattered remains of their wearers were strung throughout the treasure, a stark reminder of the dangerous creature that lurked within.

My eyes roved all over the room, searching for the spear. My naïve mind hoping that it would be left out in plain sight, that we could grab it, the dragon shifter none the wiser. I remained hopeful that Nolan's assumption had been correct, and that the dragon actually possessed what we had come for. "Who dares to trespass upon my domain," came a booming voice through the cave that caused the air to shift, a few of the coins upon the towering mound became dislodged and cascaded down the side, landing at the feet of a massive male, who seemed to appear out of thin air before us.

My attention was first drawn to his dark eyes that glowed like the embers of a dying fire within his skull. His hair was a brilliant scarlet, and his skin was extremely fair, almost translucent, from dwelling underground. The power that rolled off his body prickled my skin, causing goosebumps to form in its wake. Though he was only one male, his presence seemed to fill the entirety of the cavern in which we stood.

"I am Aisling, daughter of Queen Deidre, and rightful heir of the Druid throne. I have come to collect a treasure that my people entrusted you to protect." I spoke with confidence I did not feel, as he stared me down.

The dragon scoffed. "Entrusted is a strong word. Paid, would be more like it." Fury laced his reply. "Have you come to pay your debt, princess? Maybe then we can speak of that which you seek." Panic flooded my veins, for I did not have a cent to my name.

"How much are you owed?" Rion asked from my side. The dragon's eyes lingered on Rion, as if he was just noticing his presence, longer than necessary, his expression unreadable. A flicker of recognition followed by a twisted smile. "Interesting company you keep, princess." The smile only grew wider on the shifter's face when I looked at Rion in confusion. Before I had a chance to question his meaning, he spoke again, "Twenty-thousand pounds weight in gold. An additional fifty pounds for every year I went unpaid. Even you do not have that kind of coin." I didn't have time to unpack what he meant by the pointed comment towards Rion.

"Once, your kind offered me wine and virgin hearts to keep this land warm," he mused, bending at the waist to retrieve a broken chalice from the ground. "Now, they send daughters of fallen queens to bargain with empty hands and shaking knees." He tossed the cup behind him, the sound of metal striking metal reverberated throughout the cavern.

"I need the spear in order to defeat the false king, who has kept my people oppressed for twenty years since they invaded. Without it, we don't stand a chance," I pleaded.

"What makes you think I care what happens to your people?" My attempt to beg had fallen on deaf ears, for I was sure the dragon's heart was made of stone.

"Is there something else you would want in return for the spear?" I tried to negotiate. I pulled my mother's onyx from my pocket. "What about this?" I held out my hand, offering it to him.

He held his arms out before him. "I have no need for gems, princess. I would require more than that." He shifted his gaze to Rion, then back to me. "Would you hand yourself over to me once you have accomplished your mission to rid your lands of the false king? I have been quite lonesome and could us a beautiful face to brighten my days." The dragon stepped forward, lifting his hand.

Just before he made contact with my skin, Rion growled, "If you touch her, you die. Then, we will have nothing standing in our way of retrieving the spear."

"Ah yes, but what makes you think you have the power to do so? Many of your kind have tried. Many have failed." His glowing eyes pierced Rion. "Look at you. Same fire in your eyes. Same arrogance. The son following in the footsteps of the father, trailing after Druids and playing in rebellion." His words brought the realization that the dragon had known Rion's father. They stood toe to toe in a silent battle of wills until I interjected.

"Enough." I pushed Rion back and stepped in front of him. "I will do no such thing. First of all, I refuse to leave my mate. Secondly, once the king is gone, I intend to be there to guide my kingdom into a new era where its people need not suffer or starve."

"How very noble of you," the dragon sarcastically replied. He paced in a circle, contemplating his next request.

"I will make you a deal, princess." I could tell by the way he spoke those words that I would not like the deal.

"And what is that, pray tell?" Rion barked. The shifter sent a look of pure death in his direction, clearly unimpressed with Rion's tone.

"I was not speaking to you," he shot back. He shifted his gaze back to me once more. "Three trials," the shifter purred. "Succeed, and you may have the spear. Fail, I keep the spear, and you die." Rion grabbed my arm from behind.

"Absolutely not," Rion exclaimed.

I turned on him, keeping one eye on the dragon shifter. "We need that spear, Rion. His other demands have been unrealistic, but this gives us a chance. I don't really have a choice." Roin let out a frustrated growl deep in the back of his throat. "What will the trials consist of?" I asked the dragon.

"First, a trial of wisdom in which I will present you with a riddle. Next, a trial to test your strength, where you will face me in one-on-one combat. First to draw blood wins. Finally, a test of courage. I will present you with your biggest fears, then you will have a choice to make." The dragon smirked, as if proud of himself.

"And how do I know you will keep your word. That you will allow us to leave with the spear unharmed, if I pass these tests?" I asked the dragon before me. Rion vibrated in rage beside me but kept his mouth sealed shut.

"I am bound by my word, princess," he spat, my questioning of his honor having infuriated the dragon further. "I cannot go back on a spoken bargain."

"It's a deal," I agreed. Rion attempted once again to interject, but I sent him a silencing glare that halted him in his tracks.

"Excellent. One more thing. You must complete these trials alone. Your mate may not interfere, or the deal will be rescinded. Your magic is also off limits." Rion's agitation flowed down the bond and rattled my core.

You do not have to do this. We can find another way. Rion spoke down the bond.

No. That spear is the only way we stand a chance against the king. Especially since he possesses the sword.

The dragon must have sensed our internal conversation, for he tsked us. "Now. Now. We will have none of that. Are you ready to begin, princess?"

Rion's hand brushed my arm, barely a touch, but enough to stop me. I turned to face him, and for a moment, the firelight carved him in sharp lines: jaw clenched, brows furrowed, his entire posture coiled tight. "You don't have to prove anything to him," he murmured. "You don't owe him this."

"It's not about him," I whispered back. "It's about all of them, my people. And I do owe them." He looked like he wanted to argue, but something in my voice made him pause. Instead, he dropped his hand and stepped back, though his presence didn't waver. Always there. Always ready in case I had need of him.

"Let's get on with it then." The faster we got out of here the better. Even a placated dragon was a dangerous dragon, and this one was pissed.

"Excellent. Listen carefully, for I will not say it again. You will have three chances to answer correctly. There are two sisters. One gives birth to the other and she, in turn, gives birth to the first. Who are the two sisters?"

I repeated the riddle in my head over and over, trying to comprehend how the sisters gave birth to one another. Anxiety tore through my mind, clouding my thoughts. No answer came to me. I muttered the riddle slowly aloud in hopes that something would come to me.

I grew frustrated as my mind continued to remain blank. "Come on, princess. I do not have all night." The dragon attempted to derail my thought process with his instigation. The riddle did not refer to actual sisters but to a circular cycle. I started to recall all things that move in such a way. The seasonal cycle struck out first.

"Spring and winter?" I asked hesitantly.

The dragon shook his head with a sly smile. My heart plummeted. Two more chances. I continued my internal deliberation. The reincarnation of a soul was a prime example of a circle pattern. "Life and death?" I asked the shifter.

"Wrong again, princess." The smile on his face turned savage. "I was so looking forward to the other trials, but you don't stand a chance if you can't even answer a simple riddle."

I started looking around in a desperate attempt to find something, anything that would give me a clue. My anxiety heightened. I was sweating profusely, and my breathing was rapid. I had one last chance to answer correctly. The dragon paced before me, becoming increasingly more impatient the longer I took to answer the riddle. My eyes landed on Rion, who was fidgeting with his belt. He knew. He knew the answer, yet he could not help me.

All of a sudden, my body started to warm. Rion was sending heat down the bond. I shifted my gaze away from him to prevent the shifter from detecting his interference. He was trying to tell me something. The warmth reminded me of the sun that had beat down upon us when we first arrived in Tír na nÓg.

Confusion clouded my mind once more. The sun. The sun and the moon move in a circular pattern across the sky, but they do not give birth to each other. There are times when the moon is visible during the day.

Day. That was it. It had to be. "The answer is day and night," I blurted. "Day gives birth to night, and night gives birth to the day in return."

My heart was in my throat as the dragon cocked his head, like a predator would observe its prey. My heart pounding in my ears was deafening as the shifter remained silent. "Correct," he finally confirmed. Rion let out a ragged breath that he must have been holding. The dragon let out a laugh that echoed back down the tunnel we had emerged from. "Oh, great heir to the Druid throne. It was only a riddle. You should be fearing what lies ahead." Rion stepped forward to shield me as the shifter approached.

I feared he'd be able to hear the pounding of my heart as he drew closer. "Your next task," he began as he circled us. "Will not be so simple."

Chapter 30

Follow me," the shifter demanded, as he disappeared around his mound of riches at the center of the room. Rion and I looked to one another, a moment of doubt passed between us before we trailed after him. He guided us down an unlit hidden passage that led to another spacious room. The floors were clear of clutter, but the walls were lined with racks of weapons. "For what use would a dragon shifter need a training room?" The question popped out before I could think better of it.

"I tend to prefer my human from over that of my dragon. Though many of my kind do not, I find it tiresome." If he was offended by my question, he did not show it. "Now, it is time to see what you are truly made of, princess. What your Aos Si mate has taught you. Now choose your weapon." He gestured to the racks around him. I withdrew the sword and knife that were strapped at my side. I knew them well. Their weight. The fit of their hilts in my palms.

Rion stepped in front of me. He silently adjusted my armor, tightening each buckle as he went. "Stay focused," he murmured under the watchful eyes of the shifter. His eyes met mine, the threads of fate thrashing wildly in his emerald irises. "Just…don't die, okay?" He finished his adjustments, gave me a swift kiss, and stepped back.

Rion's nervous energy mixed with my own, as I took up my position across the room from the shifter. "That was…touching," he mocked. He held a large ruby encrusted sword drawn out in front of him. "Rion." The dragon spoke his name as though it left a bad taste in his mouth. "Stay out of the way. It would be a shame if the princess was distracted."

Rion moved behind me out of my line of sight, but his presence was always with me. *Stay focused.* I kept my face carefully blank to keep the shifter unaware as Rion disobeyed his orders once again. *Your physical strength is no match for his. You will need to be smarter. Faster. Remember all that I have taught you.*

I took a moment to calm my nerves, breathing in through my nose and out my mouth. Without the use of my magic, I needed to rely on the skills I have spent months perfecting. I had to have faith that it was enough.

I made the first move, launching myself at the dragon. My sword sung through the air. Just before my blade decapitated the shifter, he brought his own up to meet it. The impact left my arms numb with the vibrations that pulsed up my sword and into the hilt. I retreated quickly to stay out of his reach. He let out a ruggish laugh. "If that is all you've got, this shouldn't take very long."

The dragon circled me. I mirrored his movements so my back was never to him. "I have walked this earth long before your ancestors united under one banner. If you want to win, princess, you are going to have to do better than that." He wore a smile from ear to ear.

"Shut the fuck up and fight." I was already growing tired of his voice.

"Glady," he replied with a growl. He was on me in a moment. I blocked his blow and pushed forward, knocking him off balance and leaving his left open. Steel scrapping against steel filled the room as my blade moved along his. I twirled to bring my sword down on his exposed side. I misjudged his speed as the flat of his sword struck the back of my weight bearing leg midway through my turn. I landed hard on my back upon the stone floor. The air rushed from my lungs. A booming laugh ricocheted through the room.

Get up, little fox. Get up. I rolled to my side, still struggling to breathe. The shifter stood with his one hand in his pocket, leaning on his sword with the other, still laughing at my utter failure. I got to my knees and used my sword to push myself off the ground. I looked down at my leg that he had caught with his sword to ensure I hadn't already lost but there was no blood to be seen. He was playing with me, but he would soon grow tired of this game and end it. My breathing was ragged, as I took up my fighting stance once more.

"I expected more from the Druid heiress. How long have you been training? Six months?" he scoffed. "You are no match for me, princess." I gathered myself once more and lashed out once again.

The shifter wasn't expecting me to recover so quickly. He pulled his hand from his pocket and gripped his sword in order to block my blade. We flew into a dance. I met him blow for blow. The ringing of the steel calmed my nerves and focused my mind.

As we fought, I searched for any weakness that I could exploit to my advantage, but it did not appear as though he had any.

Sweat beaded at my brow and ran down my face into my eyes. I blocked his downward blow, trapping his sword between my two blades. I pushed the shifter back and retreated. I wiped my face on my sleeve and caught my breath as we circled one another. The dragon did not seem to be phased by the exertion. His breathing was even, and his skin was dry.

"It's not hard to see how the Druids lost against the Aos Si twenty years ago. What makes you think you can defeat them, if you can't even land a blow on me? What makes you think you have what it takes to rule a kingdom? Maybe in ten, or twenty years, you could be something worth my time, but right now you are nothing but a naive little girl with a death wish," the dragon instigated.

The blood ran hot in my veins. I let out a low growl in the back of my throat as the dragon laughed at my irritation. *This is what he wants. He is trying to anger you. To cause you to make a dire mistake. Do not listen to his words. Do not allow him to get in your head. You can do this.* Rion's voice filled me with renewed strength.

"Tell me, princess. What would you even do with a kingdom? You have no idea what you are doing, do you? How far in over your head you are. You allowed this moron to talk you into a battle you cannot win." I glared down at the dragon in front of me.

"I will begin by making them all pay for what they have done to my people. Every last one of them will feel my wrath." My muscles seemed to swell with strength as I spoke. My sword no longer felt so heavy in my hands. "Then, I will rebuild a kingdom where no one has to suffer."

"There is a balance to the world. You cannot have joy and comfort without sorrow and pain. Someone will have to pay that price in order to have what you seek." We continued our circular dance around each other.

"I will gladly pay that price, if it means my people do not."

"We shall see, princess. We shall see," the shifter said with a smile, like he knew something that I did not, which only angered me further. I lunged at him again, not relenting between blows. The dragon seemed surprised by the renewed strength of my strikes. I forced him to retreat a step and then another.

I came upon him with the fury of a thousand suns. Anger flowed through my arms and into the hilt of my sword. My next blow was hard and fast, but the dragon was prepared. He blocked and pushed me back. Striking out with his sword before I was able to regain my footing, he smacked my knuckles with the blunt edge of the blade. It wasn't hard enough to break the skin but enough to cause my grip to loosen. He twirled the blade, releasing it from my hands.

My sword skidded across the room with a hideous scraping noise. The shifter positioned himself between me and the blade and began to descend on me. I stepped back to remain out of reach, matching him step for step. "This has been fun, princess, but I grow weary." He feigned a yawn. "I wish to retire."

I still had my small dagger in my grasp, the last line of defense that I had. It would not be enough to defeat the shifter. My gaze shot to Rion who was vibrating with restraint. *I love you.* I spoke through the bond. I wanted him to know that before I drew my last breath.

Now is not your time, little fox. There is a rack of swords behind you. I have not interfered, because you still have a chance. My back connected with said rack. I shot my hand behind me, refusing to turn. Giving my back to the dragon would be the end.

I grabbed the hilt of the first sword my hand came across and pulled it from the rack. I brought it around to my front. It was thin and light, with vines etched into the polished steel blade. The leather on the hilt was buttery soft to prevent blisters but still allowed expert grip. It was the most beautiful blade I had ever laid eyes on.

"How strange." The dragon purred as he halted his descent. "You have chosen well, princess."

"What do you mean?" I asked as I pushed away from the rack and towards the center of the room. The shifter backed away, as well. I sheathed my dagger so I could use the sword two handed.

"That there is a Druid made blade. The only one I have in my collection, in fact. A rare find, especially now that they are no longer being forged," he disclosed. It explained why the blade seemed to hum in response to my touch, like it was meant for me and only me to wield.

I kept it out in front of me pointing towards the shifter as I grew closer. I stopped my approach at the center of the room. I took my time to determine the best way to defeat the mighty warrior. His style relied solely on his strength. If I could get under his next swing, I might be able to get a clear shot to strike.

I took a deep breath and raised the sword above my head, feigning an attack. He did as I expected and brought his sword up to meet mine. I dove into a roll off to his side and came up behind him. I spun, laying my sword upon his shoulder. As he turned to face me, my blade came across his cheek. A thin cut formed in its path—blood dripped from the wound.

The look of shock upon the dragon's face made a smile creep across mine. Rion laughed from the corner of the room that he occupied. The dragon brought his hand up to meet the cut. His shock renewed when he saw the blood staining his hands.

"Well, well, princess. Looks like you may have what it takes." I dropped my sword from his shoulder and backed away. I turned to reluctantly replace the sword from whence in came, but the shifter's voice stopped my footsteps. "Keep it."

"What?" I wasn't entirely sure I had heard him right.

"Keep it. You earned it. I can always get it back if you don't pass the next trial," he said with a wink. I looked down at the sword in my hand.

"A trade, then. This sword is not as grand, but it is well made." Rion said as he picked up my old sword from the ground and placed it in the spot the Druid sword had been.

"Thank you," I said to the dragon because that is what felt like the right thing to do.

"Prove me wrong, princess. Prove that you deserve to wield the blade of your once great ancestors." The dragon placed his sword back in a rack and came to my side. "Your final trial will be the hardest. I will allow you an hour to rest. You have earned that, as well. Stay here and don't touch anything. I will return when it is time." As the shifter left the room, I flew into Rion's arms. My limbs were sore and tired, but I ignored the pain as he braced me firmly against him.

"You impressed him, little fox," Rion stated. "He may not admit it, but he was not expecting you to complete this trial. You need to take advantage of the time he has given you and rest. I don't know what he has planned next, but it is going to be worse than this." Rion urged me to sit against the wall by one of the racks.

Fear gripped my heart and squeezed tightly. The next task was designed to test my courage. There is a fine line between bravery and stupidity. I was starting to believe that agreeing to the shifter's trials may have been the latter. "What if I don't succeed in the final trial?" I whispered to Rion who sat by my side, arm across my shoulders.

He brushed the hair that had come out of my braid during the fight away from my face. "I will not let him harm you. If it comes down to it, we will escape. We have no use for the spear if you are dead. You will use your shield to block any advance, and we'll make a run for it. Okay?" I nodded.

I leaned onto his shoulder and closed my eyes. I felt my strength quickly returning as we sat in silence. My limbs did not feel as heavy and my head was clearing. Though having a plan of escape did put my mind at ease, I had to succeed in the next trial. We needed that spear, if we wanted any chance of defeating the false king.

Chapter 31

The dragon returned in an hour, just as he had promised. "Let's get this over with, princess. Are you ready to face all the skeletons you have hidden in your closet and conquer your greatest fears?" I almost laughed. I had never had a closet in my entire life, and my skeletons would take up a much larger room.

"I am." I was straightforward with my reply. The room around me melted away. I stood on a battlefield within the gates of Lios. The dead littered the ground around me. For a moment, I thought I was seeing the dream that had plagued my nightmares for months now. However, the faces around me were unfamiliar.

Smoke and the smell of death choked my lungs, as I weaved through the bodies at my feet. I was drawn to the center of the mass, where a woman lay face down in the dirt. I rolled her onto her back to study her. Her plaited hair was the most beautiful copper. Her skin was fair and splattered with freckles.

Unseeing eyes looked back at me. They lacked the spark of life, leaving them dull. They may have once been a brilliant green, not like any emerald or jade, but a wild, untamed shade, like grass after a storm, but no more. Blood coated the front of her armor that had seeped from a deep cut across her throat.

Tears well in my eyes, as I peered down at the woman before me. I knew this face. "She was quite beautiful," a voice spoke from behind me.

"Why?" I croaked and turned to face the shifter. "Why did you show this to me?"

"You need to see what the Aos Si are capable of. What they have already done to your people." The city fell away, and I found myself in the field beyond its walls. I was no longer surrounded by dead soldiers, but the lifeless bodies of Druid men, women, and children. I pressed the heel of my palm into my aching chest. "Not even the smallest child was spared." My heart broke into a thousand tiny pieces, as I observed the slaughter of my people. Then, it knit back together with white-hot rage.

"They will pay. Every single one of them will pay," I promised through my teeth.

"As they should, but at what cost?" The world swirled again until I was standing in front of my cottage in Baile. Again, dead men and women lie scattered upon the ground. The helpless humans who died the night I escaped the clutches of the Dullahan. Their blood that had been spilt mixed with the dirt upon the earthen path, creating a thick sludge. Bile burned the back of my throat, and renewed guilt reared its ugly head.

Six months ago, I didn't have the skills to save them, but I do now. I had simply turned my back and left them to die. I wished with my entire being that I could go back in time to spare them their pain. The shifter appeared at my side. "This was the start. The first price you paid in order to set everything into motion," he declared.

The wind shifted again, and we were in the center of a burning inferno. Screams of agony tore through the air around us. Dilapidated structures were engulfed in flames, and smoke burned my eyes. We were in the heart of Baile. I dropped to my knees. "Have you had enough, princess?" The shifter asked. This was a test of my courage to assess whether I could face all the consequences of my actions.

I shook my head. "I will continue." I feared what else he would make me endure, but I would not fail. I would not give into that fear. I stood and sealed my emotions deep within me. The heat of the blazing fire faded, and I was once again within the cellar of the outpost that guarded the pass to Lios.

I watched as the abhorrent scene unfolded before me. I identified all the mistakes I made that may have changed the outcome of that night. I shouldn't have waited so long to use my magic. I had several opportunities that would have left Rion unharmed and Nora alive. I realized that the shifter showed me every instance that I had lacked courage, and the consequences had been severe.

If we were to win this war, I needed to learn from my mistakes and do everything in my power not to repeat them. "What a waste," the dragon muttered as he watched me carry Nora's lifeless body to the stairs. "A life cut short far before the Fates had ever intended."

I sent him a puzzled look. "What do you mean?"

"She was not supposed to die that night. The Fates had another plan in store, but when your courage failed, they decided to punish you for it. Her death was yet another cost of this war."

"How do you know this? The work of the Fates is not known by any mortal being." I got into the shifter's face as I spat the words at him.

"I am old, princess. I have seen the Fates meddle with the lives of many just to pass the time. Your destiny is great, but in order to see it come to fruition, you needed to be tested. You needed to find your courage." The explanation left me feeling hallow inside. I already bared the weight of blame upon my shoulders for the lives that had been lost in my wake. Knowing that it had all been to teach me a lesson stung more than anything.

I was thrown into time and space. Once again, I stood within the walls of Lios. I was surrounded by death and decay. Since my bonding with Rion the night before, I no longer feared the nightmare that had haunted me the last few months. I no longer feared he would be taken from me, for I knew I would never have to live without him.

In this version of that dream, he stood beside me, stained with the blood of our enemies. The king and his men laid dead before me. However, among the dead were Flynn and Nolan. Cian and William. Many familiar faces robbed of the chance to experience the liberation they fought for.

A wail broke free from Rion's throat, as he gathered his childhood friends into his arms. His cries broke more of my shattered heart. They were all he had left aside from me.

"This is the risk of the war you wish to fight." The shifter took up the position Rion had just occupied. "But there is an alternative. A future in which you and the ones you love survive." He sent images of Rion and I laughing in a beautiful, quaint home. Distorted visions of the children we may bring into the world flooded my mind. Flynn and Nolan joined us with families of their own. "The mainland has been left untouched by Aos Si corruption. You could live in peace there, but this is what would become of your people."

Images of starvation and suffering flashed between the visions of love. Humans lying dead in the filthy streets of their villages and left to rot, for their loved ones were either gone as well or too weak to burn their bodies. Men, women, and children chained together, their skin pulled tight over the bones, and forced into the service of the king when they could no longer pay their part of the taxes that were owed. "It comes down to a couple simple questions. Are you willing to sacrifice the few to save the many? Are you willing to sacrifice your happiness and the happiness of those you love to save your people?"

The answer was simple, but my lips would not form the word. The bond to Rion pulsed throughout my body. It wanted me to choose the path that would ensure Rion's safety and happiness. I fought against the pull of the bond. A twisting pain shot through my chest, like my heart had been ripped from the cavity and stomped on.

"Yes," I breathed. "Yes, I would sacrifice it all to liberate the humans from the oppression of the false king." The shifter's look of surprise did not go unnoticed.

"Impossible," he muttered. With a snap, we were back within the training room in the Dragon's Den. Rion leaned against the wall but rushed to my side when he saw the pain that was written across my face. "How did you do that?" the dragon demanded.

Rion's brows furrowed, showing the confusion that I also felt. "Do what?" I asked through raged, panting breaths.

"You should have never been able to put the needs and wants of others before that of your mate's," he claimed. It came as no surprise to me that the dragon had designed a trial that I would have no choice but to fail. He cocked his head to the side, like he was seeing me in a new light.

"She passed your trials. Now it is time for you to hold up your end of the bargain," Rion commanded. The shifter turned his scrutiny to Rion.

"Indeed." He snapped his fingers, and an ordinary looking spear appeared floating in the air. "I do hope you succeed, princess. I also hope that the cost, which you must pay, will not be too great." He plucked the spear from the air and handed it over. The magic that hummed from the mighty weapon was great, pulsing into my hand where it was wrapped around its shaft.

Rion and I turned to leave, but not before the shifter spoke again, "Aisling?" I looked over my shoulder towards him. "I rescind my initial assessment. You may have what it takes to make them pay for what they have done, not only to your people, but also, to the Aos Sí." Rion tugged at my sleeve to usher me from the Dragon's Den.

We walked down the tunnels once more. I told Rion of all the shifter had shown me in the last trial and the choice he presented to me. "Why was I able to overpower the bond?"

"Your will is strong, little fox. If I had been presented with the same choice, I wouldn't have chosen as wisely," he admitted.

When we exited the mouth of the cave, the sun had risen and was already descending towards the western horizon. The adrenaline from the encounter with the dragon shifter had begun to subside and left behind extreme exhaustion in my limbs. I had been awake for well over twenty-four hours, and it was beginning to take its toll. "We can rest here for a while until the sun fully sets," Rion stated as we approached our small fishing boat. I placed the spear in the bottom of the boat and laid upon one of the benches.

I felt different after everything that happened within the cavern. Surer of myself and what I was capable of. Pride welled in my heart for what I had just achieved. I had survived an encounter with a dragon that, according to legend, no one had been able to do in the past.

I dozed on and off for the next few hours, while Rion kept watch. I was plagued by the visions that dragon had presented to me in the last challenge. Though I knew I was making the right decision, I still longed for the happy life that he had shown me. The life where all the ones I loved were safe and filled with joy. I wanted to believe we would all make it out of this alive to be able to build that life from the ashes of the Aos Si kingdom, no matter how delusional that may be.

Rion shook me out of my restless sleep. "We must get going." I rubbed the sleep from my eyes, as Rion pushed the boat into the water and hopped in, taking his place on the bench in front of me. Once he had gotten us far enough away from the shore, I again adjusted the currents to propel the boat through the water.

When we reached Gorias, Rion docked the boat from whence it came and guided us down the dark, abandoned alleyways of the city. The spear weighed heavy in my hand as we crept on silent feet. Our presence went again unnoticed. Our trek back to the fairy mound was also uneventful. "When the king is gone, who will rule Tír na nÓg?"

"It really will depend. The Gods may return after the downfall of the false king, or some other Aos Si might rise to claim the land. However, there may be another option."

"What would that be?"

"You could rule the Emerald Isle and Tír na nÓg. You are

off both bloodlines. You could be the one to bring the two people together," Rion proposed.

"I am not sure I want the power over two kingdoms," I answered honestly.

"It wouldn't be two kingdoms but one. The Druids united the five human clans under one banner. Maybe it's time the Aos Si and humans do the same." I contemplated his reply. It would come down to whether the Aos Si would even accept me as their ruler, or would their disdain for humans be too great? Their minds too warped and poisoned by the king and the black magic that they wielded.

My ambitions only ever extended to the liberation of my people. I did not seek power nor legacy. All I wanted was to see King Balor wiped from my lands along with his cronies, so that the people could heal from the trauma that he has inflicted upon them. However, there was a risk that a new power-hungry Aos Si would rise. If that were to occur, it could derail all of my progress. Though ruling Tír na nÓg was not part of my plan, I would do it, if it would ensure everlasting peace. I would not make the same mistakes that my mother had and be taken by surprise.

The fairy mound came into view ahead. We ascended the slope and stopped in front of the swirling portal. The magic caused the hair to rise along my arms and the back of my neck. Just before we stepped through, a dreadful feeling slithered through my body causing me to pause momentarily. "What's wrong?" Rion asked when he saw my hesitation.

"I don't know." I peered through the dark that surrounded us, looking for some threat hidden within. "I just have a really bad feeling." I shook my head, trying to dispel the ominous weight. "It's nothing." Rion looked upon me wearily, but grabbed my hand

and pulled me through the swirling portal.

We appeared on the top of another mound. The cold struck me first, then the unfamiliar surroundings. Off to the left of the slope, where the black tower had been the night before, were the ruins of a once great outpost. Mountains loomed to the north and a city lay ahead of us. "Is that Lios?" I asked Rion, who wore a horrified expression.

"I thought this portal had been deactivated when the king took the throne. We need to go back through. Now!" Rion had barely got the words out before the clinking of armor filled the air.

"Don't you move a muscle," a malicious voice spoke from the dark. Rion went ramrod straight and stilled his movements. We were surrounded in an instant by soldiers with their weapons drawn blocking our path back to the portal. They parted down the center and a male appeared. He was absolutely massive, even from this distance. He wore gold plated armor, with a large golden crown upon his dark hair. Dark magic wafted off him casting shadows in the moonlight. King Balor.

"The boy said you would be traveling through the realms this eve." Behind the false king that descended upon us, was a soldier who held a struggling form at knife point. The hostage was male and severely beaten. His eyes were both nearly swollen shut. Blood seeped from his nose and his mouth. His clothing torn in places where blades had sliced away both skin and fabric. I let out a grasp when recognition struck me. Rion made a strangling sound as he, too, realized who the king had in his clutches.

"I'm… so… sorry," Flynn stuttered as the soldier threw him in the dirt before us.

Chapter 32

"So, this is the great Druid heiress," Balor spat in my face. Rion attempted to push me behind him, but the king stilled his movement with a pointed glare. "I will deal with you in a moment, traitor." The king was inches from my face. His fowl breath attempted to make me gag. I made an attempt to raise the spear that was still in my hand when it was ripped from my grasp.

"I have to say, you have impressed me. I am assuming it was you that snuck into The Milkmaid and slaughtered their customers. Then, preceded to free the whores. Right under my very nose," he chuckled at the utter audacity. "You may have gotten away with it, had the group of Aos Si rebels not been captured upon their retreat from the city. The women returned to their service, but I couldn't allow such treachery to go unpunished. The males were executed, but not before they gave up your rendezvous point. That is where we came across your little friend here. He didn't take long to break before we had the location of the rebel base."

"No," I gasped at what he was indicating.

He laughed once more. "Oh, yes. The rabble of a rebellion would have been problematic, but we caught the unawares in the dead of night. They were either far too drunk or buried deep within their women to notice my army coming. I remained with a group of my most trusted soldiers here to redirect all passage between realms through this portal." Nolan. Nolan was there with the cauldron.

The king must have noticed the panic in my eyes and recognized its cause, for he chuckled. "The other traitor got away, along with the cauldron you retrieved from the lake. The mermaids would never let any of my men close enough to catch a glimpse, but I have known its location for years. Thank you for that," he said with a mocking smile. "We will apprehend him soon enough."

Rion's eyes glimmered with unshed tears. All had been ripped away in a single moment. We had been gone just over a day, and we had already lost. "You have no right. These are not your lands! They are mine!" I screamed at the false king. "You do not deserve the crown that sits upon your head. You did not earn it."

He brought a hand to my face and firmly gripped my chin to force me to look him in the eye. "You will shut your pretty little mouth, before I shut it for you," he purred. Rion shot forward towards that king with death in his eyes. Black magic shot out and ensnared him in its web. He struggled against his knew bonds and growled in the back of his throat.

He didn't spare Rion another glance, as he turned my face from side to side to examine my features. "I had expected you to resemble your whore of a mother." I could no longer contain my anger. I spat a wad of saliva back in his face, arising such an anger within him that he backhanded me, nearly sending me sprawling on the ground alongside Flynn.

"If you lay another hand on her, you are dead," Rion promised.

The king laughed at his ire. "You couldn't kill me if you tried." He patted the hilt of the Sword of Light that was strapped at his hip, then gestured to Rion's magical bindings. Rion was radiating rage at this point, visibly pained by the inability to run through the king that only stood feet away.

"Fuck you," Rion cursed.

The king glared at him with disgust. "Do I need to teach you yet another lesson, boy?" I was taken back by the familiarity between them. The king caught sight of my confusion before I had a chance to conceal it. "Ah, he never told you, did he?"

I looked to Rion. *Told me what? What is he talking about, Rion?* I asked down the bond.

I love you, little fox. Please, know that is true. Rion answered me as he looked at his feet in shame.

The king laughed again as he watched our silent conversation. "I see you finally found yourself a mate, Rohan. By the way, your mother would be so proud to see you mated to a human."

"Don't speak of my mother," Rion spat at the false king before me.

"Rohan? What is going on?" The demand fell short, as my voice wavered with uncertainty.

"Your mate hasn't been entirely forthcoming," Balor stated as he shifted in front of Rion. "You see, *Rion* here is my bastard son, Rohan. Once the crowned prince of Tír na nÓg and the Emerald Isle, until he was stripped of his title and rank and banished from Lios for disobedience. The boy never did learn how to do what he was told, no matter how many times I had attempted to beat it into his thick skull." The air was sucked from my lungs, and the world spun until I was sure I was going to be sick. I couldn't even begin to comprehend the words the king had just spoken.

"That's impossible. You have no heir." I croaked. It was well known that the king had never produced an heir in the last twenty years, but no one ever had spoken of a child before the invasion.

"Rohan has been a disappointment, since he drew his first breath. His existence was not well known, even before his banishment ten years ago." I sent pleading eyes to Rion, begging him to refute the king's claims, but he still had his eyes cast to the ground. "There was a time twenty years ago, that he fought for my approval, would even kill for it. He was an exceptional warrior and cunning. I thought I might have been able to mold him in my image."

Rion—Rohan shifted uncomfortably in his bonds. "Enough. She's heard enough." Rohan's defeat was evident on his face. Tears streamed down his face, as he relived the horrors that were his childhood. I was filled with so many emotions. Anger and grief for the child that had to endure the abuse. Despair caused by his treachery and all the lies that he had led me to believe.

"I don't believe she has," the king replied to his son's pleadings. "You see, to his mother's disdain, Rohan was influential in planning the invasion. I had given him an ultimatum, either he would help me win this war, or his mother would pay the price. His decision was easy, for he would never put her at risk. I had never been prouder than the day he presented me the Druid bitch queen's head." My head spun and my stomach threatened to unleash its miniscule contents upon the ground at my feet. He couldn't possibly be insinuating what I thought he was.

The king cackled, "Ah, yes. Rohan killed your mother to save his own. Very poetic, isn't it not? I thought I had finally broken him. However, I failed exponentially. No matter what I did, he would never fully submit. He was stubborn and always causing trouble. The beatings he received for his disobedience never seemed to curb the behavior. He also refused to use black magic, though he had the best tutors that taught him the way. I had hoped, without his mother's influence, that he would eventually see reason. His mother's unfortunate demise only seemed to fuel his rebellious nature. He refused to be part of any more of my plans for the kingdom. As much as I wanted to kill him and be done with it, I felt that a better punishment was to live with his choices that led to the death of his mother."

At this point, I couldn't breathe. My lungs were paralyzed within my chest by the intense feeling of betrayal. My heart furiously pounded in my chest. I did not know if it was my own anxiety or Rion's that had increased its rhythm. *Please. Please tell me he's lying.* I begged him.

I wish I could do that, little fox, but what he says is true. His voice, hoarse with emotion, echoed through the recesses of my mind. My vision blurred with unshed tears as I looked at him. The male I had tied my life to was the son of my greatest enemy and my mother's killer.

"No." My voice cracked as sobs shook my body. "Please, no. How could you?" I shouted like Rion.

"I didn't have a choice, little fox," Rion tried to explain.

"Don't fucking call me that. There is always another choice, another path." I went for the sword at my side but was quickly retrained by the soldiers behind me. They disarmed me. My weapons hit the ground with a thud next to Flynn motionless form. The only sign of life was the shallow rise and fall of his back.

"This is all very entertaining, but I am growing bored." He strode up to me once more. "I cannot let you live to destroy all I have built in this land." His clammy hand came to the bare skin of my throat. A burning sensation, like my skin was on fire, spread from his vile touch. An agonizing scream tore from my throat.

"Stop! Please, stop. We will leave. We will leave and never come back." I barely heard Rohan's pleas over my cries of pain. I fell to my knees, pawing at my throat where the burning intensified.

"I am afraid I cannot trust your word, Rohan. Once she is dead, you will have minutes before you follow as well. Two birds. One stone. Your friend there will be dead soon, as well." The magic binding Rohan vanished and he rushed to my side. He hauled me to his chest in one fluid motion. The king and his soldiers back away. "Move out!" he called out to his men, who fell into step with him.

I writhed in pain. "I'll make it go away," Rohan promised. The pain faded, as the curse slowly moved through my veins towards my heart. My vision moved in and out of focus. It felt as though I was overcome with fatigue. My mind was clear, but I struggled to keep my eyes open. Rohan reached over to Flynn and pulled him to us. "I am so sorry," he whispered in our ears. Flynn stirred slowly.

"Rohan," he started. "I tried."

Rohan hushed him. "I know…I know you did. It's okay. Everything is okay," he croaked.

"At least…I will be with Bellamy…again."

Rion's desperate breaths tickled my cheek. Flynn's head lulled to the side—his final breath came out as a hiss. His eyes remained open as his chest went still.

Tears dripped off Rion's chin as he leaned down, placing a

soft kiss on his forehead. "May the road rise to meet you. May the wind be at your back. May the sun shine warmth upon your face, and the rains fall soft upon your fields. Until we meet again," he whispered the prayer into Flynn's hair.

He carefully laid Flynn to the side and turned his attention to me. "He had used the same curse that I was struck with at the outpost. I don't have enough time to get you to a healer." His voice cracked and sobs began to wrack his body. His body shook violently. "I need you to understand that everything I ever felt was real. My love for you is unending. I am sorry, but I couldn't tell you. You never would have allowed me to be close enough to protect you, and I couldn't live without you. Before you leave me, please forgive me." Rion's hands ran down my cheeks, framing my face in their strong embrace. I was angry with him, but this was it. I could grant him his dying wish.

"I forgive you." My tongue felt heavy in my mouth as I formed the words. The wind howled around us, whipping Rion's hair around his face, as if the earth itself was revolting against my inevitable demise. I thought of my people that would be left to suffer at the king's hands, until they could no longer go on. Oh, how I have failed them.

I flitted in and out of consciousness catching sight of Rion's face above me, coated in tears and the torment of watching me slowly succumb to the black magic, until I could no longer fight my eyes to remain open. All the happiness moments of my life flashed across my mind. All of which were with Rion. Our bonding ceremony was the last memory to filter into my mind. The intense love I had felt, now tainted by the terrible pain caused by his betrayal. The image shifted, distorted like looking through a veil of water. Everything cleared to reveal the front gates of Lios, my mother's lifeless body crumpled at the feet of my mate, splattered with her blood, eyes wild with the thrill of the kill. I screamed, but no sound emanated from my gaping mouth. I felt as my heart began to slow, the scene fading in and out of focus. My breaths came in shallow pants. Finally, I fell into the darkness, spinning wildly until all went still, as I drew my final agonizing breath.

Acknowledgments

This book would not exist without the unwavering support of those who stood by me through every chapter, every late-night writing session, and every moment of doubt.

To my husband, Syruss Windsor, thank you for your endless patience, encouragement, and love. You believed in this dream even when I struggled to, and that faith carried me through more than you know.

To my mother, Kelly L. Kingston, whose editorial wisdom and gentle honesty turned scattered words into a story I could be proud of, thank you for shaping both my book and my confidence as a writer.

To Amanda Garis, my brilliant sister-in-law, for creating a cover that captured the very soul of this world. Your artistry brought the vision to life in a way I could only dream of.

To the rest of my family and friends who cheered from the

sidelines, reminded me to eat, and never once questioned why I disappeared into the woods of my imagination, thank you for letting me wander and always welcoming me back

And finally, to you—the reader. You've stepped into these pages and breathed life into this story in a way I never could alone. May these words find you when you need them most.

Morrighan Llewellyn Lee is a writer living in Northwestern Pennsylvania with her husband and two small children. She graduated from Edinboro University of Pennsylvania with a B.S. in mathematics and is currently attending Emerson College, where she is pursuing an M.A. in Popular Fiction Writing and Publishing. When she is not writing, she can be found on stage with her original eclectic band, Anam Cara, or at a board meeting for the non-profit organization Heberle's Heartstrings—an instrument lending library—where she is their current philanthropy director and secretary.

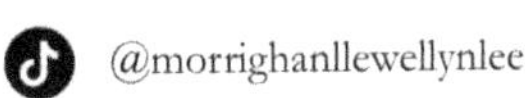

@morrighanllewellynlee

www.ingramcontent.com/pod-product-compliance
Lightning Source LLC
Chambersburg PA
CBHW070613310726
48982CB00001B/64

* 9 7 9 8 2 1 8 8 0 6 8 2 8 *